The Savannah Stories

The Wrong Side
Of The Mirror

The Savannah Stories

The Wrong Side
Of The Mirror

J.L. Lemon

Copyright © 2017 by J.L. Lemon. Printed by Lulu.com 2017. All rights reserved. No part of this book may be used or reproduced in any manner whatsoever without written permission, except in the case of brief quotations embodied in critical articles or reviews.

ISBN-13: 978-0-9909589-5-6

Published 2017

"Little Pink Houses" © John Mellencamp
"A Mother's Prayer" © Carole Bayer Sager, David W. Foster

To Dad

You are my best friend, my rock, my hero.

Thank you for your love and support.

Thank you for always being there.

You are a blessing.

I love and treasure you.

Mom,

Still love you and still miss you.

Dear Reader,

Please bear with me. I've gone off the rails again, this time with a magic mirror. The idea came to me some time ago and I really wanted to see Savannah's reaction to what awaited her and her family in the future. This was a fun book to write and way out of my usual storylines but I hope you enjoy reading it. Lord knows I had a ball writing it.

Thank you for indulging me and taking time to find out how Savannah's life turns up on The Wrong Side Of The Mirror.

J. L. Lemon

Planning is bringing the future

into the present so that you can do

something about it now.

Alan Lakein

1

"It's beautiful." My older sister Georgia ran her hand along the antique mirror's frame, inspecting it for flaws as if a thoroughbred horse stood before her, not a piece of old furniture.

In my opinion beautiful was overkill. I considered it unique but far from beautiful.

"Sturdy," she continued, still feeling it up. "Good craftsmanship."

We'd originally made the trip to the antique store for Georgia to scout out Chippendale entry tables. She found what she wanted pretty quick but that was my sister. When she set her mind to a task, it got done. No dilly-dallying for Georgia because she knew what she wanted. Me? Not so much. I'd hem and haw over things a while. I hated making big decisions (and antiques were astronomical ones for me) and I required time to sort out whether the purchase met my needs. Kinda like the mirror. I found it tucked in a dimly lit corner like a castoff. It was unusual. Old as Methuselah, showed a few dents, and the mirror looked wonky in places – but it appealed to me for some reason.

When Georgia saw me hanging around the large cheval mirror, she hot-footed it over to give an opinion. An opinion that was, like beauty, in the eye of the beholder. Some folks might say it would scare day into night. Others might call it just weird looking. It seemed my sister and I regarded the mirror with equal intrigue and semi-equal mind-sets.

I traced the carved wooden frame, noticing the smooth finish. It still retained a mostly glossy surface with few areas of wear, those being near the adjustment knobs on either side. Neither Georgia nor I could pinpoint the type of wood – Georgia bet on cherry and I thought rosewood. The owner of the antique store was no help. Minutes earlier he offered what little he knew. The mirror had been found "up north" in an elderly lady's home after she passed away. He did confirm the mirror's rarity by saying that particular company (which had no name except a strange symbol) produced the most sought after mirrors – then and now – and that a double-sided unit was almost "impossible to find anymore". He appraised the age to two hundred years old "or more" with emphasis on "more".

Georgia leaned closer, "Are you going to buy it?"

I breathed in the musty smell of old furniture and memories, trying to imagine the vast history of his antique offerings. One generation bequeathed such intricate pieces of craftsmanship to the next and so on and so forth. Even fought over them, I'd bet. Held grudges over them. But probably not that mirror, I guessed. Oh, no doubt it sat comfortably in many different houses, some parlors, bedrooms or hallways for two hundred years, looking as pretty as it possibly could. Its life spanned Samuel Morse's telegraph to today's iPhones. The horse and buggy to driverless cars. The Kittyhawk to the moon landing and International Space Station. Like I said. Methuselah. The cultural value of such a piece would outweigh its semi-homeliness, right?

I ran my hand along the frame again, wondering why the artisan chose an intertwining vine design for the frame. It was interesting, no doubt, but would it fit in with our bedroom décor? Probably not. "I don't know. It's not the right color wood for the bedroom and," I whispered back, "it's gotta cost a small fortune. I mean, two hundred years old?"

"But it's in excellent shape. Well, except the reflection of the mirror on this side." Unfortunately Georgia was correct. The mirror's reflection left a lot to be desired. It was cloudy and somewhat warped in places. The dresser at home had a nice clear mirror that made me appear a bit chubbier but was a far cry from the little fun-house experience this thing gave a person. Plus, I swore the thing made me look older. Not by much but still older than my dreaded thirty-nine. Thirty-nine years old was bad enough to endure without a mirror adding years to a woman. Sheesh. "I don't need it," I said, stepping toward a display case of cameos.

My sister lingered around the mirror. The wonky reflection on the full length cheval detracted from the urge to own it, not to mention the store owner's probable asking price.

"Try the other side," the owner suggested to Georgia. "It's in better shape."

From the corner of my eye, I saw Georgia loosen the knobs on either side of the frame then swivel the mirror to the back side. "Savannah," she gasped, "*look*."

Please don't make me want it anymore than I do. I needed it like I needed a second nose – but I wanted it like the pot of gold at the end of the rainbow.

After a mental eye roll I headed back to Georgia and the mirror, "Listen, sis, I can't afford this thing even if I wanted it – which I don't." *Which you certainly do and that fella at the counter knows it too.* The older man in khakis, brown checked shirt and caramel colored sweater vest had been eyeballing me since I migrated to the mirror. After a few minutes of appraising its condition and asking two simple questions, he pegged me as a sucker. First, the mirror looked too new to be two hundred years old. Second, it wasn't unheard of for me to inspect things without actually purchasing them. Third, I hated people staring at me and he'd done nothing short of give me a terminal case of the heebies since I showed interest in the cloudy old mirror. I needed to go home and clean house, yet here I stood surrounded with mahogany, oak and maple pieces from the Victorian age and a dozen antique clocks ticking and playing their chorus of chimes announcing two o'clock.

"Look at it," my sister beckoned. "This side is much clearer."

I turned to the mirror that showcased me and Georgia standing together. The frown faded from my features. I couldn't believe what I saw.

"We look good, don't we?" Georgia giggled, nudging me with her elbow. "Dare I say *younger*?"

Georgia joked about it but our reflections *did* appear younger than normal. Not a whole lot but those nasty little eye lines trenching a fraction deeper every year disappeared when I looked at myself. The tiny crow's feet trying to channel between my brows smoothed to flawless skin. And Georgia? She lost about five to eight years – not that she ever really showed her age. She still looked like our mama (and a thirty-something, brown-not-red-haired Rita Hayworth) despite being forty-five.

"I'll buy this thing if you don't," Georgia promised. "Just for an ego boost when I stare into it."

It was inexplicable. It embarrassed me to fawn over my reflection but damn, I hadn't looked this good in years. The harsh truth became obvious when the skeptic in me emerged, "Georgia, this is a trick mirror, it has to be. Like the fun-house stuff at the carnival."

Georgia turned sideways, sucked in her gut that was barely there anyway and chuckled at me in the mirror, "I don't care what it is. Anything that can make me look this good I'll take it." Then she made eye contact, "Unless you still want it."

I do want it, yes, but I won't spend a fortune on a party trick. I turned to the owner, "Any proof this thing is really two hundred years old?"

This drew the owner from behind the counter. Late fifties with a full crop of white hair and friendly features, the man equipped his reading glasses that dangled on a chain around his neck. He propped a thick, well-worn book across his left arm, opened it and thumbed the dog-eared pages until settling on one. "This trademark is engraved on the bottom of the stand." He pointed to a capital "A" and "C" with a circle around it. Beneath it was carved "MA" with no circle around it.

"What does it mean?" I asked.

Georgia leaned in to see the emblem. She waited for his answer.

"There's only the emblem to go by. Popular opinion holds that it stands for Acacia or something similar but the 'MA' stands for Massachusetts. This company was renowned for intricate designs like the vine-work and their pride was the double-sided cheval mirror. They stayed in business until eighteen thirty-four. The mirrors were made by a family that only specialized in those mirrors. The catalog states only two hundred mirrors were made because of the detailed craftsmanship and special imported glass. To date there are only five in existence – two being the double-sided kind. At least circulating on the open market, I mean."

So much for buying it. Only Bill Gates could afford it. The owner refused to give up, "Would you like to see the trademark?"

He bent down to show me the emblem but I stopped him, "What does the mirror cost?" The magnanimous price oughta fix Georgia's enthusiasm, I thought. She needed another mirror like I did.

The man considered the question, gave the mirror another brief going over then blurted some insane number for a supposed antique. I lifted a brow, "Shouldn't there be another zero at least? I mean as old as it is and the scarcity of it…"

Georgia shushed me then elbowed me again, only this time without much restraint. She put some power behind it. I frowned at her.

Yes, the price indicated an absolute bargain but two hundred bucks for an antique mirror with exactly one twin somewhere on the planet? Not likely.

The owner scratched his head, questioning his own judgment. "I know it sounds nuts but you two seem to like it. You're the only ones who've looked at it in six months. It's taking up space I need for my Chippendale furniture so I could use the room."

"Put your bid in now, sister," Georgia cautioned. "If you're not interested, I am."

Her vehemence surprised – and scared me a little. I stepped back, held my hands up in surrender, "Take it, *sister.* It's not worth a family rift."

Georgia stared at me momentarily then cut her vision to the old thing we bickered about. "What's wrong with me?" she asked, shaking her head. It appeared the light bulb blinked on about her sudden change in attitude. "*You* wanted it first. You found it so you should have it." For an instant it seemed she tried to gather her mental marbles, to reclaim the fun-loving sister I'd walked into the shop with. She addressed the owner, "I'll take the Chippendale table. My sister will take the mirror."

"No, your sister won't take the mirror," I replied as if she really had lost her faculties. "Georgia, we can't afford two hundred bucks for a frivolity. We've got medical bills to pay. The mirror's nice but c'mon."

The owner scampered off to ring up Georgia's sale, leaving us whispering between ourselves. Georgia crossed her arms, "If that's the case then Ennis has forgotten your bills. Dane told me he was looking at new trucks. How can he deny you a two hundred dollar mirror when he's out shopping for new wheels?"

"Ennis wouldn't deny me anything. He's just window shopping like women window shop for shoes."

"Shoes are different than Dodge Rams. Savannah, it's a nice mirror. Yes, it's got flaws but something that old does."

"I believe it's called *character*," I added.

"Indeed. It would look pretty in your bedroom. Just turn the good side out and everything will be fine."

o o o

So I came home with an old, two hundred dollar fun-house mirror. Georgia and I unloaded it from Dane's truck – the store's owner wrapped it snug in a blanket and bubble wrap to avoid breakage on the trip home. God knew I didn't need seven years of bad luck. I'd had enough of it without any shattered mirrors.

We lugged it into the master bedroom and by default decided it deserved to sit beside the dresser. Mostly because the bulky thing weighed a short ton. Later I'd get Ennis to help me relocate it across the room closer to the bed. It seemed rather pretentious to keep two mirrors (the antique and dresser) clustered together.

Both my young daughters clamored around me and Georgia while we unwrapped it. I was excited to show them the new addition. No, the mirror didn't fit into our bedroom's more modern décor. I realized that when I shelled out the two precious bills with Benjamin Franklin on them. But the damn thing just kept trying to fit in the way a lost puppy tries to charm its way into a person's heart. Only this thing started with my wallet...

With great ceremony, I cut away the bubble wrap. My girls stood in wide-eyed anticipation, telling me to hurry. When I released the blanket protecting the glass, I expected rave reviews of my choice in old furniture. Both girls froze at the sight. Their mouths actually gaped open. There were no rave reviews. Their expressions simultaneously evolved from excitement to basically accusing me of dragging a smelly, flea-bitten goat into our home.

"Yuck, Mama," two-nearly-three-year-old Anna exclaimed. "That's ugly." Despite inheriting Ennis's coffee brown eyes, his dark hair and the lion's share of her daddy's features, Anna's personality tended to lean toward mine. Abrupt and a square-shooter. Nature remembered to supply my ten fingers and toes but neglected to stuff some diplomacy between my ears. I'd hoped our youngest inherited a kinder, gentler demeanor like her father. Or at least a nature that didn't incite riots.

"*Really* ugly," Anna stressed with such vehemence *really* emerged as *weelly*. She helped herself to the bubble wrap strewn across the floor and proceeded to pinch several bubbles, giggling with every pop.

"You've got a mirror. Why'd you bring *that* home?" The question came from Lily, mine and Ennis's four-year-old, the child who exercised the aforementioned diplomacy with regularity until now. This kid looked eerily like me in the face. She inherited my blue eyes and chestnut colored hair and by her gradual growth, I predicted her height to rival my five nine someday.

"I thought it was pretty," I replied, cringing as Anna wrung the bubble wrap between her hands. It sounded like tiny firecrackers exploding.

"It's not," Lily said, grabbing the other end of the bubble wrap to join her sister. Both girls bestowed upon me an expression forewarning that because of that mirror they probably wouldn't trust my judgment on choosing their clothes in the future. If I considered that old cumbersome thing pretty, I had a screw loose, they seemed to say. "Okay, pretty in a different kind of way," I amended. Another series of tiny firecrackers snapped beside me. I calmly requested, "Girls, please put the bubble wrap down." They refused.

Georgia walked in the bedroom armed with glass cleaner, paper towels and a separate dust cloth smelling of lemon furniture polish. "I think it's pretty in every way," she handed the glass cleaner and towels to me and began wiping the frame down with the lemon rag. If I believed in reincarnation, I'd bet my sister was either a drill sergeant or obsessive compulsive maid in a former life. Yes, cleanliness was next to Godliness but too much of it was next to nuttiness, especially when it involved toothbrushes and toothpicks – Georgia's favorite detailing tools.

My girls gave their aunt the same look they gave me when I declared the mirror pretty. Meanwhile I busied myself polishing the glass. I started with the most unflattering side (the one that made me seem older) and did what I could to improve its looks – *and* mine in its reflection. No such luck.

I swiveled the mirror to polish the clearer side. I chose that side to display simply because it lopped a few years off my current age. Every woman in the universe desired a mirror that not just flattered but added a youthful touch to the image staring into it. I could sell this thing for three times what I bought it for, I thought, maybe more. But I wasn't stupid. I was keeping my version of the Fountain of Youth no matter what.

"There," Georgia nodded her approval. "Get rid of the dust and film and it looks good." She waited for verbal agreement. I gave it. My kids scrunched their faces like they ate a pickle.

"Where is everyone?" a voice called from the living room. Ennis was home and I dreaded to see his reaction, especially after enduring our girls' critiques.

"Daddy," Anna shouted. "Mama bought a ugly."

I pursed my lips. *Thanks kid, I owe you one.*

Lily corrected her sister, "It's a mirror, Anna. An ugly mirror."

Ennis rounded the corner to the bedroom. My big strapping Texan stood six feet two inches tall, had beautiful brown eyes and his dark brown hair cropped in a business man's cut. Those beautiful brown eyes settled on the cheval mirror and narrowed. Then the dragged-in-a-smelly-goat frown set in, "What is that?"

"Daddy, it's a *mirror*," Lily sighed, frustrated with correcting everyone.

He scrutinized the antique from the doorway, shifted his vision to me. "Why is this *mirror* in our house? We've got one right there," he pointed to the dresser.

"Yes," I deadpanned, "our oldest reminded me of that. Ennis, I couldn't resist." My mind raced for reasons (not excuses, of course) why I lugged such a piece of worn imperfect and apparently ugly furniture home. Now I knew how Charlie Brown felt when everyone saw his Christmas tree... "It's over two hundred years old. Oh, and there's only two left in the world." That's all I mustered. *I guess you were right, Linus*, I remembered Charlie Brown saying. *I shouldn't have picked this little Christmas tree...*

And like Charlie Brown's friends, my husband wasn't happy. In fact, he reacted as if I'd hurled yellow snowballs at him and hit my target, "It *looks* two hundred years old and I don't care if there's a million or one of them. Savannah, how much did this thing cost?"

Georgia cleared her throat, "I hear Dane calling for his supper."

I grabbed her arm, "No, you don't. You're part of why it came home with me so you'll suffer the wrath too. Ennis, it cost two hundred dollars." I tilted my chin back, "Go ahead. Hit me with your best shot." This was my customary answer when I knew he was upset with me. He never laid a hand on me so I felt safe in saying it.

"Mama's a drama queen," Anna accused.

Sometimes I wanted to kick my brother. My kid learned that phrase from her Uncle Seth, bless his overly outspoken heart. When a female complained, his answer? She's being a drama queen. "Don't you have a date with Big Bird or something?" I shot back as nicely as possible.

My sister barely corralled a laugh at the exchange. "Not that it matters," she told Ennis in my defense, "but the rarity of it means it's probably worth a lot more than what she paid."

That jogged my memory, "He said he wanted rid of it to make room for Chippendale stuff – and Georgia bought an entry table so you're not the only Rutherford brother in for a surprise."

"But it's ugly," Anna repeated.

"So you've said." I glanced at Lily, shooing her toward her sister, "Take her outta here. She's not exactly helping."

With the kids gone, the three adults opted for the blunt approach. Ennis started it, "We can't afford to buy things like this, babe. We're trying to pay off bills."

I slowly turned in Georgia's direction, blasting her with the old *I told you so* sneer. It didn't deter my sister, "Ennis, c'mon. It's a mirror. Okay, it's not perfect, it doesn't completely match the décor but she loves it."

"I don't go to antique shops that often," I told him. And this was why I didn't, I nearly finished. "I love the mirror, Ennis. It may be ugly to you and the kids but I'm glad I bought it."

"I hope you're still saying that in another month." He waved it off, shook his head in hopeless surrender, "Why couldn't you bring home shoes like other women?"

2

Every time I passed by the mirror, I paused, marveling at my slightly younger image. We'd had the mirror three days. Long enough to inspect it closer, appreciate the nicks and dents and wonder who or what put them there. The old thing must have had an active life considering the scuff marks on the bottom of its base. I laid it flat in the floor to observe the manufacturer's trademark, placed a piece of paper over it and rubbed a pencil lead over the emblem. While I worked, the symbol gradually darkened until I felt satisfied with the results. Now I could look up the manufacturer myself. Or try to. The store owner – a guy who dealt with antiques every day – sure offered no hope of finding an actual name.

I'd just lifted the mirror back on its base when a young voice called, "Mama."

I turned to see Anna holding an empty plastic cup. "What's up, buttercup?" I asked.

Anna not only physically favored her daddy but used those features and traits to her advantage. She batted her soulful brown eyes to get her way and armed her persuasive, charming smile as backup. Anna skipped the eye thing and went straight for the smile while extending the cup, "I want some juice please."

She and I headed for the kitchen. I opened the fridge for the orange juice. Anna held the cup steady between both hands while I poured. Once topped up, I returned the carton to the fridge while Anna indulged in a long drink.

"Thank you," the girl said toddled off to the living room to watch Sesame Street.

"You're welcome, baby." I headed back to the bedroom, took another look at the strange emblem. I wouldn't know a Chippendale from a Queen Anne to a Sheraton (I considered the last one a hotel, not furniture). Georgia studied antiques for years and threw out terms and names like Piecrust, Davenport and Pembroke the way preachers quoted the Bible. She knew the names of manufacturers, styles, and the times and places things were made. But she'd never seen the emblem carved on the bottom of my cheval mirror. I halfway regarded the thing with caution, afraid the store owner duped me into buying a twenty year-old mistreated reproduction, not a rare antique.

Once I picked up Anna's toys and returned them to their rightful place for the hundredth time that week, I'd research the emblem best I could and pray I hadn't fallen for a clever line of bull.

I bent down to pick up Anna's latest deposit in our bedroom. I'd reunite the giraffe and monkey to the plastic play zoo in our daughter's bedroom. Pieces from a Disney princess play set joined the impromptu toy party, these placed in front of the dresser beside the mirror. I leaned down and stepped forward to retrieve the small replicas of Sleeping Beauty and Snow White.

An unexpected dizziness struck me, knocking my equilibrium askew. I reached for the dresser to steady myself but the combination of bending and lightheadedness overwhelmed me. I tilted toward the mirror and panicked, groping again for the dresser. Nothing stopped me. I fell straight at the mirror, realizing the inevitable outcome. Before my shoulder crashed against the antique, my last thought was *my new mirror is history…*

I closed my eyes, expecting my head to smash into the mirror, busting the glass and splintering the old wooden frame. I expected shards of glass to not only litter the floor but slice a gash in my scalp or hands. I expected complete disaster.

I did *not* expect something to pull at me. Not some*one* but some*thing*. Not a sudden yank but a steadily increasing pressure towing me in one specific direction – into the mirror. I reached out where the dresser should have been but again my hand swatted air. I gradually lost the battle until a quick, powerful jerk ended the fight once and for all. There were no solid handholds, nothing tangible to grasp. I flew through a bright vortex and I felt quite certain I'd knocked myself stupid when I fell. But I was still scared to death. None of it made sense, even if I'd suffered a concussion. I'd been in a coma before and never experienced the Dorothy and Toto Ride from Hell.

My heart pounded, my arms flailed and hand grasped for things that should be there but weren't. A blinding light forced my eyes shut again to close out the glare. No sound registered. Nothing. Just dizzying chaos.

I caught a whiff of a familiar smell. In the turmoil surrounding me, I recognized it as my mother's perfume. That light, flowery essence of Mama floated to me stronger by the second, sending me back many, many years. Of her standing at her own dresser, applying that expensive perfume (Daddy always bought her a bottle for her birthday). Of walking into a room and catching a whiff of Mama, knowing she'd been there.

The light dimmed. The solid feel of a floor beneath me registered. I was lying down – with no signs of broken glass or injury to speak of. I chanced feeling around me. No glass shards, no indication of any problem. Just carpet. Soft, thick carpet. My hand brushed a stumpy wooden table leg. When I stretched my legs, my feet bumped a big, solid piece of furniture. *Great. I've knocked myself straight into a concussion. That's what's wrong with me.* It had to be because I still smelled my mother's perfume – and it mingled with the delicious aroma of chicken fried steak, mashed potatoes and gravy.

Cautiously I opened my eyes to narrow slits. They popped wide open at the sight around me. *Yep. A concussion. No doubt about it.* I sat up, surveyed my surroundings, stunned by what I saw. I was in the living room (specifically behind the sofa) of my childhood home in Augusta. A room transformed back over twenty years. I ran my hand along the cream colored sofa's fabric backing. *Mama replaced this old sofa months before her cancer diagnosis. And that end table... Daddy broke that while he and Seth lifted the sofa to move it to his truck.* What the hell was going on?   Wait, I assured myself. *None of this is real. It's all a vivid memory, a product of a concussion. That's all, Savannah. That's all.*

I levered to my feet, deciding to enjoy the trip back in time because I'd pay for it later. Concussion headaches punished people tenfold for getting conked, sometimes for weeks.

Once upright I saw Mama's prized cherry wood coffee table – without dents and rings from Daddy's scotch glasses.   Beside an arrangement of blue hydrangeas sat my American Government textbook. When I'd forget the book (which was often) my boyfriend Roy Carlson lent me his for the fourth period class.

Beneath the front window stood a cherry wood console table. Mama's medley of framed photos lined the surface in a neat row. Hers and Daddy's wedding picture, Seth and his family, Georgia's high school graduation and me holding one of my golf trophies.

A quick glance up the stairs revealed the whole picture gallery still intact along the wall. Since Mama's passing Daddy removed a few pictures mostly of her, saying they were too painful to see. I not only understood but agreed. Some memories hurt more, not less, as time marched on.

In that brief time, my equilibrium settled down and my heart followed suit. Everything seemed so real, not vague or faraway like a dream. The couch felt soft to the touch, the wooden picture frames solid. How did I get here and why was I here – and how did I get back?

In the entry the grandfather clock ticked away with its lazy swaying pendulum. The mechanism cranked up to chime the quarter hour. Five-fifteen.

A key turned the front door lock and when the door opened, I found myself leaning against the sofa for stability as I watched *myself* (as a teenager) bolt through the door holding a letter in my hand, "Mama! Mama! Look!"

"My goodness, what's got you so excited?"

My mother's voice. I heard it loud and clear from the kitchen. I straightened, anticipating – hoping – to see my beautiful mother appear in the doorway. She asked what inspired the outburst. Standing there, watching and waiting, I knew what that teenager wagged in her hand. The acceptance letter from Georgia Tech University. I'd received my golf scholarship.

The girl took off for the kitchen after dropping the heavy golf bag in the corner of the entry. I recalled that day with nostalgia and a bit of sadness. Still, witnessing it brought a smile to my face.

From memory I knew what the teenager would say. *I did it, Mama. I made it. I finally made it.*

My mother stepped into view. She wore black slacks and her usual pink floral apron over a blue button down blouse. She held a dish towel in her hands. I'd seen her like this a million times. So youthful and gorgeous even in her mid-forties, especially when she broke into that radiant grin. The mere sight of her after all these years brought tears to my eyes, a lump to my throat. Instinctively I went to her, my arms open,

"Oh Mama, I've missed you…"

She stared past me, drying her hands on her trusty dish towel, "Tell me what's going on."

Younger Me ran by (missing me by an inch) and right into Mama's arms, "I did it, Mama. I made it. I finally made it."

"Slow down, sweetheart," Mama laughed. "What's got you so fired up?"

I reached to touch her, to show her I was there – hoping she'd feel it, maybe turn to me and *see* me. After all, I could touch the couch and the carpet – what a true gift to feel my mother's hand again or her cheek and have her beautiful green eyes center on me and smile from ear to ear.

My hand disappeared in her image, sinking completely through as if I grasped thin air, not flesh and bone. A sense of emptiness overwhelmed me. I could see and hear her but the one thing I wanted so badly to do – to feel her warmth enfold me in that hug – was impossible. Instead I watched a memory replay one of the happiest moments in my life – while I stood by swiping away my own tears of heartbreak, yearning and sorrow.

Younger Me stepped back, raised the letter in triumph. From arm's length I saw the interlocking "G" and "T" on the letterhead. "I got the scholarship to Georgia Tech!"

Mama beamed that special smile reserved for the most joyous moments of her life – Seth's wedding, Georgia's first book contract and later my sister's marriage to Matthew. Now my college scholarship rated among them. I saw the pride in her eyes when she said, "You've worked so hard for this. Excellent grades, practiced every day. Look at all you've accomplished already. Imagine what you'll do in years to come." Her eyes sparkled with tears, "My baby is the first Prince to attend college. I'm so proud of you."

And standing there, her exuberance broke my heart. Mama crowed to anyone with ears and a moment to spare about her youngest daughter's scholarship to Georgia Tech. And in Augusta, Georgia, a golf scholarship meant as much as a football scholarship in Dallas, Texas. The cruel reality was I screwed the whole scholarship in the ground when I heard her cancer diagnosis and began drinking myself into a stupor.

But less than two yards away, Teenage Savannah danced with chaste bliss, unaware of the tragic future soon to befall the family. She only knew she pleased not only her mother but her siblings and probably her daddy too.

Mama eagerly reached for the letter, "Let me see it."

I remember handing it over with such rapturous glee my hands trembled. Mama held them in her steady grasp, telling me to calm down or I'd faint. She reverently smoothed the letter's folds before reading aloud. Her enthusiasm mounted with every word, "'...we are sure this scholarship will help you live your dreams and achieve your goals. Thousands of applications are considered but only a few are selected. We are happy to announce that you are among those chosen.'" Mama again threw her arms around her teenage daughter. That hug would stay with me forever – the strength in it. The sheer delight. I remembered her giddy laughter. Her euphoria when she called Georgia and Seth. My mother reverted forty years that afternoon, revealing a childlike whimsy rarely seen outside those four walls. "This calls for a celebration." Mama winked, "I have just enough time to whip up a peach pie for my college girl."

A flash of bright light blinded me, disorienting me until I reached for the sofa for balance. I groped for a handhold anywhere in that room – at least I assumed I was still in a room. Nothing solid met my touch. I decided the floor felt safe enough so I crouched down, keeping my hands flat against the floor. My head spun the way it did when I rode the Georgia Scorcher at Six Flags. Then everything stopped.

Seconds earlier I braced my palms on the soft carpet, curled my fingers in the nap. Now I clutched thick clumps of grass. The air smelled earthy and sweet like mid to late spring. I opened my eyes. Towering trees and manicured grass surrounded me. Birds chirped high above, singing their songs, trying to impress potential mates. A wave of cheers and applause rose in the distance.

I pushed to my feet, brushed grass clippings from my jeans. From this perspective I realized I stood at a tee box on a golf course. The eighteenth tee. Behind me a group of around fifty people marched their way in my direction. Golfers. Coaches. Families – dozens of spectators and supporters. I'd been thrown into the finale of one of my tournaments.

The mass of people stopped a respectable distance away while the golfers and coaches assembled behind the tee box. There I was with my teammates dressed in black slacks and maroon polo, the latter embroidered with our high school mascot – a fierce looking Razorback – on the upper left chest.

We (Cross Creek High) played Westside High School and their best player and I had a running rivalry that bordered on ridiculous. Trash talk, intimidation and an occasional insult weren't unheard of. Our coaches spent more effort watching us to ensure we used the clubs on the little white balls and instead of each other.

Broad shouldered, built like an Olympic-trained Swede Brittany Tully slid her driver from her golf bag, stroked the shaft in a way that seemed on the verge of obscene.

I stood two inches taller but in a contest of sheer muscle mass she outranked me by a mile. If we were vehicles she'd be considered a Mack truck while I qualified in the SUV range. She and I locked horns many times – thankfully I won most of those battles.

"You're going down, Prince," she bent to stab a tee in the ground. She placed the ball on top then smiled back at me. "The Bomber's about to crash."

She'd used my nickname (one I never asked for or approved of) to needle me. The local paper labeled me the Augusta Bomber because I could drive the ball further than most girls my age. I thought the name was silly and impossible to live up to. Plus it encouraged opponents like Brittany Tully to use it against me.

"So shut up, hit the ball and prove it," was the Bomber's cool challenge.

"Girls," Coach Warren (my coach) cautioned.

"Yes, Coach," Younger Me complied. Warren realized Tully started off mild with the taunting only to escalate quickly. Plus he knew I had a temper and the last thing anyone wanted was a bitch-fest at a golf tournament. It made for bad press but her long golden ponytail sure tempted me to yank on it... Repeatedly.

One glance at the scoreboard explained Tully's desire to fluster me. We were tied for first place. This hole determined the winner – or forced a playoff, something no one wanted in the sticky heat. I tried to recall what tournament it was but Brittany and I competed dozens of times and tied for the lead on occasion too.

"Go Bomber," someone in the crowd yelled. I turned to see Georgia give Younger Me a thumbs up. My sister evidently heard Tully's remark and countered it. I loved my sister more every day for that. She attended competitions with the dependability of a mother. Mama attended when she could but later on the cancer began taking its toll and no one knew it. My boyfriend Roy hung with Georgia when he could attend but that day he must have had an away game with the baseball team.

Brittany stepped back, took a small practice swing. "Bring your fan club today?"

"At least I have one," I'd replied.

"Cut it out." This time Warren meant it. Tully's coach joined in.

No one playing high school golf in Augusta mistook Tully for human.   She swung her clubs like a machine and enhanced her confidence to the point of galling hubris. Oh, she had talent but most of it resided in her tongue. I was sarcastic but Brittany redefined the word. She and I halfway got along on the golf course (with plenty of competitive banter) but we never hung out after a game. That day however, a burr got under Tully's saddle, as Ennis might say, and her acid tongue strafed more than usual. "Sorry, Coach," she winked at me. "Just giving Georgia Tech a little of what Florida State's gonna do to her. That's okay. Guess not everyone can make the big league."

Ah. So she signed with Florida State. Good for her. Not so good for me, I remember thinking. I'd never be shed of her since both GT and FSU were in the ACC. Big league, my eye. I got a scholarship offer from Florida State too but I liked Georgia Tech, their campus and their "Southerness".

Tully's coach stepped closer to her, mumbled something. She nodded. Whatever he said managed to set her so straight she refused to look at me.

The coach stepped back, "Let's play golf, girls. Nicely."

The hole was a par four. One good swing of my driver shortened it to a birdie try – if I didn't foul up. Brittany's shot sailed down the fairway. Chin tilted at her customary cocky angle, she waltzed back to her bag, shook out a pristine white towel and wiped the club head.

Now I remembered this encounter. Younger Me approached the tee, placed the ball and took two practice swings. I watched her line up the shot then pause. Golfers were weird people. They were superstitious beings whether they admitted it or not. Some counted their practice swings. Others mumbled a word or phrase before swinging. A few chanted one line over and over then cut loose with their shot. I paused before swinging the club, replayed the shot in my mind – just to narrow my focus one last time. Swing it true, I always reminded myself. Swing it true.

Younger Me drew back the club (I had a hell of a backswing then) then the club sliced the air on the downswing until the ball exploded off the tee. It flew straight as an arrow between the lane of trees and landed on the fairway where it rolled far past Tully's shot.

Georgia gave a rousing cheer behind me then added a loud two-fingered whistle. It was the only "unladylike" gesture my sister possessed. During my games she let it all hang out, rooting for her baby sis, making sure I knew she was there for me.

Younger Me turned and gifted Georgia with a smile and wink saying *I showed her.* Once my younger version packed up her driver and the two other competitors hit their shots, they all trekked down the fairway.

Somehow in this crazy movie, I flash-forwarded, skipping the second shot with my wedge that ended up on the green. Brittany looked flustered. Younger Me was not. My competitor pursed her lips, shook her head at the green.

"Hey," Younger Me said in a pleasant voice, "it happens. The green slopes more to the right than it looks."

"It doesn't happen to me, Savannah. Not me," she huffed,

suddenly losing her bravado. "I just knew I had that putt." Then she waved Younger Me toward the green, "Go ahead. Go win another trophy. Just leave something for the rest of us this season, will you?"

Younger Me wiped down the putter before approaching the ball marker. I needed to retain my poise and concentration. I'd hunkered down behind my ball marker four feet from the hole. As with their swing rituals, golfers also tended to gravitate to particular ball markers. Some used British coins, others U.S. coins. Not just any coins either. I knew golfers who only used dimes. Another a six pence piece. I used a 1943 steel wheat penny that belonged to my Grandpa Prince, the man who introduced me to the game. I placed the coin face up with Lincoln's pronounced proboscis pointing toward my ball to line up my putt. Tully used an Australian twenty cent piece with her birth year. It had a swimming platypus on the back. I always knew Brittany's marker because she and the platypus shared one specific trait. They both had big mouths.

My putt was different from Tully's. Hers sloped right. Mine left. And, like hers, it sloped more than it looked. I'd played that course often. I knew the details of the greens better than she did. Younger Me assessed the slope and line of the putt then stood to address the ball.

Pause. Deep breath. Pause again. *Wait. Was that slope as steep as I judged it to be?* I remembered asking myself that question.

Watching the tense moment unfold, I recalled a Ben Hogan quote came to me at the time, one that rattled my concentration and with it, my confidence. *The most important shot in golf is the next one.*

Any golfer, especially one sweating bullets during a tournament could vouch for that.

Younger Me dipped to one knee, gave it another look. Yes, it was that steep. She rose, addressed the ball and paused. The putter drew back about three inches then tapped the ball. The little white orb arced away from the hole as I'd expected. It closed in on the hole, slowing and curving toward it. The putt looked good. I'd compensated perfectly for that slope. Then, like Tully, fate gave my ego a kick in the pants.

The little white orb threw on the brakes. A few gasps rose from the crowd. Me? I couldn't breathe. My heart stopped then sank to my feet. I screwed up, I thought at the time, and I watched in horror as it eased to a halt right at the rim of the hole. No one made a sound. Then I heard Tully behind me – *Oh my God, she missed. I still stand a chance.*

In those brief seconds I prayed the damn thing might win that championship for me. I stared at it, nudging my hips for body English. Just an eighth of an inch. Less than a quarter inch and I was either a champion or a joke, depending on the ball teetering on that precipice.

"Go in the hole!" Georgia's yell shattered the silence around us. Her scream scared me into a temporary back spasm when I wheeled to face her. The crowd erupted into a huge cheer. Georgia stabbed a finger past me, "You won! Savannah, you won! Look!"

Younger Me turned back to the hole. The ball was gone and Tully's high-spirits bottomed out to miserable resignation as she held her hand out. "Congratulations *again.*"

My younger version shook the hand with a gracious Thank You then glanced back at Georgia who feverishly clapped her hands and beamed from ear to ear. Who needed superstition when I had Georgia, a living lucky charm, to help me out?

I didn't know it then but that was the last tournament I'd win before my mother's cancer diagnosis.

The bright light returned. Shielding my eyes with my forearm, I wondered where I'd end up next...

Children's voices floated to me from far away. Two girls. Maybe the mirror sent me back to childhood. When I opened my eyes, I would see myself toddling alongside Georgia who clasped my hand in hers, taking her tagalong sister to the park or a friend's house.

"It's mine," a young girl (indeed a toddler) demanded.

"No, it's mine," the other girl (this one older) answered.

This was not a flashback to my childhood. Once my hearing cleared and mind focused, I realized the arguing pair belonged to me.

Opening my eyes revealed I laid right where I fell: at the foot of the mirror near the dresser. I must have knocked myself cock-eyed with the fall. It could explain the crazy bright light and dizziness but revisiting the past, especially with such vivid clarity and realism? Doubtful.

"Mama got it for *me*," Anna insisted.

"She bought you one. Yours is Cinderella, mine's Aurora."

"She got *that* for *me*!"

"No, she didn't!" Lily yelled.

I prayed one day soon the deep sisterly love Georgia and I shared might bloom and flourish with my girls. Lily tried but Anna apparently felt displaced because of the time Lily and I spent on golf lessons (as if I never spent time playing dolls and other games with Anna).

It occurred to me that age, time and hardships forged that deep sisterly love between me and Georgia. Our bond strengthened thanks to Daddy's temper. We spent a lot of nights holding each other while one cried. Georgia bore his beatings with few tears unlike me. It took years to develop the ability to endure that abuse without shedding a drop. Knowing she was there to comfort me helped more than she realized. Other experiences and arguments only sisters understood fortified our close-knit relationship. I was proud to call Georgia my sister and someday I hoped Lily and Anna shared that unbreakable bond. For now, however, they fought harder than cats and dogs.

I had only seconds before a pair of irate children invaded the room and there I lay prone on my belly facing the dresser looking indescribably silly.

Children's footsteps pattered down the hallway. The two girls drew to an abrupt halt in the doorway, Anna nearly colliding against her older sister's back. What a sight I must have been. The two stood motionless and wide-eyed like two owls in a tree. Lily asked, "What're you doing in the floor?"

"Thought I lost something under the dresser," I lied.

She sank to hands and knees to peek beneath it, "What'd you lose?"

I maneuvered to a sitting position, "That's okay, hon. I'll look later."

"You need a frashright," Anna suggested with absolute conviction.

I wasn't sure if she massacred the name *flashlight* by accident or on purpose because her daddy had a habit of obscuring words as a joke. I'd heard Ennis refer to it as a *frashright* before so I nodded to my little girl. "I'll get one later and look." Once on my feet, I inquired, "Why were you fussing?"

Lily held a sky blue t-shirt, showed me the front, "Anna thinks you bought this shirt for her."

I glanced at the blouse. It depicted Sleeping Beauty, Lily's favorite Disney princess, dressed in her signature flowing pink dress. Above Aurora's head was "Up all night, sleep all day". Anna's shirt, also blue, had Cinderella in her blue dress with "I'm looking for my Prince Charming" written in pink across the front. There was no way to mistake the two shirts, at least in my opinion. So I explained, "Anna, honey, this one is Lily's shirt. Yours has Cinderella on it, remember? And, if I recall, it needs washing." *Note to self. Before doing anything else besides breathing, wash that shirt before civil war breaks out in this house.*

"I wanna wear hers," Anna pouted.

I gathered the two close as we walked back to the living room, "Lily's is too big for you. Let me wash your shirt then you can wear your own."

"No!"

I took a breath, looked at the clock. The flashbacks lasted only ten minutes though in my opinion it lasted a lifetime as weary as I felt. I restrained my frustration at Anna's hissy fit. Instead I directed her to the laundry room. Two calendars hung on the wall about kid high. We designated one calendar per daughter, Anna chose Mickey and Minnie while Lily opted for Disney princesses. When the girls performed extra chores or just plain got along, we had them place a sticker (we bought a variety) on the appropriate day. Each week they accumulated enough stickers, we gave them a choice of reward for the week – or they could hold out for an end of month, more expensive reward, as long as they collected enough stickers to pay for that item. That meant getting along and not driving the tall people crazy.

Yes, I admitted in layman's terms it was called bribery but in a harried parent's world, there were moments we valued sanity more than kid-rearing ethics. Every parent resorted to it whether they admitted it or not. It started off small with a binky when the baby cried for hours on end. Years later it escalated to candy at the checkout before other shoppers lynched the stressed-out parent for not silencing their screaming child (please, honey, for the love of God *be quiet* and you can have the M&Ms). So far the calendar thing seemed to work.

I pointed to Anna's calendar, "Sweetie, see all the stickers on your Mickey Mouse calendar?"

Red-faced and arms crossed, she nodded a grumpy *yeah*. I continued, "You've got enough for the Tigger coloring book you wanted. Is that what you *really* wanted this month?"

A vigorous shake of the head. Still no headway on breaking through the mad spell. Oh, this kid was just like me as a child. I cringed each time she got angry because I saw myself at that age. I tried again, "No, you wanted that soft, cuddly Pooh Bear, right? To get him, you have to have more stickers."

No acknowledgment. Her frowny-face intensified, the corners of her mouth practically met her chin.

Lily, though, raised her arms in victory, "I've got more stickers than Anna!"

My vision cut to her, "You're not helping. I'm trying to explain why she wants as many stickers as you have."

"Because then she'll get Pooh Bear!" She topped off her enthusiasm by jumping up and down, "I'm getting my Aurora necklace! Yay!"

Bending to one knee in front of Anna, I agreed, "Lily's right. Is it worth fussing with your sister if you lose out on Pooh Bear? He'd be mighty nice to snuggle with at night."

I let her mull over my words. My littlest girl stared hard at the calendar. After a second or two she sighed, surrendering the anger, "I want Pooh Bear."

I smiled, "There's my girl–"

"And my shirt."

"And your shirt. I'll get right on that." Anything to save another argument.

3

A blizzard of papers weighed down the dining table, each stack serving its own purpose. Checking and savings accounts, credit card bills, utilities, insurance. Then there was the meat of it. Our income. Ennis and I sat in the middle of this mess toiling over every detail.

Unexpected expenditures stole a yolk or two from our nest egg. Hospital costs from the last year sank its teeth into our savings. Our financial status remained stable for the most part but we faced a decision. Did we want additional income or keep the status quo?

The captain of Zone 5 wanted Ennis for his detective squad. In theory the move would raise his salary close to mine but it also split us up professionally. For years we worked Zone 2 together, sometimes as partners, sometimes not. While good for my husband's career and our income, this opportunity separated us at work *and* home. He would take the late shift at Zone 5 whereas I kept the day shift at Zone 2. In a moment of pure honesty I told him we'd barely be married. The separation, the weird hours, and the fact Zone 5's residents weren't as sedate as Zone 2's. While we recorded more larceny and residential robberies, Zone 5 logged more murders. Not a great way to instill that warm, fuzzy feeling in Savannah.

Ennis stared wistfully at the direct deposit showing my monthly salary, "We can sure use that pay bump I'd get. I'd earn nearly as much as you."

This was the second time in twenty minutes he stated the obvious. So I reciprocated, "And *I'd* get a decent pay bump if I was promoted to sergeant. We can sure use *that* money and you wouldn't have to transfer."

"Sergeants do make a good chunk of change." A wary frown crossed his features, "But you said you weren't ready to take that step."

Ah, so he *did* listen on occasion… "Well, I've been studying and making inquiries to sergeants in other precincts about the job. I don't like the idea of you leaving our station. No offense to Zone 5 but on occasion they encounter crazier people than we do in Two. You know the stats between our zone and theirs."

Now *he* looked worried, "I'd love for you to get that promotion but you might get transferred if you get it. I hadn't thought of that."

I shrugged, "It's a chance I have to take if you want more income. Maybe Josh could talk to the bosses and keep me where I am. Or you could take the test."

He hemmed and hawed at that. "Yeah," he drew out the word. "But like you said, you've been studying and if you get promoted, you'd make more than I would. Man, this is getting complicated."

"You know the pros and cons. The money versus the hours and separation. We still have time to think on it." Please don't take the transfer, I begged in silence. "The captain said by the end of the month. We know our financial status and estimated savings at our current income."

"I do want to check with–"

"Stop it, Anna!" Lily shouted.

"It's my doll!"

"It's *my* doll! Give it back!"

"No!"

"What's wrong now?" I told myself to calm down. The conversation with Ennis upset me every time we broached the subject. The girls' screaming and arguing increased in frequency since Jeffrey Holland abducted me then Anna. Supposedly he hadn't physically hurt her (this according to her and the doctors) but the emotional toll wreaked havoc on our baby daughter. Jeffrey's stunt transformed our well-behaved baby into a bold, mouthy mini-me. I did not appreciate this side of my girl when she picked fights with Lily or outright defied me or Ennis. Right now I wanted to tear my hair out, "What is going on here? And *don't*," I warned, "shout and scream the problem at me."

The girls tilted their heads to meet my gaze. Lily gulped, "Uh-oh. It's Mama Ice."

Over the years I developed what Georgia called a "look". When my kids argued, I gave them that "look" and their mouths snapped shut while their eyes expanded to saucer size. She christened it Mama Ice. My unofficial mob boss name. Mama Ice was a magical expression that settled fussing in stores, in cars (one glance in the rearview mirror), and at home. To my surprise it had a side benefit. It also worked on my sister. Not often but it did. The biggest drawback to Mama Ice: my kids began using the term, even in public.

I blew out a breath, "Don't 'Mama Ice' me. Daddy and I are having a serious conversation. What are you two fighting about now?"

In that short amount of time, Anna managed to hide the doll behind her back. I leveled the "look" at her, extended my hand, "I heard the word *doll*. Let me see it."

Anna didn't immediately surrender it. Lily pointed, "It's behind her back."

"I'm waiting," I told Anna.

"Anna, show your mother the doll," Ennis barked — but not too viciously. Ennis Rutherford possessed no sharpness of the tongue — at least not like his wife. And when it came to his kids? Feh. Talk about a softie. Over the years I heard him apologize to Lily and later Anna just for sounding abrupt when he should have been steaming angry.

Head hung low, Anna withdrew the doll from behind her back. I recognized it as Lily's Barbie. A tiny headache pecked at my temple. Jeffrey's aftershocks kept rearing up with our baby. For a dead man, he still managed to cause hell in our lives.

I rubbed my temple while dipping to one knee. My tone gentled, "Honey, why do you have Lily's doll? You have one of your own."

"I wanted it."

"Would you want Lily to take your dolls?"

She shook her head, refused to make eye contact. I tilted her chin up, "Lily doesn't like it when you take her dolls either. If you want to play with one, ask her first. Will you do that?"

Anna toed the carpet, kept a solid grip on that Barbie. Ennis stepped behind me, put a hand to my shoulder, "Anna, Mama asked you a question."

"You'll ask your sister before taking her things?" I asked again.

Her mouth puckered then her lower lip pouted, "Yes, ma'am."

"Then hand her the doll and say you're sorry."

To my utter shock, she did. She gave the Barbie back to Lily and offered what I considered a sincere apology. Lily begrudgingly accepted it to keep the peace. Our four-year-old possessed a maturity (and tolerance) not found in plenty of adults.

Ennis's hand gently tightened on my shoulder. We're making progress with her, it seemed to say. I touched his hand, praying he was right.

4

No one except me and God were privy to the mirror's secret. It would stay that way. Telling any reasonable human being that I fell into a mirror and relived my past? No thanks. I liked my jackets *without* leather straps dangling from the wrists and waist.

I did, however, like my mirrors usable so the next afternoon I allotted half an hour to research replacing the silver on the mirror's back side. I wanted to use both sides, not just one. Most of the front side's silver remained intact but that back side – whew. It needed serious help. Places spotted the surface where the backing eroded, leaving patches of clear glass while other areas clouded up in murky splotches at the top and bottom. Left alone it certainly lived up to its "antique" status but I bought it because I liked it, not for its status. I wanted a functional mirror – one that worked right, at least in regards to showing a person's reflection accurately. The back side of the damn thing made me look old. Well, *older* and I hated that. It gave me a slightly wonky fun-house appearance but my reflection also revealed additional lines on my face and more silver in my hair.

The online how-tos listed everything I needed. A mirror. Protective gloves. Protective eyewear. A concoction including something called nitric acid to remove the mottled, cloudy backing and another referred to as resilvering chemicals. What it neglected to say: forget the whole thing and call a professional. Who was I kidding anyway? I lacked the fortitude and ability to resilver anything. Hell, I couldn't even gold leaf a paper mâché bowl in school, what made me think I could refurbish an antique mirror?

Tracking down those professionals straightened me out pretty quick too. The cost ranged from doable to outrageous. I ditched the chemistry experiment and jotted down a phone number instead. It beat buying the equivalent of a Hazmat suit, chemicals and still rounding up privacy from the kids for the project. Having them flit around my efforts spelled disaster – including emergency rooms and uncomfortable meetings with police detectives asking why I felt possessed to expose small children to caustic substances.

I turned off the computer and headed back to the bedroom. I swiveled the bad side of the mirror to face me. Yech. I looked awful. I swore those little wrinkles at my eyes appeared deeper in that fun-house reflection. Just as my hair, of course, seemed a tad shinier with silver.

"If you were a man, I'd slap you for making me feel ancient," I told the old mirror. I ran my hand along the side, searching for a seam to separate the frame. Before I called anyone I wanted to ensure this endeavor was possible because I wanted that good side preserved at all costs. To do that, the mirror had to be disassembled.

I braced my hands, one on either side of the frame. The heel of my right hand rested against the mirror itself. The wooden seam holding the two sides together refused to budge when I pried at it. Once, twice then three times I tried. By then I wondered whether a professional repair place stood a chance of taking it apart. I gave another small tug on the sturdy frame when I felt a tremendous pulling sensation at my wrist.

Over the last couple of days, I'd grown accustomed to the feeling. The mirror became a window into the past, transporting me to happier times. Interaction with people in the memories wasn't allowed however inert objects were fair game such as the sofa in my first trip back in time. The mirror paid for itself by becoming my own personal retreat where every journey produced laughter and joyous moments any sane person would, literally, pay money to experience again.

So far I'd returned to see my glory days in golf, I spent time with my mother and my grandparents. I'd teased Georgia about her boyfriends and swiped a sweater or two from her closet. I'd relived the day I met Ennis. The mirror also gifted me with a Christmas morning only two years earlier when Lily was nearly three. She passed the stage of screaming like a banshee in the mall Santa's lap and now actually liked him. He'd graduated from a big, creepy, bushy-bearded monster to a jovial grandfatherly type who dropped in on Christmas Eve to leave her lots of nifty toys.

I jokingly told her that any other man breaking into our house would leave in handcuffs and a knot on his head. With a deadly serious frown, she put me on notice, "Do not arrest Santa." She omitted the *or else* portion of her warning.

On Christmas Eve our daughter went to bed too excited to sleep. When Ennis and I checked on her an hour later, the kid was wide awake. Two hours later – zonked out. We found ourselves struggling to sleep as well, whispering to each other our predictions on how she'd react to seeing Santa's gifts.

The mirror allowed me the pleasure of viewing that reaction from a different perspective – as a bystander to the little family of four. I witnessed my little girl's sleepy features coming to life once spying her new toys – delivered personally by that jolly old elf that Mama promised not to arrest. I laughed when she bounced on her toes, mouth hanging wide open in wonder and excitement. Then she dashed to the Christmas tree to touch every toy just to ensure they were really there and it wasn't a dream. She'd marveled over the stack of carefully chosen cookies reduced to mere crumbs in the saucer. The glass, once brimming with whole milk (only the best for Santa) now stood empty, its contents consumed by her favorite annual visitor and a little note beside the plate thanking her and Baby Anna for the goodies.

Watching the scene, I held a hand to my stomach, remembering the heartburn after downing half the cookies and my share of milk while Ennis ate his portion. We both giggled like kids upon watching our daughter's reaction to Santa's visit.

This time, however, I resisted when the mirror pulled at my wrist. Regrettably I had no minute to spare, save the allotment of thirty minutes to search for information regarding mirror repair. The family needed feeding, kids needed bathing and Ennis and I continued toiling over transfers and promotions.

But it seemed the mirror had other ideas. The heel of my hand disappeared into the mirror and, as if a giant hand clamped onto my wrist and jerked, I lurched toward the antique. The force drawing me into it overpowered me and I had nothing to brace against to stop my progress.

The usual blinding light flooded my surroundings, making me shield my eyes. The brightness quickly dimmed back to normal. My cell phone cranked up with Elvis Presley's "A Little Less Conversation". Was this the present or past? A tiny wave of dizziness rolled through making me focus on staying upright, not which time zone I'd fallen into. These trips into the past really played hell with my equilibrium so I braced against the first thing I felt – the dining table. My eyes opened to see myself dressed in my navy blue pajamas. What looked like Present Day Me glanced up from the sergeant's exam study guide, checked the caller's name then clicked onto the call. "Hi, Sonya."

Sonya Porter, the church's organizer extraordinaire. I was a year younger than her, seven inches taller and a hell of a lot less energetic. Trim and what I called cute, she kept her silky black hair in a bob ever since I'd known her. If life were a cartoon, she'd have been Betty Boop.

I often wondered if fate put her and Georgia in charge of a project if they wouldn't master it and carry on to more challenging ventures like world domination. A natural born leader, Sonya sweet-talked her way into a business owner's heart to hold bake sales at their store's entrance. She batted her eyelashes at the church congregation and with a deep Georgia brogue reminiscent of my sister's, reminded us all to be generous with our contributions to fundraisers because *this is for a good cause, y'all.* If that failed to draw in the cash she pressed harder for donations or assistance. Over the years I'd heard her compared to one of those scary, overbearing aliens on Star Trek who stormed the galaxy declaring *resistance is futile.*

I assumed the fundraiser leadership role twice and that was enough for me. I organized two golf tournaments, one for adults, the other for the kids and parents (the latter being a miniature golf tournament). Twice ended up being two times too many. We priced the tickets affordably while I suggested discounts for kids and senior citizens. Everyone liked me. Everyone wanted me for more committees. I wanted peace and quiet while working in the background so Sonya assigned me a new job. As she phrased it, I'd *help get the word out.* I happily accepted because I was good at it. When a car T-boned a family of four from our church, it left their Chevy totaled and all four in the hospital. Crippling medical bills began rolling in and Sonya elected me to *get the word out* to the news media for donations. The community's efforts paid for a decent chunk of the cost. But no, fundraising and I shared a silent partnership. I'd quietly help it on its feet while Sonya Porter encouraged it to take its first steps then trained it for the Boston Marathon.

Grasping the dining table, I assumed the mirror threw me into the past again. I'd had many of these phone conversations with Sonya so they all went about like this:

Sonya: *It's fundraiser time. Can I count on you to pitch in?*

Me: *Yes, I'll pitch in.*

Sonya: *Oh, you're such a doll.*

Me: *Thank you, Sonya. I'm glad someone thinks so.*

I stood, waiting to see the tone of the call, waiting for the *It's fundraiser time. Can I count on you to pitch in?*

"Remember that bake sale I mentioned a while back?" my friend asked.

My brow lifted, amazed I actually heard Sonya Porter's voice from three feet away. It blared from the receiver, the words flying the way she buzzed around at church. Like a bee on nectar overload.

"Are you organizing it already?" Other Me asked, visibly stunned.

"You think Saturday's too early? I know it's short notice for everyone. I barely got permission from the store's manager to set up outside that day."

Of course she got permission. Sonya Porter could talk her way into the White House to sell brownies and come out with funds for a new church building. She possessed that kind of charm.

She continued, "I know you're probably working but we sure need some cakes if you could swing it. How about it, Savannah? Can I count on you to pitch in?"

I and my other self cringed. This wasn't a conversation from the past. I stood, confused while Other Me fretted. For one insane moment I questioned if this was a glimpse into the future. If so, I was screwed. I had to work that coming Saturday and Friday was my only day off. *I might be able to swing a cake on Friday. Two at the most.* Other Me concurred, "Sure. I'll bring a butter cake and cherry chocolate cake. Sound good?"

"Sounds divine. Could I squeeze an apple cream coffee cake from you too? Those sell *so* fast. And I'd love to have the recipe for myself, hint, hint..."

Yeah right. Hint, hint, my eye. She was as subtle as the mallet in Whack-A-Mole. This moment was *not* a memory. This conversation had not occurred yet. Sonya never tried prying three cakes from me – ever. And what did Other Me say? "Okay, but it'll take most of the day to do this. I'll have to drop them off on my way to work Saturday along with the recipe."

"Super duper!"

I rolled my eyes in unison with Other Me. I hated that phrase, especially when expressed with such passion. In that instant I wanted to slap Ms. Super Duper for her assumption I'd have time to bake three entire cakes while taking care of kids, running errands and preparing supper.

Sonya gushed, "Savannah, you're a doll and a lifesaver."

Another flash blinded me. I held on to the table that seemed to soften then vanish from my grasp. Once the light dimmed, I opened my eyes. I'd returned to the bedroom. My hand still clutched the mirror's frame as if I hadn't moved. I stared at the mirror, my brow furrowed, my brain still spinning. It finally dawned on me that the two sides of the mirror possessed two different powers. The near pristine side sent me to the past. The cloudy, unsightly side – the one I considered repairing – threw me into the future.

"Mama, Anna fell and scraped her leg. She's yelling for you."

Lily's voice drew me from my thoughts. It took a second to process the fact Lily asked for help. "She fell? Where is she?"

"On the porch."

I abandoned the mirror for more important things. Faint, muffled toddler wails drifted into the bedroom. An unsuspecting soul might assume my baby girl teetered on the edge of death. Anyone with kids, however, realized small children considered almost any boo-boo a life-threatening injury. I consulted with Lily before wrongly judging, "How bad is the scrape?"

My kid wasn't impressed, "I was hurt worse when I fell off the swing at school."

Anna's weeping grew in volume the closer I got to the door. "Hold on, baby, I'm coming," I called, hoping to settle her down before the neighbors summoned the cops for neglect. In the back of my mind I made a mental note to pick up more Band-Aids at the store. And flour, cherry pie filling, apples and butter, just in case Sonya Porter decided to make a last minute phone call to me.

O   O   O

After supper, I put aside an hour to study for the sergeant's exam. For the last couple of months during my study time, Ennis kept the girls busy or ran interference for me with their questions or issues. I appreciated his help since the test was only weeks away.

I changed into my pink pajamas while Ennis finished up the dishes. The girls occupied themselves in the living room and I actually heard laughter from both. Amazing.

The guide, a notebook and several pieces of scrawled on paper covered the dining table. I'd already halfway filled the spiral notebook with in-depth notations about certain questions and scenarios presented in the guide and from sergeants I'd spoken to.

I equipped my reading glasses, cracked open the exam guide and with a heavy sigh, commenced reading. The past weeks grated on me. I couldn't understand why Ennis suddenly obsessed about money. His fixation caused such an upheaval with him that he planned to abandon our cozy arrangement of working together for greener pastures because the Zone 5 job paid more. And the second I mentioned (in jest) taking the sergeant's exam, he'd jumped on board the way fleas pounced on a dog. I sobered fast at that point. He wanted more income and he damn well meant it. Even at the cost of time with me and our children, it seemed.

I did not want a promotion to sergeant. In my mind sergeants equaled higher paid traffic cops – traffic cops that directed other cops, not cars. I enjoyed being a detective, not a boss. The promotion to sergeant seemed a natural progression of my career, I guessed, but I'd planned that step for my mid-forties. A Southern philosopher once said, "You sit in a garage for twenty years, you don't turn into a master mechanic but you don't turn into a Buick either." The twenty year landmark on my career fast approached so I employed one of Daddy's pearls of wisdom. Shit or get off the pot.

"Hey," Ennis called while soaping up a skillet. "Got one for you."

Oh great, I winced. Another pop quiz. Ennis sprung these things on me lately and it got on my nerves. Interestingly enough, I caught him nosing into the study guide as often as I did. At that rate, he'd know the test better than I would.

I removed my glasses, sat them aside while trying not to sigh again, "Shoot."

"Here goes. As a sergeant – God, I love the sound of that. *Sergeant Savannah Rutherford.*"

I hated to correct my hubby but, "Technically it would be Detective Sergeant Savannah *Prince*, at least during business hours but what the hay. What's your scenario?"

"As a sergeant you observe one of your officers approach a person who she suspects is selling cocaine. The officer questions the person, does a pat-down search of the jacket to find the dope. As her supervisor you should tell the officer that type of search is what?"

Well, that test didn't take long. I put my glasses back on, "The search is not justifiable because she only had reasonable suspicion." Praying that ended the little inquisition, I thumbed through the guide until coming across the hot pink sticky note I used for a bookmark. The whole book resembled a rainbow. Different colored sticky notes fanned out from all sides except the binding. I jotted my own Cliff Notes to alert me of my weak areas. Review Again, one read. NEED SERIOUS HELP, said another in bold capital letters. One afternoon I found two notes I hadn't written. Ennis penned his own that read "Keep up the great work" and a second one "I love you". Hard to get too angry with a man who took time for such thoughtful gestures.

Over the weeks Ennis transformed into an energetic cheerleader. I appreciated that too. The written part of the exam was only half the battle. The oral exam came later. If I cleared the written hurdle, my next ordeal (and most stressful) took place in front of a board of my superiors (lieutenant and above) who would determine if I qualified for the supervisor's job. Could I keep my troops in line and performing up to speed? Could I handle crisis situations – and how would I handle them?

I'd mined other sergeants in the department for valuable nuggets of information. The most insightful advice I received came from a sergeant in Zone 1. Brush up on the frequency of particular crimes in the city because the subject will be discussed during the oral portion. The administration wanted resourceful officers in charge, ones who kept current with the city's issues. Study the problems, he said, and come up with basic ideas of how to combat those problems before walking into the oral exam. Other scenarios to mull over, he continued, were large-scale crime scenes and multiple crime scenes.

Personally, I needed a Tylenol. At best I'd walk out of the oral exam with a racing heart, sweaty palms and a migraine. At worst, I'd faint or keel over from a stupid coronary.

"I've got another if you're interested," Ennis so graciously offered. He'd finished washing the dishes and graduated to drying the skillet and casserole pan with a dishcloth.

"Let me get some bookwork behind me first. I want to review something first."

The girls charged into the living room screaming about another stolen toy. I bit my lip to corral my inner thoughts. Children really didn't need to hear those colorful words but, damn, between Ennis, the kids and my self-doubts, I stood no chance of passing that daunting test.

Lily headed straight for me to plead her case. Remaining outwardly calm, I glanced over my reading glasses at her, "Yes?"

"Don't bother Mama right now. She's busy," Ennis told her.

I found that ironic. He could interrupt me but the kids couldn't.

He added, "Tell *me* what happened."

Lily didn't appreciate being redirected. She frowned at him, "Anna took my doll again. Then she hid it from me."

I flipped pages until coming to the Review Again note, "Uh-oh. No sticker for Anna today which means Pooh Bear might *stay* at the mall." That threat usually worked on young attitudes. Eventually.

Lily turned back to me, "Mama, she–"

"Talk to *me*," Ennis reminded. "Mama's studying."

Was he kidding? No one except the hearing impaired could concentrate in that house. My expression told him as much.

Lily crossed her arms, pouting and waiting for Daddy to serve up justice. We'd given Anna leeway earlier about stealing Lily's dolls and my husband enjoyed playing Switzerland.

"Daddy," Lily whined and stomped her foot.

Ennis screwed his mouth to the side. This was a bad sign. He needed serious help channeling his Daddy Ice role. Me? I personified Mama Ice and exercised it with regularity, "Anna, give Lily her doll. *Now.*" I blew out a breath, "I'm tired of playing bad cop, Daddy. Brush up on your supervisor skills. That's an order from Soon-To-Be Sergeant Savannah." I started to bury my nose in the book again when my cell phone rang. Rolling my eyes, I leaned my head in my hands. Why the hell did I even try to study for this test? Honestly, I wasn't sure I wanted the promotion and apparently no one in my family or the outside world wanted me to have it either. I glanced at the Caller ID then froze. It was Sonya Porter.

No more than three hours ago I watched this very scene unfold – if she asked for three cakes, that was. "Hi, Sonya." Funny how a person managed to sound congenial when they suffered a bad case of dread.

"Hi, Savannah. I hope I didn't catch you at a bad time. Were you and the brood eating supper?"

"No, my brood and I are digesting right now. What's up?"

"Remember that bake sale I mentioned a while back?"

Inside, my stomach dropped. Outside, a rash of goosebumps rose along my arms. My mind emptied of everything except that earlier experience. Sonya's phone call. The request for three cakes, not two. Sonya calling me not only a doll but breaking protocol and adding "lifesaver" to the list of accolades. Unbelievable, I thought. The mirror amazed me but now it kinda scared me too. Had it predicted this phone call? If so, what else could it foretell?

"Savannah, are you there?"

Sonya's voice broke my daze, "Yes. The bake sale." *Yeah. The bake sale you originally scheduled for two weeks from Saturday.*

Sonya forged ahead with her idea and the enthusiasm I wish I had about the sergeant's test, "You think this Saturday's too early? I know it's short notice for everyone. I barely finagled permission from the store's manager to set up outside that day."

How did I tell her Saturday sounded insane? I didn't. I lied and told her it sounded fine.

"I know you're probably working but we sure need some cakes if you could swing it. How about it, Savannah? Can I count on you to pitch in?"

Oh yes, I was ready for that question. "How about an apple cream coffee cake and a cherry chocolate cake?"

I opted for the apple cake to ward off any mention of three cakes. I smiled, confident I forestalled the request. This future vision thing could come in handy. I might learn in advance what people wanted for their birthdays – and learn how I did on the sergeant's exam too.

"Sounds great except could you swing a butter cake too? Yours is always so delicious."

My brain stumbled over that pothole as it cruised along, thinking of all the advantages of seeing the future. What the hell happened? In the vision she raved over the apple cake. Now she preferred the butter cake. I shook my head. Apparently the future dictated three cakes. Period. No deviation allowed. "And a butter cake. I'll drop them at your house Saturday around seven thirty. I have the eight to four shift."

"Super duper! Savannah, you're a doll and a lifesaver. I can always count on you."

Yes. Unfortunately she could. We wrapped up our conversation. It overwhelmed me to think about baking three cakes in a day. The shock must have shown because Ennis just stared at me. "Do you have enough time to do three cakes?"

No but, "I'll have to make time."

He covered my hand with his, pressed a soft kiss to my cheek, "You gotta slow down, babe. You've been running like a scalded dog since Holland was killed."

Said the man who harped about a sergeant's exam day and night. Slow down? I took several weeks off work to heal after Jeffrey Holland tried to kill me. The massive blood loss triggered a heart attack so not only did I have to heal from shoulder surgery but also keep appointments with my brand new cardiologist. The damage and resulting surgery to my shoulder caused problems requalifying with my gun. It took weeks for that too. Jeffrey attacked me on July first. It was late October now. The frequency of people asking *how are you doing* fell dramatically but the reminders lingered. Nightmares reduced in number but returned from time to time when I groaned myself awake drenched in sweat. Residual aches and pains in my shoulder and arm flared up when I overworked it or lifted heavy objects. Or my hand began to shake. I developed a tremor in my right hand when I held the gun too long. Try aiming for the bullseye with a tottering gun hand. Not a real confidence builder.

Some solid citizen killed Jeffrey Holland so we had no more worries about him. Since then I crammed for the sergeant's exam and fielded church members who ran on enthusiasm, determination and probably gallons of caffeine. Slow down, my husband suggested. I nearly laughed.

5

The next evening after shift I vacuumed the house to spruce it up. Less work for Friday when I'd slave in the kitchen baking three cakes. If Georgia found out, she'd call me screwy. She'd be right.

I repositioned the mirror into place, leaving the cloudy (or *old, fat side* as I called it) facing me. Once I tidied up the place I intended to take another trip into the future – if the mirror allowed it. The antique cheval taught me when it closed for business, it turned off the lights and bolted the door. It decided when to let me in and what moment it transported me to.

I reached to the glass on a whim. Pleasant warmth met my palm. Certain trips to the past first greeted me with the sensation of sunshine on my right hand and forearm – the mirror's version of the pre-flight announcement of *fasten your seat belt*.

I slipped my fingers and wrist into the mirror's glass slow and easy like dipping my toe in the bathwater to test the temperature. Hot metal (or what felt like it) clamped around my wrist in an uncomfortable grip and wrenched me toward the glass, yanking the way an angry, impatient parent tugged a rebellious child along. *Now,* it seemed to say. *You're coming with me now.*

Like hell I would. I pulled, trying to reclaim my hand but my shoulder throbbed from the strain. The mirror denied my retreat. Arrows of pain shot from beneath my collarbone (where Jeffrey carved the number ten), down my arm and across my back. Visions of torn muscle, and another hellacious ordeal with surgery to repair the damage engulfed me in a cold shroud of sheer panic. I had to protect that shoulder.

I held a hand to the pain, bracing it while the unrelenting invisible force hauled me through the mirror. The bright light moved in and stability moved out, giving me no choice except brace myself for the ride.

The hot grip released, leaving me prone on my belly and my shoulder still aching. The mirror unceremoniously dumped me on a thick carpet of jade green grass. A brisk, bitter wind blew across my face and arms. Shivering, I pushed to my knees, cradled my right arm. I closed my fist then released it, testing the fingers, wincing at the steady needlelike tingling. I gently rolled my shoulder. The prickling sensation spread up and down my arm. Careful, I told myself. No surgery, no doctors, no way. I'd baby it the next day or two. By Friday it would be ready to whip up a cake or three.

Manicured grass stretched for hundreds of yards around me. Sturdy, old trees with large billowing autumn colored canopies towered over the area. Vases of flowers protruded from the ground in front of me, each one brimming with bold colors. Next to the grave in front of me sat a stone bench with the name "Charlie" boldly engraved across the front. I recognized the surroundings. Ennis and I visited the cemetery when we bought our plots.

The abrupt realization scrambled me to my feet to read Charlie's cemetery marker. We'd bought our final resting places beside a man named Charles Denman whose family placed a stone bench at his grave to sit and rest when they visited him. The two plots beside him were the only available ones in this beautiful area of the sprawling cemetery. We liked the established trees shading the graves and the quiet, peaceful lack of horns and usual traffic noises. Somehow where I stood seemed too familiar – the view around me but most of all, Charlie's bench.

I glanced down to see a brass marker reading, "Charles A. Denman", his birth and death dates and the inscription "Love Makes Memory Eternal". I wheeled and accidentally bumped into something solid. That something was a mahogany casket draped in a flag. Mere feet away a police honor guard stood at attention, each member wearing dress blues and white gloves and holding rifles in their hands.

One of us, either myself or Ennis, occupied that heavy, polished box. The breath left my lungs. My legs liquefied, the knees threatening to buckle. I hugged my arms tight around me to battle another gust of chilling wind. This could not be happening. Of course it's not, the logical part of my brain concurred, because it hasn't happened *yet*. But it will, the emotional side shot back, or the mirror wouldn't show this to you.

Our preacher continued the eulogy while I squinted, trying to see past the dense fog obscuring the assembled masses at the funeral.

An additional bitter gust parted the mist to reveal a massive crowd of police officers gathered behind the family. Mine and Ennis's families.

I turned to the casket, reaching toward it then jerked back, afraid to touch it. *Which one of us is in there – me or Ennis?*

"…the soul is alive and well in the kingdom and the glory of our Lord…" the pastor continued.

Huddling in heavy coats, the assembled crowd stood shoulder to shoulder with a multitude of officers in dress blue uniforms, half a dozen of the latter braced on crutches. All stood in reverent silence, listening to our preacher's heartfelt tribute to the departed. I estimated more than a hundred people paid their respects along with our families.

Dane and Georgia sat in the front row, his arm around her. In their best Sunday attire, they bore the freezing cold and wind while shielding our kids from it. Lily was still a child, maybe eight or nine but exercised a natural maturity as she sat beside Georgia in a blue dress and brown and black tweed coat. My sister held her hand.

Little Anna, now about six, sat in Aunt Georgia's lap, snuggled tight in her embrace. She shrank down as small as possible with the pink coat's fur hood pulled up to block the wind. There was another child, a boy, sitting in Dane's lap. The toddler in the small black suit and matching wool coat could've been my nephew except my gut told me this boy was my son. He looked amazingly like Ennis, complete with an unruly cowlick at the back of his dark hair.

Ennis and Dane's mother also sat in the front row. Immediately behind her sat Ennis's brother Cal and his family. The remaining seats in the second row consisted of Seth, Leah and their kids and Ennis's youngest brother Jake. The biggest surprise sat between Lily and Mama Rutherford – my daddy. He wore a black suit, white shirt and sported a close, perfect shave. I hadn't seen him so gussied up – or somber – since Mama's funeral. In the immediate crowd behind our families I saw Captain Josh Hunter and his wife then John Mathis, Christine Clark and several others we'd worked with over the years.

Meanwhile, I scoured the crowd for any sign of me or Ennis. Neither of us were there.

"…leaves behind three little angels – Lily, Anna and Daniel…"

I'd been so engrossed trying to find the two of us, I missed another part the preacher's eulogy – but not our children's names. Tears welled in my eyes. Daniel. Ennis's middle name. That *was* our son! Ennis finally got his baby boy.

My sister dabbed tears from her eyes with a Kleenex as Daniel, squirming on Dane's lap, whined, "Where's Daddy and Ma? I want them."

Dane hugged him close, "I know you do, buddy. We all do."

"It's okay, baby," Georgia assured with a pat on his leg. "We're about finished then we'll go home to supper."

The pastor continued with a prayer. The crowd bowed their heads and I approached Georgia demanding, "Georgia, who's in the casket?" In my panic I forgot no one heard or saw me. When she ignored me, I reached to her, to shake her by the shoulders. My hands met no flesh, no bone just like my trips to the past when I tried hugging Mama. Maybe if I yelled the question – in my sister's face. "Who's in the casket!?"

She stared straight through me, right at that polished wood coffin. Fine. If the mirror denied me interaction with people, maybe it still allowed interaction with objects. My hands touched soft blades of grass, after all, and I about froze solid from that damn blustery wind so I could open the casket.

I reached for the flag draped atop the coffin, to lay it back. To my utter frustration, my fingers, as with Georgia, went through like I grasped thin air. Somewhere between my arrival and now, the mirror changed the rules. Swift anger washed over me at the roadblocks that damn mirror erected. It put me here, for God's sake, the least it could do is let me find out who died. "Let me in, you sorry bastard. Why did you bring me here if–"

A sudden, debilitating pain impaled my brain, dropping me to my knees. I pressed the heel of my hand to my temple. Auras of colors swirled behind my eyes as if I peered through a kaleidoscope. The pain's intensity prevented simple coherent speech until I shoved my hand hard against my throbbing temple. It was, without question, the worst migraine onset I'd ever experienced. "Tell me if it's me or Ennis. I need to know who died. *Please...*"

Did I, only a day earlier, crow about a hocus pocus mirror being fun? Spouting drivel about advance notice on birthday gifts and results of exams? Good idea in theory. I forgot about the flip side to that marvelous possibility. The *darker* flip side.

People faded, the casket disappeared into a bright white flash that drove the pain to my soul. I reached for the casket, straining with all my might to grab it and hold on. An invisible fist closed around me, squeezing until I thought I'd explode. Then, as quick as it began, the pressure and pain vanished bringing instant relief, rendering me boneless, exhausted and on the verge of tears.

I felt a rhythmic patting on my right shoulder and thigh and both increased in urgency when I moaned. My eyes opened to my girls standing beside me (I ended up on the bed). Both stared at me. Two small hands continued patting me, Lily on my shoulder, Anna on my thigh. They'd been trying to wake me.

Lily looked up at something and I followed her vision. My left arm stretched above me with fingers splayed wide, still reaching for the casket that moments ago eluded my touch. My short, panicked breaths settled while I regained my senses. Tears slid down the sides of my face from pain and sorrow. I was back home in the present – and still had no answers.

I patted Lily's hand. The repeated blows, gentle as they were, stirred a minor pang where the surgeon repaired my shoulder. "I'm awake now, hon," I said. "Thank you both."

"You had a bad mightmare," Anna whacked my thigh once more for good measure, "but we woke you up. You're okay now."

That's debatable, I wanted to say. *I don't feel okay, not when I know either me or Ennis just flew away in that damn casket.* "Yes," I lied, "I'm okay now."

Lily's gentle touch swept away my tears, "You're crying."

"It was a very upsetting nightmare," was all I mustered.

"A doozy?"

I nodded. Another of Ennis's colloquialisms. He used "doozy" to describe anything from a traffic accident to a stubbed toe. Lily considered the word noteworthy enough to adopt and use frequently.

Lily shook her finger at me, "Aunt Georgia says it's too much sugar."

"Aunt Georgia doesn't know everything," I reclaimed my bearings enough to recognize a lecture coming when I heard one. Propping on my elbows, I stared balefully at the mirror. I hated the thing now.

My oldest argued, "Yes, she does. She's older than you."

Talk about deflating. When my own child labeled my sister a genius and me somewhere in between, that fell into the category of humiliating. I mean, I wasn't exactly a turnip. "She's smart but she's not Einstein, kid." I sat on the side of the bed, waited for my equilibrium to catch up. "Where's Daddy?"

Lily pointed to the window, "Outside raking leaves. Who's Ine..." She struggled with the name at first but finally got it, "Ine-stine?"

"A guy not smart enough to get a haircut when he needed it. Why don't you and Anna go help Daddy? There are lots of leaves to choose from."

Anna shook her head, "Nuh-uh. What if you have another mightmare?"

I reassured, "Mama's not taking another nap for a long time, believe me. You two go help Daddy for a while." *Because I need back in that mirror.*

Anna spread her arms, "Give a hug, ladybug." Lily seconded the sentiment with outstretched arms. I smiled. Our rhyming exchanges began one day I asked Lily, "What's up, buttercup?" The trend progressed to *howdy do, kangaroo* and, of course, *give a hug, ladybug.*

We three shared a good supportive squeeze then I tried my sea legs. So far so good. I blew the girls a kiss as they made their way to the door.

Lily unexpectedly paused and turned, "Mama?"

"Yes?"

"Who died?"

Before I collapsed, I sat down again. The question shocked me back to reality, sorta the way hearing my four-year-old utter the dreaded "F" word a while back. She'd overheard it at school and, like "doozy", thought it was a dandy little word for almost all occasions. Once my fifteen minute lecture concluded on how *not* dandy that term was, she promised not to use it again – and I promised to tan her hide but good if she did.

Who died, she asked. I'd been talking aloud, apparently, and the kids heard every word. Struggling for a convincing reply, I finally gave up, saying, "No one died, baby. I had a bad dream, that's all." Not just a bad dream. The worst ever.

To my relief, she accepted the answer with a shrug. I waited for the front door to close before climbing off the bed. I scowled at the mirror, "Tell me who's in the casket. I need to know." I reached, hoping to reenter the mirror's foreseeing side. My knuckles bumped the glass. I pushed at the mirror. Maybe a little more pressure, I thought. *Hell, all I have to do is get close to this stupid thing and it sucks me in, why won't it take me when I* <u>want</u> *to go?*

The mirror swayed on its base, refusing me. I grabbed the wooden sides of the treacherous old thing and shook it, ground the words between clenched teeth, "Let me in."

After several minutes, I sighed, resigning myself. I shoved my fingers through my hair, still idiotically lambasting the inanimate object, "Listen, you piece of sh–"

"Mama."

My mouth snapped shut and I spun on my heel, grateful I hadn't completed my sentence. Lily stood at the bedroom door with hands clamped to her hips. A frown rumpled her cute features. She pulled Anna into the doorway, "You're not having another one of these, are you?"

She sounded thirty-four, not four. My mind drifted to little Daniel. Ennis's mini-me. In years to come he'd be a heartbreaker. Then I returned to the present, intending to reply to Lily's inquiry, "Daddy and I haven't discussed–"

"Please, Mama," she cut me off. "Just say no." And everything will be fine and no one will get hurt, was the implied conclusion.

I glanced at our youngest. Anna Rose, our usually neat as a pin child (neat as a toddler could be, that was), stood covered in mud. Her shirt, jeans, hands and most of the face smeared in gooey brown mud – except the two spots reserved for two huge brown eyes staring up at me. There was a child in there somewhere. The trick was finding her.

Any urge to chuckle vacated the premises pretty damn quick. The sheer amount of work needed for cleanup surpassed what patience I had left, "What happened?" My vision dropped to the floor, praying there weren't muddy footprints to clean up as well. A muddy child and her filthy clothes were enough.

One thing was for sure. Having children wasn't for sissies. Neither was marriage. Grandma Culberson called marriage a fairytale in reverse. A woman started off at a ball in a beautiful dress and ended up cleaning up after all the little people.

Arms crossed with one brow raised Aunt Georgia style, Lily explained, "There's mud in the flowerbed and she was making mud pies."

That put the mirror on hold. I'd deal with it later. Right now I had to strip and bathe a mud monster before her chocolate coating dried. I put a hand to my youngest girl's back (about the singularly clean area on the child) while lamenting, "Anna, Anna, Anna..."

On the way to the bathroom, I breathed a sigh of relief at the status of our carpet. At least Lily had the presence of thought to remove Anna's shoes before traipsing her inside. I thanked Lily for her forethought and for bringing her sister inside instead of blasting her with the garden hose.

"You're welcome, Mama." She followed behind us and when I glanced back, her lip curled at Anna's messy clothes. "I don't see why we need more kids, do you? This one's keeping us busy enough."

6

I tossed and turned all night without a wink of sleep. I reran the images through my mind, slowed them down to grasp details if I could. From what I noticed in the vision, our kids were older by four or five years. We had a son – Daniel – who appeared around three or so.

While Ennis snored beside me, I searched the disturbing images for clues. The sea of suits and dresses. Uniform cops and detectives packed in shoulder to shoulder. The faces I recognized revealed no clue as the deceased's identity. I missed the telltale "him" or "her" in the eulogy, leaving me to battle my own fears and assumptions. The bottom line: our kids were at least one parent down. Maybe two. However if we'd both passed away, Georgia and Mama Rutherford would have scheduled a double funeral. I know my sister that well. She would avoid additional stress on the kids and themselves and nothing piled it on like two separate funerals.

One of us, Ennis or me, still lived and breathed somewhere in that vision. But where? What kept the spouse from attending the services? A hospital. One of us died, the other was injured somehow.

I wanted rest and sleep. My mind returned to the scene, obsessing over the casket. If only that damn mirror would let me in! For the next few days I tried everything from sweet-talk and a gentle touch to outright threats with a hammer to get into that mirror. It still ignored me.

At one point I presumed the mirror broke, at least its ability to show me what I needed to see. I'd just have to cope with the fact someone would die and I didn't know who. Yeah. Right.

Tell that to my overtaxed, sleep-deprived brain running on worry that night *and* my upset stomach. The emotional strain stretched me to my wit's end until I grabbed the damn mirror, shook it. "I'm taking you to the landfill. You're bad luck. I don't want a refund. If you're not going to help me fix this, I want you outta here."

I fetched the brown blanket the store owner wrapped it in for safe transport home. God knew I didn't want it breaking on the way to the dump. I shook the blanket open and draped it over the mirror. The blanket slid off. "Oh, no you don't. You're leaving whether you want to or not," I vowed, realizing anyone who heard me might think I was more cuckoo than a clock factory.

I tossed the blanket over the top again, this time making sure it stayed put before going after the strapping tape.

At the doorway, I heard the *whoosh* of thick material slipping to the floor. Now I was mad. It wanted to play games (yes, it sounded crazy but I toed that line pretty close anyway). The mirror played cruel games that toyed with people's lives and kept them awake at night to mentally suffer their worst fears. No. No more. It was leaving. That day.

I forged ahead for that strapping tape in the garage. Back in the bedroom I squared off with the old magic artifact. I thrust the roll of tape at it, "I'm done with you. Go suck seagulls into your vortex from hell. I hope they peck you to death."

I retrieved the blanket once more, tossed it over the top. I reached under the soft fabric to straighten it over the mirror's adjustment knobs on either side. When I tried withdrawing my hand, something grabbed my wrist, yanked me forward. The instinct to resist kicked in but the dresser stood out of reach. Plus, why resist now? This was what I fought days for. That thought vanished when one violent jerk knocked me and the mirror off balance. It seemed to taunt, *You wanna see the future? Then get ready...*

The world moved in slow motion. The descent to the floor. The mirror falling with me on top of it. My free hand extended to cushion my impact because shards of shattered mirror caused more issues than I cared to deal with. I squeezed my eyes tight just before crashing against the floor... Except I never collided with the floor. Instead I continued falling. For an instant I opened my eyes to nothing but a white abyss surrounding me. My legs and free arm flailed because the grip on my right wrist tightened while it pulled me faster and faster through the blinding light. I closed my eyes again, praying I hadn't screwed up by taunting the mirror. Yes, I believed it had a personality and possibly a form of intelligence. Similar to the way people sweet-talked their cars into starting on cold mornings.

The sensation of plummeting intensified. I imagined this was how people on a plane felt when the bottom dropped out during a storm, leaving the aircraft diving toward terra firma at breakneck speed.

The feeling abruptly stopped. I did not smash into the ground to my surprise. The grasp on my wrist disappeared. The ringing in my ears faded to a different noise. A helicopter's rotor whirred in the near distance.

I stood still, afraid to open my eyes. That trip into the mirror rated as the worst yet for screwing up my equilibrium and hearing but at least my feet finally found purchase and my hands rested on warm, *firm* metal. I sucked in a deep breath, hoping to regain my bearings when another grasp – this one human – clamped on my left wrist and jerked me to my knees.

"What's the matter with you? You wanna get killed?" A man shouted. His words echoed as if he spoke from deep inside a well. I kinda regretted bullying the mirror into taking this adventure. Then without question, I *utterly* regretted it…

My eyes opened at the same time several loud, short bursts of gunfire split the silence. My vision met Ennis who, along with me, crouched behind a cruiser. His hand still held my wrist to the point it hurt. I tugged against his grasp however his one solid yank sent me to all fours on the pavement as a round of bullets strafed the car. Bullets clanked against metal along the passenger side from front to back. A few stray shots ricocheted off the pavement behind me. I crouched tighter, smaller beside the back wheel.

Being dropped in the middle of a gunfight certainly got my attention. My heart cranked into overdrive until blood roared in my ears – but I wasn't dizzy anymore. Fighting for one's life tended to shift their focus to simple survival, not inconvenient maladies.

Radio chatter erupted in frantic bursts with officers giving their locations and the brass giving orders. On previous visits to the future I only observed the action. This time I lived it in full color, 3D reality including bullets, panic and pain, the latter of which registered as a burning ache in my thigh about four inches from my groin. I looked down to see blood staining the pavement and soaking my slacks. Before the mirror tossed me into this living hell, I'd been shot.

"Savannah, *stay down*," Ennis ordered. He chanced a quick glimpse over the hood of the sedan then fired off two shots at a high trajectory across the street.

"What happened?" I asked.

"The gunman shot another cop over there," he pointed down the street. "That's six of us that I know of."

Try seven, dear. Not six.

He assured, "The reinforcements should be here any minute then we can get inside."

I surveyed our surroundings. This was not our police precinct. We were stationed in Zone 2, our building on Maple Street resembled a large residential home. This was a square brick structure located in a street mall type structure running a block in length. The Zone 5 station.

Ennis took the job. Zone 5 wasn't a horribly high crime area of the city. It covered Midtown, Piedmont Park, The Botanical Gardens, and Georgia Tech University. Other areas of town were nightmares to work in but apparently Zone 5 had its share of crazies too. The plate glass windows lining the front of the station – one with the Atlanta Police insignia – now gaped, their empty frames ringed with jagged knives of glass. The gunman shot out every one of them, littering the sidewalk with millions of sharp shards, one now embedded in my left palm. When Ennis jerked me to the ground, a piece jammed itself into the base of my thumb. It throbbed like a bee sting.

I leaned against the cruiser to pick the glass from my hand. Ennis glanced my way, "You get cut?"

I nodded, easing the sliver from the flesh with a wince. Blood pooled in my palm, dripped on the concrete. Ennis handed me his "non-blowin'" handkerchief and I wrapped my hand tight and closed my fist to apply pressure to the wound.

"Where's my gun?" I asked him.

His vision darted around me, "You just had it. Did you drop it?" Then his brown eyes expanded at the sight of my blood-stained slacks, "Is that from your hand?"

Several shots rang out from inside the building. A short barrage rang out from across the street. The radio came alive with shouting about the "idiot" on the building shooting at the helicopter that quickly retreated a safe distance. So much for help.

Another voice, this one I guessed was the Zone 5 captain, barked from the radio, "Rutherford, you and Prince try to make it through the window while we cover you."

Ennis ignored him. Instead he repeated his question, "The blood on your thigh – is it from your hand?"

I located my gun behind the cruiser's back tire and laid it in my lap in case I needed it, "No. I caught one in the leg." And I sure began feeling the effects too. Past the burning pain a small wave of wooziness rolled in. It obscured my focus, both mentally and physically. "I guess it's worse than I thought."

More shots. The gunman strafed the building twice. Chips of brick and puffs of mortar went flying. And they expected us to run fifteen feet and leap through a broken window? I couldn't run three yards, much less run for my life. And if I tried, I'd endanger Ennis. I refused to do that.

"We can't, boss," Ennis called once the firing stopped. "She's been shot in the leg. It's bleeding pretty bad."

Blood soaked his handkerchief around my hand. I squeezed the blood from it, rewrapped it. The dizziness set in heavier, causing the world to tilt off-axis. I pressed my back against the cruiser for stability and prayed the bullet hadn't nicked an artery in my thigh. I needed to stay conscious to help Ennis. I reached out to him, "Lemme have your belt. I'll try to stanch the bleeding."

Ennis unbuckled his leather belt, slipped it through the loops, "Need me to do it?"

"Yeah. Go ahead," I wiped the growing perspiration from my

brow. I wondered if Ennis sensed the growing weakness in my voice. Things took a sudden turn for the worst. Ignoring my injured hand, I braced myself with both hands to stop the world from spinning. Meanwhile the gunman sprayed the cruiser again. Rounds ricocheted off the trunk, others pierced along the passenger side with a distinct metallic clunk.

More shots came from officers and detectives inside the building. At that point I didn't care. I only wanted my husband safe so I changed my mind about the belt, "Ennis, go. I'll handle the tourniquet."

"I'm not leaving you."

He growled it at me with a glare capable of maiming most people. I took no offense because I saw the fear in his eyes. "But I'm a hindrance. Someone will help me to safety. They're working on it. Please, for God's sake, go. You can make it if they give you cover."

His answer was silence. Furious silence. His lips pursed. His vision narrowed again. He snaked his belt under my thigh, wrapped it above the wound then cinched it down hard enough it sent molten lightning through my leg and hip. I cried out, barely curbing the desire to slap the shit out of my husband. I wasn't entirely certain the brute force was necessary for the bleeding or this was payback for my asking him to leave. Either way, I clenched my teeth against the pain, "Ease up, Superman. You're killin' me."

"I have to keep pressure on it," he said then bore down again until I whimpered. He, of course, ignored me and examined the leg closer, "It's bleeding like a stuck hog."

I felt my strength waning. I remembered the symptoms of blood loss from Jeffrey's last attempt to kill me.   Profuse sweating, fatigue, lightheadedness and nausea. All were present and accounted for.

I prayed just one good shot took out the gunman because at this rate I'd be dead before help came. "Can't they bring in a sniper from our station? It's only a few miles." My speech began to slur – or I thought it had.

Evidently Ennis heard it since he tipped my chin up, "Savannah, hang in there." He turned to the window, "We need help now, boss. She's trying to lose consciousness."

"We've got two officers working their way to you," the voice said. "Look to your left."

From the corner of my vision, I saw movement. Indeed, two cruisers behind ours a pair of officers crawled on their hands and knees toward us.

They took turns dashing between cars to the one we employed as a shield. One officer huddled tight beside me while the other circled around Ennis to the other side. They were both young but not rookies – both someone's son and according to the older officer's left hand, also a husband.

The married officer appraised my leg with one brief glance. His vision lifted to mine. I saw in his face what I already knew. I needed a hospital quick because it was hard to recover from being dead. I gave a tiny shrug, "Wrong place, wrong time." Problem was, it was literally true thanks to the mirror.

He turned to the window, "We're in position."

The captain acknowledged. I wiped the cold sweat from my forehead. My breaths grew shorter, more ragged as moments passed. My mind clouded and my hands trembled. Oh yes, I recalled every second of Jeffrey's cruelty and how the body reacted when the blood slowly emptied out. To me it ranked in the top three worst ways to die next to burning alive or being buried alive...

The officer slipped his arm around my waist, "Hold on tight, Sergeant. That's all you gotta do."

Little did he know. If I couldn't get back to the real world (which meant I needed to survive this hell), holding on tight didn't mean beans. *Wait,* I thought. *He called me Sergeant, not Detective.* That nugget derailed my train of thought, making me question when I'd received the promotion *and* wonder who the hell was stupid enough to give it to me.

"Sergeant?" the officer pushed for an answer. "You ready?"

I laid my arm across his shoulders, got a firm handhold. "Ready when you are."

The other officer joined Ennis who planned on falling in behind us to provide cover.

"Ennis," I waited until we made eye contact. "Be careful."

He flashed me a thoughtful smile, one that eased my mind and assured I'd be okay. He added a wink, "You too, sugar. See you inside." Then told the officer assisting me, "Take care of her."

"I'll do my best. Okay, on three," he said and I felt his hand tightening across my waist and hip. "One, two..."

I drew in a deep breath, grateful I had help making it inside the station. *Lord, please protect us–*

"Three," the officer finished and immediately I pushed with my good leg and my free hand to help him lift me to my feet. Little did I know my efforts weren't required. The guy must have bench pressed four hundred pounds. My feet scarcely hit the ground while he toted me toward the door. I felt like a child in his embrace but was grateful for his strength and speed.

The good guys cut loose with a hail of bullets toward the gunman. I looked over my shoulder, "Ennis, hurry." I wanted to grasp him, to tow him along with us however my escort already approached the station door.

The shooter fired off another volley. Bullets struck bricks, plinked off cruisers, shattered meager remains of windows. I reached back for Ennis who, with the second officer, returned fire while retreating to the door behind us.

"Ennis, come on," I begged, tightening my hold across the cop's burly shoulders. A syrupy molasses of dizziness swirled between my ears, bringing on a bout of nausea. The mere motion and speed of the last few seconds took a toll.

There were few things in life so satisfying as feeling your true love snuggled against you. It felt right. It felt perfect. It felt like home. When Ennis's back pressed against mine, his momentum pushing us through the open door, my heart eased a small degree of its rioting. We were mere feet from safety.

The gunman sprayed bullets in a stream of death, keeping his finger steady on the trigger since we took off running.

The instant my officer and I crossed the threshold, he hauled me toward a desk that had been upended for a makeshift shield. "Is the ambulance in back?" He shouted this at no one in particular.

"Yeah," a nearby officer replied then answered the shooter's fire with three shots of his own. "Engine's running and ready to go."

I searched behind me for Ennis. I did not see him. "Where's Ennis?"

"I'm right here," said the voice I'd prayed to hear.

I turned to see the most glorious sight in my life. Ennis standing beside me, safe and sound.

He took over from the officer, slid his arm around my waist, "Let's get you some help."

More shooting erupted from the building across the way. This time I saw the potted plant near the door collapse to the floor as the terra cotta pot shattered then disintegrated beneath it. The destruction zigzagged left and right as bullets bounced along the floor, splintered chairs in the waiting area and aerated a wastebasket I'd been standing next to. A fiery arrow of pain pierced my right hip, buckled my knees and sent me to the floor. I'd released the belt and the wound in my leg leaked blood in a thick, constant stream. The dizziness flooded in and the only thing sharpening my focus: The fact Ennis fell toward me, his body aligned with mine.

The top of his head clipped my chin when he landed hard and heavy. The impact drove the air from our lungs, leaving only enough to groan with (which we did). His weight inflamed the aching wounds, thickened the cloudiness sweeping over my remaining consciousness.

I wrapped my arms around him, "Ennis, are you okay?" Something warm and wet soaked my blouse. It spread above my breasts and trickled around my neck and shoulder producing a weird sensation as if someone poured warm syrup on my skin. I heard him cough. I lifted his head until his wide eyes met mine. This time I demanded an answer, "*Ennis?*"

"I…" he shakily pushed himself to his elbows. Tears glistened in his eyes. His mouth opened and blood spilled out onto my chest. He tried to speak. Words gurgled out in the form of, "I'm sorry."

This was not happening, I told myself. But the warm, wet blood pulsing from a hole beside his Adam's Apple refuted that claim. It *was* real. It *was* happening. There was no way he'd survive that wound. The bullet struck the carotid artery. My precious husband would die in my arms and I could do nothing to save him.

I pressed a hand to the fountain gushing from his neck, "Hold on, Ennis. *Please* hold on." I caught an officer's attention, demanding, "Get him to the ambulance quick! He's been shot! Hurry!"

The color drained from Ennis's cheeks, his eyelids drooped, "Too late." His efforts forced a pool of warm blood to dribble between my fingers.

It can't be too late. *No!* I silently implored the damn mirror.

Ennis can't die! Don't let him die! "Hurry! Get him to the hospital!" I screamed at the cops ducking behind furniture despite no shots being fired. In that moment, I hated them all because every second they hesitated guaranteed Ennis's death.

"Savannah..." he tried to swallow back the blood. It didn't work. His strength waned. His weight steadily settled against me as his body surrendered to the inevitable. I kept pressing hard against the flow coming from the hole in his neck. I pressed so hard he begged me to let go. I didn't. I would never let go, I told him. I loved him and pleaded with him, "Please stay with me, Ennis. Don't leave me. Please *don't leave me...*"

His eyes gradually closed, his shaking arms buckled and he collapsed against me. He still breathed short, uneven breaths, "...vannah," he pushed my name past the pooling blood. I barely understood him now. His voice faded to a whisper while he struggled to draw breath, "I... love... you." His head fell heavy on my shoulder.

I hugged him close as tears streamed down my face. I fought the urge to sleep but the black veil of unconsciousness prevailed. It descended fast, giving me only enough time to declare four last words to my dying husband, "I love you too."

7

I drifted awake, alone and flat of my back facing the bedroom window. The scent of Irish Spring and Ennis lingered from his side of the bed. I breathed in deep, savoring that unique bouquet and the assurance things were back to normal. I was home with my husband and kids.

The sun blared through the cream colored curtains, brightening the whole room to a blinding afternoon intensity. Good Lord, what time was it? Ennis already stirred in the kitchen – I heard the subdued clank of a pan on the stove. I was grateful to be home again, both of us safe from gunmen, both of us still alive.

Other noises filtered in. A mockingbird sang an upbeat melody in our oak tree. Children's whispers tuned my hearing to the bedside. Our girls. One murmured *is she awake* then another replied *yeah*.

Something made me pause to listen closer. They sounded, I don't know, older than Lily's four and Anna's two-nearly-three years old. I turned to the whispering pair. Yes, our daughters were the mumbling culprits – and yes, they were older. Taller and older. Not only that – three, not two children stared back at me. Lily, Anna, and a toddler likely named Daniel.

Dressed in white slacks and black sweater decorated with wildflowers, Lily stood tall for her age (around nine). Her features reminded me of my own at that age except her blue eyes possessed warmth that put a person at ease or charmed them to her will. Her silky chestnut hair grew in long, loose waves draping down her back. The countless changes in those few years left me speechless. She fast became a woman – and thanks to the mirror I'd missed it.

Anna, about six and sporting black jeans and a hot pink t-shirt, changed from cute to comely in those few short years. She was a stunning sight in her own right with those big, persuasive brown eyes, dimpled cheeks, and wavy umber hair that darkened over the years. She looked so much like Ennis it amazed me.

The toddler resembled both me and Ennis. Mama's smile, Daddy's gentle, friendly features and his stubborn "Alfalfa" cowlick. Our boy sported a fetching presence in his beige striped polo shirt and khaki colored pants. He looked absolutely precious.

Cute as he was, he shouldn't have been there like I shouldn't have been. The mirror stuck me in one of my worst nightmares and refused to send me back home.

"Good mornin', Ma," the boy beamed.

"Hush, Daniel," Anna admonished. "It's only good if Mama isn't crying." Sadness shadowed her features. "And if Daddy was here."

Lily, who really favored me by that age, gently thumbed away my tears, "You were moaning so we tried waking you up."

I held her hand, taking comfort in her warm grasp, "Thank you, baby. What time is it?"

She referenced the clock on the nightstand, "Two. Daniel just finished Sesame Street."

Two? I never slept that late. Of course I'd never buried my husband either. Weird how I knew I'd spent time in the hospital (and why) but somehow I jumped from the scene at the station to the house – which didn't bother me since I'd been in the hospital enough over the years. I had no idea how much time lapsed from the shooting to "now". I only knew I hadn't returned to the correct year in time. Since I hadn't gone back, I grimly turned my attention to living in this nightmare of the future.

My first thought was my children were home alone and that spawned images of further misery if they got into trouble. Nine years old or not, Lily couldn't handle running a household alone and it wasn't fair to ask her to try.

I tried propping on my elbow to sit up when my hip reminded me how tender it was. Movement awakened the soreness in it and my thigh causing me to wince. I flopped back to the pillow uttering a muted groan.

Lily put a hand to my shoulder, "You're supposed to rest."

I doubted I'd ever rest again. Chores needed doing, meals needed cooking, kids needed care. Bills needed paying so I added reviewing finances to the growing to-do list. As for my job, who the hell knew its status or what station I reported to for my shift? It all seemed insurmountable. "I can't, sweetie. You three need to eat supper and I have to find something to *fix* for supper."

"That's why I'm here." My sister appeared at the bedroom door. "The kids are fine," she softened her voice. "Well, except worrying about you, I mean."

Lily said, "Uncle Seth and Aunt Leah asked how you were doing."

Not so good considering my world collapsed without Ennis and I found no way to get home again where he was alive. For now though, I felt like hell physically and emotionally. Memories of blood pouring from his throat and mouth haunted me. I rubbed my fingers together, remembering the warm, sticky blood seeping between them, of it pulsing against my palm and pooling on my clothes. Every lost, precious drop stealing his life and our life together. "Tell them I'm still breathing. That's as far as I go."

"You're looking better today." Georgia's voice drew me from the horrific images tormenting me. I glanced at her as she gave me a thoughtful smile, "She looks more rested, doesn't she?" She'd asked the owl-eyed threesome standing beside me. They obediently nodded but we all knew the truth. No matter the optimistic spin someone put on it, I looked like crap and I knew it.

I propped on my elbow again, bearing the ache of my hip. I asked Georgia, "What day is it?"

She stepped to the bedroom window, fingered the curtain aside. She heard the mockingbird too. "It's Friday. Why?"

I rubbed my temple. I'd had a powerful headache. The muscles in my temple and along my jaw felt sore to the touch. The tendons in my neck stretched tighter than a drum. I didn't remember the actual migraine but Lord, when Georgia yanked the curtain cord, the light streamed in so bright my brain contracted in my skull and I expected to see Jesus at the far end of the tunnel. I squinted, held a hand to block the light until my sister closed them again. I thanked her then asked, "When was the funeral?"

Lily's brow wrinkled. The action accentuated the quirky little curve at the corner of her left eyebrow, giving it an adorable sideways S-shaped arch. What wasn't so adorable: my girls appraised me as if I'd recited the question backwards.

Lily looked at Georgia who patted her back with an assuring, "It happens during times like this. Don't worry. It's probably the emotional and physical trauma plus the sedative they gave her yesterday."

"What?" I asked.

My sister eased onto the side of the bed, her gentle touch swept my hair behind my ear, "The funeral was yesterday. You were pretty groggy when we brought you home from the hospital last night. It's no wonder you have your days mixed up."

"No more mixing up." Anna shook her finger at me, "Straighten up and fly right."

The comment sparked an instinctive smile – then it vanished. Straighten up and fly right, Ennis always said. Anna picked it up and occasionally used the phrase even back in her nearly-three-year-old world.

I nodded, "I'll try."

"Girls, go sit at the table." Georgia shooed them out, "I've got a snack waiting for you. Take your brother." She waited for them to leave but Daniel lingered by the bed, a grin curling around his thumb stuck in his mouth.

He tottered around his aunt reached out to me with his free hand. He removed the thumb long enough to say, "Good morning, Ma."

The boy insisted – despite what his sisters said – that it was a good morning so I obliged him. I kissed my palm, pressed it to his cheek then held his hand in mine, "Good morning, sweetheart."

Georgia smoothed his hair, "Go see your sisters, honey. Mama and I need to talk." The boy toddled off, satisfied and humming a catchy tune he probably learned on Sesame Street.

Georgia turned to me, "I've never seen such devoted kids. They must know where you are and what you're doing at all times or they panic." She lowered her voice to a whisper, "You tolerated Lily's presence in the bathroom amazingly well. I don't think I'd have been as gracious, not when I need privacy to do my business. I'm hoping she'll settle down now that you're home."

My kid followed me to the *crapper*? Holy hell. Talk about role reversals. I'd hoped I was fifty years away from my daughter helping me to the bathroom. The idea weirded me out but it currently rated way lower than, "Why wasn't I at the funeral? I'd never miss Ennis's funeral."

One involuntary grimace later, she answered, "It's hard to attend when the hospital won't release you. I told you to calm down yesterday morning but you refused to listen. When the doctor ordered another test, I thought you'd kill him. The closer to four it got the more out of control you were. It's no wonder they sedated you."

I clenched my teeth. "I missed my husband's funeral because of a test?" *Dear God, if I ever see that doctor again, he'd better run for his life...*

"Calm down, hon. That expression is partly why they sedated you. I expect that's why your memory is foggy this morning. They knocked you on your butt."

Well, she was right about the foggy part. My brain floated in a wasteland of facts, the only solid ones being I *was* married (now supposedly widowed), my kids *were* still my kids (plus one) and my sister looked and sounded exactly the same as always, just a tad older and grayer.

She clasped my chin, made direct eye contact, "I want you to eat today."

Yep, same ol' Georgia. Bossy as hell. "I'm not hun—"

"Savannah," she used her she-who-must-be-obeyed voice, "the last few days you've barely eaten enough to get by. Before you say no, Lily keeps asking me how to 'make Mama eat'. She's nine but she's mature enough to see how unhealthy this is." She whispered, "At least eat to appease her."

My sister perfected guilt. I called it "the gift that keeps on giving" and when Georgia climbed on her bandwagon, she made it count. According to her, I verged on starvation. According to her, my daughter obsessed over my lack of appetite. Well, according to me, I wasn't the least bit hungry and if we hadn't had children I'd still be on a hunger strike. But we *did* have kids and they deserved a mother who woke up at a reasonable time, kept food on the table and some semblance of a smile on her face. I suffered a devastating loss with Ennis but so had our kids.

I waved Georgia off the bed, "I'll get up and try to eat."

She kissed my cheek, "I know it's a difficult time, hon, but you can do this. You've got us to help you."

And I was thankful, I told her. I couldn't imagine bearing the emotional pain alone. Trying to sit up without reciting every R and X-rated word in my vocabulary proved harder than stone. My right hip cranked up a symphony of throbbing that went into my back and down my leg. I leaned to roll onto my left hip to relieve it. Georgia helped me by sliding her hand beneath my shoulders to steady me, "Try to get up. It'll take the pressure off."

Oh yeah, easy as pie. Right... I braced one hand on the nightstand, my other in her strong, steady hold. I managed to curb the cussing and settle for a groan.

"Stand there a minute, get your balance," she instructed, still holding firm to me with one hand then slid her other arm around my waist.

Like I'd willingly take a step at that point. Only a gun pressed to my skull would prove successful in moving me. I waited for the dizziness to ease then glanced around. Crutches leaned against the wall beside the nightstand. A set of fluffy pink slippers reminiscent of the nineteen seventies sat in front of my feet. Wearing those garish things rated up there with licking toads for kicks but I'd wear 'em since (I assumed) the kids chose them for Christmas or my birthday. Of course, I could have lost my mind for a day, licked a toad, and bought them myself.

Georgia assisted me in slipping on my robe then zipped it for me with a proud, "There we go."

"We? You got a hole in your hip too?"

A tiny smile played at her lips, "Good to see that sense of humor back, even if it is raw as a steak." She seemed impressed with something then shed light on the subject, "Your balance is better than last night so the sedative must have worn off."

Probably so, I agreed until the room developed another dizzying spin I clearly remembered from my drinking days. Georgia steadied me, told me to sit down. I declined since I dug deep for the courage to stand in the first place. I looked to my right and got a shock that called for another tranquilizer – or a swift belt with a two by four. My mirror was gone. "Where's the mirror?"

"What mirror?"

I leaned out for the crutches but fell short on reach. Georgia handed them to me. I equipped them with a pained grimace and hobbled to the dresser, "The antique cheval I bought last..." I stopped cold. I had to remember this was not last week. This was four years later, "The one I bought years ago. I had it next to the dresser."

Recognition dawned on Georgia, "Oh, that mirror."

"Yeah, that mirror. Where is it?" I bordered on panic. If that mirror went missing, I feared I might be stuck in the future forever. With no Ennis. With no idea what the hell led up to his death. How could I live in this time without him, knowing he was actually alive and well in the real world? "*Where is it, Georgia?*"

My sister regarded me with a concern suggesting I suffered more than physical instability. "You really don't remember. I think I need to call the doctor. He never mentioned this degree of memory loss being a side effect of what happened. You've been fine until this morning. With your memory, I mean."

"No doctors," I preached. "Just tell me where my mirror is." Outside the bedroom I heard whispering. Girl's voices talking back and forth. The kids were listening. I distinctly picked up certain words and phrases. Why's she asking so many questions, Anna inquired. Lily shushed her to be quiet.

"Girls," I called, "Aunt Georgia made those snacks for you. Better go eat them."

Scurrying sounds of feet running down the hall told me they obeyed. I turned back to my sister, waiting for an answer.

"Honey, the mirror is gone. Ennis tripped and broke it after Daniel was born. He felt so bad about it too."

In my mind a heavy metal door clanged shut and a lock snapped. *I'm stuck here, locked in the future because my portal home broke.* I couldn't explain how the mirror worked, I only figured I needed the mirror – not broken shards – to get me back home. Hopeless and incredulous, I repeated, "He broke it? It was stouter than Mount Rushmore, how did he break it?"

"He tripped like I said. He heard Daniel crying in the night, got up to grab his robe and fell over it. It was a wonder he didn't get kill–" her mouth slammed shut, shook her head. A heartfelt apology followed, "I'm sorry, hon. It just slipped out."

I barely heard her past *Ennis tripped and broke it.* I could not wrap my mind around the fact my mirror was toast. How did I get back to the real world where Ennis vacillated over transferring to Zone 5? To the reality where our children equaled only two, not three?

Georgia squeezed my hand, "Let's get you fed and bring some color to your cheeks. You need nourishment."

No, I needed my husband. I needed my life back the way it was. I started forward on the crutches to discover my armpits ached as if I'd been hung on a fence for days. I pushed against the handles to relieve the strain then realized my arms hurt too. I rolled my eyes as I headed out the door. I was a complete wreck.

The house hadn't changed much over those few years. A new sofa (this one potato colored for some reason), and a pair of tall dracaena plants bookended the TV stand. Family pictures still lined the mantle. The kids, the Rutherfords, Mama & Daddy, Georgia's family and Seth's. A conspicuous hole glared out between the kids and the Rutherfords. I remembered that photo. One taken of me and Ennis at our wedding just after saying our "I do's". I pointed to the mantle, "The picture?"

Georgia answered easily now. I assumed she grew accustomed to my strange amnesia. "You took it down last night when we got home from the hospital. Said it was–"

"Too painful to see," I finished, knowing what I'd say no matter when I lost my husband. Georgia gave a solemn nod.

The kids sat at the dining table, all quiet, all staring at me. I felt like a lab rat.

Georgia pulled the wooden dining chair out for me. The chair at the head of the table. Ennis's. Anna sat to my left, Lily to my right and Daniel straight ahead. "Pull up a chair," I told my sibling.

She shook her head, "I've got a chair right here," she pointed to a lone dining chair positioned out of the way – right where she could monitor my food intake.

I gratefully removed the crutches, braced a hand on the chair seat and gingerly eased down. The hip sent a flare of fire along my leg to my toes. I tried braving the pain by wincing but the blistering words stampeding through my brain could have sent a shiver down Satan's back.

Georgia took the crutches, leaned them in the corner, "I'll get your lunch."

"What *is* for lunch?" I inquired. The ache eased a degree, allowing me a tentative smile at the kids. Lily and Anna's mouths curved slightly but Daniel giggled across the way. He was happy. Mama was up and about and apparently in better shape than the past few days. My children expected a semi-normal mother, not a loon raving about a long gone mirror (which I'd work on later if possible). I'd try my best to act compos mentis for their sakes – before they and my sister carted me off to the asylum.

"I made chicken soup for you," Georgia answered from the kitchen. "You always like it when you're sick."

Well, that was true. She put canned soup to shame with her homemade concoction. And it healed a cold in record time. I just wondered if it cured insanity because if I failed to return to my real life soon, I'd put a whole new spin on berserk.

I surveyed the saucers sitting in front of the kids. Georgia's "snacks" consisted of Ritz cracker and peanut butter sandwiches for Daniel and for the girls: a large graham cracker slathered with cream cheese and topped with strawberry slices. My sister verged on genius. Daniel already plowed through one of his Ritz treats and Anna eagerly ogled her snack but politely waited for her gimpy mother to receive her lunch before diving in. Lily, on the other hand, watched me with an intense, invasive stare that compelled me to glance away.

My vision passed across the morning paper Georgia had folded and placed on the arm of my recliner. Above the fold in bold, black letters a partial headline read *Second APD Detective...*

"Sweetie," I asked Lily, "hand me the newspaper, please."

She hesitated, looked toward the kitchen. Either she wanted to run the request past Aunt Georgia first, or Aunt Georgia laid down the law. No more bad news for Mama.

I nodded, waving her to go ahead, "It's okay."

She dutifully fetched it but hid it behind her back, "You promise to eat?" Now *her* voice held a note of authority. Plus, she held my paper hostage until I answered her. She'd been around her aunt *way* too much.

I crossed my heart, "I promise to eat what I can."

She handed it to me. I unfolded it. The whole headline read "*Second APD Detective Laid To Rest*". Ennis's death was still front page news. The photo beneath the bold lettering showed a sea of uniforms crowding the cemetery. Most from Atlanta, others from surrounding departments. I saw nothing but row after row of saluting officers. The urge to weep lodged in my throat.

Lily put me under her microscope, scrutinizing every nuance of my expression, so I forced back the emotion, swallowed the lump and skimmed over the article before my sister caught me. According to the paper, two cops died in the attack, Ennis and a uniform officer. Six others were wounded, including me. I read on. *A married father of three, Rutherford was fatally shot outside the Zone 5 stationhouse on Monday when a gunman opened fire on the precinct. Rutherford's wife, a sergeant with the department, and five others were also injured...* My vision drifted to the photo of Ennis. My heart squeezed in my chest but I resisted the urge to rub it since Lily continued to eagle eye my every move.

Below Ennis's photo was the bastard who killed him. My vision locked on his name. Shaun Ellis. Mr. Ellis, twenty-one, attended Dartmouth University and scored not only excellent grades in his classes but points with the rowing team. So what made Shaun Ellis drop his oars and pick up an M4 assault rifle and get trigger happy on us cops? Because New Hampshire was a far cry from Georgia and an M4 with four ammo boxes (two still full when cops found them on the roof of the building) meant either Mr. Ellis nursed a grudge against the South in general or a grudge specifically against Atlanta cops.

He looked like grandma's angel with a baby face, chubby cheeks and charming smile. I'd bet my retirement women flocked to this young man, jockeying for his attention and probably more. He appeared competent, intelligent. He did not look like a killer. The article quoted his parents as saying he was a gentle boy who (of course) never hurt a fly.

Newsflash, Mom and Pop. You missed the moment when Sonny Boy snapped and went postal on a dozen cops with his trusty M4. My face flushed as my blood pressure skyrocketed. I wanted to kill that little bastard myself but a police sniper beat me to it. The article got worse. Ellis's goal upon graduation was to enter politics and push for gun control, thus magically reducing gun deaths across the country.

I pursed my lips. Yeah, right. Gun Control? Reduce gun violence? Did anyone else see the twisted irony? So once Sonny Boy, the caped crusader against citizens owning firearms, got his wish and relieved everyone of their Second Amendment Rights, what did he intend to do then? Legislate cars, knives, food and water out of existence too? Because driving killed, knives killed, people choked on food and drowned in water. And not everything was murder, not like Mr. Ellis's grand stand.

I read further to realize that *had* been his goal, according to a note he left behind at his dorm. To show why guns should be removed from everyone's possession – and to show how irresponsibly law enforcement used *their* weapons. Six months earlier his brother Darren Ellis, upon exiting the bank he just robbed, thrust a .45 at an officer from Zone 5 and pulled the trigger. Darren's aim lacked the accuracy of his liberal-minded sibling. The shot missed. The officer's didn't.

Shaun Ellis's siege had been payback for his brother's "tragic, unnecessary death" but I called it revenge for law enforcement doing their sworn duty. Protecting the public from a dangerous criminal.

The paper vanished from my hands as Georgia stripped it away, "Stop reading that. You did it every day in the hospital and ended up crying and needing a sedative."

There was that word again. Sedative. Hated to tell my sister but no sedative on this planet would put my lights out if she didn't hand that damn paper back, "Today I won't end up crying or needing meds. Give it back."

She refused to. My eyes narrowed at her, "Georgia, give me the paper. I am not going back to bed, I promise you that." *Because I've got too much work to do. I have a name and face to work with. I just need to talk to Mathis or Josh. Probably Mathis.* The captain and Georgia aligned together against me – for my own good, they always said. I suspected this time I'd get nada from Josh Hunter as per Georgia's marching orders.

My sister and I stared each other down. Lily leaned back in her seat. Anna stopped eating. Daniel only muttered an *uh-oh* upon seeing us square off. I tried again, this time nicely, "I want to finish that article and eat. Please allow me to do that."

She appraised my expression. Seconds stretched into years until she relinquished the paper, "So help me if you fall into that depression again or you don't eat, I'll put you over my knee, little sister."

The girls exchanged wide-eyed stares, probably curious if it could actually happen and who would win the battle. In my condition, I realized the answers were *yes* and *Aunt Georgia.*

I blustered for dignity's sake, "If you get me over your knee, good luck getting me upright again with this bum hip and leg." The kids relaxed when our voices softened. They resumed eating and I laid the paper aside to dig into Georgia's chicken soup. No one made tastier soup than my sister. I'd even heard people who hated soup rave about it. As good as it tasted, my vision kept migrating to Lily's graham cracker slathered in cream cheese and perfectly arranged strawberry slices.

With a hopeful, almost pleading look, my daughter pushed her saucer toward me. I smiled, touched by the thoughtful gesture, then eased it back to her, "Aunt Georgia made that for you, sweetheart, but thank you."

My sister's jaw dropped as if I'd mentioned taking up square dancing before day's end. "*You* want one?" she asked.

I couldn't fix what happened to their daddy but I could ease my kids' concern for their mother. "Please," I said. "It looks delicious."

That simple request produced the widest smile I'd ever seen on my oldest child. Georgia joined her, adding a confident wink for her young collaborator. My sister grasped my hand, gave it a gentle squeeze, "I'll be right back."

O O O

I'd spoken to friends, family and coworkers who extended their condolences. Since learning the gunman's name I tried on several occasions to call Mathis who never seemed to be available. The desk sergeant finally told me he'd left for his daughter's wedding after attending Ennis's funeral. Being desperate, I dialed Josh Hunter's number but he'd taken a three day vacation "at his wife's request" the sergeant said. Michelle Hunter reminded me of Georgia. The take-charge type. For years she wanted Josh to put in his papers so Ennis's death probably reopened that old wound. Today was his day back so I'd call again.

Every day the mailbox brimmed with sympathy cards and condolences. What wasn't delivered by mail was brought via uniform officer. Stacks of cards and letters addressed to me in care of the police department piled up. I'd jumped from the shooting to the following Friday so days of mail accumulated in that time. I sifted through mail that expressed "our thoughts are with you", "with deepest sympathy" and "so sorry for your loss". I was never so grateful for a Sunday in my life. At least there would be no mail. Friends, extended family and strangers sent cards. They came from different states, the furthest – Alaska. Shaun Ellis's rampage went nationwide, covered by networks and newspapers alike.

After so many days, I missed hearing Ennis's voice and seeing his face – yet I still couldn't bring myself to look at his picture. I missed snuggling with him in bed. I missed his laugh, his jokes, and his smell. On Monday (Day Four), Georgia caught me pressing my nose to one of his t-shirts. I inhaled deeply, remembering only days ago when we both spent the afternoon playing hide and seek with the kids. When I kissed him, he embraced me, wrapping his sun-warmed arms around me. He smelled like heaven and home.

Monday afternoon Dane arrived with their six-month-old daughter Eden. If one thing in the future scenario actually happened, I prayed it was Eden. The moment I laid eyes on that tiny angel, I cried with joy. My sister's dream finally came true with the chubby, wiggly bundle swaddled in her pink blankie. In my "normal" life, she and Dane struggled to conceive, trying everything short of adoption (which they seriously considered) to have their own child. At long last my sister was a proud, doting mother.

Dane stayed with the kids while Georgia drove me to my appointment with the estate lawyer. Nothing prepared me for that meeting. After expressing his sympathies, the lawyer began the task of reading Ennis's will. Hearing my husband's last wishes read (and dissected) by a stranger brought the harsh reality crashing in on me. Whether now (in the vision) or later (in the actual future), one of us would sit in a seat facing a lawyer, hearing these words read and made official.

Ennis and I both knew each other's wills but hearing the lawyer's businesslike manner while reading it bothered me. No, it angered me. My husband's life encompassed more than a house, some savings and stocks and a damn Dodge. He was my husband and partner, my best friend and soul mate. He was a father of three beautiful children who loved him dearly. He was the son of a devoted couple who raised him with a gentle, profound love and helped mold him into the fine man I married. So having Ennis basically referred to as an asset I needed to cash in inflamed my temper to explosive proportions. If Georgia hadn't been there, I might have climbed over that lawyer's desk and strangled him to shut him up.

While I stewed, he listed the documents necessary to finalize my husband's passing – account statements, copies of bills, his life insurance policy, the house deed, the papers for his Dodge and on and on. To his surprise, I'd brought most of them with me anyway. I came home with a number, a migraine and a date for probate court. The number indicated how many death certificates I required to officially inform everyone this side of the universe that my husband was deceased. That "formality" – as the lawyer called it – wouldn't occur until we attended probate court. Then my title would officially change from *married* to *widowed*. The appointment, paperwork, and will reinforced the gravity of my situation in a short four years – or *now*, if I failed to return to my current time. Damn it, I was thirty-nine, not forty-three. Ennis and I had two children, not three. And my husband was *living and breathing*, not dead in the ground.

A deep, overwhelming depression set in on the way home. I stared at the to-do's written on the note in my hand realizing Ennis's life – and death – boiled down to legalities and lists. When Georgia and I got home, my appetite (what little there was) had long disappeared but to appease the masses I nibbled on a ham and cheese sandwich Dane prepared for me. He wanted to help, to comfort me however he could, but I found it difficult to even look at him since he and Ennis favored so heavily. I spoke to him while averting my gaze (I'm sure he noticed this but he said nothing). I apologized for my behavior and confessed that right then, Ennis's image – in any respect – broke my heart.

I ate three bites of Dane's ham and cheese "sammy" (Ennis's personal nickname for sandwich) before nausea kicked in. I excused myself and headed to the bedroom. I passed by the mantle where I'd returned the picture of Ennis and me together (hoping to restore some normalcy to our lives). I tilted the photo face down. No one said a word.

On Day Five – Tuesday – Lily's crying woke me up at eight-thirty. Since I'd arrived on the wrong side of the mirror, Lily followed me everywhere, including the bathroom. Georgia at least allowed me privacy for that. My oldest daughter did not. I hated to admit it got on my nerves but when a person couldn't even pee without their kid repeatedly knocking on the door asking for a status report, that toed a pretty thin line with me. Her paranoia worsened over those few days. Saturday night she tiptoed in the bedroom, stood by my side. The question went unspoken. I lifted the covers, invited her in. She snuggled in and I held her close.

I'd hoped the closeness helped until I heard the mournful weeping coming from her bedroom Tuesday morning. Her room was next to ours so the sound traveled loud and clear. I hurried to wrestle my thirty-nine (not forty-three) year-old bones from the nice warm bed, equip the crutches then stumped to her room.

One lone crazy man caused this. He killed Lily's daddy, wounded her mother and instilled the base fear in my child that she'd be left without either parent.

I stopped at the closed bedroom door. Georgia spoke to Lily who sniffed back tears. Tuning my hearing, I caught my sister softly assure, "Honey, you need to remember Mama's okay. I know you miss your daddy. We all do–"

"Why won't she retire? She could work with you at the bakery." She unleashed another round of uncontrollable weeping, "No one dies at bakeries."

My heart squeezed in my chest. I rubbed at it, trying to will away the pain of my child's inconsolable sorrow. It was time to broach this subject – and time for honesty.

I knocked on the door, waited for Georgia to respond before I opened it. My oldest child huddled in her aunt's embrace, clung to her as if her life depended on it. She clamped her lips tight to smother the sobs battling for freedom then lifted her red, tear-streaked face to meet my gaze. Her accusing expression shocked me. It wasn't *I hate you* but more in the neighborhood of *I'll never forgive you.*

"Baby, what's wrong?" I plodded to her bed, laid the crutches aside and eased next to her. I stroked her cheek. She pulled away, hugged Georgia tighter.

Don't take it personally. She's upset about losing Ennis. I only prayed she didn't hold me responsible for his death for some reason. Seeing her reject me to seek comfort in Georgia's arms hurt me in a way I could only explain as a mother's ache. It went to my soul.

My sister must have seen it in my expression since she reached for my hand, held it, "She misses Ennis and is afraid she'll lose you too."

I noticed she failed to mention Lily's suggestion at trading my gun for an apron. *No one dies at bakeries...* No, but bakeries didn't pay the bucks I needed to keep the bills paid and food on the table either. A sergeant's salary paid considerably more and we needed every penny, especially now that we were essentially a one income family. For the immediate future, I had to keep my job and that would make me as popular as a leper with the kids.

I eased my hand down her back, "Lily, nothing will happen to me."

There was that accusatory glare again, "You can't promise that. Look what happened to you and Daddy. And I remember Jeffrey..." Controlling her emotions became an overwhelming struggle to the point I wasn't sure if she'd lash out or burst into tears. She chose a mix of both, "He nearly killed you and you still wouldn't quit your job."

Yowch. "Honey, I–"

"You don't love us enough to quit."

I winced on that one. It hit the intended mark. Right in the heart. Georgia lightly scolded her, saying *you know that's not true.*

Anna and Daniel peeked around the corner, probably too terrified to venture in. But they both awaited my answer. Especially Anna.

I kept my voice calm and even, "Lily, you, Anna and Daniel are the most important people in my life. I love you so much–"

"No, you don't. You love your *job,*" she accused.

"I *need* my job. I'll have desk duty. Nothing can happen to me there." I reached to touch her cheek but she retreated closer to Georgia. It was difficult to tell who my sister felt sorriest for, Lily or me.

"Lily," she said, "let her heal more before we mention retirement. She misses Daddy too and needs time to think about the future, to figure out what's best for you, Anna, Daniel and herself. Right now is little soon to make those decisions."

The urge to cry rose in my throat, "Sweetheart, please listen." I wanted to hug my daughter whether she welcomed my embrace or fought it. I needed the feel of my baby in my arms, to reassure her. And to reassure myself that I wasn't alone. I'd lost Ennis. That dark finality grew each day, threatening to drag me into its abyss. I shored up my voice, "I promise to think about retirement but I can't right now. There are so many bills coming in that we need the money."

I received no clemency or understanding. "Aunt Georgia and Uncle Seth offered to help," she shot back. "I heard them."

"Yes, they did and I appreciate their generous offers but," I swallowed however the lump in my throat refused to budge, "we need to learn how to live without Daddy now. That's going to be the hardest thing we've ever done." Tears slipped down my cheeks, "And if we need them, Aunt Georgia and Uncle Seth will be there but we'll do this ourselves if we can. As for retirement, I understand you want me to quit and I would if I could." Something I never expected to say, much less mean, but I did.

Georgia's brow lifted in a question. I confirmed, "Yes. I would." I put a hand to Lily's knee, grateful she didn't pull away, "But I have the funeral, the hospital, the other bills and everything else to contend with. I don't want to disappoint you, sweetheart, but for now I have to keep my job." I gave her knee a tiny squeeze, "I promise when things settle down, we will sit down and discuss what to do next, including my job."

Georgia helped things along by reminding, "See? I told you she'd listen. And she promised to talk with you later about it. Your mother never breaks her promises, you know that."

"I know," she sniffled. "I just miss Daddy so much."

Her sadness hit me right in the mom part of my brain, not to mention my heart that broke with each tear she shed. "I know you do, baby. I miss him too." I extended my arms, praying she accepted the offer. Without hesitation, she bailed straight into my embrace and held on with an unbreakable, earnest ferocity that defined my girl's love for me. I wasn't alone after all.

O   O   O

Don't invite me to your pity party. My colleague John Mathis cataloged a ton of such sayings. My personal favorite: *I'm sorry. I don't speak Whinese.* He embodied a smattering of memorable people in my mind – the pre-Jacob-Marley-in-chains version of Scrooge (bah-humbug!), Budda with his rare gems of wisdom, Archie Bunker with his unvarnished opinions and prejudice and last but not least a dash of little boy needing a mother's softer presence to offset Scrooge and Archie. The last usually fell to me despite the ten year age gap (he was older).

For all his weird ways and shortcomings, John Mathis was a good man. Sure he surpassed the usual weight limit for cops years ago and eighty percent of the time his personality made porcupines seem like walking feather pillows. But he'd also seen plenty of injustice and death on the job and after a point it affected a cop. It made him gruff, temperamental, caustic and unsympathetic toward others – unless he liked them. Thankfully Ennis and I fell into that exclusive category. That morning, Day Five, I decided not to throw a pity party. Instead I'd search for a way home. In short that meant searching for another mirror.

When I bought the mirror, the antique store owner mentioned only two double-sided mirrors on the market. I intended to track that other one down by any means necessary. A long shot but what else could I do?

"Georgia," I called, gimping to the kitchen by way of those hateful medieval crutches. I thought I remembered the name of the antique shop but needed confirmation. I only hoped after four years my sister could verify it. Last week (in the world where Ennis was alive) we'd visited a number of antique stores. Junk & Disorderly, Good Old Days, Top Drawer Antiques and one other store. Vintage Treasures, was my best recollection.

I thumped through the living room and rounded the corner of the kitchen to find Georgia in a blue blouse and jeans, leisurely propped against the cabinet. She busied herself thumbing through my cookbook. "I need to look through this more often," she said, seemingly impressed. "Where'd you get the chicken pot pie casserole recipe? Dane and I would love it."

I recognized the dish from a church fundraiser long ago – well, five years ago to be exact which dated it to "fairly recent" to me in my "Ennis Is Alive World". "A church fundraiser for Vacation Bible School five years ago. Sonya Porter and I exchanged recipes. My chicken stew for her chicken pot pie casserole."

Georgia's mouth dropped, "How do you remember that far back? You've got a much better memory than I do."

Nope. Just, "Doesn't seem that long ago to me." I nodded to a pen and notepad I kept by the phone, "Copy the recipe. It's delicious."

"Thanks." She collected the paper and pen, nodded to the dining table, "Get off your feet. You look miserable. Is it your leg and hip?"

"No, my armpits. What'd I do, use the crutches for pole vaulting down the hospital corridors?" I grimaced as I leaned them against the neighboring chair.

Georgia exercised her best *you-poor-thing* frown, "No. You

weren't very steady on your feet at first so you relied on them to support your weight." She sat down, jotted down the first few ingredients for the casserole. Every second that passed made me edgier. I wanted her to have the recipe – hell, she could take the whole book if she'd help me get back home.

"Would you like this for supper or does the," she flipped back through the book to another recipe, "beef stroganoff sound better?"

"The girls like chicken pot pie so it'll be fine, though I bet Daniel takes after En–" *I bet Daniel takes after Ennis and prefers* anything *beef,* I was going to say.

Georgia reached across, patted my hand, "Yes, he does take after Ennis. A meat and potatoes man. So we'll have beef stroganoff tonight and chicken pot pie tomorrow."

"Dane's gonna think you've moved in. You need to get back to your life, Georgia. You've got a baby, a husband, the bakery and other responsibilities. You're wearing yourself out. I can manage."

"*Hush, Savannah.*"

The surprisingly sharp scold took me aback. She immediately apologized then turned away, silent for several seconds. Her voice tightened, "We nearly lost you both. It was the most helpless I've felt next to Mama's passing and when Jeffrey abducted you that last time. Dane and I have Eden's care worked out. He understands and encourages me to stay here as long as I need to be here. It was," she brushed tears from her cheeks, "the most empty feeling at the funeral. Holding your children without either of you there. We all felt lost. So pardon my French but *shut the hell up* about getting back to my life. You are my sister and you *are* part of my life."

I inadvertently stepped on her toes by saying I could manage without her. I could but I dreaded trying. She wanted to help and Dane, a typical Rutherford, understood that. I grasped her hand, "Thank you for being here for us, sis."

She nodded then stripped a tissue from the box on the table – an essential item added by Georgia since tears ran like rivers around the house these days. She blew her nose hard enough it honked like a miniature congested trumpet. I chose that time to mention the store, "Do you happen to remember the name of that antique store? The one where you bought your entry table and I bought the mirror?"

"Antique store?" She blew her nose again. No trumpet that time. "The one on Broad Street?"

"Yes, that one. Was the name Vintage Treasures?"

"No, it was Attic Treasures. Why?"

"Would you drop me by there later this afternoon? I want to see if he can find another mirror for me."

"Savannah," her brow dipped, "why are you preoccupied with that mirror? Not long before Ennis stumbled over it you planned to get rid of it."

How thoroughly stupid of me. Sheepishly I answered, "I want another."

A tiny humorous smile played at her lips. All signs of the tears disappeared. Now incredulity replaced them, "If I remember correctly, the owner mentioned only two mirrors in existence at the time – and you'd just bought one of them. What are the chances *anyone* can find the other – if it's still in circulation and in one piece?"

"I'd like to ask him to try."

"Honey, I'd love to take you but he closed the store six months after we bought the table and mirror. We can call around and see if another store can track the mirror down but honestly you stand a better chance of winning the lottery."

Getting the other mirror *meant* winning the lottery but Georgia was right. It would take a miracle to find the other cheval.

Early that afternoon Georgia supplied me with the Dunwoody and Metro Atlanta phone books. Atlanta's weighed more than the tablets Moses toted down the mountain. I called every antique store listed. Nothing. Georgia covertly listened in and later my kids joined the audience, except they exercised their portion of my genetic contribution. Their sharp tongues.

"That mirror was ugly," Anna declared.

"I know," I replied, a bit defensive. But no one understood its true value. I said it before Anna did, "You called it *A Ugly*."

"Mama, it was creepy," Lily piled on. "You were obsessed with it."

I doubted that. Okay, I took some trips back in time but those trips added up to less than six. I put my oldest on the spot, "Obsessed how?"

She recoiled, looked to Georgia for guidance. My voice remained normal, not accusatory in any way. I sensed the subject had been a sore spot in the past because of her reaction.

Georgia motioned for her to proceed which she did, "You started acting weird after you bought it."

"About a week or so afterward, if memory serves me," Georgia added.

The timeline coincided with the moment the mirror zapped me into this particular nightmare. I listened closer now, "Go on."

"The worst was when you got really angry at Daddy for transferring to Zone 5. You, um," Lily averted her gaze to Georgia again, apparently uneasy with her forthcoming words – or possible backlash from me.

"Remember?" Georgia took over. "You accused him of not discussing his final decision with you. You both squared off in that vicious argument."

Lily averted her gaze, "It was horrible."

"When Lily called me and Dane to intervene we knew it was bad." She blew out a breath, "It *was* pretty explosive when we arrived."

By now my oldest shrank down in her chair, "You and Daddy kept shouting at each other."

I placed a hand on hers, the other on Anna's, "Girls, I'm sorry we fought. At the time I guess I thought I knew better than Daddy." As it turned out I did though I'd never tell the kids. "Neither of us meant to scare or upset you. He wanted more money for us and transferring to Zone 5 and my sergeant's promotion provided that."

My sister shook her head, "I never understood your bizarre behavior until now."

Bizarre behavior? I cocked a brow at her. Wasn't fighting in front of the kids bizarre enough?

Georgia continued, "When I took you aside you insisted something bad would happen to Ennis – and yourself – if he transferred. I admit I thought you'd lost your mind. You got hysterical about him being in danger. In retrospect, you were right but how did you predict it?"

Good question. Before the mirror dumped me in that gunfight at the station, I had no clue who'd died or how. There was only one explanation in my opinion. I'd experienced this "future" before. Oh dear God. I rubbed my forehead, feeling a pang starting. *Am I stuck in a "Groundhog Day" scenario?* If so, how? And why didn't I remember going through this before? How many times had I sat at the table with Georgia and the kids having this same conversation? It didn't matter how many rotations of this "Groundhog Day" hell I'd been through because the mirror was gone. Broken. Did this mean I repeatedly failed to change Ennis's mind about transferring so the mirror said "Game Over" and forced me to endure the rest of my life without him? "I said that?" I asked, dumbfounded. "I said we were both in danger?"

According to Georgia's expression, my incessant questioning of my past must have alarmed her but if I'd forewarned Ennis, I wanted to know. Before she mentioned a doctor or something worse, I waved off her frown, "Just refresh my memory. I actually told Ennis we'd both be hurt if he transferred?"

Lily bowed her head, mumbling, "You told him he'd die."

My mouth gaped. The hairs on the back of my neck bristled from shock and surprise that I'd say such horrible things to my husband (even in a moment of anger) – and say them in front of our kids. "I did not," I defended, hoping someone might agree with me. "I wouldn't do that."

My daughters avoided my gaze. "You did," Anna said.

The girls emotionally retreated from me. I figured they viewed me as a heartless monster. I prayed that when they peered up again I didn't see hatred in their eyes saying *I wish you'd died and not Daddy.*

My voice abandoned me, leaving a tremulous whisper in its wake, "Georgia, tell me I never said that. I love Ennis." Tears gathered in my eyes. Grief overwhelmed me that I not only fought with Ennis but that I'd been so callous to him. "Why would I be so cruel?"

She touched my hand that felt ice cold. I welcomed the firm, steady warmth of her grasp. "You were terrified, Savannah," she said. "Raw panic and anger caused you to lash out. To be honest you were incoherent and rambling. You talked about the mirror then told him he'd be killed if he transferred. I tried giving you a Valium to calm you down but you got physical with me. You're strong anyway but add anger and you're unstoppable."

"Did I hit you?" Then added a plausible excuse, "I can't remember." I couldn't believe I'd hit my sister. Of course the past few minutes proved I was apparently capable of anything.

"No, hon, but you scared the dickens out of me. I backed off quick."

"Forget the Valium. You should have hit me with a hammer if I really said that to Ennis and fought with you."

"You were upset and felt betrayed that he accepted the job without telling you first. I'm not sure why you mentioned the mirror or why you insisted he'd die and you'd get injured but you *were* very specific. You told me it would happen on a Monday after you and Ennis stopped for lunch at the café down the street from the station. You mentioned the gunman across the street and the wounds you and Ennis would suffer. You predicted the whole event point by point. It gives me chills."

She suddenly shuddered. The tremors vibrated through my hand and arm. I noticed she neglected to describe where the bullet struck Ennis. For the kids' sake (and mine), I offered my thanks. In the real time, the "event" hadn't happened yet but my mind didn't see it that way. I still felt him slamming on top of me, forcing the breath from my lungs. His struggle to push his body off mine to relieve me of his weight. The warm, sticky blood oozing onto my blouse and down my neck. The effort it took to draw his last breath – to declare his love for me. Yes, in my mind, it *happened*. In my normal, present time, it *hadn't*. But telling the heart and brain to be logical when a person saw, felt, heard and wholly experienced those final moments? When those final moments were as real and strong as their love for their dearly departed? There's no such thing as logical.

My sister gently squeezed my hand, "We need to pull together right now, like we always have as a family. That means instead of tracking down another mirror, why don't you concentrate on healing and we'll help where we can. Right, kids?"

They all nodded, Daniel putting more effort into the action than the girls. "Get well, Ma." His enthusiasm reminded me of Ennis and his perpetual optimism.

"I'm trying, baby." I looked to my girls, expecting to see loathing or even hatred. "Girls, I can't apologize enough for my actions back then. You have to believe I'd never hurt Daddy or any of you on purpose. Never."

"We know," Lily replied as sadly as I felt. The memory of my actions still stung, I could see it in her eyes. "It hurts to remember it though."

Anna slid from the chair and embraced me, "We love you, Mama."

"Very much," Lily finally smiled, joined the group hug. It was the best feeling in the world to have those arms enfold me so tight. Hot tears streaked my face – not tears of sorrow but of relief…

8

That afternoon darkened with slate gray clouds and a colder wind. The forecast called for cold rain and brisk winds by evening. I watched a dreary shroud obscure the beaming sun and bright blue sky. By noon, the winds kicked in, bringing with it a chilly rain. The cold front blew through early.

Since Ennis's funeral the local rag moved on to other topics. Shootings in bars, car accidents, politics and football news. At the top of all this cheery news sat a cheesy caricature of Santa Claus. With Thanksgiving a couple of weeks away, the paper decided to bombard us with a most annoying fact. "48 Shopping Days Left Until Christmas" it read. Damned idiots. Not everyone would have a Merry Christmas. If the mirror didn't return me to the present soon, I'd need to shop for children who would only ask Santa to bring their father back. If it would work, I'd sit on the old man's lap too. As for that nagging newspaper, I wadded it into a ball and threw it away.

Just after one o'clock, an officer and his wife braved the inclement weather, dropping by with a casserole and offers of help if we needed it. With Thanksgiving and Christmas on the horizon they said, a man's assistance might come in handy, or another pair of hands to tend to the kids and let me catch up on rest.

Since my release from the hospital, these occurrences increased in frequency. Cops helping cops. The men usually offered manual labor in case I required repairs around the house. Their wives pitched in with food and volunteered to babysit or do housework. Law enforcement took care of each other but Southerners in general naturally gathered around to help. In was in our blood.

At three o'clock Dane arrived, carrying their six-month-old bundle of joy. He'd driven over to stay with me while Georgia toted the kids to Kroger with her.

My first order of business was to steal time with baby Eden. I settled on the couch and took the angel in my arms. I cooed at her, tickled her tummy. Her brown eyes widened with surprise then she broke into a smile and a giggle. I saw Georgia in that grin. Eden favored both her Mama and Daddy and inherited that laid-back Rutherford demeanor unless she was wet, muddy or hungry.

In five days I learned her favorite lullabies (Frère Jacques and Hush, Little Baby), her preferred game (Peek-A-Boo) and her favorite foods. Spending time with my niece became a rare bright spot in the trip to the future.

Eden gurgled and grinned at me as I cradled her close. We exchanged quite a conversation in baby talk. I discovered she enjoyed both Mama and Daddy's reading abilities and that she considered Dr.

Seuss's work among the classics (an assumption I made from her rapt attention while I quoted his work). As for food, she kept Georgia busy mashing apples, carrots and an occasional banana (and fortifying it with formula) to satisfy her expanding palette. Forgetting one apple, Dane said, meant Eden mutinied by nightfall.

I joked with Eden about inciting mutinies and riots. That was Aunt Savannah's job, I said, so don't put me out of work. The baby giggled which inspired one from me.

Dane patted my knee, "It's good to see you smile and laugh again, Peach."

When I looked up, he offered me a reserved smile. He bore such a strong resemblance to Ennis, my smile faded a degree. I fought the urge to instinctively look away, forcing myself to face my brother-in-law. After all, he couldn't help his genetics. "Having my family around me, having your support and," I motioned to Eden, "holding my little niece keeps me going. I haven't said it but I know you're hurting and I want to support you too."

"Hearing your laugh is loads of help for me. Gives me hope. Hope for us all."

We chatted a while longer then I excused myself to make phone calls. My brother-in-law wasn't the nosy type, thank God, so I needn't worry about eavesdroppers, not until Georgia and the kids returned – and my time ran short.

I started with antique stores. No matter what Georgia said, I needed another mirror or I feared I was doomed to die in this version of my life, one I'd lived at least one other time, maybe more. Every phone call met with failure. Some stores never heard of the mirror's manufacturer (or *trademark* I should say), others specialized in clocks, glassware or larger furniture such as dining sets or armoires. Thought I found one encouraging possibility at a shop two miles away. The manager referred to his catalog, spent several minutes researching the auctions and offers from other dealers. I stayed on hold for fifteen minutes biting my bottom lip. I eyed the clock the whole time, expecting the front door to open and a group of excited kids to stream in.

The manager clicked back on with dismal news. There were no mirrors by that manufacturer currently for sale or auction. He suggested I try back in a few weeks or months. *Hell, in a few weeks I'll be nuts. They don't normally allow cheval mirrors in the booby hatch, especially ones the patient claims are magic.* I thanked the manager and focused on the next task that afternoon.

I gathered the courage to dial Josh Hunter's number at work. His usual businesslike voice softened once he realized it was me. "How are you doing?" he asked.

"Getting by. Met with the lawyer yesterday. I have an appointment in probate court next week."

"One day at a time, Savannah. One *step* at a time. You've got family and friends waiting to help. If there's anything I can do, let me know."

"Thanks, I appreciate it." I paused a moment to group my thoughts. "Now that I think about it, would you look up the date Ennis transferred to Zone 5? I forgot it…"

"Sure." Computer keys clicked in the background. "Savannah, you sound exhausted. Can't this wait until later when you're more rested?"

"Actually I need the date now."

"Give me a minute. The computer's slow." He paused a moment then, "You planned a beautiful service for Ennis. He would have been proud. Just sorry you weren't able to attend."

I choked up, not trusting myself to speak without completely breaking down. For something that hadn't actually happened yet, Ennis's death seemed as real as my being stuck in this hideous future forever.

"Listen," he said, "be with Georgia and your kids. Forget starting a crusade for answers. It will never make sense and it won't ease your pain."

In normal circumstances he'd have been correct. But I sought to *prevent* this tragedy, not mire down in my sorrow for empty answers. I swallowed, praying to prevent a total breakdown, "Please, Josh. I need to know the date."

Reluctantly he spilled the information. Back in my thirty-nine year-old life, Ennis would transfer in two weeks – to a precinct destined for disaster four short years later. I had to get back home as soon as possible – *if* possible. I grabbed a piece of paper and pen, wrote down the date. Focusing on my goal ebbed the rising tide of emotion. I sniffed back the tears, shored up my voice, "Got another minute?"

"For you, yes."

"Just a couple of other questions."

He sighed, no doubt frustrated that I ignored his advice. "I'll do what I can. Go ahead."

"Did Shaun Ellis have a record?"

"Savannah, come on." Now his tone firmed to his boss persona. "Don't clutter your mind with this. You've got other matters to tend to."

I gently argued, "I'm curious about his past. Did he have a record?"

He mumbled something about not letting things be. "Hold on, I'll check."

I heard the computer keys clicking. After a few seconds he replied, "Minor stuff. Possession of marijuana a few years ago, breaking windows at a rival high school, stuff of that nature."

"How about his brother Darren Ellis?"

He took a deep breath then mumbled about me being hard-headed. "You realize this isn't healthy, right? Dwelling on this will only destroy you and we all need you, especially your kids."

"I'm not dwelling," I replied in a calm voice. "I'm only asking questions. Both Ellis brothers are dead so what else can I do?"

"You're searching for reasons and answers for why this happened. There aren't any but people do it after losing a loved one. Believe me, there aren't any answers."

Yes, there are, but I can't tell you that. "No, no answers. But there are facts. Josh, please help me. Just look up Darren Ellis and I'll be satisfied."

"Yeah," he harrumphed, "sure you will."

While he referenced the brother's record, I pressed the pen to the page, ready to write. I planned to take notes as if he'd assigned this homicide case to me. *My husband's* homicide.

"Okay. His past is more extensive than his brother's. He had an arrest for assault four years ago then seven months after that – before Halloween – he robbed a Marathon Gas station and shot and killed the attendant. They issued a warrant but he disappeared until he robbed the SunTrust bank and was killed by cops."

"Disappeared?" I was confused. "You mean no one saw him until six months ago?"

"According to the records, the detectives came up empty on family, friends and informants."

"No girlfriend either, I suppose. Can't imagine why. He was such a sweet, upstanding citizen."

"No, he had a girlfriend. Jessica Shepard. In her statement after Darren was killed she said they'd been together on and off for five years."

"S-h-e-p-a-r-d?"

"Yes – wait, what are you up to?"

"Just asking questions. What did she say about Darren?"

"That's the thing. The detectives never knew about her until after the SunTrust robbery. Apparently she and Ellis had been living together the whole time. Moved around from place to place is what the report says. She was from out-of-state and for some reason they couldn't find a record of her anywhere. No Georgia driver license, no credit cards, no apartment lease or car registration with that name. The only reason they found out about her is she claimed the cop killed Ellis after he dropped the gun."

"How would she know unless she was there?"

"Savannah, stop. Stop investigating a case that's closed. You need to heal."

I tried backing off a tad, "So the cops never got a chance to interview her after the Marathon homicide because no one knew about her, right?" I wanted to make sure I took accurate notes.

"Hardheaded and impossible," he grumbled away from the mouthpiece. He sighed, "Yes, that's right."

"And Darren's family and friends shut down on the detectives."

I kept jotting while he added, "Maybe if the detectives would have pressed them harder, they might have given Darren up, we'd have arrested him and..." Josh's words trailed to silence.

"I know," I replied softly. *None of this would have ever happened...*

"I'm so sorry, Savannah. If only they'd found him earlier..."

Yes. If only. Then I'd still have my husband and our kids would still have their daddy.

"Get some rest, my friend," he said. "If there's anything Michelle or I can do, call me. I'll check in with you later."

"Wait," my voice wavered precariously on the edge.

"What?" The word fell almost as a thoughtful whisper in my ear.

"Where did Darren Ellis and his family live four years ago? What address?"

"Savannah," his sternness warned he was finished granting favors that day, "none of this matters anymore. Concentrate on yourself and your kids right now."

Another hasty glance at the clock. I almost felt Georgia driving down the street, pulling into the driveway. "I promise to hush after you tell me the address." I hated repeating myself but, "It's important to me."

He hesitated. Then hesitated longer. I'd sparked his curiosity – and inadvertently roused the *boss* side of my captain instead of the friend side, "Why? What are you going to do?"

"I haven't got the time or energy to *do* anything. I only want to find out where they were living back then."

It took another minute before he released the information to me. I wrote the address down. I wrapped up the conversation with him and had secreted the note in the pocket of my not-so-stylish loose-fitting sweatpants. I took a pit stop in the bathroom which took for freaking ever since I had to employ walls and towel racks to pull myself vertical again. I planned to hobble back to Dane and Eden, spend more time with my cute niece and pretend nothing happened when Georgia returned home.

I equipped those terrible crutches, steadied myself then embarked on my short journey when the bedroom door opened, sending me back a step.

Georgia blocked my exit. All three kids flanked her. They stared at me like executioners facing a condemned prisoner. I was in big time trouble for whatever reason. Was it the trip to the bathroom that upset them? That I'd gone alone without my usual escort? "I couldn't wait to pee. Sorry."

Georgia crossed her arms, "Will you ever stop being a cop?"

Okay. This wasn't about taking a leak. Since only one thing could provoke that particular question, I opted to plead the Fifth. I figured Josh Hunter couldn't clam up about our conversation. So I stood there hanging on those crutches like a wounded monkey, waiting for hell to break loose.

Indeed, Georgia wagged her cell phone, "I just hung up from Josh. He said you were inquiring about Shaun Ellis and his brother. You're already drowning in grief, why make things worse by digging into those–" she pursed her lips tight, trapping a scalding epithet behind them. "By digging into their lives?" she finally finished.

I fussed with the crutches because my left arm ached, "I'm trying to find answers. It *will* help, Georgia. Finding this out is a great help to me."

"Tell me how."

A sudden rage erupted inside me. Anger that no one understood my urgency for such pertinent information (despite their obvious unawareness of the "mirror" conundrum). In one sense I appreciated their efforts to insulate me from the details revolving around Shaun Ellis's rampage. It showed they cared. In another sense it infuriated me that they tried blocking me at every turn. Hunter spilled the information out of sympathy. Chances were he paid dearly for that decision once my sister finished with him. Now she climbed on me about my inquiries. She apparently forgot one thing. I was no ostrich.

"Savannah, how will it help? Tell me." Georgia's temper flared but not too hot. She shooed the kids toward the bedroom door, "Your mother and I need to talk."

"Let 'em stay because there's nothing to tell. I wanted the information and I deserve to know what led up to the shooting."

"So you can crawl in bed and cry your eyes out?" She pointed to the door, "Kids, now."

Only Anna and Daniel backed to the door. Lily stood her ground.

"So I can cope, Georgia. So I can deal with Ennis's death and this," I shook one crutch to make a point. "It won't fix anything but at least I have the information." *It won't fix anything now – but later? Maybe.* "Kids, stay put."

My impudence surprised Georgia. She did a doubletake, staring at me like I was a stranger. "Why on earth would you choose to relive such a tragic, traumatic experience? Immersing yourself in details that change nothing but only cause you more pain. It makes no sense to me."

"You haven't lost–" now *I* pursed my lips tight, cutting my sentence short. *You haven't lost your husband either...*

She sensed every word, "No, I haven't lost my husband. But I nearly lost my sister in a senseless shooting that did claim her husband's life. I'm trying to help you, Savannah. We all are so when you obsess over Shaun Ellis, yes, I get angry. You need to heal and that means staying away from that name."

"You don't understand," I shot back. "This information is vital to my…" The weird feeling beneath my left arm began throbbing and spreading through my arm, my chest. I steadied myself on the corner of the dresser when a tide of lightheadedness rolled in. Balance abandoned me and an invisible foot stepped on my breastbone, compressing my lungs, stealing my breath. Fear replaced my anger. I remembered the symptoms of my last heart attack and I was diving headfirst into another. The desire to argue with Georgia vanished. Instead I opened my mouth to ask for help – but nothing emerged.

Our brusque exchange fueled Georgia's frustration. Cringing, I pressed a hand to my heart while she advanced on me, preaching the whole way, "Well, *you're* important to *me* and I'll move mountains before… Savannah?"

"Mama?" Lily rushed past Georgia to me. "What's wrong?"

I tapped my chest. All four converged the instant my knees gave way. The crutches clattered against the dresser then to the floor that raced toward me. I was powerless to stop myself. Georgia caught me in her arms, eased me to the floor. I squeezed her hand hard enough she winced, my eyes wide with a terror I'd rarely felt.

"Calm down, honey," her gentle tone should have assured me but her eyes betrayed her. We were both scared shitless. Georgia glanced over her shoulder, "Dane! Call 911!"

I held tighter to her hand, "Don't let go, Georgia. Don't let me go."

She touched my cheek, "I'm staying right here, sweetie. I'm not going anywhere."

"Mama…" Lily fell to her knees beside me, lifted my trembling fist into her hands. Anna and Daniel claimed their place beside her. "Don't you die too," my oldest begged.

"No one's dying," Georgia said with absolutely certainty to console the kids. My sister regained her composure and slipped into General Georgia mode, taking control in the midst of chaos, "Lily, she needs an aspirin. Go get one and bring the nitroglycerin pills too."

Through a filmy haze I watched my girl dash from the room. Georgia's face filled my vision, "Try to relax."

Dane hovered behind his wife, cell phone to his ear and talking a mile a minute in his Texas twang. Somewhere I heard Eden crying. My eyelids grew heavy. For a moment my world went black, drifting into semi-consciousness.

Soft, trembling fingertips touched my lips. Georgia. "Hon, open up. You're clenching your teeth."

I forced my mouth open to receive the aspirin. She grasped my jaw to open it wider. She positioned the aspirin between my molars, closed my mouth. *Crush it. Save yourself. Don't die in front of your kids. Crush the stupid pill.*

"Chew, Mama. Chew it," Lily pleaded. Anna joined in and Daniel tried his best to root me on.

I gnashed my teeth but mainly from pain because the upper part of my body ached in agony. I crushed the aspirin and swallowed. The debilitating pain clenched me in its fist, crushing my chest and squeezing my arms. "It hurts," I cried. "Dear God, it hurts." Tears streamed from my eyes. I prayed it eased up because anymore pressure would kill me.

Georgia held another pill to my mouth, "One more, sweetie. This one goes under the tongue."

I forced my jaw open, tried lifting my tongue enough for her to drop the pill in. She nodded with a tremulous smile, cupped my jaw to close it.

"Peach, the paramedics are on the way," Dane assured. "Hang on, sugar."

That struck me odd. *Sugar.* Dane never called me that. Ever. Ennis always bestowed that endearment from the time we met to the day he died. A new sensation combined with the pain, changing my confusion to a different kind of panic. Something pulled and stretched my body like taffy. It started at my feet, spread up my legs to my waist and into my arms. When I looked at my arm it appeared perfectly normal – but it sure didn't feel normal. It hurt like hell. I expected to hear bones pop and muscles snap. The stretching reached my shoulders and neck.

I'd reached the threshold of excruciating pain when a body surrendered to the agony and shut down the conscious mind. Jeffrey's ruthless beating accomplished that. Now I approached that threshold again. The kids' pleas and tears drifted further and further away.

Georgia's fingers stroked my gradually numbing cheek. I barely felt her or my kids touching me. My sister's worried features clouded behind my eyes. Dane's words and Eden's cries muffled into nothingness as the black steel curtain dropped like a door on my mind.

o   o   o

I didn't know how long I'd been out. Voices surrounded me. Georgia. Dane. Three other adults. The stretching abated but the crushing pressure in my chest and radiating pain in my back revved to a higher, more crippling level.

I chanced a peek, praying I'd ended up at the hospital. No such luck. Nope, I was still at home lying on the floor. The difference? I laid in the living room, not the bedroom. That, however, paled in comparison to the two biggest surprises of all. One, somehow I'd split from myself the way the mirror presented the past to me. As a spectator but this time a spectator who still suffered the excruciating symptoms of a heart attack.

The second and most astounding shock – my children were not children anymore. My three babies matured into adults and were dressed to the nines in their Sunday best. Lily, whose resemblance to me deepened in those years, appeared around twenty-five. Our beautiful Anna probably attended college now. And Daniel (now rugged and tall) favored his daddy more and more and looked freshly graduated from high school.

Georgia and Lily flanked Older Me. My sister caressed the cheek of the stricken form lying in the floor – and *I* felt it too as well as Lily's warm touch brushing her mother's arm and Anna patting her hand. I heard them and felt them but could not interact with them. No one heard my cries for help – *my* cries, not the other, older me lying motionless in front of the TV (ironically tuned to a rerun of Grey's Anatomy). No, *she* was unconscious, unaware of the hell her younger version endured.

"I knew something was wrong when she didn't show up for church," Anna said. "But I never expected this."

Daniel bent to one knee, stroked his mother's arm – which *I* felt standing several feet away. "When I called this morning she told me she was tired. She didn't mention having any problems with her heart. I should have dropped by to pick her up then I'd have been here to help."

"No one could have predicted this," Lily told him. "At least she was able to reach me at church. I called 911 on the way here. It's up to Mama and the paramedics now."

Daniel stole a quick look at his watch, "If they'll just get here."

Dane, still on the phone, explained, "The dispatcher says they had to detour because of roadwork."

Daniel rubbed the back of his neck (one of Ennis's habits). "Why didn't she call 911 instead of Lily? I don't understand."

"She was scared," Georgia said. "She wanted her family. Since your daddy passed, she's clung harder to us. She wanted us to be with her."

Lily pressed her hand to the side of my neck. I felt the gentle pressure and her cool, trembling fingers.   Unlike her unflappable demeanor with her siblings, I saw the chaste terror in her blue eyes. She turned to Georgia, "There's a pulse but it's weak."

Anna – normally the stoic one, at least as a child – sounded less composed when she nestled my hand to her cheek, "Hang on, Mama. The paramedics'll be here any minute."

Daniel lifted my other hand in his. His gentle, compassionate grasp felt like his father's.   The warm hold settled my own shivering, at least from across the room. The body surrounded by her loved ones showed no signs of movement except short, ragged breaths. My son held my hand to his whisker-roughened cheek, "Ma, you're the strongest woman I've ever known. Fight to stay with us. We need you."

"Did she chew the aspirin?" Anna asked Lily.

Lily brushed the hair back from my forehead, "She chewed it once. You did good, Mama. You did real well."

Dane, meanwhile, rattled off an update to the 911 operator and again asked where the ambulance was.

I rose to my feet with a fist against my breastbone to combat the pain.   I struggled to the group. The woman lying prone looked fifteen years older or so than my current age. Silver generously streaked her hair not in slashes the way Grandma Culberson's had but threaded itself elegantly (at least to me) throughout the brown tresses. The lines at her eyes trenched deeper, not just from age but the pain gripping her and her face contorted in an agony no one should have to bear.

Older Me drew a labored, noisy gasp. I noticed we did this in unison, only my own breaths sounded slightly deeper, less labored. We simultaneously exhaled. My effort surfaced short and pained, hers long and gentle. Then it occurred to me. As I watched my older self's face relax, the mouth slacken, it hit me. *I'm watching myself die. These are my last moments, my final breaths.* Surrounded by my family, waiting for an ambulance that took its sweet time, I would die in the living room and meet Ennis at the Pearly Gates. Together again after so many lonely years apart.

"I'm here," a young woman in a blue skirt and matching silk blouse bounded in the front door. A pair of spike high heels dangled from her right hand while her left smoothed her long, windblown hair into place. I knew this woman in years past. I grew up with her – or a woman closely resembling her. With her abundance of luxurious brown waves cascading to the middle of her back and beguiling emerald green eyes, Eden Rutherford inherited most of her mother's features, including the svelte figure. Nature gifted her with the Rutherford loft so she stood tall, close to my height. She was a beautiful sight to behold. Three steps in the door she stopped cold, staring at Older Me, "How is she, Mama?"

Georgia struggled for an answer so Lily replied, "Her pulse is weak but so far she's hanging in there."

Come back to me, sugar. Ennis summoned from beyond. *I'm right here with you.*

In the last minute the pain deepened and intensified. My older self's expression mimicked mine, only with an ashen complexion. She moaned. Her fingers slackened on Anna and Daniel's hands.

"Savannah," Georgia called in a voice I'd not heard before. Sheer, utter panic. She jabbed her fingers against the side of my neck and for the first time in my life, I watched my sister lose her composure. "No!" She positioned her palms over my breastbone. "Don't you leave us, not right now," she ordered through the tears choking her voice. Not a request or plea. An order. She locked her elbows and pressed down, "You'd better fight to stay with us, do you hear me?"

Whether Older Me heard her or not, I got the message loud and clear. In my life I've learned many essential truths. Besides never underestimate the power of a mother's love, another adage came to mind. Never underestimate the power of terror or an older sister. I'd read about people who lifted cars off loved ones after an accident. My sister's first compression buckled my knees. I did not sink to the carpet. I *slammed* to the carpet with an impact sending shockwaves reverberating from my knees to my teeth. The woman possessed the strength to lift a Mack truck off of me, not merely a car. Eyes narrowed and preaching harder than a reverend at a revival of lost souls, Georgia put the same muscle into the next compression.

Ribs, I (myself) begged her. *Watch the ribs 'cause I need 'em.* I reached for her, hoping to stop her because her efforts might have helped my older self but they were flat-out finishing *me* off. I couldn't breathe, my heart raced in a funky rhythm and every time she pushed, I nearly passed out.

I swatted at her to shove her away. My hand swiped through her image. No amount of yelling, flailing or kicking at her would break her concentration or cease the compressions. She couldn't see, hear or feel me. Georgia's efforts failed at reviving my older image but anyone who knew my sister realized she never gave up. The compressions kept coming in a rhythmic onslaught.

By trying to save me in the future, they were actually killing me in the present. My sister's hot tears fell on my cheeks while she labored to keep me alive.

"Come on, Mama," Lily pleaded. "*Live.*"

Savannah, I'm right here, Ennis called. *Come back to me.*

I looked for him. He sounded so close – beside me – but he wasn't there. "Ennis," I moaned. "Help me."

Paramedics filed in, unloaded their equipment, quickly examined the woman on the floor. One unlatched a plastic case. When he dragged out the defibrillator paddles I backed away begging the paramedic to stop.

Though Older Me would probably not consciously feel the shocks, I most certainly would.

His partner stripped open my blouse while the other prepared the defibrillator. He placed one cold paddle beneath my right clavicle covering Jeffrey's number 10 and the other over my left lower ribs.

The other guy turned a dial on the machine then counted *one, two, three* much like Georgia had performing CPR. Only at the count of *three* it felt like a Clydesdale kicked me in the chest. I collapsed on the floor, temporarily stunned senseless – all while Older Savannah lay lifeless. The paramedic recharged the damn thing to hit me again. The Clydesdale kicked once more sending a new, unfamiliar pain from head to toe. "Stop! Please stop," I screamed to the paramedic determined to shoot another round of lightning into me. "Ennis!" I cried. "Help!"

I prayed God rescued me before I literally fell over dead. Another countershock surged through me. It drained the last of my energy and hope of returning home to my family. I couldn't move, couldn't think and could barely draw breath. "I can't... go any... further. I can't." I laid my head down to sleep. A peaceful sleep. Sleep free of pain and people manhandling and shocking the shit out of me. In the distance, as I drifted off, I heard the paramedic say, "I'm sorry. She's gone."

O O O

A vigorous shaking gradually roused me awake. Frustration and bone weary dread set in. I imagined the paramedics still hovering over me wielding those lethal paddles and one of them piping up with a cheery, "We got 'er back, folks. We'll plug 'er in again if she even *thinks* about closing 'er eyes."

At that point I *wanted* to be dead but I experienced no blinding white tunnel or welcoming relatives. Only an annoying combination of rocking and shaking that sparked irritation and dizziness. Apparently there was no peace alive or dead.

"Leave me alone," I whimpered. "I'm dead already."

The shaking evolved to a violent wobbling that jarred my whole body. Why couldn't people take a hint? They tried to save me, I gave them credit for their efforts. But for God sakes, "Let me go to Mama." *Where there's no pain, no suffering and hopefully no paramedics slamming me with defibrillators...*

"Sugar," a man's voice called. The hand on my shoulder gave me another solid shake, "Savannah, *are you alright?*"

Ennis! It was Ennis! Goose flesh rose along my body not only from not just relief but amazement. The mirror finally brought me home. Tears seeped from my closed eyes. Tears of joy. *Thank God I'm really home.*

More hands, these smaller, touched mine that still clutched my chest. "Daddy," a little girl said, "why is she shaking? Is she hurt?"

Lily. She sounded four again, not in her mid-twenties. I felt Anna patting my arm, telling her mama to wake up from the "mightmare".

Before chancing a look, I evaluated my physical condition, measuring whether I honestly suffered a heart attack or not. Despite my clenched fists pressing against my breastbone, the pain vanished and my breathing slowed to normal. I felt exhausted but otherwise fine.

"Lily, get me the phone," Ennis directed. "I'm calling 911."

The mere threat of 911 made me groan. I fumbled for Lily's hand to gently restrain her. Nobody would sic those sadistic paramedics on me again, not as long as my mouth formed words and my feet could carry me to safety. "No 911," I moaned.

My eyes opened to see Lily staring back, our noses only inches apart. She virtually shouted in my face, "She's awake, Daddy!"

Yep, I was home. Thank God indeed.

Anna showed her approval with frenetic applauding. Ennis chose not to celebrate yet. His brow sank instead, "What happened? We heard you scream then found you on the floor clutching your chest. Do you need an ambulance?"

Call one and you'll need their help, not me... After what I went through, I'd give him a lump on his head if he laid a finger on that phone. Any phone. "No, no ambulance please. I'm okay." Except I wasn't, at least not emotionally. I'd watched myself die – and experienced every level of misery and pain involved in the process except the actual checking out part.

Lily wrinkled her nose until she resembled her father, "You don't look okay."

"No, you don't," Ennis agreed. He started to stand, "I'm calling anyway."

My hand shot to his wrist, gripping it so tight he cringed. "No 911," I warned. My vehement reaction drew him up short. He eyed me as if I'd gone mad. I risked releasing him but reclaimed his hand. The firm warmth of his grasp eased the panic raging inside me for days. Ennis was still alive. I was holding proof of it.

His brow sank further, "You probably hit your head when you went down. I'd feel better if you were checked out."

"No 911!" Anna shouted at her daddy. "Mama doesn't want it."

By his frown Ennis resented his youngest child's outspoken

nature. He replied back, "Then Mama better have a good reason for dropping like a fly." He switched the expression to me.

Their exchange gave me time to concoct a believable lie, "I tripped and went down. Simple as that – and I did not hit my head."

His lips pursed. The fortunate (but sometimes *un*fortunate) aspects of our marriage meant he read my mind. He memorized my mannerisms, tells and quirky phrasing so accutely he knew a white lie from a whopper. Despite my best efforts, he'd sensed the lie. Sure enough, he shooed the kids from the bedroom, "Girls, your mother and I need to talk. Go to your rooms."

Lily voiced her discontent, "But Daddy–"

"Now," was all he said.

The two slunk toward the bedroom door as if he'd threatened to roll them up and bowl them out. Before vacating the room, Anna shook her finger at him, "No 911."

Our baby girl grew quite a backbone the last couple of months. Before she saw Jeffrey Holland's handiwork on her mama, Anna Rose verged on painfully shy. About a week after my return home from the hospital, she blossomed into a bold, talkative, opinionated child. Sometimes too opinionated.

Ennis huffed, "She's getting so mouthy. I dread her teenage years."

"She looks like you and acts like me." I hoped for a laugh or a smile at the very least. I got nothing.

He touched my cheek, "Let me call the paramedics. Or I'll take you to the hospital, how about that?"

He presented it in a palatable enough way. Kinda like *what's your preference - Italian or Mexican food tonight?* My answer? Neither.

Hospitals had weird, overbearing doctors who did obnoxious, unkind things to people. Had he forgotten where I met Jeffrey? It wasn't exactly a church supper. No, the serial killer's day job was emergency room physician. A surgeon. I wasn't about to leave again anytime soon whether via mirror, ambulance or personal chauffeur to the ER. "Ennis, I'm okay. I promise." *I'm just elated to be home with you and the girls. You don't realize how wonderful it is.*

The weakness subsided and my legs regained some strength so Ennis helped me up, steadying me with an arm around my waist. The bedside clock revealed five minutes passed since the mirror whisked me off to my private rendezvous with our future. I felt as if I'd aged thirty years and spent half my life in the future, not five minutes.

"Slow and easy," Ennis prompted until I sat safely on the bed.

Ennis settled beside me, "Tell me the truth because when we tried waking you up, you weren't making sense."

"What, was I speaking in tongues?"

The attempt at humor irritated him. "You were begging someone to stop whatever they were doing. You cried for my help and said you were dying."

I shrugged, "Could have been a nightmare about Jeffrey." What else could I say? It seemed the only plausible excuse.

"You never begged Jeffrey Holland to stop, not like that. You sounded so mournful."

I pecked a kiss to his cheek, "Ennis, I'm fine. I can't explain it all but I feel fine."

He took my hand, his thumb stroking back and forth in a tender caress. "I was afraid..." he stopped mid-sentence. "You were lying so still for a minute. When you started groaning and grabbing your chest I thought it was—"

A heart attack. My husband feared losing me as much as I feared losing him. I gave his hand a squeeze, reassuring, "Stop worrying. I've got tons I need and want to do before that happens." Number one on my list – change the future to our benefit.

9

It may not have been a heart attack but it certainly did not prevent everyone from overreacting. Ennis started campaigning for an appointment with my cardiologist. When I declined, he enlisted the General. General Georgia spent fifteen minutes melting the phone lines from her house to ours, explaining the importance of a follow-up appointment. If not for me, she said, for Ennis and the girls. My sister used guilt the way warring countries duked it out. Sometimes she employed a surgical strike, others a blitz attack.

The next morning I found myself on an exam table with Dr. Montague (long *a*, silent *ue*) wiring me up to more sensors than a nuclear power station. My sister accompanied me at Ennis's behest since he had to work. God blessed me with three mothers. My mother Charlene (who passed away years ago) and two surrogate moms called Georgia and Ennis. Figuring out which of the last two earned the Biggest Mother Hen award inspired plenty of headaches and I'd suffered enough of those the last few days. So I sat there like a good little girl and let the doctor do his thing.

The night before my unnecessary jaunt to the doc, I lugged the mirror across the room from the dresser. This created a generous open space for us to navigate the area without fear of tripping and killing ourselves or the mirror. The future taught me one thing. Plan ahead. If the mirror wasn't there for Ennis (or anyone) to trip on, I could preserve my window into the future – and hopefully fix some things in the process. When we crawled into bed that night Ennis discovered the mirror tucked in the corner across the room. He asked why I'd moved it. It was in the way, I said. My husband just smiled.

"Ennis said she was incoherent a minute or two," Georgia happily volunteered to the doctor. Not content on leaving the comment as is, she threw in, "And Lily said her whole body shook and she kept crying *no, no, no* like she pleaded with someone."

Okay, now I sound nuts. Thanks, sis. "Ennis also says I'm incoherent before I have coffee in the morning," I defended, "and Lily was scared because I fell."

"Mrs. Rutherford, please," Dr. Montague pressed a finger to his lips, shushing me. "Not during the test."

I obeyed. Anything to expedite the process. Georgia opened her mouth to say something else – probably another anecdote. Maybe Anna swore I belted out a chorus of "John Jacob Jingleheimer Schmidt" or more appropriately "Boom, Boom, Ain't It Great to Be Crazy?"

I fired off a do-it-and-I'll-thump-ya-but-good expression that almost always worked on my kids. Georgia closed her mouth.

A few minutes passed when the doctor removed the sensors. I

buttoned my blouse, careful not to dislodge the cotton ball taped in the crook of my arm. The earlier blood work would return normal, of that I had no doubt. They didn't diagnose time travel trauma with vials of blood and centrifuges.

He took a while to examine the ECG results, removed his glasses and appraised his patient. I recognized his expression. Our girls used it when we uttered the phrase "clean up your room" – and their looks accused us of saying it in ancient Greek dialect.

"No pain since yesterday?" Montague asked, still stumped at the results in his hands.

I shook my head, "I'm pretty sure I just pulled a muscle in my chest." Yes, I lied to my doctor. Everyone did and I felt safe doing so because I'd bet money I hadn't had a heart attack, at least not in this time zone.

Plus, I needed my sister to calm down. Georgia wound herself in a knot since Ennis told her what happened. The Mother Hens held a powwow, labeled me a flight risk and Georgia appointed herself my escort (I called it *warden*) for the day. She'd go "for moral support" she said but I knew otherwise. She'd inform the doctor of details best left unsaid – the ones Ennis told her about and suspected (correctly) I would ignore. And she'd done a fine job since the doctor crossed the room's threshold. The phrase *I'm talking and I can't shut up* came to mind.

Dr. Montague lifted his vision to mine, "You said you remember falling but not crying out or having chest pain?"

I remembered everything but I had enough doctors in my life

without adding a shrink. One mention of what really happened and off to the crazy farm I'd go – in a straightjacket. I repeated myself, "I was going to the dresser for something and I tripped. I remember reaching out to grab the dresser so it's logical I might scream from fear of falling."

Georgia didn't buy it. She crossed her arms. I shot her the I'll-thump-ya glare. She pursed her lips but didn't say a word. No, neither she nor my husband bought the tripping excuse. They thought I dropped from a weak heart. With what I experienced after plummeting through Alice's rabbit hole, I should have keeled over from cardiac arrest two seconds later but my heart proved it was strong as an ox no matter what my family thought.

The doctor continued, "The attack in July caused a small amount of damage but according to these results, you didn't suffer another attack yesterday. I don't know what happened but it wasn't a heart attack. I can refer you to–"

I raised a hand to stop him, "No more doctors please. No offense but I can only handle so many of you guys."

The corners of his mouth curled into a tiny smile, "I understand but if you get concerned about your heart again, let me know."

I eased off the table, nodded toward Georgia, "I won't have to, Doc. I've got an army of tattletales in my midst. You'll know before I do if anything goes wrong."

O O O

Georgia chauffeured me home in her Tahoe. The doctor's visit only halfway eased her mind. The General spent the time verbally troubleshooting everything from my medications causing dizziness to, believe it or not, developing a food allergy. I highly doubted hamburgers caused my problem. No, I secretly blamed the mirror from hell.

On the way home, Sonya Porter called to remind me of Saturday's fundraiser for the church. Yes, I told her, I would deliver the cakes bright and early Saturday morning. I clicked off the call to have my sister question my sanity. "After yesterday? Savannah, you should be resting, not on your feet all day baking *three* cakes."

"I promised to make them and I will," I argued mildly.

Georgia capitulated, "Then I'll help you. Friday I'll be over and between the two of us, we'll get it done and you won't be overworked."

I thanked her. If anyone could streamline an arduous task it was my good and loving General. And with the mirror's antics and my newfound goals regarding the future, I'd have taken a beating to avoid standing in a kitchen baking my brains out. I had bigger issues now. Ennis depended on me – he just didn't realize it. His decision on the Zone 5 job came to a close within two weeks – less if the mirror's vision was correct. At some point between now and two weeks, Ennis would agree to the job without consulting me. And yes, I'd get hot about it too, but this time I'd try not to blow sky high.

"We're close to that antique store where I got the mirror. Let's drop by right quick." Because I wanted a few choice words with the owner. To the tune of *why are you selling instruments of Satan to unsuspecting customers?*

"What for?" she wanted to know.

"I want to ask him a question about that mirror."

"What question?"

"Where did it come from?" The bowels of hell, no doubt, but I intended to wring it out of the man before I socked him in the nose for suckering me. "And I don't mean the elderly woman's house. I mean its actual origin. He knows more than he's saying."

"Why? Is there a problem with the mirror?"

I nearly laughed except I kinda resented her marathon third degree. I'd tolerated it all morning at the doctor's office. The mirror was my business alone. "It's not unusual to research an antique's origin, is it? You do it."

Georgia shrugged a shoulder, "I'll browse while you chat with him."

Beware of anything you buy there, I wanted to say, because the place is probably owned by Stephen King.

10

Going to an antique store equaled a miniature vacation. A person stepped back in time the moment they entered the place. The days of Lewis and Clark, the Alamo, War of Northern Aggression (the "Civil War" to the Yankees), or if the person was truly fortunate they found a piece from the days of Washington, Jefferson and all that Constitution business.

Artisans back then took great pride in their handcrafted creations and took equally great pains to stamp, impress, or paint a maker's mark on their work. My specialty (which equated to general knowledge) was glassware. Georgia educated me on the finer points one day when I picked up a carnival glass bowl. My sister, the walking encyclopedia of antiques. I could identify several maker's marks from memory and offer a vague history of a few choice manufacturers. But a mirror from the Twilight Zone? Not a chance. So it was up to Mr. Attic Treasures (or Mr. Fowler) to school me on the manufacturer because I had a decent idea where the damn thing was made.

The antique brass bell above the door announced our arrival.

The older man, Fowler, behind the counter, peered over his morning paper, "Y'all come back for the pie cabinet?"

On our last trip, Georgia mulled over buying a maple wood pie cabinet with tin doors bearing a wheat sheaf design. The owner did everything to sell it except swear Dolley Madison herself once owned it.

The old cabinet's allure kicked in, drawing Georgia to give it further consideration. She eased her hand along one of the punched tin doors, "Not today."

My instinct said otherwise. If she kept stroking it, I'd tell her to give it a good home. To my surprise, she abandoned the cabinet for a display of glassware saying, "My sister has a question about the mirror she bought."

She started with the depression glass then the Vaseline glass and satin glass offerings. She examined a pink satin glass cake plate with the keen eye of those experts on Antiques Roadshow.

Her last statement deflated his enthusiasm to borderline apathy. I don't want to answer questions, I want to sell things. I already have your money, his expression told me, so go away and play with your satanic mirror. "I doubt I have an answer but shoot."

Do not tempt me. That mirror caused a myriad of problems in my life. Yes, it forewarned me of the dangers awaiting Ennis and myself four years from now – *if* they were accurate predictions. "Was that thing manufactured in Salem, Massachusetts?"

His eyes tightened. Was that umbrage I detected behind those silver-rimmed glasses? As though I called his only child uglier than the east end of a westbound horse?

He folded his paper a bit too briskly, slapped it onto the glass display case beside him. Without consulting his "Antique Bible" he replied, "Peabody, Massachusetts to be precise. Quality made from top to bottom and well worth what you paid for it."

I raised a brow, "Hop, skip and a jump from Salem maybe?"

He crossed his arms, "About five miles or so."

I checked Georgia's progress. She moved to a carnival and cobalt blue glassware display which brought her closer to our conversation. I mumbled to the owner, "Any of those craftsmen or crafts*women* get hanged or burned at the stake?"

"Listen, if you're unhappy with your purchase and wanting a refund," he nodded toward the All Sales Final sign looming on the wall behind him.

That pissed me off. I was way past wanting my money back. My expression said so.

His vision darted past my shoulder to Georgia. I'd hit a nerve with my last question so I pushed harder, "I know why you discounted that mirror and it was not to make room for Chippendale side chairs. That's why you shoved it in a corner out of plain sight."

"Ma'am, listen," he continued in a hushed voice, "use the clearer side of the mirror and you'll be happier. It looks better anyway."

That sounded suspiciously like *he'd* taken a trip or two on the magic mirror ride... "You said they imported special glass for it. Where did the glass come from? I want to know everything about that—"

"Did you ask your question?" Georgia innocently (I think) bounded into the conversation.

"Yes, now I'm waiting for answers. Give me a complete history of that thing. You said the company was Acacia."

He reached beneath the counter where he stocked the price guides for antiques, "I believe I said it was rumored to be Acacia, not that it was Acacia."

"Acacia. Like the tree?" Georgia asked.

"No, ma'am. That's spelled differently."

We both waited for him to elaborate. He didn't so I urged, "Could you spell it for us?"

"Yes, ma'am. It's A-c-a-c-i-a."

I looked at Georgia. She looked at me. We both rolled our eyes. I tried again, "Not the tree. *The mirror's supposed manufacturer.* Could you spell *that* for us?"

He still remained bent down behind the counter, his voice muffled as he spoke, "No, ma'am, because I'm pronouncing it phonetically. It may be spelled entirely different. As I said, it was rumored to have a name but the books only have the trademark I showed you before."

He finally stood up, hefted a heavy book onto the glass topped counter with a labored sigh. He spelunked the well-worn pages of the three inch thick tome, thumbing through it from memory instead of referring to the table of contents. He stopped then spun the book to face me, "See? Just the trademark 'AC' and the 'MA' for Massachusetts." His finger slid down a list of facts regarding that old, mysterious mirror including number of pieces made, location of the manufacturer, the trademark, and its age. Apart from that, the information amounted to zero. The box beneath the manufacturer's name remained frustratingly empty. Of course to sell an item, how could someone say *Made by Lucifer* in good conscience?

Uncovering the history of this strange mirror-making company fell to me and my old not-so-reliable friend the internet. I dreaded it worse than baking three cakes in one day.

o   o   o

The Mother Hens convened once Georgia and I arrived home. While they discussed the doctor's test results, the girls presented me with a pretty bouquet of six fully bloomed purple roses cradled in a wrap of dark green tissue. Lily resembled a pint sized beauty queen holding the arrangement in her hands. She explained that Daddy drove them to the "flower shop" and let them pick whatever they wanted as a gift.

Georgia and Ennis huddled in the living room exchanging secretive whispers so I took that opportunity to fill a vase with water and ask the girls for help with the flowers. "You girls know how to brighten my day. These are gorgeous. Thank you."

Lily approached her work with a keen, discriminating eye, positioning the flowers to her satisfaction. Anna plopped a rose in the arrangement's middle, causing Lily to frown her disapproval but she left it anyway.

Task completed, we spent a brief minute admiring our work when Lily took my hand, tugged me toward the back door, "Time for golf practice."

"Honey, Mama needs to rest." Georgia and her owl ears. My whole life I swore she could hear a pin drop at the South Pole. On a snow bank. During a raging blizzard.

Georgia dialed down the protest before hurting Lily's feelings, "She's had a long morning. Maybe tomorrow she can practice with you."

"Nah, I need a diversion," I smiled at my daughters. "Let's go, girls." So far Lily's interest in golf burned as fierce as mine when I was young. She religiously practiced the game, asked for advice and followed instructions very well for a child her age. My main goal for her at this point – to have fun.

Long after Georgia left and we'd eaten supper, the kids settled down to play and Ennis plopped in his chair for the American League Division Series (his Rangers made it again this year). I absconded to the computer for research. The magic word for antiques was *provenance*, or the history of the piece in question. I quickly discovered to have *provenance*, first you must locate the item somewhere in the vast confusion of the Internet. Try finding a mirror with no actual manufacturer on record. To feel like a complete and utter moron, a person should type the words "magic mirror" into the browser search bar and hit the enter key. The screen inundated me with Snow White references and lots of ads for plain old mirrors that acted normal. "Time travel mirror" produced more hysterical results, showing videos of how to use a normal mirror to travel "back in time for a second." For that to possibly happen, one supposed scientist said the mirror had to be about the size of our planet. Mine was considerably smaller than Mother Earth and went backward *and* forward in time – *twenty years at a time*. Guess I blew *that* theory all to hell.

I spent an hour searching the Internet for the mirror's *provenance* only to find one website showing drawings of men and women dressed in pilgrim outfits hard at work carving wooden mirror frames. It showed the weird symbol but listed no name. The scant information it gave stated the types of cheval mirrors they crafted and how long they remained in business. No website pinpointed the origins of the *special imported glass*. The closest I came: Slovakia. Then I hit a complete dead end.

I put the amateur antique sleuthing aside to search for Darren Ellis on social media. Another dead end. Ditto for Jessica Shepard, at least a Jessica Shepard living in Atlanta or surrounding suburbs. As a last, desperate resort, I plugged the name Shaun Ellis into Twitter. Two seconds later I decided I'd lost my mind. It rained the name Shaun Ellis, flooding the screen with more choices than the cereal aisle at Kroger. I gave up Twitter and turned to Facebook, hoping for better and fewer results. I loved how high school kids used Facebook. They considered anything from a football game to a hangnail meaningful. They documented tongue piercings, pranks and bullying with photographs and chronicled details worthy of any forensic tech. Nothing was off limits.

As much as I hated social media, it proved a valuable tool in police investigations. Teenagers enjoyed being heard and loved being popular.

Four years from now Shaun Ellis would be knee deep in studies at Dartmouth and pushing oars for the rowing team. I envisioned him, even in his high school years, to be well-groomed and decked out in high dollar threads with a big fancy Ivy League ego to match.

The Facebook search dampened my optimism of finding Shaun. Out of an almost insurmountable number of people named Shaun Ellis, I narrowed the search by city. Much more manageable. The address I procured from Josh during my trip into the future corresponded with the high school district Shaun attended now. *Let's just see what the little shit's up to four years before he destroys everyone's future including his own...*

My initial guess panned out. The profile picture showed a young man with short ash blond hair, a baby face and the smug smile of a lawyer. The teenager seemed quite proud of his life and himself. He hailed from New York State then his family moved to Atlanta two years ago. He really missed New York, he wrote. *And, personally, I really wish you'd all move back.*

He attended North Atlanta High School, an International Baccalaureate school located in Zone 2. In his profile Shaun bragged about his memberships to the National Honor Society, Mu Alpha Theta (Math Honor Society), Men of Excellence and the Chess Club. I tried not to throw up.

I sneered at the next tidbit he volunteered to the world. Young

Mr. Ellis's aspirations leaned to the political side. He stated his life's ambition as "leading the gun control movement into great, unprecedented success". To back up that lofty statement, he listed Coalition to Stop Gun Violence, Brady Campaign to Prevent Gun Violence, Violence Policy Center and CeaseFire as his causes. Interesting how in four years his "goals" would become a tragic joke on the police, my family and the public. His aim (interesting choice of words, I thought) was to promote gun free homes and families because guns were a public health threat. *Unlike blockheads who don't understand life and try to legislate everyone into stupidity.* I glared at the screen. Unbeknownst to Mr. Progressive, while he busied himself tossing law-abiding homeowners' guns in Lake Lanier, those same homeowners instantly became vulnerable to attack by criminals who still had *their* guns. Anyone with sense knew the outcome of swiping away a person's protection. Most cops did not support asinine rants like Shaun's. We wanted good and decent people armed.

Ellis listed a brother Darren and posted pictures of them together palling around and teasing the way brothers did. Shaun's clean-cut, baby face contrasted against his older brother's wilder, unkempt style. Darren's hair needed three inches lopped off and his face and Gillette apparently parted ways several weeks earlier. Darren's arm slung across Shaun's shoulders, the former's eyelids drooping in an alcohol soaked haze. He offered a tongue-lolling sleepy smile while squeezing Shaun's cheeks into a fish face.

I clicked to Shaun's postings where I learned more about this future revolutionary pencil-pusher. Without realizing it, teenagers (and people in general) allowed the world to see their personalities on social media. Dogs or cats, religious or atheistic, outgoing or shy, modest or egomaniacal. Not so smart for privacy's sake but great for law enforcement.

I read Shaun's postings to familiarize myself with him, his thoughts, phrasing. A kid didn't normally attend Dartmouth for sports. For the record I'm not an idiot. I went to school, got decent grades and brought home a spiffy diploma. But this kid used words Merriam-Webster never heard of (I think he made them up). Five, six and a few seven syllable words stretched longer than a passenger train. The more I read, the more I saw a lawyer in the making. He spoke primarily about himself, his accomplishments, goals and his plans to reach The Top. In four years he'd make it to the top alright. The top of a building. Not exactly what he had in mind.

Shaun and his brother were worlds apart. One possessed ambition in spades, the other was a repeat offender. Studying Shaun's face in the pictures with Darren, I saw a younger brother searching for acceptance from the older one while the older one sailed along oblivious to it all. It proved two things. One, National Honor Society and Chess Club aside, Shaun still sought acceptance from his sibling and two, Big Brother Darren was this kid's Achilles Heel.

11

After settling behind my desk early the next morning, I cranked up the department computer to search for Darren Ellis and his girlfriend Jessica Shepard. Ellis's record already bore scars of a youth gone wrong. Vandalism, theft and assault. His brother the genius, who in four years would take aim on Ennis, me and other cops, so far stayed off law enforcement radar.

"What're you doing here, kid? Thought you'd take a sick day."

I looked up from the computer to see John Mathis in the doorway. A rumpled blue suit hung off his round physique, the jacket draping open to reveal an off-center, color-coordinated tie. John's good mood surprised me. Usually he grumbled around the station, barking orders to rookies and scowling at the rest of us. Today he approached with concern and a kindness I rarely experienced.

I peered over my reading glasses, "I would have if I was sick. Ennis bend your ear again?"

"Told me what happened. If it wasn't your ticker, maybe you need a new-rologist. One of those brain guys."

"John, it warms my ticker that you care. My problem isn't in my brain so I don't need a neurologist and Montague cleared me of any and all infractions *and* infarctions."

When he nodded he resembled a fat bobblehead doll, "I heard Montague is good." He pronounced it Mon-*tuh*-gyoo, not Mun-*tay*-g. My doctor corrected such errors. I did not. Especially with John Mathis, the original Mr. Cranky Pants.

"Okay," Mathis capitulated, "I won't bother you about it but listen, you gotta stay upright on my watch, understand? I ain't answering to your better half if you keel over."

I saluted with a wink, "Staying upright will be my priority today, Detective."

He shuffled his way down the hall, shaking his head. My decision to clock in that morning displeased more than Mathis. I heard about it from Ennis, our kids, and Georgia. But with no money, I said, we can't pay bills because we're fresh out of pixie dust. No one laughed.

I swiveled back to the computer, typed in Darren Ellis for a last known address. The note I wrote from my foray into the future lay on my desk, ready for verification. Indeed, the address matched. The Ellis family lived exactly where I'd been told. Later that day, I'd head out and visit them. For now, I put that aside for my current case: a home invasion resulting in a double homicide. The mid-forties couple, Joe and Lisa Stewart, resided in the upscale Chastain Park area. Large homes with yards and mortgages to match, and small, expensive cars to park in their expensive garages. Ennis, Mathis and I worked the case for days with precious little to show for our efforts. Generic witness statements (maybe they saw a guy, maybe not or maybe the car out front was black, not red) left the trail cold.

I heaved a small sigh, wishing I could tackle the Ellis visit that morning instead of slog through the same interviews over and over hoping to find a nugget of useful information on the bogged down case. I began re-re-reading the neighbors' statements, such as they were. Then I ran across a gold nugget. A man matching Darren Ellis's description was spotted walking down the Stewart's street the night of the murders. Okay, a witness description did not automatically slap cuffs on him but it gave me a reason to investigate him further. Sorry, *legitimately* investigate him further. That's when I dug up another piece of gold, this one so sizeable I considered it a small jackpot. While poking into the Marathon Gas homicide (what I could within my limited capacity), I discovered that security cameras caught Darren Ellis at the Chevron a mere four to five miles from the Stewart house the night they died. That gave me compelling, bona fide grounds to dive headfirst into Darren Ellis.

"Why aren't you home resting?"

My shoulders dropped. Oh goody. Captain Josh Hunter, my superior officer and *other*, part-time mother made his requisite appearance.

No wonder the man's hair constantly grew grayer and grayer if he shouldered his own life plus everyone else's. I smelled Georgia all over this visit. She'd probably called him to jack me up about going home.

How my sister managed to wrap these men around her little finger amazed and annoyed me.

I removed my glasses with a sigh, turned to face him, "Because the doctor confirmed I'm fit as a fiddle. No heart issues at this time. That status is subject to change if Georgia and Ennis don't stop updating the masses on my every move."

Captain Hunter pursed his already downturned mouth. Yep, this was Georgia's handiwork. She relayed the whole appointment to Hunter, probably embellishing the facts enough that he felt obligated to suggest taking a sick day which I would not do. Time ticked down on the Zone 5 job for Ennis, mine ticked down on our future together.

Josh exercised his obligation to my sister by saying, "Sure you're up to it? You never take enough time off when you have problems. Only time I can remember is few months ago after Holland's last abduction."

"That wasn't by choice either. I couldn't requalify because I couldn't shoot straight. Rehabbing my shoulder after the surgery saved me. Well, that and practicing at the shooting range."

He winced, "Severed tendons do take a while to heal."

It took months to recover from Jeffrey Holland's last hurrah. I visited the shooting range several times a week after finishing rehab. My hand and arm trembled from the strain of my lightweight .38, a complication from the injury and surgery that continued affecting my aim. After so many failures at the range, the family mentioned retirement. They touted a career change, comparing it to an everlasting Christmas vacation, or so it seemed. I never told them but if I'd put in my papers, I wouldn't consider it retiring. I'd considered it a personal defeat and a giant victory for Jeffrey. The day my aim held steady enough to qualify, I'd pretended I pointed that barrel straight at Holland's nose and pulled the trigger. The results weren't stellar but they got me back on the job.

Hunter abandoned his quest, "If you need a half-day, tell me. Mathis can fill in on the Stewart homicides. On another note, I just got a call from Detective Welch in Zone 5. He wants to know why you entered a search for a Darren Ellis."

His statement caught me off-guard. Since when did detectives mind another detective running a name? Did Welch sit at his computer watching for these notifications the way day traders eyeballed their screens for sudden market trends? Hunter left the impression Welch sounded miffed. Ennis had met Welch and described him as laidback.

I waded into potentially treacherous waters with caution, "Why can't I do a search for this guy without being summoned by the principal? Is he upset with me?"

"I think he wants help but can't bring himself to ask for it. He's under pressure from his captain to find leads on that Marathon Gas station homicide. Ellis is the prime suspect, right?"

"M-hmm. And I'm working a home invasion/double homicide. Darren Ellis is on security video at the Chevron on Riverdale Road an hour before the Marathon homicide. That's less than five miles from the Stewart house. My job description says check out all possibilities – as remote as they are – so that's what I'm doing. I'll call Welch and square up with him and smooth any ruffled feathers."

Hunter hated dealing with upset (or potentially upset) detectives and I was his number one problem child for making waves. He hemmed and hawed a second until asking, "Ennis made a decision about Zone 5 yet?"

"Hope not because he promised to discuss it with me first."

"Time's running short on the deadline."

Time was running short on a lot of things I wanted to say. "He knows."

"The sergeant's exam date is closing in too. Still thinking about taking it?"

"Thinking about it is all."

He handed me a sheet of paper crammed with handwritten questions. He shrugged a shoulder, "I put together a list of questions I asked when I served on the oral exam board. And some tips that helped me through my own interviews with the board."

It touched me that Hunter went to such lengths to help. I looked over the pointers. "Answers should be only one to two minutes. Exercise a few hours before the interview." There were other bits of advice but one struck me odd, "Put a tic-tac between my cheek and gum?"

Hunter explained, "Keeps your mouth from going dry."

"Thanks. I hadn't thought of that." I reviewed the questions and felt my stomach drop. A couple of them sent a shiver along my aspirations, "'What changes need to be made in the sergeant's position and why?' Oh brother..." *I'm toast.* "'What are my strengths and weaknesses?'" *Oh, yes. Burnt toast.* "'What do I have to offer in this position?' Josh..."

"Relax. We'll work through it together if you like. I'll help any way I can."

"I like very much because I'm studying the ethical, organizational, disciplinary and legal scenarios. Not how to hype myself."

"That's your biggest obstacle. Yourself. See me after shift when Ennis can look after the kids. We'll work on your self-promotional skills."

I was grateful to him, considering a promotion would probably mean a transfer for me.

"Remember if you're promoted, that seat you're sitting in might belong to someone else."

Thanks for the reminder. I wrinkled my nose, "And that is why I usually throw the emergency brake on the idea. I don't want to leave your command. We've had a good professional marriage, don't you think?"

My hesitancy seemed to brighten him up a bit. He nodded, "But if you decide to further your career, I'm not standing in your way." Hunter tossed out a surprising offer, "I can always campaign to keep you here. No promises but it's worth a try."

I chuckled, "I'd love to see the look on John's face if I became his boss." As equals we got along fine. Through the years I relied on his seniority and experience to fine-tune my skills. I spent the first years of my detective career taking orders from him – or strong suggestions as he called them. But Mathis taking orders from me? The mirror oughta run that scenario by me for laughs, I thought.

Hunter's brow rose, "Lemme see what I can do – if that helps your decision, I mean."

I thanked him because frankly, I felt at home in our cozy little station. I'd spent my entire career in the place and I hated the idea of transferring – unlike someone else I knew.

I called Welch to introduce myself and tell him my interest in Mr. Ellis. After learning that Ennis Rutherford – official candidate for transferring to Zone 5 – was my husband, he lightened up. Once he heard the reason I poked around for Darren Ellis (the Chevron sighting not far from my double homicides) the man really warmed up to me. He seemed more than happy to accommodate my request for previous addresses for Darren. It resulted in three locations, the last one I already had. The residence of Robert and Aileen Ellis, Darren's parents. Wet Blanket Welch offered no hope there. "If you enjoy ramming your head into brick walls, you'll love his mother," he forewarned. "She musta used Charlie Manson's parenting guide for those boys. One's a murderer, the other's an asshole."

O   O   O

The Ellis family lived in a modest home in a relatively safer part of town. Forty years ago the city finished paving the streets for the addition and the sidewalks ran smooth and perfect along the newly planted yards. The neighborhood now suffered the plight of most aging areas. Crack and pothole repairs resembling zebra stripes and black dinner plates marred the once smooth street and spindly weeds protruded from sidewalks and curbs.

I'd been in this area before, just not often so I drove slower down the street to find the Ellis house. Mostly single story homes painted to fit in – browns, whites, tans and grays. One radical took John Mellancamp's song to heart and painted his house pink. It stood out like a sore thumb in the conservative palate around it. Then, on cue, the damn song lodged in my brain repeating the chorus until I hummed along with it. *Ain't that America, for you and me. Ain't that America, we're something to see...*

I passed Fords and Chevys aligned together in driveways. A lawnmower sat beside a garage waiting to grind through thick Kentucky bluegrass. Big Wheels and kid's bikes spotted nicely manicured lawns or were parked near porches. *Ain't that America, home of the free. Little pink houses for you and me...*

A one story, brick home came into view. It had a nice green lawn, an oak tree and a small flower garden filled with withering chrysanthemums. Beside the front door an American flag swayed lazily in the temperate breeze. Such a humble home for two murderers. Darren already claimed the title but in a few years, the teen behind those walls would shock the nation by shooting eight cops and killing two, including my husband. Ain't that America, I mused darkly.

I angled to the Ellis curb, parked beneath the shade of the large billowing oak and took a moment to review my strategy – and slip on my cop persona.

Making my way up the drive, a wind chime's gentle melodic song serenaded me from next door. After thumbing the doorbell, I waited… and waited. The blue Malibu parked in the drive indicated someone should have been home so I thumbed the bell again. This time a lock snapped open, followed by the door.

A woman about my age stood in jeans and red pullover blouse, holding a compact and inspecting her makeup. Ringlets of reddish-gold hair fell to her nape, making her resemble a grown up Little Orphan Annie. Without making eye contact, she acknowledged me with an impatient, "Yes?"

"Mrs. Aileen Ellis?"

She nodded, "Yes, what is it? I'm busy."

I retrieved my badge, held it for her to see, "Detective Prince, Atlanta Police. I need a moment of your time, please."

She eyeballed her watch, "If I *had* a moment but I'm on my way out."

"Won't take long, I promise."

"I don't know where Darren is. That's why you're here right? Like all the other cops? *I don't know where he is.* Now can I leave?"

Um… No. "May I come in a moment?"

Aileen inhaled sharp and deep as if gearing up to tell me *buzz off* – or a decidedly more colorful version of it. Instead she stood aside, releasing the breath in a long, annoyed sigh, "Why not? But I have no answers for you."

I stepped inside, placed my badge back on my belt and quickly assessed the house. Neat, with mulberry colored sofa, comfy looking chairs and hardwood floors. "I'm not here about the Marathon Gas station robbery." I left out the word "homicide". Robbery sounded bad enough. Homicide had that ring of "death penalty" to it no mother appreciated hearing.

She tucked the compact back in her purse then stopped. "Then why are you here?"

"I'm working a case in Chastain Park and someone mentioned seeing a young man about Darren's age and description–"

"You mean the murdered couple? God, you cops're trying to pin everything on him, even this Chastain Park bullshit."

"Mrs. Ellis, I never accused Darren of killing anyone. He was seen at the Chevron on Riverdale Road fifteen minutes before the Stewarts were murdered. I have witness accounts describing Darren walking down the street, not committing a crime. I need to get his witness statement, see if he noticed anything unusual that night when he passed by."

"And I look stupid to you, right? Stupid enough to hand you an address so you can drag him off to Norcross for his execution?"

"My interest in your son goes no further than a witness account of what he may or may not have seen that night on Pineland Road. The Marathon robbery isn't my case. It's not even in my precinct."

She retrieved her handbag, slung the strap over her shoulder,

"Still doesn't change the fact I don't know where he is. Listen, I'm gonna be late for my appointment. Are we done?"

I supposed so since she'd dug in deeper than a soldier in a foxhole. Score another for the Brick Wall. Mrs. Ellis forced me to find another avenue to saving Darren's life. If a cop didn't shoot him dead in four years then Shaun would never pick up a weapon and mow us down. By saving Darren I saved us all. I hoped.

Time for my backup plan. "Does Darren have any siblings I could speak with?"

"He's got a brother." Aileen wheeled, shouted at the hallway, "Shaun, come talk to this detective. And don't forget to do your homework. I'm checking it when I get home." She rolled her eyes, "Maybe I can get *this* one to graduate."

I nodded and stepped aside to let her pass, "Thank you for your time, Mrs. Ellis."

His mother closed the door behind her, leaving her kid to fend for himself with me. At first it bothered me. Most parents wanted to be present when a cop questioned their child. Not her. *I'm busy,* she said. That explained a lot about why her boys grew up with police records.

When I turned back I came face to face with the boy who would later kill my husband. Thirteen at most, Shaun Ellis appeared to be in the throes of puberty. Acne pock-marked his forehead and cheeks, a far cry from the smoother, lightly stubbled jaw on the front page four years from now. He inherited the "baby face" syndrome that plagued many boys and I saw how his features fooled people into believing he was a harmless, nice young man. But his mouth cured that quick.

"What do you want?" Shaun accused in a hostile New York dialect.

I introduced myself, extended my hand. It was the hardest thing I'd done in a while, offering to shake the hand of a killer. Technically not a killer yet, of course, and that was the reason I embarked on this crazy journey.

Shaun stared at my hand, shoved both of his into the front pockets of his jeans. He tilted his chin back in a defiant gesture.

I pointed to the sofa, "Let's sit down."

"No thanks. Bottom line is I don't know where my brother is and if I did, I wouldn't tell you."

His accent drifted in and out. He struggled to enunciate without it but anger overrode that effort. I assumed he worked at losing the brogue since Dartmouth students probably didn't speak "Soprano".

Maybe I'd stir him up enough he'd revert to his native Yankee tongue. "As I told your mother, I need his statement for my case."

"Lady, I wouldn't tell you the time of day, much less where my brother was. I rememba what happened to Amadou Diallo, Malcolm Fuhguson and dozens of other people. I'm not about to set Darren up to be executed."

I did a mental eye roll. Yeah. Amadou Diallo and Malcolm Ferguson. Nice jab, kid, but, "This isn't New York, Shaun. You can't lump Atlanta in with other cities–"

"Cops ah all the same," he advanced on me. "Yah speak with yah guns. Yah bully, beat and murder honest, hard-workin' citizens."

Not old enough to drive, vote or drink but he had all the answers for the law enforcement rube he tried to intimidate. Down here in these Bible thumpin', football lovin', sweet tea drinkin' parts, we called those know-it-all individuals "morons". And as for intimidation, I grew up with a daddy who used willow branches and his fists to make his point so it took a bigger threat than a small-time, showboating barely-teen to spook me. Calm and professional, I held a hand in a stop gesture, "That's close enough."

"Yah gonna shoot me if I take anotha step?"

"No, I've got other ways to bring you down, young man, so stop before I use them."

He heeded my tone – but kept the scowl for effect. His bluster amounted to sad, pathetic and comical. Mostly pathetic.

"I'm sorry you have a lowly opinion of law enforcement," I said, "but that doesn't change the fact I need a witness statement from Darren."

"You can't even find him. The Donut Patrol spent days talking to me and my mother. Then they send you to beg me for Darren's location?" He laughed, "This is hillbilly heaven."

…Said the man who couldn't decide which accent to use – American or Corleone.

I tried one last time, "You're mistaken, Shaun. I'm not begging you to give him up." Yes, I lied through my teeth and cared less and less as seconds ticked by. "Darren is wanted for murder in another precinct."

Not a lie. "When my colleagues find him – and they will – they'll try to bring him in unharmed, I promise you that. But if Darren puts up a fight, has a weapon or threatens them, I cannot promise he won't get hurt or possibly killed. It depends on your brother." True. "You, on the other hand, can help him by either disclosing his location or contacting him and suggesting he turn himself in. Then no one gets hurt." Maybe.

Ennis's face flashed in my mind. The fountain of blood spurting from a hole in his neck. I winced when the memory of my husband evolved to him landing atop me in the police station.

Shaun pulled his hands from his pockets. They were tight fists. "Get outta hea, Detective Whoevah-The-Hell-You-Ah."

I watched those fists blanch white as the angry young man ordered me out. He needed lessons from Jeffrey Holland on how to frighten me – plus more age, experience, muscle and smarts. "*My name*, Mr. Ellis, is Detective Savannah Prince. Keep that fresh on your mind because we'll be seeing each other again." My vision drifted from his fists to the coffee table a few feet away. A Sports Illustrated swimsuit issue mingled with a Cosmopolitan and Vogue. I thought that odd but not as intriguing as the bright yellow Post-It note stuck across the SI model's ample bosom. Without being obvious, I quickly read the scribbled note. *Boo, give this back when you're done.* The mailing label was addressed to Darren Ellis.

Young Mr. Ellis stabbed a finger toward the door, "I said get out before I help you out."

I smiled slyly, wagged a finger at him, "Careful there, Shaun. Do that and I'll call the Donut Patrol. Drag 'em away from their glazed goodies and they get mighty prickly, especially when one of their own is manhandled. They'll haul you to jail then your mama'll have to divide her time between Norcross and juvenile hall to visit her boys."

12

Bright and early Friday morning my sister knocked on the door. For a woman who owned a bakery and clocked in around or before five, she adjusted her early bird nature to accommodate my family's not-so-gung-ho enthusiasm. Our breakfast consisted of bowls of cereal complimented by a side order of complaints about going to school. Ennis joined the chorus, grousing about our stalled case. I sympathized with him except my mind focused on Darren Ellis and preserving my future with Ennis.

The constant stress took a toll. I'd obsessed over Ellis until insomnia, fatigue and nausea set in and my back ached from the strain and worry. In short, I was grateful to see Georgia's smiling face that morning.

Before her arrival I gathered ingredients to expedite this ridiculous bake-a-thon I committed to. By eight fifteen, my back already complained of overuse so I popped an aspirin.

"Remind me again," Georgia said, reviewing the trio of recipes on the cabinet. "Who is Sonya Porter?"

The Commandant to your General, I nearly blurted then thought better of it. Miffing off the good-hearted General was not on my agenda, especially in my stoved up condition. Georgia took the nickname well but why take a chance?

Sonya was a good friend, always polite and reliable but she also had that Type A personality that turned several people off – that last tidbit I'd keep to myself. She excelled at making money for the church, either by guilt or by basically assuming everyone wanted to participate. I always contributed a dish or cake or two (never three until now) not because I felt I needed to, but because others benefited from the effort. The members of our church were caring and very giving when others needed help. They provided tons of moral support and meals for me and my family while I recovered from Jeffrey Holland's attack in July. And Sonya Porter led the way. So uttering any disparaging remark about Sonya, however mild, went the way of tossing around the "General" nickname that day. Not gonna happen.

"You remember her," I told Georgia while handing her an apron. I opted for the one declaring *You Can't Scare Me – I Have Two Daughters.* "Sonya came to the hospital a couple of times to see me. She's short, about five-two, skinny as a nail and bobbed black hair."

"Is she the one who kept delivering meals from church members?"

"And her own meals too. You were here when she brought the hobo casserole for supper one night."

My sister's nose wrinkled then she swallowed hard, "I remember that casserole. How did you ever keep that stuff down? It looked terrible."

"It tastes much better than it looks. Ground beef, potatoes, carrots, onion, garlic and a can of mushroom soup – which Sonya removed the mushrooms because Ennis can't stand them." I teased, "Want the recipe?"

She shuddered all the way to her toes, "*Heavens no.*" She still appeared unnerved at the idea even while heading to the pantry for the dry ingredients. "She's much better at delivering pretty meals than making them."

"Georgia," I scolded good-naturedly. "I can't believe you said that."

She toted back a five pound bag of flour, hefted it onto the counter. "You eat with your eyes first. That's all I'm saying."

I detected resentment more than disgust. I figured Georgia blamed Sonya for strong-arming me into baking the cakes. Fact was, I'd committed to baking them long before being hauled to the cardiologist. "Sonya swipe your good cutlery or something?" I joked.

She reached in a cabinet for a measuring cup. Georgia traversed my kitchen as expertly as her own. She should have. She'd spent several days in it preparing meals for me and my family while my shoulder healed and I regained my strength. If anyone asked me, my sister rated with the saints.

Leveling off a cup of flour, she used the same terse tone, "I honestly think if you told her what happened the other day, she'd understand. And if she didn't," she stopped to look me squarely in the eyes, "I'd *make* her understand."

In my mind I watched my sister back Sonya against a wall, read her the riot act, ending it with *back off or you'll answer to me*... That was Georgia. Beautiful, congenial and well-spoken – but deadly as a viper when protecting her family.

I took up a knife and rocked the blade through a handful of walnuts for a quick rough chop. "Georgia, she's not a Nazi. She's... driven. Very goal oriented."

"So am I, sweetie, and my goal is to prevent you from having a setback. Jeffrey caused enough trouble, I'm not about to let anyone else. How much flour?"

"Two cups." I dropped the controversial subject, hoping she might too. To defuse the situation and her rising annoyance, I thanked her for helping with the cakes.

The strategy coaxed a smile from her, "You're welcome, hon. You've pitched in at the bakery for years so it's nice to help you for a change."

My mind wandered to Darren Ellis again. I made it a point to regularly check Shaun's Facebook account for updates since the kid exercised his chatty nature online. He'd mentioned a visit from the "Atlanta Porcine Department" and ended it with "I smell bacon." His description of me (thankfully he omitted my name) delved into a personal nature, saying I'd look good on a spit and served with an apple in my mouth. I wanted to squish his Yankee baby face in the muck he said I was full of.

"Has Ennis decided on the transfer yet?" Georgia asked. Her eyes bulged at the sight of my nuts, or rather the size of them. "You can't use those. You've chopped them too small. What's wrong? You seem preoccupied."

I scraped the now powdered nuts into the trash, placed another handful on the cutting board, "I'm a little tired and my back aches today–" My mouth slammed shut. What the hell was I thinking? Telling Queen-Frets-A-Lot about my maladies only invited doctor's appointments so I recovered as best I could, "It's nothing to worry over. I've done a lot of computer work this week so it happens." I mentally crossed my fingers, praying my excuse worked. I hurriedly answered her original question, "Ennis told me he might take the job. That's as far as I get with him on the subject. I did suggest *he* take the sergeant's test and stay at Zone 2."

"That's the best idea yet – if he can stay there, I mean. More money and you don't work across town from each other. What did he say?"

I pursed my lips and I sped up my chopping, careful not to annihilate the nuts.

Georgia winced, "Nothing good, I assume."

Not quite. Hubby wanted to remain warm and snug as a detective. No big decisions, no command headaches. Did I salivate at the idea of supervising detectives, reviewing their reports, assigning duties and maintaining records and statistics? Good Lord no. A person paid for that promotion. Yes, they received a fatter paycheck but gained a gigantic headache for it too.

My pent up bitterness poured out, "No, Ennis doesn't want the job. He wants me to shoot for the promotion. Like *I* want to be a boss. I enjoy being a regular ol' detective."

"You've been studying for the test though. Don't you get regular hours being a sergeant? You'd get more time with the girls."

I finished chopping the nuts and sat the knife aside. It was time to set the record straight, "The hours are better, yes, and I'd love the extra time with the kids but I've been studying because he wanted me to. I planned to wait four more years then try for the promotion. It has a decent pay hike but he's the one nagging about our income, not me. We can manage on our salaries. We can't afford new cars like the neighbors or private schools for the girls but you and I went to public school and did just fine."

Georgia lifted her hands in surrender, retreated backward a step, "Whew. Opened a can of worms, didn't I?"

I apologized for the acid retort and gentled my voice, "I feel guilty that I don't want the promotion. I sound selfish like I'm denying my family but I'd rather put in a few more years as a regular ol' detective *then* make sergeant." I grabbed an apple and started peeling it.

The spicy warm scent of cinnamon drifted past when she tapped the two teaspoons into the mixing bowl. "Then do it," she said. "Don't let Ennis push you into a career move you hate."

"Ennis doesn't push, Georgia, you know that. He *suggests*." Lately he *strongly* suggested.

"Hon, I'm serious." She'd abandoned the dry ingredients to face me, "It's not been four months since your last encounter with Jeffrey. It took weeks to requalify with your gun because of the physical damage and surgery. Ennis is a wonderful man with lofty goals but he wasn't the victim. You were. Don't upend your life in a way that'll cause more stress. You've had enough."

I loved my sister but there were days I downright adored her. I smiled, "Thanks, sis. I'm going to have another talk with him and try to convince him to take the test. I'm scared that he'll accept the job across town though. Separation, different hours, the part of town." Not to mention a crazy gunman waiting to kill him...

"Zone 5 isn't as dangerous as 3 or 4 is it?"

"Statistically, no." But wait four years. "I just don't have a good feeling about it."

My cell phone rang just as I graduated to chopping apples. "Could you get that for me?"

Georgia glanced at the Caller ID, "It's the station."

"Put it on speaker."

"You're sure?"

"Yep. If it's Mathis it'll keep him G-rated. Plus I need to multitask today."

Georgia clicked on. She seemed intrigued to discover why work interrupted my day off. Truthfully I was too. The desk sergeant apologized, "Sorry to disturb you on your day off, Detective, but I didn't know what else to do."

Georgia offered to take over chopping duty while I spoke to the sergeant. I politely declined. She went to preheat the oven while I continued drawing the knife blade smooth and steady through the apple slices. "Go ahead," I said.

"Detective Welch at Five keeps hounding me for an update on a Darren Ellis. Wants you to call him."

"Will do, Sergeant. Thank you." I ended the call rolling my eyes. And men said women perfected nagging...

Welch called my cell twice sometimes three times a day (when he knew I was at work) on the pretext of Ennis transferring to Zone 5 and to establish what a valuable asset he'd be to their team. Then Welch threw in a casual mention of Darren, a veiled prompt for me to update him on any progress (or lack thereof). His call to the desk sergeant surprised me since he normally dialed me direct.

Welch ensured I had his home and cell numbers in case I ran across Ellis on his off duty hours. "Call me any time, any day. I want this bastard," he'd said. He wasn't the only one. The pressure to solve big cases like the Marathon Gas station homicide increased each day. The public groaned when departments resorted to psychics and Ouija boards but when someone's desperate, they'll do anything, especially when their job is in jeopardy. And mayors, chiefs of police and others higher in the pecking order had ways of saying it without actually saying it. Welch and his partner felt the pain from every direction, so he'd take any help available, even from a long shot from across town. On her day off.

I left Georgia stirring apples and nuts into the cake batter and made good on my promise to call my eager colleague. After the brief conversation, I returned to the kitchen where I found my sister deep in the process of stirring cherry pie filling into chocolate cake batter. The woman amazed me. She shot a revolver with such accuracy she'd ace the police department's requirements. She cleaned a house faster than a maid on uppers and she cooked and baked with the speed and expertise of a Le Cordon Bleu graduate. She was a marvel on two legs. At that rate, I'd be able to drop off all three cakes that *evening* instead of on my way to work the next morning.

"Isn't Darren Ellis wanted for that gas station shooting?" Georgia asked.

I nodded, "He's been off the radar since then too."

"So why is that detective badgering you about him? Do you have a lead on his location?"

Not really, I replied. "Ellis – or a guy matching his description – was seen near my double homicide. So we're both hoping to catch him before he does anything else." So I stretched the truth a bit if "near" meant five miles. My sister need not know this or the ambiguous explanation might stir her curiosity. Georgia and curiosity meant bright lights and endless questions until I spilled the truth or lost my temper, neither of which mixed with baking all day in a hot kitchen.

Georgia shivered, "That's frightening to think he went on a spree across the city. You're convinced he's still here and hasn't left town?"

You want a spree? Wait until you see his brother in four years. I shook my head, "He's still here, I feel it. Just wish I knew where."

"I hope you find him soon."

"Me too. The gas station shooting is only the beginning if we don't get him off the street."

13

Sunday

Finally free of the fruit juice stain on his belly, Winnie the Pooh smiled sappily up at me from the laundry basket. He looked positively high. I wanted a bite of whatever happy shroom he found in the forest because a day's worth of washing never inspired joy in me.

I'd soldiered through an early morning of our "lean, mean cleaning machine" freshening up the big people's clothes and removing the tiny people's gook like smeared chocolate, swipes of jelly and spaghetti mishaps. I truly pitied our washer.

By ten o'clock, I threw another load into the washer and hefted the basket full of dry ones to the dining table (our impromptu folding table). That load belonged to Anna. The last one was Lily's.

Ennis pitched in to help fold Anna's clothes then halfway through, a Eureka moment struck him and he absconded to the bedroom with phone in hand. "I'll be back shortly," he sang his way behind closed doors. The sudden change from ho-hum to high-spirited confused me but it was nice to see someone getting a thrill that morning.

I turned my attention to the girls who sprawled on the floor to watch TV, elbows propped up and their chins in their hands. Anna laid close to Lily, little sister mimicking big sister right down to the sighs and laughs during the program. They'd spent the last thirty minutes reliving Princess Ariel and her adventures for the hundredth time – and parroting the dialog by heart. It delighted me to see them getting along for a change.

Ennis emerged from the bedroom, his cheerful mood in full swing. I'd heard him talking on the phone since going AWOL from laundry duty. Whatever the conversation entailed, it hadn't dampened his enthusiasm.

He danced past the girls humming a song I hadn't heard except on an oldies radio station. Frank Sinatra may have aced singing "All The Way" but my husband hummed with the best of them. His rendition brought a smile to my face as Mr. Light-On-His-Feet breezed up to me and daintily relieved me of Anna's Winnie the Pooh shirt I'd begun folding. Hubby must have swiped a magic mushroom from Pooh, I mused, cause this guy was on Cloud Nine.

Ennis clasped my hand, drew me close to dance. I gladly accepted.

Mesmerized, the girls watched us (apparently we were more interesting than Ariel) while we glided across the living room floor in faded jeans and casual garb. I joined him in humming the song while we danced.

This was the man I fell in love with. The impulsive romantic.

The fella who presented me flowers just because, "I wanted to see you smile". The thoughtful Texan that left little love notes in places I'd find them. The man who slipped that diamond wedding ring on my finger meant everything to me.

Ennis slowed our spontaneous waltz to a stop and bent to kiss me. I went to tiptoe, meeting him halfway. At first his soft, warm lips teased mine then we shared a long but G-rated kiss that grossed out the kids enough they walked out protesting and leaving Ariel to fend for herself.

Still luxuriating in his snug embrace, curiosity got the best of me, "What spurred you to dance today?"

"Excitement. I've got excellent news."

I nudged his hips with mine, bobbed my brow, "Don't leave me in suspense. If it's that good, we could celebrate after I run the kids next door to Katherine. She owes me a favor."

"Get ready to collect because I called Major Wilkins about transferring," he said.

My heart sank. Earlier, when I'd heard him on the phone, I had no clue he contacted the commander of Zone 5. As the mirror predicted, he'd made his decision to transfer without me. The poignant moment in each other's arms now left me cold as if he suckered me into applauding his shot playing Russian Roulette (no pun intended) – using a fully loaded weapon.

I stiffened in his hold, "Exactly where was I in the decision making process? You promised to include me."

He tightened his embrace, blew off my irritation, "I know, I know. But Wilkins and Captain Shaw told me if I didn't take it, they'd offer the job to Christine. Baby, we need that money."

He made our situation sound critical as if our next meal depended on that transfer. So I ignored the comment, "Does Christine seem interested in it?"

My question eclipsed his bright and shiny mood. The luster of his smile dulled a degree, "That job is mine. Think of what we can do with that money. Remodel the bathroom, add a deck out back. We could finally afford to convert the back bedroom into a nursery, top to bottom, new wallpaper and everything."

Oh, I laughed to myself. *He thinks he's getting sex after this? What was that saying about people in hell wanting cold water?* "You're getting ahead of yourself, aren't you? A nursery?" And who the hell ever mentioned a deck? What was next, a swimming pool?

From the corner of my eye I saw the girls peeking at us from the hallway. A memory from my "future" foray flashed in my brain. Lily and Anna both mentioned a knockdown drag-out fight between me and Ennis – all revolving around his decision to transfer. I took a breath, told myself to ease up on my temper which nearly amounted to removing a pressure cooker's lid while it whistled.

He sighed, "Well, how about a new couch or a dining set? Anything we might want instead of giving it all to insurance and bills? What's wrong with you and this transfer? You've never wanted me to take it."

I shrugged from his arms. He chose to heave bombs, not shoot bullets in this argument. Yes, I felt the transfer was a terrible idea but I never told him so. Apparently by my silence he assumed he gained ground on the argument and steamed ahead, "And I don't understand why you balk at a sergeant's promotion–"

"So do you," I shot back. "You won't even study for the test." The girls cowered behind the wall. I imagined how confused they were. For two people who expressed their undying love moments ago, we were fast draws on our tempers. Transfers and sergeant exams meant nothing to them. They only understood we went from dancing to warring.

"You've been on the job longer," Ennis defended. "You make more. If you don't want a promotion, what's wrong with me wanting a pay bump?"

"Nothing."

He dropped each word with deadly finality, "Then you should be happy I accepted the transfer."

No, I wanted to tell him, your presumptuous and impulsive nature *should* render me mute with disbelief. Instead words cascaded into my mind, filling it with humdinger comebacks, five alarm criticisms, and blistering expletives that should never grace the ears of any child or decent adult. My mama would have slapped me for thinking them and Daddy… Well, let's just say Savannah's sitting days would have vanished for at least three weeks.

Chilling silence fell between us as we squared off. Ariel and Prince Eric shared a hearty laugh on the TV. Our daughters, on the other hand, still quietly recoiled in the hallway daring an occasional peek. Ennis visually dared me to further my comment – or unleash my profane lecture about including his wife in crucial decisions. We both battled the overwhelming urge to lash out. We both gradually lost that fight too. I wanted an answer to why, after stewing over the job for weeks, he felt the sudden urgency to leap in the deep end without consulting me. His betrayal sank to the bone. By agreeing to that transfer, he signed his death warrant and set in motion my future as a widow. He didn't know it, of course, and I couldn't tell him how I knew. Except my tongue, for some reason, never got the memo, "Ennis, if you take that job, you're going to–" At the last second, the tiny rational part of my mind engaged, snapping my mouth shut with a graphic reminder of our girls' devastation in four short years. I remembered the nine and seven-year-olds' accusing stares – as if I, not Shaun Ellis – pulled the trigger on their daddy when I said *you'll die if you take the job*. Today I would change that part of the future and not utter that sentence in front of our kids – or I'd end up jumping in front of a speeding bus from the guilt.

Hands on hips, Ennis demanded in a tone hot enough to breathe fire, "I'm going to what?"

I eased back a step. Fear of Ennis never entered into it. I wasn't scared of him. Fear of my own anger, of what I might say, forced me to retreat physically and mentally. I rephrased the fateful "going to die" into a generic, "I think you'll regret leaving. You're happier in Zone 2 and should stay but that's my opinion." *For what's that's worth*, I mumbled, marching to the bedroom. On the way I snatched my cell phone from the dining table. I'd call Georgia once safely locked in the bathroom (my usual haunt during bad arguments). My loyal, level-headed sister always talked me down in distressing situations. This qualified as unconditional, nuclear meltdown distress.

Fingers clasped my arm a shade too hard. "Why are you walking away?" Ennis sounded furious that I refused to stay and wallow in the argument – in front of our kids.

Despite my calmer tone, I shot him a withering glare, "Because before this turns uglier, and believe me Ennis, it can and will get uglier, I'm leaving the room." I nodded to the hallway, "*Our girls* are hearing everything."

We both glanced over. Lily and Anna shrank back like small cowering turtles withdrawing into their shells. I suggested, "Let's talk about this when we have time alone."

"No need to talk. I told you–"

"Yes," I jerked my arm free with a wince, "you've decided to take the job. Have you told Major Wilkins you're taking the transfer? Is that what you were doing on the phone?"

Ennis simmered. He replied with carefully enunciated words, "I wanted to tell my wife first."

"Your wife thanks you," I about-faced to the master bathroom and closed the door. I braced myself against the cabinet, focused on trying those deep breathing exercises the health experts advise people to do before they pop a blood vessel and keel over. By the end of two minutes I concluded those people were either overpaid or I was hopeless.

My thumb shakily tapped the phone's screen to bring up Georgia's number. The phone wobbled in my trembling grasp so I changed hands to my left which quickly reminded me how inept I was as a Southpaw. Blood pounded through every artery and vein until pulsing in my hands, feet and even my ears. Unless I dialed an ambulance, I needed to stay away from all conversations. I'd give myself time to truly settle down before disturbing Georgia. In my mood, she'd rush over or call the cops, thinking someone needed to intervene before violence ensued.

I opted to check Shaun's Facebook account again. I'd done this on and off during the week with no luck. I expected nothing less today.

The boy's arrogant smile taunted me from the screen, reminding me of that old, annoying tease *I know something you don't know* or perhaps it conveyed a simpler message to the detective staring back at him. Something to the tune of *oink, oink...*

Scrolling through his postings, I sneered at the bastard who referred to civil servants as smelly barnyard animals. He wrote more overblown rhetoric about gun control, law enforcement's "fascist" tactics and yes, a personal mention of Yours Truly for good measure. He bestowed upon me a moniker so obscure it drove me to the online dictionary for enlightenment. Hmm... So this was how Dartmouth students cuss, I thought. Then I wanted to tear that Yankee twerp into as many pieces as there were letters to that disparaging epithet. Between that idiot and my husband, I'd lose my mind or my health.

Facebook time-stamped Shaun's latest activity at ten-thirty that morning. I nearly closed the app when I realized another posting appeared during my snooping session. This one from a Jessie Shepard. I stared at the name, not quite believing what I saw. I checked his list of "friends" which, for the last week, had not included that name or Darren's – but it was there now. Returning back to the posting, a spark of hope ignited when I read *Need 40 bucks, Boo. Be here at noon.* Ms. Shepard used Shaun's nickname, the very one I'd seen before on a Sports Illustrated in the Ellis living room – with Darren Ellis's name on the mailing label. A hundred bucks said Darren sent the message via his girlfriend's account. Considering no cop in the present time except me knew about her, anyone might assume she was Shaun's main squeeze, not the on-again off-again girlfriend of his brother, a cold-blooded killer.

I quickly dialed Welch to tell him about the new posting. He treated it with excitement of a weather update, "I need more than a gut feeling to assign people to follow Shaun. We don't have a clue who or what this Jessie is to Ellis anyway. And if it's a girl, this could be a teenage tryst and '40 bucks' is code for nookie."

I played along, "Then she'd better have an IQ of 140 if she wants in his pants. Anything less would be slumming for him, at least in his opinion. I really believe Darren is writing on Shepard's account. Remember the SI swimsuit issue had Darren's name on it, along with the note. He's communicating with his brother the only way he can. Through friends. You said yourself the phone records from the home and Shaun's cell are useless. They both know you're checking them. Darren's in hiding, he needs to eat so he uses a friend's social media account because you don't recognize the name."

"Neither do you."

"But the name 'Boo' and the mailing label are the keys. It's worth tailing Shaun just to see who he's meeting, don't you think?"

He hemmed and hawed. Several seconds elapsed when, "How confident are you about this? Cause I hate being laughed at."

"I'd stake my life on it." And Ennis's and a few others...

Still plenty skeptical, Welch conceded, "I'll assign a coupla of plainclothes to follow the brat. But if we find out Jessie's a girl and she and Shaun are just knocking boots, I'm gonna be mopping the jail the rest of my career and you'll be holding the bucket for me. I'll let you know what happens."

Um... Well, "I'd like to see the arrest if Darren's there."

"Sure. It'll save the brass time if we're both there. If we're right, they'll congratulate us. If we're wrong, they can line us up for the firing squad right there in the street. Better get on the road because noon is an hour away."

O   O   O

An unusually early beginning to Autumn blew through a week earlier, plummeting temperatures to freezing levels and turning the city's foliage into a patchwork of Fall hues. Driving to the Zone 5 station on Spring Street, I noticed trees turning for the season, their leaves the color of sunrise, honey and scarlet. Halloween crept up on us and I thanked goodness our girls already had their costumes. Lily decided on Sleeping Beauty and Anna chose a ladybug (give a hug, ladybug).

That morning summer returned, abruptly kicking autumn aside for a rerun of heat and humidity. The sun blared hot and bright by eleven-thirty, heating the muggy air to the eighties. I wore jeans and a lightweight pullover blouse to stave off the miserable heat if possible.

The drive from our house in Dunwoody to the Spring Street station amounted to nearly twenty miles – the same distance from home to our station on Maple Drive. I encountered heavier traffic from the few churches that let out early. Due to work, household responsibilities or other situations, we sometimes attended Sunday evening services and that day would be one of them (if Ennis and I were speaking by then). Waiting until the late service would pay off, however, if Darren sat behind bars before we sang the first chorus of "What a Friend We Have in Jesus" with the congregation that evening.

My cell phone rang halfway to the station. Welch called to divert me to another location. My vigilance on Facebook paid off. Undercover officers tailed Shaun from his home to an older area known for smaller, lesser maintained houses. The undercover cops saw Darren answer the door to his brother and reported back to Welch who then called me.

"Ennis with you?" Welch asked.

"He stayed home to watch the kids." I'd chew off my tongue before confessing we'd parted ways on a very sour note. Our argument escalated when I walked out the door to Ennis's veiled accusation I put work before our future together. In my lifetime I'd been hit, shot, and incurred various other injuries and indignities but nothing went quite as deep as Ennis's final words that morning. He'd never understand the importance of nabbing Darren Ellis. I never expected him to but I'd do anything to save everything near and dear to me, including my crabby, overly vocal husband.

"He's okay with you doing this alone?"

"No," I answered honestly then proceeded to lie through my teeth, "but everyone else is too busy to babysit. How's it going on your end?"

"Still waiting to hear if they picked Shaun up yet. I'll be glad to bag that asshole too. Keeping us in the dark about his murdering brother. Oh, and 'Jessie' is apparently 'Jessica'. Darren's friend or girlfriend, I guess. Uniforms said she and Darren barricaded themselves in the house the second they saw them. Never got 'em outta there so we called SWAT in. This'll take a while. I hope you weren't planning to watch the game."

The Falcons could survive without me. Ennis not so much. "I'd rather be cuffing a killer."

"Me too. Then I'll sleep tonight knowing I still got a job. I'm pulling up now. How far are you?"

"About three minutes."

"When you get here, park down the block with EMS."

When I arrived I pulled to the curb near two ambulances. Their engines idled and the paramedics lounged in their seats. They knew the routine. Nothing got done in a hurry in these situations.

Welch and the patrol units parked at the curb of the small house. It sat in the middle of the block of similar homes needing painting, lawn mowing and other maintenance. Trees throughout the neighborhood fell victim to the "flash freeze" the prior week. Brittle brown leaves carpeted yards and the street, the hot breeze rustling and tumbling them along the curb gutters.

I got out of the Charger to a sore, stiff back and a pinging nausea. I attributed it to Friday's baking marathon, the excitement of this moment and that morning's argument with Ennis. Nothing upset a stomach like betrayal.

Half a block ahead Welch leaned against the hood of his sedan, arms crossed, waiting impatiently for SWAT to coordinate their plans. *Everyone has a twin* the saying went. From a distance Welch and Mathis favored enough they looked like brothers right down to the age, height, fat belly and same taste in suit. Up close I changed my initial judgment. Yes, they kinda favored but Welch had friendlier features and demeanor, plus his tie laid straight down the middle of his chest, not cocked slightly off kilter.

SWAT surrounded the modest, white clapboard house with a sickly elm and a For Sale sign out front. This rundown home tucked in the middle of downtown protected the man who started my husband's murder in motion. I wanted the bastard cuffed and stuffed in the far reaches of a prison, tucked away for the rest of his life. If he remained alive, so did Ennis.

Officers cordoned off the area, diverting traffic. To Welch's relief, SWAT geared up for entry into the house. I jogged up to Welch who hitched his thumb at his sedan. "Get a vest." He tossed me the keys. "They're finally ready."

I unlocked the trunk. The black bulky bulletproof (what a misnomer) vest fit snug when I cinched the Velcro straps. I equated it to a halfway inflated life preserver. The vests prevented most small caliber handgun bullets from penetrating the skin but the impact of a shot left a painful bruise bigger than a fist. Easier to recover from at least. It performed decently yet it played hell on a person when they felt on the verge of puking. It trapped heat, restricted movement and was generally a pain. Less than two minutes wearing the damn thing, my chest and back developed a moist, uncomfortable sheen of perspiration – and that managed to rile my nausea.

Once officially strapped in, I withdrew my .38 to add to SWAT and Welch's firepower, took a position behind his detective's sedan. "So did I miss anything?"

"Only that Ellis and Shepard have been squatting in this house for weeks. Neighbors said they knew Shepard stayed there but not Ellis."

"And of course no one called to report squatters in the house."

He snorted, "I guess you believe in the Easter Bunny too. These people barely open their doors to us. Forget calling to report a crime."

The SWAT commander gathered his troops for a last minute review of their plan. My sweat glands continued to work overtime beneath the vest and my stomach still percolated. I understood Welch's irritation now. We both wanted closure on Darren Ellis. Welch for professional reasons, me for personal ones.

He continued, "I guess Ellis and Shepard depended on his brother to supply them with money and food. They were good. No phone calls, no communication that we found at all." He looked at me in amazement, "Only when you kept track of Shaun Ellis's Facebook account did we make headway on this case." Then he smiled, "You did good work. No telling how many lives you saved by stumbling onto Jessica Shepard's name – and the note on that magazine."

Oh, I had an idea, but if this failed, my efforts to save Ennis failed. If Darren Ellis escaped SWAT and the squad of officers at the street, he'd disappear into oblivion. Short of following that punk brother of his, I had no way of finding him after that.

I dabbed perspiration from my forehead just as the SWAT commander gave the go signal. Welch and I hunkered behind his Ford, weapons trained on the small house. I held my breath. Seconds dragged on. My heart hammered in my chest, frantic with hope and anticipation of Darren's arrest. My gun hand trembled and before Welch noticed, I braced it with my left, steadying it. I hated Jeffrey Holland but I doubly hated him on days like that. His scalpel-happy ways destroyed my solid, reliable aim.

Please, I silently urged the SWAT guys. *I'm depending on you to grab this murdering asshole before our lives are destroyed.*

Muffled gunshots rang out from inside the house. Another round of shots fired off, sending every cop on the block diving for cover behind their cars, behind trees and homes. We curled tight, withdrawing a whole lot like our girls when Ennis and I fought that morning.

Bullets rocketed out the large picture window facing the street, shattering the glass and striking random objects. They zipped through tree leaves, ricocheted off curbs, and plinked off cars.

In those instances, besides *get the hell down, idiot,* my thoughts centered on my family. I squeezed down tight behind the car, centered my mind on the portrait on our living room wall. It was, without question, the grandest picture I ever saw. Ennis looked sharp in his black suit, the girls cheek-pinching adorable in their little dresses (white with pink trim for Lily, lilac with lavender for Anna) and I rounded out the foursome in a wine colored dress. Ennis hugged Lily close in his lap, I held Anna in mine. Our smiles told the world how much we loved each other, how blessed we felt with our girls. That picture kept me sane during moments when all hell broke loose. It kept me focused on going home alive.

Frantic chatter crackled over the radio in Welch's car. The SWAT leader. One short burst of gunfire followed by a two quick shots brought an unsettled, eerie peace to the neighborhood. More chatter on the radio. The SWAT leader announced "all clear" then summoned the ambulances down the block. The two parked beside my Charger revved their engines, lurched forward, speeding toward us with emergency lights flashing but no siren wailing their approach.

Welch and I holstered our weapons. My hand shook harder than a rookie's on her first armed robbery call. No one felt secure around a cop with a wobbly aim so I tucked the .38 away quick. Then I noticed he swiped a hand down his face and sighed a sigh I recognized. The one every cop recognized. The one meaning *Thank God I'm going home to my family tonight.*

The ambulances screeched to a stop behind us. Paramedics bailed from the cabs, unloaded the stretchers, tossed their equipment bags on board and took off toward the house.

More minutes ticked by. Every cop on the street stared at that house. And waited. No noise, no voices, no traffic. Just maddening silence. For the uniforms and detectives outside, the world shrank to a small single family dwelling that had seen its glory days forty years ago. The little old house harboring a murderer and his girlfriend.

A SWAT member, his assault rifle lowered at his side, opened the front door. Jessica Shepard, hands cuffed behind her, emerged first. She fought against the SWAT officer's hold, writhing to go back inside. Her cries penetrated the quiet neighborhood. *You shot him* she screamed along with a scathing string of profanity no bar of soap or backhand could cure.

The officer pulled her aside for the paramedics to exit with a stretcher occupied by a person in jeans and green t-shirt. A third paramedic straddled the patient, his hands pumping the person's chest while the unforgiving gurney bounced and rattled along the uneven sidewalk. In that short span of time they'd started two IV lines, slapped a heart monitor and oxygen on the wounded individual.

They wheeled the stretcher past us, giving me a fleeting glance at Darren Ellis. With that single glance I realized the oxygen, IV fluids and heart monitor were window dressing for a shop closing for business. He caught a bullet beneath the sternum and another in the left side of his chest. Blood soaked the green t-shirt, giving it an odd brown shade as it blended with the fabric – but pure crimson pooled beneath the paramedic's gloved hands, seeped between his fingers with every compression. Darren would not live four minutes, much less four years when his death would inspire his brother to gun down any cop in sight.

The paramedic aboard the stretcher, red-faced with sweat ringing his armpits and a damp stripe lining his spine, never slowed the compressions. He grunted through the strain and exertion of each one until his partner called him off to load Ellis into the bus.

Welch's hand on my arm urged me back a step. The touch shattered my daze of the surreal scene. With another grunt (this one by both paramedics) the stretcher lifted into the ambulance. The monitor continued droning the steady, flat tone. Before two uniforms closed the bus doors, one EMT already stripped Darren's shirt open, another readied paddles to shock the young man's heart.

An icy shiver crawled up my back despite the hot sun beating down on me. Darren Ellis's future entailed being pronounced D.O.A. at the hospital but what about mine and Ennis's future? The breath I released combined *Thank God I'm going home to my family* with *what happens now*? What did Darren's premature death mean four years from now? Had Welch's colleagues grabbed up Shaun? If so, perhaps that forestalled his vengeful rampage on police for killing his brother. Hard to shoot cops if he was behind bars. Despite the unknown repercussions of that day's events, a certain sadness crept in. Not for Darren but his mother. The loss of a child consumed a parent until their broken heart surrendered its pain in this earthly world. My only true regrets were Darren chose a life of crime and that choice robbed his mother of a son.

14

The SWAT commander updated us on what happened inside the house while we relieved ourselves of those hot, uncomfortable vests. Darren Ellis, armed with his own assault rifle, charged from a back bedroom spraying bullets in every direction he saw a uniform. Except for a graze or two, the officers escaped unscathed. The men in blue, however, demonstrated how it was done. Quick, clean and accurate. Now Darren sat in God's office atoning for his sins.

Two detectives from Zone 5 headed to the hospital while Welch and I returned to his station to update Captain Shaw.

I detoured to Kroger for Emetrol to ease my nausea. Normally I popped a Tums however the last several days called for the granddaddy of over-the-counter help. I opened the lid convinced such stressful weeks would give Mother Teresa an ulcer or a nervous tic so surely I was allowed an occasional bout of queasiness.

I swilled down a guesstimated tablespoon then waited for it to kick in on my way to the station. It barely touched the nagging sickness. I'd begun to wonder if I caught a bug or if my nerves went so bonkers I needed a vacation.

I parked my car at the back of the station then hoofed it around the building to Welch's car.

Media vans from the local news stations assembled en masse down the street. Word traveled fast about Darren Ellis's death. Before the reporters converged on us, I slipped into Welch's passenger seat, grateful for the cold air conditioning blasting from the vents. I angled one at my face then noticed Welch did not look happy.

"What's wrong?" I asked.

He stared at his phone as if he contemplated violence. "This job, that's what. They missed Shaun Ellis. He gave 'em the slip. Little bastard's slicker than greased shit. And to top it off, Mike just called." Mike Nelson was his partner. "He said Internal Affairs swarmed the hospital after hearing Darren Ellis died." He turned to me with a glare that pressed me back in my seat then proceeded, "He said there's another swarm headed our way. I guess it's okay Ellis shot at us but not okay we defended ourselves. They want answers from you, me, and anyone involved. Making sure we didn't violate a murderer's civil rights or give his accomplice indigestion when we broke down the door."

Oh, I wished he hadn't mentioned indigestion. I leaned back, sighing and wincing back a small wave of nausea. He commiserated longer on Internal Affairs while I yearned for another dose of Emetrol. IA cops got a bad name and a lot of them deserved it. The hinky ones twisted an honest cop's facts to meet their agenda. I always questioned whether Internal Affairs awarded commendations for every cop they disciplined, suspended or fired.

"...bastard walks in that gas station, blows away a hard working Joe Blow for eighty lousy bucks – a father of two, mind you – and takes shots at *us* then we shoot the bastard dead and Internal Affairs labels *us* the criminals." He bashed the steering wheel with his fist, "Assholes."

I agreed with him, hoping he'd calm down soon. I expected an IA interview so why didn't he? A cop couldn't crap without IA finding out and questioning them about it. Actually Welch's mild epithet surprised me. Most cops cut loose with more colorful descriptions of IA and honestly, I doubted even Internal Affairs liked *each other,* much less other cops.

I waited out his tirade until he wiped his brow, sighing, "So, is Ennis joining our happy crowd or does he know yet?"

I caught the not-so-subtle hint, "You mean have I given him permission?"

He shrugged a shoulder, "Wives hold a lot of clout."

Apparently not this wife. To salvage my dignity and skirt the issue I said, "It's his decision, not mine."

Welch killed the engine and we climbed out of the car. Before IA arrived, I wanted to fortify myself with more Emetrol, "Give me a minute and I'll meet you inside–"

The crack of gunfire split the air, first a single shot then another eight to twelve in quick succession. People fled in every direction, running for safety. Welch sought refuge behind the detective sedan parked in front of his. I dropped between the cars, scurried on all fours until safely beside him then pulled my .38 from the holster.

Reporters jumped in their vehicles, flooring them in reverse to escape the gunfire. As usual they retreated far enough for their safety but remained close enough to exercise their camera's zoom lens. Within seconds the entire block belonged to three people. Detective Welch, me and the shooter who positioned himself exactly where he'd been in the mirror's version of the future. On the building's roof across the street.

I pressed my back against the car's sun-seared fender, trying to calm my raging heart and catch my breath. The sturdy metal behind me relieved the immediate concern of eating a bullet but the heat radiating from it also escalated my sickness to urgent levels. I didn't want to hark up my cookies in front of Ennis's soon-to-be colleague but this day tested my constitution beyond its limits.

Welch grabbed his knee with a grimace, "Son of a bitch."

"Are you hit?"

"No, but I hit the ground on my bad knee." For retribution, he fired off two shots toward the building opposite us.

I joined him, not caring if my hand shook itself to pieces in the process. The ambush terrified me because before scrambling safely behind the fender, a bullet zipped passed my thigh in a frightening near-parallel to the mirror's scenario.

The shooter sent off a cascade of bullets at us. I jerked my arm back, cradling the upper arm from the searing pain. It felt like a burn from a red hot stove.

"What happened?" Welch demanded, leaning closer to see.

I clenched my teeth against the sensation spreading to the elbow and shoulder. The bullet grazed the flesh, stripping the skin until a film of blood seeped to the surface. "Glancing blow," I said. Road rash from a bullet was better than the alternative because six inches closer and I'd have taken that shot in the chest.

Bullets sprayed the station, sending puffs of mortar and chips of brick flying. The shooter fired into the windows that collapsed in giant shards then shattered on the pavement.

For an instant I remained paralyzed, stunned that I narrowly escaped a fatal wound *and* that my actions hastened the gun battle between Shaun Ellis and the police. What happened four years in the future unfolded now because I found Darren Ellis and he died four years ahead of schedule. Only instead of Ennis, Detective Welch joined me between Shaun's crosshairs.

"It seems like this asshole's only aiming at us. Who is this bastard anyway?"

Oh, just an angry teenager who blames us for killing his brother. "I don't know," I lied, "but we'll find out at his autopsy."

For a Yankee pacifist, sixteen-year-old Shaun Ellis sure got cozy with that assault rifle mighty fast. He strafed the car shielding us, his accuracy drastically improving. I shrank down, trying to envision that beautiful family portrait at home. My mind, however, kept repeating the same thing. *Six inches...* Six inches and Ennis became a widower. Six inches and the girls lost their mother. No more *give a hug, ladybug* or giving Lily golf lessons. No more snuggling in bed with Ennis or savoring his tender kisses. *I want to go home to my family, Lord. I want to make up with Ennis, to stop arguing with him about the transfer. I want to hold my husband and girls tight in my arms. Please let me go home.*

My heart pounded with such force, each impact felt like a hammer slamming into my chest. I felt my pulse in my fingertips and toes and warm, slick sweat popped out on my face and along my back. And that damn nausea intensified until I held the back of my hand to my pursed lips, hoping to keep the embarrassment to a minimum.

Down the street every television station in Atlanta pointed their cameras at us. What a sight we were. Two detectives hunkering behind a car while a nutcase tried to ventilate us. I prayed none of my family tuned in to watch Days of Our Lives, Dr. Phil or whatever aired that time of day. They'd get a live shot of this nightmare instead.

Welch's cell phone rang. "Yeah," he barked at the caller. He sounded aggravated more than scared, "We'd sure appreciate the help. We're a little tired of being targets. Prince needs medical attention. A graze but it's a mess... Yeah, *anything*. We need something – a helicopter, sniper, atom bomb. Just get him, will ya?" He clicked off then turned to me, "Boss says they're bringing SWAT and snipers in." He reached in his suit pocket for a handkerchief. "Take this," he motioned to my arm.

I laid my gun aside to press the hanky to my wound. I pursed my lips tight against the raw ache.

Sirens in the distance closed in on our location as Shaun threw another volley our way. The car windows shattered into small chunks of crystal, leaving gaping holes as more shots ripped through them. The entire car sank a few inches when bullets pierced the tires, leaving a hissing noise that not only deflated the Goodyears but my expectations of getting home soon – if at all.

A shout echoed from across the street, "Yah killed my brother! I'll kill all yah bastards!" That mixed-up New Yawk accent unconditionally confirmed one person held that gun. Shaun Ellis ended his tirade with another two shots, one for me and one for Welch. The bullets plinked exactly where we crouched down – at the wheel wells.

"Well, I guess we know who it is now," Welch joked with a grim frown.

"Yeah, and he might wanna look at me again." The thought of that uppity little asshole pinning us down like cowards sent my temper soaring. I grabbed my gun, reached around the trunk, aimed up at the building across the way. I fired two shots, "I'm a *bitch*, not a bastard! Get it right!"

Welch couldn't help but smile, "A little touchy about gender, are you?"

I leaned against the wheel with a pained sigh, "Only when cornered by teenage halfwits who think they're smarter than me."

Ellis rewarded my bravado with a personal shot that ricocheted off the trunk only inches from my head. I nearly lost my cookies.

"I believe he got the message," Welch said. His phone rang again and mine cranked up with Elvis Presley's "A Little Less Conversation". I cringed at the caller's name, plugged my left ear to block the approaching sirens, "Kinda busy right now, Georgia."

"I just saw on the news there's a shooter at a police station here. Hold on. They're showing a live shot now." Then she panicked, "*Oh my God, you're <u>there</u>. I'm looking right at you.*"

Thanks, Channel 11. I glared at the camera pointed at our horror show and spoke clearly and concisely into the receiver, "I didn't exactly plan this, Georgia."

Her voice softened, "Lily, go check on Anna. I'll be there in a minute."

Lily? Anna? Why would Georgia be with the kids? Now *I* panicked, "You're at the house?"

"Yes, Ennis asked me over to babysit while he met with a Captain Shaw. Don't worry, the kids aren't seeing this on TV."

My heart sank to my stomach. The world moved in slow motion upon hearing those words. "Ennis is here? Right now?" Despite my best efforts, Ennis found himself in the middle of a gunfight that shouldn't have happened. I turned to the large jagged holes that served as windows ten minutes ago. Was my husband among the wounded or worse, one of the dying?

Shaun cut loose with five more shots. I crouched even smaller knowing Georgia saw everything thanks to the nosy media.

My sister sounded on the verge of tears, "Savannah, don't you move one inch, do you hear me? Not one inch."

"I won't. Georgia, *is Ennis here right now?*"

"He just walked out. Let me check the driveway."

"If he's still there, keep him from leaving. Please stop him."

Those seconds lasted forever. "Ennis, wait!" Georgia shouted loud enough I yanked my cell away from my ear. She finally toned it down for me, "He says he coming down there to help."

"No. Do not let Ennis leave. He will get killed. They're bringing in snipers. That's all the help we need. Swipe his keys if you have to but *keep him home.*"

"No one's swiping my keys," Ennis barked in my ear. In those brief moments during my tirade, he'd commandeered the phone. He sounded as hot as I was, "You really think I'm leaving you out there alone?"

"Ennis, they're bringing in snipers. We don't need any more targets around here. Please stay home. Take care of the girls. I'll be there when this is over." I spent two minutes on the phone (it felt like an hour) convincing him to stay away. After the call, I sagged against the car with great relief that he listened.

Incredulous, Welch hung up from his call, "My wife is watching this on TV."

I checked my arm. Blood soaked the handkerchief. The stinging ebbed back to a mild ache. "Ennis and my sister are too."

"Heard you toeing the line with Ennis. Did it work?"

I nodded, "I don't remember my hero being that stubborn but he is."

A sudden burst of gunfire erupted from across the street. Shaun aimed at the small parking lot beside the station out of our line of sight. A groan emerged from that area.

Welch heard him too, "Perfect. A casualty of this trigger-happy moron." He yelled at the shattered station window, "Officer down on the west side of the building."

I went to all fours, flinching when I put weight on my arm. I intended to lean out and call to the uniform to check on him – while still protected by the fender.

A hand wrapped around my ankle, "Where the hell are you going? To your funeral?"

"*No.* I wanted to ask him how bad he was hurt."

The grasp on my ankle tightened while he repeated his previous plea for assistance, "Officer down on the west side of the building. He needs help and we can't do it without our families collecting our death benefits."

I retreated back to the fender when my phone rang. Georgia. Again. What part of *I'm busy* could she not grasp? I answered the call, "Yes, Georgia?"

"*Savannah Charlene, I told you not to move!*"

Well, *that* made my ears ring. "Stop yelling and stop watching the television. This'll be over soon."

She lectured, "Plant yourself beside that car and wait for help."

"There's an injured cop back there."

"If I see you twitch," Ennis had grabbed the phone again to continue Georgia's reaming out, "you will see a side of me you never thought existed, understand?"

"Ennis, I was not–"

"Savannah," he spoke but mostly snarled, "I'll spank the spit outta you if you don't *stay put*!"

Few things rated more humiliating than my husband threatening to spank me at bullhorn levels over a damn phone. Welch heard every shouted word. He lifted a brow.

I flushed the color of a Maine lobster and capitulated to Ennis for fear he'd elaborate on the supposed corporal punishment he planned.

After the call Welch's mouth curled into a sly grin. Anyone with two brains cells could see the images flitting through the man's head. *Well, not so fast, buddy...* "It'll be a cold day in hell before I let him do that," I vowed.

"I dunno. You may get more than Internal Affairs working you over tonight. He sounded pretty pissed off." He finished the comment with a chuckle. "Ennis has a point though. You don't want that third eye Billy the Kid's so eager to give you."

We stared in the gaping holes that once served as windows to the police station. The place was devoid of officers and citizens. The patrol sergeant's desk stood abandoned, the phone ringing somewhere behind it.

Shaun gave us a reminder of his presence by firing a long burst from the assault rifle. We both hunkered smaller behind the car.

Police units sped along cross streets down the block. Sirens converged from all directions. The cavalry finally assembled to save us –

at least I hoped so. Shaun apparently noticed the police reinforcement because his weapon fell silent for several seconds.

Welch took the opportunity to yell, "Our friends are here! You're toast now, you crazy son of a—"

"Welch," I nodded to the news media committing this moment to their cameras for the world to see.

That sucked the wind from his sails. He sighed, "Dumbest thing ever invented. Reporters."

"Dumb or not, we don't need any more trouble."

Shaun strafed the car again. A bullet bounced off the pavement, struck the undercarriage of the car. A second zipped past my leg. With his aim (or luck) improving, I curled beside the wheel even tighter. Georgia would have been proud.

Welch cocked his head, "You hear that?"

"Hear what? My ears are ringing from the shooting and my family shouting at me."

"It's the chopper." He chanced a look upward. His eyes darted across the powder blue sky until he smiled, "There he is."

Now the rhythmic whirring of the blades penetrated the fog of panic and the incessant, almost painful ringing in my ears. I tilted back to see an officer leaning out of the copter, his foot braced on the skid. In his hands: the most beautiful rifle I've ever seen. The helicopter hung, suspended in air as the officer stared down the scope to zero in on Shaun Ellis.

A shot rang out but it wasn't from the sniper above us. "That didn't come from the helicopter," I told Welch.

He shrugged, "Maybe another sniper got him. As long as the little bastard's out of commission I'll be happy."

I gave a nervous nod, wondering what had happened but too scared to move because my phone would ring again. God only knew what Ennis might threaten me with next.

The helicopter remained in position, the officer's rifle still trained on the roof across the way. The pain in my arm made a genuine resurgence. I just needed it bandaged and something to ease the aching. Then I needed my family. I *really* needed my family.

Elvis started singing again. And I hadn't budged an inch. The caller was Ennis. "Before you say anything," I warned, "I haven't wiggled one centimeter from this spot." *And so help me, if you mention spanking again...*

"They cut the media's feed. What's happening? Are you okay?"

That's how a person recognized a panicked Texan. When they rattled off words faster than a Yankee stuck on fast forward. I tried calming him down, "I'm okay. The sniper's here. We heard a shot so we're just waiting now."

Welch's phone trilled with a call. He answered halfway through the second ring, "He's down?" He tapped my shoulder, "They got the son of a bitch. Let's go."

A released a long, pent-up breath, struggling to maintain my cop persona a little longer. The family portrait raced to mind. The happy family of four remained intact – healthy and considerably shaken, but intact. I swallowed hard, bit back tears blurring my vision while informing Ennis, "It's over."

"I'm leaving right now." His truck door slammed. The engine cranked. "Babe," he said.

Hot tears slipped down my cheeks. To hell with the cop in me. I was a woman scared out of my mind, afraid I'd never see my family again, "Yeah?"

"I love you." His voice choked with emotion, "I'm glad you're safe."

"I love you too. See you soon."

Seconds after our conversation ended, dazed officers filed out of the station like victims of a tornado emerging to assess the aftermath. Everyone gave the newly aerated detective's sedan a wide berth, their mouths slung open in amazement and shock. They looked at the car, the building then us. A cluster of uniforms gathered around me and Welch. Three ambulances raced one after another to where we stood. Welch and I waved the paramedics off, pointing inside the station and telling them about the wounded officer that needed help.

At the behest of Captain Shaw I took up residence on the back bumper of the second ambulance while a paramedic bandaged my arm. He updated us both on the officer beside the building. Shot in the side, on his way to the hospital but the outlook seemed encouraging.

Welch limped around the scene with his swollen knee to get the lowdown on Shaun Ellis. We weren't sure if he was dead or wounded. At that point, it honestly did not matter to me.

Once police allowed them within filming range the media stormed the area like the Allies at Normandy. They jockeyed for prime real estate and of course Channel 11, the one that got me in deep shit with Georgia, claimed the best stake. They centered on me for some stupid reason. From the cordoned off area down the street, they aimed their camera at me just as I unloaded my breakfast into a barf bag. One of those real Kodak moments.

In eighty degree heat, the paramedic wrapped a blanket around me because I shivered from nerves and shock. I could barely keep a straight face and a bone-tired weariness set in. A uniform fetched a Sprite for me to sip and I bummed a piece of Trident from an EMT to help settle my stomach.

Before the big department brass swooped in with their Inquisition, first Lieutenant Ramsey then Captain Shaw and finally Major Wilkins took turns asking questions. Despite their gentle handling of the situation, the redundancy added to my fatigue. I kept checking my watch wondering where Ennis was. I couldn't wait to hold him in my arms.

I was in the middle of the major's redundancy when Ennis raced by without noticing me and stopped cold at the sight of the shot up sedan. He leaned onto his knees, catching his breath and, I assume, fighting the urge to puke as I did earlier. He spotted Welch, "Where's Savannah?"

Welch pointed at me, "Some detective you are. She's right behind you."

Ennis spun to face me, owl-eyed. The blood drained from his cheeks leaving him ashen.

"Need a seat?" I patted the bumper, "There's room."

He zeroed in on the bandaged arm, "You got shot."

"I got grazed." I glanced to the paramedic who vouched for me.

Before I could say another word, Ennis planted his lips on mine in a demanding, passionate kiss that sent shivers through me. I liked this kind of hello. I liked it a lot.

Major Wilkins uneasily cleared his throat, "I'll give you two some privacy," then discreetly ambled away.

I parted from the steamy kiss whispering to Ennis, "Missed me that much, huh?"

"More," he smiled.

Welch gimped up beside Ennis to tell me, "You won't believe this. Remember you said the shot didn't come from the helicopter? You were right. The dumbshit on the roof shot himself."

"Shaun Ellis committed suicide?" That stretched the limits of plausibility, kinda like saying John Wayne was actually a woman. Nuh-uh, no way. Not computing. Cowards and insufferable egotists such as Mr. Ellis chose other routes to their Maker, preferably one where someone else pulled the trigger.

"He's not dead but he ain't going anywhere for a while either," Welch continued. "The guy in the copter said the idiot had a handgun in his waistband. He pulled it and starting running for the fire escape in back of the building. He tripped and shot himself. In the plums."

Ennis flinched, "He nailed himself in the nuts? Not exactly Mensa, is he?"

I chuckled. If my husband only knew. Before this, Shaun Ellis was destined to attend Dartmouth – and yes, his IQ was higher than mine – but I knew how to handle a gun. He didn't. As odd as it sounded and inappropriate as it was, my chuckle bordered on erupting into a boisterous laughing fit. I dialed it down to a smirk. Shaun Ellis, the smart ass, shot himself in the giggleberries. Let's see Mr. Ivy League explain *that* to a trauma surgeon.

15

That evening after touching base with Georgia and Seth, I settled in for supper. Ennis let Ronald McDonald prepare his and the girls' supper and picked up a nice, juicy Rocketburger for me. For dessert, he dropped by Georgia's bakery for a fresh peach pie. It was the best meal I'd had in ages, especially once I plucked the jalapeños from my burger. After puking to the ninth power that afternoon, I possessed no desire for a repeat.

By five o'clock, exhaustion set in. Georgia called to recite a list of to-do's for wound care and pain relief, as if I was a novice in the injury department. *Yes, Georgia. Yes, Georgia. Thank you, Georgia. Love you too.* That was the best way to handle my sister when in mission mode. "Yes" her to pieces.

Six rolled around. Things thankfully settled down. Until six thirty-five. The phone jangled maniacally on and off for two solid hours. Our network affiliates graciously shared their footage with everyone this side of Creation so the whole world heard about the psycho using Atlanta cops as target practice. Ennis fielded calls from his family in Texas, a handful of my relatives and plenty of friends, mostly from church (and yes, Sonya Porter led the crowd).

I changed into my pajamas and robe. Facing the mirror, I tied the robe at my waist, not caring that the image staring back looked a tad older than I cared for. Truthfully that evening I felt rather elderly for my age.

No one could guess some semi-homely, weird old mirror predicted a person's future. It bore scars, a few decent scratches and needed work but it turned out to be the most valuable belonging I'd ever bought and worth every one of the two hundred dollars I shelled out.

I leaned closer to ensure no one overheard me, "I think Ennis and I will be okay." I stroked the smooth interwoven vine along the frame, "Thanks for the forewarning."

The girls started a ruckus in the living room, yelling about dolls again. The day's events drained me of energy *and* patience. I gripped the mirror, wanting just a moment's peace and quiet. I winced at a sudden pressure on my wrist. The mirror wanted another adventure but I did not. After the day I'd had a journey into the future would finish me off. I pulled against the force dragging me into the unknown. In the living room both girls yelled at each other.

"Anna, give the doll back to your sister!" I ordered as the mirror jerked me through once more. This time I had no time to prepare, no chance to gain my bearings before the world tumbled askew.

Apples, cinnamon and strong brewed coffee wafted to me, caressing my senses. I sat in a wooden chair – a dining chair I guessed.

When I opened my eyes, I sat at the dining table in jeans and a blue pullover blouse (no pink floral pajamas). Two women joined me at the table, one to my left, the other to my right. I recognized them from the earlier vision when my older self suffered the ultimate unfortunate event called death.

Our girls were adults. Lily (in her early twenties) opted for chic style with white Capri pants and peach colored blouse. Anna (maybe just cresting the Big Two-Oh) shared her mama's choice of attire with comfortable jeans and pullover blouse, the latter being fire engine red. Bold and loud, just like my baby girl at two-nearly-three-years-old.

Now that I wasn't keeling over from cardiac arrest, I could fully appreciate our beautiful, grown daughters and what I saw took my breath away. As a child Lily heavily favored me. Age and maturity retained the basic resemblance but God finessed those features into a woman with her own individuality. She inherited my blue eyes and brown, wavy hair. But He gifted Lily with eyes prettier than any sapphire and silky chestnut hair that tumbled in soft waves below her shoulders. He topped off this masterpiece with a dazzling smile persuasive enough to bring men to their knees. As evidenced by the previous vision (with the heart attack) He gave her courageous strength to endure hard times, a commanding presence during emergencies and mixed in a generous amount of Southern compassion. I was so proud of her. She grew up with me for her mother but God molded her into a lady, elegant and well-spoken, gentle yet tough when required, and loved and admired by all who met her, I'd bet the farm on it. And on the golf course? I imagined my girl put my abilities to shame.

I looked at Anna. My, how she'd grown from that chubby-cheeked toddler to a blend of Ennis and myself (mostly Ennis). Her eyes were the color of sunlight shining through whiskey and her hair a luxurious sable mane a bit longer than her sister's. I could only imagine her sheer beauty at Sunday services. Perhaps wearing a darling navy blue dress with matching heels, her loose waves tousled by a warm Atlanta breeze. In my mind, I saw her. Well-worn Bible in hand, her purse tucked beneath her arm while she picked up the pace to the church door, hoping to grab a seat up front for the sermon.

Both girls giggled at my stunned bug-eyed stare. "Doll?" they said in unison.

Anna snapped her fingers to break my daze, "Earth to Mama. I don't have Lily's doll."

Lily smirked, "And it's been quite a few years since either of us played with Barbie and Ken."

I shook my head, trying to adjust to the enormous changes around me. The girls looked at me as if I'd gone loopy. "Sorry," I apologized. "Must have had a senior moment."

"At fifty-six?" Anna rolled her eyes good-naturedly, "You're not exactly ready for the old folks' home."

Ah, so she inherited my sarcastic wit. I forced a small chuckle but found nothing humorous about this situation. The mirror did it again, throwing me into the deep end of a bizarre future then left me to flounder my way through it. I'd make the best of it one more time.

First, I surveyed my surroundings. Several items occupied the dining table. Three half-full cups of steaming, aromatic coffee sat beside three saucers with forks propped on the sides. A practically perfect apple pie (missing a sizeable section) played centerpiece to our get-together. The burnished golden crust looked tender enough to melt in my mouth and I could almost taste what surely was a delicious cider-flavored filling. Georgia's work. Had to be. My pies rated okay but nothing compared to hers. I considered indulging in a second piece since I missed out on savoring the first.

Anna dabbed the corners of her mouth with a napkin, patted her barely-there tummy, "Excellent pie, Mama. Yours has always been my favorite."

Mine? That piece of art was *my* effort? This wasn't the future, this was a dream and so far I loved it.

Lily chimed in, "Mine too. Aunt Georgia cornered the market on peach pie but your apple pie is out of this world."

I thanked them while Lily reached forward, tapped a small stack of papers in front of me, "So do you think forty-three is too many? I culled it down from fifty."

I peered at the page, squinting to read the blurred writing. Lily nudged a pair of glasses at me, "These might help."

Embarrassed, I slipped them on offering a sheepish thanks. The writing, unlike the situation, cleared right up. The page had two columns. In each Lily wrote a list of names in a graceful, sloping cursive. She'd drawn lines through a few names to mark them off. It finally dawned on me. This was a guest list for her wedding. I had no clue what to say except, "Forty-three sounds reasonable."

"You're sure? Since you and Daddy insist on paying for the wedding, I don't want you strapped for money later on."

I glanced over my specs, "I assume you're planning just one wedding?"

She eased into a gorgeous smile, "Yes, just the one." She paused a moment. I sensed another issue looming on the horizon so I waited. Considering the delay, she labored over the phrasing. Finally she braved into it, "One more question and please don't get angry. Can I invite Daddy to the wedding?"

I did a doubletake. What an odd question. Why wouldn't she invite him, I asked.

She and Anna exchanged a look. I wasn't sure if those frowns questioned my sanity or not. Lily continued tiptoeing into the subject for some reason, "I assumed you'd both be uncomfortable with each other."

Since when? "Uncomfortable?"

Anna took over, "You gotta admit the temperature drops when you're in the same room together. He's agreed to do whatever you decide. He mentioned maybe coming for the wedding but skipping the reception. Does that work for you?"

No, it does not and I said as much. I asked Lily, "Why would I want Ennis excluded from the most important day in your life?" I needed coffee to shake off the residual cobwebs of this visit to the future.

The conversation veered into strange territory so fortifying myself seemed natural. I lifted the cup, took a tentative sip. Tasty. So I went back for another.

They looked at each other again. This glance *did* doubt my mental balance. Lily cleared her throat, "Did you two call a truce while we weren't around? Because you can't stand each other since the divorce."

She said the word *divorce* at the precise time I swallowed. Not a good thing. Coffee went sideways down my throat, launching me into an uncontrollable coughing fit.

Lily seized the coffee cup from my hand before I spilled hot liquid all over me and her guest list. Anna raced to the kitchen to draw up a glass of water. I dared a small swallow then another until regaining my composure. "What!?" I croaked. *Divorce?* I turned to the wall showcasing the beautiful family portrait I loved. A minute ago, that portrait showed a smiling family of four. Ennis, me, Lily and Anna. Our family together and happy.

My horrified vision saw no portrait and no sign the portrait ever graced our family home. In its place hung two individual eight by tens, one of Lily, the other of Anna. Both looked like high school senior portraits. Ennis was gone. Any photos of us as a couple were gone. What the hell happened to our marriage, to *us*?

Anna sat down, put a hand to my knee, "Mama, are you feeling okay?"

Play it cool and calm down, I cautioned myself. That was easier said than done. Closing my fingers around the glass, I wished for a slug or two of Jack Daniel's just to liven it up a shade – and help me cope with this bombshell. Devastating news deserved a good belt of the strong stuff, not a wholesome glass of water. "Sorry," I said with a tremulous smile. "Swallowed wrong." When had Ennis and I divorced? I intended to wheedle answers from our girls just as soon as I wrapped my mind around this "reality".

Anna's brow still pinched with concern so I patted her hand, tried to sound convincing, "I'm fine, sweetheart. Really." *No, not really. I'm stunned and outraged at me and Ennis both...* Another forced smile later, I crowed, "My oldest baby is getting married so there's a lot to celebrate. Invite Ennis. He deserves to be there and it won't bother me because my attention will be on the beautiful bride and her equally stunning maid of honor." *Liar, liar, pants on fire... Your attention will also be diverted to cornering the ex-husband and asking some very pertinent questions.*

To recoup my poise, I busied myself scanning the papers beneath the guest list. One diagramed the hierarchy of bridesmaids, groomsmen, flower girl, ring bearer and other active participants of the day. Lily's attention to detail reminded me of Georgia. Anna was listed as maid of honor, of course – and cousins (Georgia's daughter Eden was mentioned first and Seth daughter Lindsey second) plus friends (I assumed) served as bridesmaids. I did not recognize anyone on the groom's side – or the groom for that matter. My daughter was engaged to an Anthony Stafford. I slowly perused her notes and other material included in the stack. A bridal magazine bookmarked with Post-It flags came next. She'd marked a page called "Cranberry & Champagne – A Perfect Autumn Wedding Palette". In their cranberry colored strapless gowns, bridesmaids flanked the bride in her white dress. The bouquets consisted of champagne colored roses ringed in deep red calla lilies. Right now our daughter mixed her attire in eclectic ways, colors that clashed or wild ideas of different colored socks. But I envisioned that child all grown up and in this wedding gown. I nearly cried.

To prevent that I sat the magazine aside, regeared my mind to the business at hand: Lily's computer printed draft of the invitations. Ennis and I were listed as separate parties. Divorced in marriage, divorced in name and divorced from our manners apparently, judging from the girls' reluctance to say Ennis's name in my presence. It read *Mrs. Savannah Rutherford* (then on the next line) *Mr. Ennis Rutherford request the honor of your presence at the wedding of their daughter Lily Christine Rutherford to Anthony Reimer Stafford...* Grown children, weddings, divorces – it seemed so Alice-in-Wonderland.

On the list beside the invitation's draft, I noticed one important omission, "I don't see Daniel on the list anywhere. You didn't include him?"

Simultaneous confusion crossed their features. Lily spoke first, "Who's Daniel?"

A crooked, sly grin curved Anna's lips, "Mama, have you got a boyfriend?"

The two broke into a girlish chant of *Mama and Daniel sittin' in a tree...*

It flustered and annoyed me. "No," I interrupted their merry little song, "he's your br–" I barely stopped before blurting *brother.* A thread of unease wound through me. Something was wrong. In the other visions Ennis and I had three kids – Lily, Anna and Daniel. Now the baby disappeared from this version of the future. I proceeded carefully now, struggling to adapt to *this* twist as well, "Daniel's not my boyfriend. I met him some time ago and I was sure you girls knew him too."

Anna spoke her mind, "Mama, it's truly okay for you to have a beau. Don't be shy about it. Lily and I want to see you happy again. You've been all about work since the divorce. You're basically full time at the bakery. You need a man in your life, not more work."

Lily's hand gently clasped mine, "Seventeen years is too long. You're lonely. Anna and I see it in your eyes. Listen, Tony's uncle James is retired from the Birmingham PD. He'll be at the wedding and we want to introduce you. He's very interested in meeting you..."

Her voice faded as my mind tried to wrap around another verbal bomb my daughter dropped on me. The divorce occurred within a year of Ennis transferring to Zone 5. What had happened to split us up? And so damn quickly too? God, I really needed Georgia. She'd tell me why without getting emotional. The girls worried about me and the last thing I wanted was them thinking I'd lost my mind. Hell, Georgia was used to thinking I had.

"...if you and Daniel aren't an item, it couldn't hurt to go to dinner with James. Mama, have you heard a word I've said?"

I drifted back to hear Lily's question. In that brief time I devised a subtle way to broach the subject. "I'm sorry, sweetie. I was remembering back when Ennis and I broke up."

Her nose wrinkled, "Why? I prefer you in a good mood, not your 'Ennis and Sheila Mood'."

Anna shivered, "I second that motion. Let's change the subject."

"No," I encouraged. "I'd like to discuss it with you both. You girls never got a chance to honestly voice your feelings about it all."

Lily reluctantly spoke, "I don't think it's wise to delve into it again. You get too upset."

I crossed my heart. It worked on the girls as children, maybe it still would. "I promise today I won't."

Anna's dark eyes zeroed in on the gesture. She seemed to read my mind, "We're not kids anymore, Mama. Your heart is the reason we *don't* want to talk about it."

"Anna..." Lily cautioned.

"What?" She fussed, "She's already acting strange this morning and now she wants to relive that? Might as well dial up the ambulance and have them on standby."

I kept my voice composed, "I understand your concern but I'll be fine. It's important we talk about it."

They looked at one another. Anna shrugged with a dismissive wave at her sister, "Fine but *you're* calling Aunt Georgia if anything happens. I'm not weathering that storm too."

They already alerted me by mentioning another woman's name. Sheila. What happened with her? For most wives the obvious answer was "affair" but Ennis sleeping around on me? Get real.

The girls clammed up. Neither chose to start the conversation so I would, "The obvious place to begin is Sheila."

Lily's jaw set, "I told Daddy if he came to the wedding *she's* not welcome. That was *my* rule. She's not my mother and never will be so don't worry about seeing her."

A combination of disappointment and inner rage sparked inside me. He had, hadn't he? Had an affair with this Sheila then divorced me to marry the "other woman"? Oh, for the love of God... "It's your decision who attends, sweetheart." *But thank you for your loyalty. At least someone understands the concept.*

Lily shook her head with a decisive, "She may have married Daddy but what she did to you back then, I'll swing a chair at her if she shows up."

"Be careful," I wanted to keep the tone semi-light. "They don't allow conjugal visits in the city jail."

My oldest child's face soured, "A lieutenant using her department connections to try and have you fired? Unconscionable, homewrecking tramp."

"Yeah," Anna chimed in, "I'll take up a chair and we'll *both* wail away on the bitch." Then flinched, "Sorry for the language, Mama."

I felt rather confident that, "I've called her worse."

Cheeks scarlet red and fists clenched, Lily proceeded, "She

provoked you into that fight the way she goaded Daddy into filing for custody of us." The longer she spoke, the angrier she grew. "She wanted you penniless and alone – and nearly succeeded."

I covered her shaking fists with my hand, "And you thought *I'd* get riled. Settle down, hon. It's in the past."

"The heck it is. If Daddy attends the wedding or reception, she'll be there wrapped around him like kudzu. *'Oh, Ennis',*" she gushed, flapping her hand and batting her eyelashes like a Southern belle turning on the charm. "'*Honey Buns, My Brown Eyed Baby Love–*"

"Don't forget *Cupcake*," Anna deadpanned.

"Right. *'Cupcake, be a dear and fetch me a glass of champagne.'*" She sagged in the chair, "Ugh. You get cavities just listening to her. Mama, you don't realize how grateful we are that you fought so hard for us. I'd have killed her if they'd won custody."

"And I'd have held her down for Lily," Anna vowed. "Hammer Sheila Bennett into the ground."

Lieutenant Sheila Bennett. Slept with Ennis. Provoked me into a fight. Probably turned me into Internal Affairs. Tried to steal my kids. Yep. I had the basics now. When the mirror tossed me back to my thirty-nine-year-old life, I'd track the bitch down before she and Ennis encountered each other. One thing really bothered me though. "I can't believe Ennis condoned how she treated me – or the fact she tried to get me fired."

"No one could stop her," Lily said. "He tried. When she picked us up from school that day and sent you into a panic to find us? That was her idea and he demanded they bring us home. She asked him if he wanted custody of us or not. He said yes. She told him to back off and let her handle it."

"How the hell did she lure him into her bed?" I mumbled to myself – or so I thought.

"She set him up," Anna replied. "I know you don't believe that but she did."

Lily fired a blistering glare at her, "Shut up, Anna Rose. You'll upset Mama with that kinda talk."

Anna backed off, patted the air in surrender, "Fine, fine, whatever you say. But Mama seems fine. *You're* the one blowing a gasket."

"Well, you never heard Mama cry herself to sleep like I did. I remember all those nights. She thought he'd take us and move back to Texas. She thought she'd lose us, her job, her pension and everything that–"

"Girls," I tried to break up the growing discontent. The argument, however, took on a life of its own.

Anna shot a hot glare at her sister, "I might've been young but I remember the fights. I didn't want Daddy to take us either. I wanted us to stay a family. So did you."

"So did I," I stated flatly.

That deflated most of the anger revolving around the table. Lily shook her head, "She's so Polly*anna* when it comes to Daddy. I love him too but he destroyed our family."

"Sheila destroyed it, Lily. I don't approve of what Daddy did but you know Sheila can talk herself out of trouble or someone else into it."

Lily crossed her arms, "And that, baby sister, is called a sociopath."

My surroundings flashed blinding white. I closed my eyes to shut out the glare. The girls' voices fell away. A soft, melodic tune "A Mother's Prayer" replaced it. When I opened my eyes I stood at the entrance of our church's sanctuary. The mirror dropped me smack-dab into the wedding day. I prayed for no disasters since the stupid antique possessed a penchant for such things.

Arrangements of red and cream colored roses tied with champagne colored ribbons hung at the ends of each pew. Approximately sixty formally attired people (not forty-three as originally suggested) crowded the frontmost seats and every person present turned in my direction.

In an odd moment of déjà vu, I noticed my wine colored dress fit Lily's color scheme as well as it fit me. The ankle length chiffon dress reminded me of the one I wore for our family portrait that no longer hung in the living room (in the future). The dress I wore for the wedding however looked far too elegant for me. Had Lily chosen it for me? Georgia maybe?

"You ready, Aunt Savannah?"

The deep voice startled me. I turned to a tall, handsome man in a blue suit that – with the exception of his eyes – favored Seth. My mouth nearly gaped. *This* was Dylan, Seth and Leah's youngest child. The little boy I'd held, the toddler who loved drinking his "gingerella" (ginger ale), the youngster I'd cheered at little league football games, was grown up and approaching thirty. That boy grew broad-shouldered and lofty like his father. He offered me his arm with a smile, "Time for the mother of the bride."

I linked my arm in his and we started down the aisle. "A Mother's Prayer" flowed from the instrumental intro to the softly sung lyrics, the words tugging at my heart, the sheer power of them stirring sentiment so deep I swallowed back the rising urge to weep.

I pray you'll be my eyes
And watch her where she goes
And help her to be wise
Help me to let go

I figured out that mothers consisted of love, milestones, memories and paranoia. We were rainbows of emotions, jugglers of tasks, traffic cops of trouble, nurses and doctors, therapists, guidance counselors and more. There wasn't a monetary sum large enough to pay a mother for her years of service. But a day this magnificent? Worth every sleepless night, every argument (however ridiculous they seemed) and every tear of worry and frustration. Watching their child go from crying newborn to a mature, happy adult was priceless to any parent.

I pray she finds your light
And holds it in her heart
As darkness falls each night
Remind her where you are

My eyes grew misty the longer the song played. Dylan patted my hand, whispered I should calm down. It occurred to me that I grasped his arm in a death grip. I muttered an apology. He just smiled.

Toward the front I spied Seth and his wife Leah. Georgia and Dane sat in the front row (I assumed Lily made the arrangements for me and Georgia to sit together). My sister smiled as we approached. The song concluded, giving one last try at causing the bride's mother to collapse in a sobbing heap:

> *Every mother's prayer*
> *Every child knows*
> *Lead her to a place*
> *Guide her with your grace*
> *To a place where she'll be safe*

I dabbed a single tear, released a shaky breath when we stopped at the end of the pew and Dylan kissed my cheek. I took my place beside Georgia who claimed my hand with a hushed, "You look so beautiful in that dress. Lily has good taste, doesn't she?"

Yeah, in clothes. But what about men? Dressed in camel colored suits with burgundy ties, the groomsmen filed in, giving me a chance to regroup. Then best man followed and finally Tony Stafford walked down the aisle. I sized him up. At least he wasn't decked out in tie-dye or leaving the impression he tooled around in an old Volkswagen van adorned with bumper stickers saying "Cure Virginity" and "Old hippies never die – they just go to pot".

By his height Tony stood taller than Lily who was my height. Short brown hair, clean shaven and nice looking, he had an easy smile and friendly face. In that tux he looked handsome and polished but what about after the formalities of marriage? I'd seen plenty of hopeful, starry-eyed brides after the courting, vows and honeymoon. I visited them at their homes to separate the "happy" couple from killing each other or I'd gone to the hospital to document bruises and broken bones. I'd heard "I tripped" and "he didn't mean it" and "he just had a bad day" more times than I could count.

Tony caught my eye and smiled. I returned the gesture with a private meaning. *You'd better be good to my little girl or* _you'll_ *end up at the hospital with more than bruises and broken bones. Remember that, young man...*

The bridesmaids (all dressed in strapless dark red gowns) included Lindsey, Eden, a couple of women I didn't recognize and last but not least, the maid of honor. Anna, wearing her cranberry colored gown, absolutely glided down the aisle. With her slender figure, a touch of makeup and her hair in a stylish updo, she was pure splendor in motion and as graceful as a model on a catwalk.

During her trek to join the bridesmaids she displayed a bashful yet proud smile. In that instant I saw my baby hugging her teddy bear Dallas to her heart. The little girl who insisted "frashrights" were the answer to any darkness issue, and I saw the child who replied to my *I love you* with *love you more.* How did mothers survive these events without losing their composure and looking like complete idiots?

On cue, Georgia offered me a tissue. I took two. I'd need a box before they exchanged vows.

The organist paused, waited a brief few beats then cranked up Mendelssohn's Wedding March. When I looked back toward the entrance, the loveliest sight I'd ever beheld stepped into the crowded room. Lily surveyed her guests, her vision sweeping across the gathering as if personally welcoming them.

Another step. She centered on me with that girlish grin I already recognized in her four-year-old features. I smiled and winked at her. *You look beautiful, my baby girl. Enjoy this moment. It is yours. Remember how happy you are right now and I pray the feeling lasts a lifetime...*

Dabbing tears, I watched Lily glance up at her escort with the love and devotion she bestowed on me.

My heart stopped. Father and daughter stood arm-in-arm for the walk down the aisle. Ennis beamed down at Lily. He gave her hand a tender squeeze. The proud papa. In the quiet moments at night I'd given this event a trial run. My musings paled in comparison to the scene before me. The only dark cloud looming over the special occasion was the fact Ennis and I weren't together anymore. Otherwise it was spectacular.

Ennis's gaze passed across mine then darted back, his gaze sharpening for an instant. His smile wavered but he maintained his role as they progressed down the aisle. He nervously nodded to me. I nodded back in acknowledgment but couldn't help seeing a traitor in my midst considering the bitter custody battle the girls spoke of. But that was a different Ennis, I reminded myself. In my thirty-nine-year-old world we were still married and loved each other.

Throughout the procession he glanced to me again and again. The pair approached the preacher who asked, "Who gives this woman to be married to this man?"

Ennis responded without hesitation, "Her mother and I do." Before leaving Lily and Tony together at the alter I heard Ennis speak to her betrothed, "This is my little girl. My princess. Take good care of her." Or else, I read between the lines. The bride's parents parted ways on a sour note but we agreed on something. Our daughter.

Ennis turned, unsure of where to sit. Georgia leaned closer to me, "Don't worry. Lily's got you covered."

I had no idea what she meant until Dane discreetly lifted a finger, a sign for his brother to sit beside him. So that's what *got you covered* meant. Our daughter left no room for confrontations by placing two buffers between us.

By seating Ennis beside Dane, it left him within a very long arm's length of me beside Georgia. The seat next to Ennis remained empty. At least he'd adhered to Lily's demand. No Sheila Bennett.

Upon closer scrutiny the years hadn't been kind to him. His once youthful features showed the strain of a stressful, unhappy life with deepening lines at his eyes and streaks of gray in his hair. Ennis chanced a smile at me. For an instant I thought I detected a hint of regret in his expression.

The blinding light returned, fast forwarding me to the reception. A group of people gathered with the bride and groom chatting with them. Tony drew Lily closer by the waist. They shared a long kiss. The two looked very much in love or "stupid-happy" as I called it.

Once the "I do's" wrapped up, Tony and Lily turned their attention to matchmaking. According to Tony, his uncle, James Hendricks (he preferred James, not Jimmy) looked drastically different than Ennis. James stood about my height – Ennis towered five inches over me at six-two. James sported a stocky round build in his white shirt and blue suit while Ennis, still slim and muscular, filled out his gray suit/white shirt combination with a burgundy tie. James buzzed his flaming red hair in a flattop and grew a bushy chevron shaped mustache. Ennis kept his coffee colored hair at a respectable length and the worst he ever sprouted was five o'clock shadow. The two were complete opposites. And I'd bet cold, hard cash it was not an accident.

I considered Hendricks nice looking however against Ennis, he was merely average (but I was biased *and* still married in my thirty-nine-year-old life). My daughter insisted I meet James to broaden my horizons on men and get me a hot date. I never pegged Lily for a Georgia clone but my sister's ways apparently rubbed off on my kid through the years. Barbie and Ken? Been there, done that. Up next: Mama and James.

I hated to tell her. He wasn't my idea of a lifelong mate, not that I was looking for a mate, of course. I recalled Georgia saying *you eat with your eyes first*. She meant it in regards to food but it also applied to physical attraction. The moment I saw Ennis Rutherford I fell hard and fast. James Hendricks? Nice try, kids, but he wasn't my type no matter my marital status.

Before introducing us, Lily took me aside for a crash course on Mr. Hendricks. Divorced ten years, four grown kids (three boys, one girl), loved fishing and traveling. Watched British comedies, listened to jazz, and read the classics.

Across the room, Tony huddled with James, providing him Cliff Notes on me. As if the older folks were incapable of asking our own questions. We were cops, for God's sake. Our jobs hinged on asking questions – but the kids meant well...

Lily unbuttoned my jacket's topmost button then adjusted my blouse to show a shade more cleavage. Sprucing up my attire to her liking, she proceeded, "His hobbies include chess, playing the guitar, and woodworking. He builds birdhouses. Tony says he sells them for good money too. Mama, give him a chance. He's a great guy."

But worlds apart from Ennis who enjoyed crime dramas, country songs, and whose musical acumen amounted to lullabies to our girls and hymns at Sunday services. He'd rather hunt or go bowling instead of learning guitar. Ennis also worked with wood – but the two-by-four and sixteen penny nail kind of construction, not petite, intricate birdhouses.

I appraised myself. She really wanted me to like him judging by the modifications she made to my outfit. One brow raised, "You finished with my makeover?"

She smiled her approval, "You look sexy."

To her dismay, I gathered my blouse and did the same with my jacket. Not to look prudish but to look more like myself. I only walked down Cleavage Lane with Ennis, not some guy I'd never met before.

Behind Lily, money exchanged hands between Seth and Dylan. Dylan lost a bet, apparently regarding Lily's spur-of-the-moment wardrobe adjustments.

Lily crossed her arms, shook her head good-naturedly at me, "Same ol' Mama. You'll never change, will you?"

"Cool it, kid. I'm not cut out to look 'sexy'. I'm not exactly built like Raquel Welch, you know."

"Who?"

"Nevermind." I nodded to Tony's little powwow across the way, "Well, let's move this along."

"You sound as happy as a condemned prisoner," she linked her arm through mine to personally escort me. "Loosen up," she whispered, "and don't be so businesslike. Kiss him if you feel the urge."

I laughed. She didn't understand. James and I were cops. Cops kept things businesslike, at least at first. It came naturally. My kid nearly fainted when, after the introductions, we only shook hands – no romantic hand kissing, blushing or coy *how do you do*. Just a regular old handshake sufficed.

While the kids wrote us off as lost causes, James and I settled into an easy conversation but gave each other space. In our exchanges I discovered he'd retired a year earlier (at fifty-eight) as a sergeant and loved the job. That's what we spent the majority of our time discussing. The sergeant's job.

During our chat, he offered multiple times to fetch me a glass of sparkling punch. I declined, adding that the Arnold Palmer (iced tea and lemonade) suited me fine, thank you. Lily made sure to include my signature alcohol-free "mocktail" on the menu.

Lily, Anna and the rest of my family supervised our progress from afar. We parted company on an upbeat note and a friendly kiss on the cheek. We'd agreed to share dinner one night soon. The families high-fived Lily and Tony for playing Cupid. I hated to tell the brood but James and I agreed to dinner for the sole purpose of discussing our careers as cops, not for a fling and a ring.

He headed to the restroom and I visited the bar for a refill on my Arnie. Despite it being a glimpse into the future, a deep, unexpected sadness crept in. I watched couples dancing, laughing and talking but mostly I centered on my girl – who wasn't a girl anymore but a woman. My firstborn no longer answered to Lily Rutherford. She was Lily Stafford now, wife to a man I knew nothing about but prayed he treated my baby well and treasured her as Ennis cherished me – or did until he met a particular lieutenant...

The room's cacophony subsided. The festivities wound down and soon I'd say goodbye to my daughter and her new husband as they departed on their honeymoon. Ennis and I should have been side by side witnessing this milestone in Lily's life. Instead we stood on opposite ends of the room with everyone tastefully monitoring our positions and moods. I couldn't remember when I felt so (strange as it sounded) alone.

I sipped my drink then turned from the bar. I froze with the glass halfway to my lips. The growing silence in the room became painfully apparent because who dared to venture near? Ennis.

An unfamiliar mix of unease, anger and bitterness churned in my stomach. I'd never experienced that upon sight of Ennis and I regretted I felt it now.

Seth's mood darkened upon seeing Ennis approach me. Without breaking his stare at the back of my ex-husband's head, he placed his drink on a nearby table. His expression detailed how he intended to divert Ennis away from me – directly through a stained glass window.

Leah put a hand to Seth's arm, stopping him. She shook her head, whispered something to him.

Dane scrambled to Ennis's side, caught him by the elbow, "Don't do it, bro. It's a bad idea."

Ennis and I held a steady gaze. With an ambling gait I was all too familiar seeing, he continued toward me despite Dane's caution. "Let go," he replied, "I know what I'm doing."

"No, you don't. That booze is giving you false confidence. Remember the last time you two saw each other?"

"That was two years ago. *Let me go.*" Ennis slung his arm, freeing it from his brother's grasp.

Thirty feet away Lily, Anna and Georgia stared at us in wide-eyed alarm as if a bomb counted down to detonate.

Dane whispered something to his brother who stated with finality, "We'll be fine. Leave us alone."

Dane reluctantly hung back while Ennis stopped within arm's length of his now ex-wife. He tried to appear casual and relaxed but I knew Ennis's facial tells as he knew mine. The man was scared shitless.

The corners of his mouth lifted a degree, testing my mood, "Hello, Savannah."

"Hello," I answered, not sure how to further the encounter. Obviously our prior meetings turned into high noon with words at twenty paces.

No matter what happened in the past, I refused to ruin Lily's wedding. Not for Ennis or his corrupt, conniving lieutenant.

The light reflected off a gold band on his ring finger. Still married to her. Lily forewarned me of it but seeing a different ring on his finger affected me more than I expected. This was not my Ennis, I reminded myself. This was *a version* of him like the version of me that lived seventeen years in solitude, unmarried except to my job.

He slowly leaned toward me. The room fell dead quiet. Soft, warm lips pressed to my cheek. I nearly closed my eyes to enjoy the sensation and the sentiment I felt in the brief kiss. He retreated only mere inches, his voice gentle and sweet, "You look gorgeous in that dress. And those beautiful eyes. I've always loved your eyes."

Yep, the booze went straight to his head. I smelled Uncle Jack on his breath but he'd not imbibed so much he slurred. "Thank you," I replied, ignoring the "eyes" comment. "You look nice too."

Our families cocked their ears to eavesdrop on our conversation. Ennis sensed this, I assumed, because he nodded to the vacant back corner, "Could we talk a minute?"

"About what?" I saw images of him and the mystery woman

Sheila Bennett writhing together in bed, touching and kissing (and other, more intimate activities). I imagined him massaging her feet the way he massaged mine. I imagined her massaging a few things on him as well. I thought of them eating together, laughing together, and being a regular married couple.

Ennis surveyed the crowd, many of whom planned a particularly ungracious and expedited departure for my ex should he step out of line. He backtracked, whispering, "Just to chat." He touched my hand, the one missing a wedding ring on the third finger. He composed enough courage to say, "This time I want to talk, not argue. Can we do that?"

Don't know about you, darling, but, "*I'm* not destroying our daughter's wedding. Are you?"

His fingers ever-so-delicately clasped around mine. I sensed his trepidation and fear I might slug him or worse, pull away. We moved to the back wall, eased into a couple of chairs. From the corner of my eye, I saw my family inching closer to us. Ennis retained his hold on my hand, "How've you been?"

"Okay, I suppose. And you?"

He shrugged a shoulder and attempted a smile. I always loved how his eyes smiled with his mouth but the man sitting beside me showed no genuine happiness in the gesture. His warm brown eyes held caution, "Keepin' on." He looked at the glass in my hand, "Jack Nicklaus?"

"Arnold Palmer."

"Oh, yeah. The Arnie. I remember you enjoy those. More than

a Yoo-hoo, if I'm correct."

"You are."

Ennis spent several seconds observing the guests then centered on our daughters. He heaved a wistful sigh, gently squeezed my hand, "The girls are the most beautiful women I've ever seen next to you. We did good. We did real good."

Did I hear nostalgia in his tone? Even a hint of sadness? I nodded to his statement – we had done well with our kids, no denying it. I wondered why he became so melancholy. Was his marriage turning south? According to Lily, he and Sheila hadn't had children. That's why they wanted full custody of ours. I suppose I taught them a hard lesson on trying to strip my kids from my arms, home and my heart.

"I appreciate you allowing me to attend the wedding."

I recoiled slightly at his wording, reclaimed my hand, "I didn't *allow* you. We are her parents. We should both be here."

I'd spoken soft and low to avoid prying ears but Seth edged toward us with the express intention of kicking Ennis's ass. I shook my head. Ennis saw him grudgingly back off. My ex's shoulders slumped, "I didn't mean it the way it sounded, I swear. I meant to say that no matter what happened between us, I love our girls and want to be in their lives."

"As I said, you should be." The exchange grew increasingly awkward. Years of being a cop and a mother taught me to recognize a fishing expedition. He wanted something but his whipped puppy act grated on me. He treated me like I foamed at the mouth and threatened to pounce. After what Lily and Anna told me, I had every right. He broke our marriage vows then worked in concert against me with this Sheila Bennett, her conspiring to strip my job and pension while he tried to steal the kids.

I leaned back, crossed one knee over the other while he leaned forward onto his, clasped his hands. I stared at his wedding ring while he ruminated on his next brilliant announcement. I didn't have to wait long. He halfway laughed, "Dane's probably right. I don't know what I'm doing but I do know how I feel."

A knot formed in my gut. Here it came. The booze lowered his inhibitions and loosened his tongue. Whatever he planned to say he'd probably regret the next morning so I offered him an out, "How much have you had to drink?"

He seemed tense, almost embarrassed, "Not near enough."

"Maybe you should rethink your feelings. They could be influenced by Uncle Jack's oil." I should know since I spent plenty of time with the master whiskey-maker's magic juice.

"We've both been there, haven't we?"

I bristled. Judgment? From him? After what he'd done to our lives? People laughed and danced around us. I supposed many of the younger women were college friends of Lily's. Tony's friends and family acted more reserved than the crowd, choosing to gather in small groups and drink quietly. Or they feared what my family feared. A firestorm.

Ennis shook his head, "Shit. I'm screwing up again. Savannah, I didn't mean it that way. I'm sorry."

"Ennis, say what you're going to say. The kids are getting ready to leave on their honeymoon." Actually the reception's chatter and revelry picked up shortly after Ennis and I sat down together. I supposed the majority of guests figured the bomb had been disarmed though our families remained on guard, their discussions subdued. I imagined the conversations ranged from amazement to chaste horror regarding our close proximity.

Ennis hemmed and hawed, raked a hand through his graying hair, "Okay, here goes. I regret everything, especially leaving you and trying to take the kids. I let Sheila influence my decisions on how to handle the custody situation. After she lost her job she agreed to stay home and raise the girls but I doubt they'd have turned out so good-natured if we'd gained custody. God knows they hated her enough."

Stop saying the name Sheila. "And they still can't stand her." *Zing! Gotcha, buddy.* I blinked, appalled and ashamed that I'd allowed this version of the future to turn me into a sour, almost despicable divorced wife.

His interlocked fingers tightened. Yep, my shot hit the bullseye – and I hated myself for it. His mouth quirked in annoyance, "I know. Anyway, I'm sorry."

"Let's forget it," was all I felt safe saying on the subject. "They're grown and they love us both very much. They shouldn't have to love who we marry."

Ennis glanced back at me, "Mind if I ask you a question?"

Yes. "What?"

"Why haven't you remarried? The girls said you had a couple of serious relationships. It made me wonder why you never took the leap."

Finally. Something I felt qualified in answering. "I took that leap once. It was enough." Or it should have been. Before furthering that comment, I quickly occupied my mouth with a sip from my glass.

He flinched, "I deserved that one." Then pointed in the direction of Tony's uncle, "Saw you talking with that fella over there. He dresses like a cop."

And that meant what, exactly? I held my tongue, replying instead, "Tony's uncle. He's retired from Birmingham PD and Lily insisted we meet."

"Any hope for him?"

"Might be nice to share supper with but not my bed or golden years."

Anna and Lily tiptoed closer. Anna spoke first, "You coming to blows yet?"

Lily nudged her with an elbow, her expression questioning her common sense, "What she means is you seem to be kinda getting along."

I waved them off, "We don't need our young'uns babysitting us. Go have fun."

Lily beamed. To me, she was a stunning beauty. "This is the best wedding gift you can give me," she said. "To see you actually talking." Tears glistened in her eyes as she wrapped each of us in a hug, "Thank you."

"Happy Wedding Day, Mrs. Stafford," I smiled. "Your father and I expect grandchildren soon so you and Tony have *lots* of fun on this honeymoon."

Anna shook a finger at me, "I'll remind you of this moment when the first crying brat lands in your arms."

One brow lifted as I stated the obvious, "I survived you two, didn't I?"

Ennis leaned back, claimed my hand again, "We've both been blessed with a couple of sweet, beautiful girls–"

"Leave you alone for one minute," a female voice growled, "and you're right back with her, cozying up."

Ennis stiffened. The girls bowed up. My sister, brother and Dane sat their drinks down then converged on the interloper. Dylan shrugged from his suit jacket, handed it to his sister and joined us. Me? I sat clueless to the woman on the warpath but guessed by everyone's reactions, the party crasher's name was Sheila Bennett.

James Taylor's "How Sweet It Is" continued playing for the dancing couples who missed the initial fireworks on our end of the room.

Ennis gaped in wide-eyed surprise as Sheila grasped his wrist, jerked our platonic handhold apart.

She scowled at me in red-faced, almost wild rage, "Let my husband go, *Sergeant*." She spat the last word in an attempt to put me in my place, considering she'd once held the rank of lieutenant. Difference was I retired from the job. According to Lily and Ennis, the department booted Sheila from hers.

I rose to my feet, my vision narrowing at the woman who'd poached my husband. She appeared to be around my age, maybe younger. To me (Ennis's reject) she certainly fell short of arm candy but for an unscrupulous tramp she wasn't half bad. High cheekbones framed features that could, with great effort, appear amiable. She used her piercing green eyes to impale her victims – so far the count held at two – Ennis and me. Her wavy nutmeg brown hair (courtesy of Clairol, not God) draped long enough to catch a man's attention and stir a woman's resentment, though any longer might be considered witchy. Topping everything off was a sleek, catlike body that advertised a vigorous exercise regimen. Yes, jealousy and I became close-knit pals in those brief seconds. Except for her treacherous manner of finding a husband, I supposed the woman was pretty. I *did* possess one thing she lacked. Height. Wearing only mid-heels I stood three inches taller than Sheila Bennett who marched in on four inch spike heels.

I didn't care if Sheila Bennett was a giant or a Lilliputian. I couldn't care less if she wore a tiara and ball gown and called herself Cinderella. She dressed for an occasion no one invited her to and my daughter's displeasure brought out Mama Bear. I squared my shoulders to help Seth bounce someone out and that someone was Ennis's wife.

Anna's hand seized mine. She tugged at me but I stayed rooted to the spot. She leveled a strict warning, "Mama, come with me." When I ignored her, she visually searched out Georgia. My sister wound her way through the mass of family to aid Anna's cause.

Lily bowed up at the deranged female scowling at me, "Are you deaf, suicidal or just stupid? I told Daddy you weren't welcome so get out."

Georgia reached for my other arm until I slung her hand away. I stepped within inches of Bennett to address her with a lethal calm, "This is my daughter's wedding and she wants you out. You can go willingly or be helped out the door."

To my surprise, Sheila brazenly confronted me. Oh yeah. I saw crazy dancing behind those emerald eyes but I'd back Lily's wishes until hell froze – or an ex-lieutenant went flying out a window. I met her gaze for gaze, hoping she sensed every homicidal notion raging through my mind.

The room fell quiet when the DJ cut the song short, ending James Taylor's vow of *there's you and there ain't nobody else*. Couple by couple the guests became aware of our confrontation.

Bennett's nostrils flared, the ragged, shallow breaths reminding me of a bull ready to charge, "You touch me and I promise you'll regret it."

I stood my ground, "If you don't leave in the next three seconds, we'll see who has the regrets."

James Hendricks parted the crowd by employing his cop voice, "Comin' through. Step aside." We needed an objective face to intervene because my current mindset dug in as Mother of the Bride, not a retired police sergeant.

By the time he approached us, he slipped into full business mode, speaking cop to cop with me, "What's the problem, Savannah?"

"Ennis's wife. She wasn't invited. I think you see why."

Seth fought his way to the forefront, joined James, only my

brother crossed his arms and centered on Ennis, not Sheila. Like our daddy, he still presented an imposing figure, even in his older years.

Ennis retreated a step from both men standing sentry and put a hand to Sheila's waist, "Come on, babe. Let's go."

Sheila shrugged away from him and nailed him with an asinine accusation, "What were you doing? Angling for a roll in the hay?"

I took her arm and not very gently either, "Shut your mouth, listen to your husband and leave. You probably remember my temper, especially when you screw with my kids. This is Lily's day and I'll be damned if you'll ruin it." I looked past her to Ennis, "Get her out of here. *Now.*" Whether Sheila heeded my warning or not, Ennis certainly did.

He towed her by the elbow, her narrowed vision locked on mine, "This isn't over, Savannah."

"Yes, it is," I stepped between her and the girls who seethed with jaws set, ready to join the fray.

James followed the not-so-happy couple outside, ensuring they left the building while the family gathered around me. My shoulders sagged and I sighed, grateful for James and Seth's quiet intervention.

Anna held her hand up, "High five, Mama. Way to go. The wicked witch is gone."

I shook my head, motioned her to lower her hand, "But so is your father and Lily wanted him here."

Lily appeared to take the disturbance well. Tony cuddled her close from behind. She shrugged, resigned, "At least she let him attend the wedding..."

I began to add my two cents when the room flashed white. I already knew I was traveling again, either to another moment in the future or back to the present.

My eyes opened to find my fingers gripping the mirror's frame until the knuckles blanched. The mirror sent me home – a very quiet home. Since Lily's birth I'd not heard much silence between those walls so I tiptoed into the hall, peeked into the dining room. The girls roosted opposite each other at the table. They patiently waited for their daddy who emerged from the kitchen and served them both a glass of chocolate milk, "Drink up."

Lily reminded, "I need my straw."

"Me too," Anna chimed in.

Ennis propped hands to hips with a teasing, "Your mama spoils you," before going in search of their special Krazy straws.

I ambled from the hall as Ennis placed a straw in each of the glasses, "Anything else you ladies need?"

It was hard to imagine this man not only divorcing me but abandoning his girls for a woman he barely knew. The coup de grâce: trying to steal the kids from their mother and their home. The man serving chocolate milk loved his family. The man in the vision fell for Lieutenant Bimbo's siren song. I had to fix this before Sheila Bennett entered the picture. The trick, as with Darren Ellis, was figuring out how – and not screwing it up this time.

The girls giggled, answered his question with a shake of their heads. Ennis took his leave by way of a gallant bow.

"Bet I can drink mine faster," Lily challenged her sister.

"Nuh-uh," Anna wrapped her lips around the straw and started sucking like a noisy mini-Hoover. Lily hurried to catch up. Four small puckered cheeks frantically siphoned the milk through the straw's curlicue bends. Lily won the contest but Anna posed serious competition already. In a couple of months Anna might surprise her sister.

Ennis pulled out a chair, motioned for me to sit, "The bar is open, ma'am. What's your pleasure? An Arnold Palmer perhaps?"

The difference in the two men then and now still astounded me. I nodded, "Much obliged, barkeep."

"I aim to please our prettiest customers." He hightailed it to the kitchen, leaving the girls polishing off every drop of milk with loud slurping noises and laughing about it.

The fridge opened and liquid poured once, then twice. A spoon clinked against the glass as he stirred in extra sugar.

Soon my husband toted out the tumbler of tea and lemonade, complete with two fat ice cubes chilling the glass. With it he carried a plate holding a sandwich and generous serving of Cheesy Puffs. The man knew the way to my heart. "What's this, Chef Boyardee? A bonus?"

"You only ate half your hamburger so I slammed together a ham and cheese sammy for you." He sat the plate in front of me, "Black Forest ham straight from Kroger's deli, Swiss cheese with extra holes and only the cheesiest puffs from the factory. Especially for you."

Nope, this wasn't the same guy from the future. I found his presentation humorous, "Extra holes, huh? Clever way of glamming up a ham and cheese sandwich."

"Ah," he corrected, "a *hot* ham and cheese sandwich. I nuked it for you."

I smiled, "A sign of true love. Thank you, Chef Ennis." When he sat beside me, I tried envisioning him with another woman – especially the rabid shrew in the vision. The kind, thoughtful man who brought my special ham and cheese "sammy" and Arnold Palmer, the man who pampered and protected me since I'd met him? No, that old mirror got that scenario wrong. Damn wrong.

I dug into the sandwich and moaned. The succulent, smoked ham combined with the warm, melty cheese... Oh yes, he'd "nuked" it just right.

While I chowed down on the sandwich, Lily eyeballed my Cheesy Puffs. Anna stared longingly at them too. I scooted the plate within reach of both, "Leave me five."

Four small hands attacked the plate. When they retreated they left exactly five Puffs behind.

Ennis leaned closer, "When you're rested up, you and I need time alone." He kissed beneath my ear with a whisper, "I'll show you how this grateful citizen appreciates your sacrifice."

"Daddy," Lily whined while crunching a Cheesy Puff. "Don't be gross."

"You can't even hear what I'm saying," he volleyed back. "You're eating."

"Mama's blushing. That's all I need."

I laughed, "Honey, we old people need special time together sometimes. To discuss our aches and pains–"

"And pull a few muscles in bed," Ennis blurted.

I nudged him with my elbow, "Pipe down, Pops. Our kid's already protesting."

"You're right." He sat beside me, stroked my arm with a feathery light touch, "Welch said they're talking about a commendation for your work."

Little did my spouse realize I put my back into this case for our future, not just to nab a killer or arrest his liberal-minded, bad-aiming brother. I certainly hadn't considered a commendation. The department could keep it. The biggest gifts sat at the table with me. "That's nice," I said. "But I'd rather have your reward for my hard work rather than the department's."

Lily chomped another Cheesy Puff, "What's a divorce?"

My jaw clapped shut so fast I bit my tongue. Meanwhile, Ennis's eyes rounded, "What?"

"Where did you hear that word?" I tried not to sound cartoonish with my now lisping tongue.

"From you," Lily struck back.

"I never said 'divorce'." And I hadn't.

"Yes, you did."

"No, I didn't."

"Yes, you did."

"When do you think Mama said that word?" Ennis attempted to

derail our absurd back and forth.

"This afternoon.   Mama's got a magic mirror like the Evil Queen."

The sandwich fell from my hand, dropped to the plate. Oh sweet Lord. A magic mirror. Forget the fact our kid put me in the same category as the Evil Queen. She knew about the mirror. A growing sense of panic billowed inside me like a slow motion mushroom cloud. How, my rioting brain clamored, had Lily discovered the mirror's power and what had she seen and heard besides the word "divorce"?

Ennis's mouth curved into a crooked smile. He leaned to my ear, "Vivid imagination." Then he asked Lily, "A magic mirror? Did it say you were a thousand times more beautiful than any other woman? Besides your mama, of course."

I highly doubted it. The mirror in our bedroom made the Queen's look rinky-dink. The Queen's knocked her down a peg or two. Mine kept destroying my future with Ennis.

"No," Lily replied. "I looked in it and saw you fighting."

Her tone came across mature and matter-of-fact. She truly wanted answers – not an adult's placation.

"Fighting?" Ennis asked. He turned to me as if the mere notion sounded preposterous.

Lily made a not-so-nice face, "You yelled at each other, called each other names. Me and Anna hid under my bed."

I swallowed hard – mostly because my mind still reeled in disbelief and my stomach percolated a volcanic eruption. If I opened my mouth, supper would come out, not words.

"Lily, mirrors show your reflection, that's all," he assured. "You must be remembering a bad dream because mirrors can't show you something that never happened."

I wish you hadn't said that. That can of worms should really be kept closed – and welded shut. My hand went to my stomach, cradling it.

"*Yes, it can. It's magic.*" Lily crossed her arms, "I touched it and saw you and Mama fighting." Our kid morphed into a miniature Perry Mason, leading us in small, gradual steps (with Ennis's help) to her ultimate conclusion that *I can prove it.*

"Tell us exactly what you saw and heard," he prompted.

I rolled my eyes, stifled a groan. The man just could not stop himself. Ennis still believed the child made up a story. His expression said so. Meanwhile I stewed a hundred different ways – foremost being my gut, my mind and my heart. A disaster lurked on the horizon and Ennis unwittingly monkeyed with the eject button to our marriage. "Maybe," I chanced speaking, "we don't want to know. Lily said we fought. That should be enough."

Lily's blue eyes settled on me with a steady, unblinking stare that seemed rather accusatory. I actually squirmed in my seat. Correction. Perry Mason *on steroids.* But I'd never confess my experiences in that mirror, not to anyone, not even my pint-sized lawyer daughter.

"You told Daddy to get out of the house."

Anna swiped a Cheesy Puff from Lily's stash. Lily never noticed because she busied herself grilling Mama and Daddy.

"But I've never told your daddy to leave the house and I never said divorce. Ever." Yes, I sounded defensive because I was. And furthermore, "I never intend to either." Not if I nip Sheila Bennett in the bud...

The mere notion of my kicking him out inspired him, of all things, to crack a joke, "What did I do to deserve being tossed out?"

You slept with another woman, that's what. To my credit, I kept quiet but, like Lily, crossed my arms in protest to his cavalier attitude and the whole situation.

"Mama caught you with a lady," Lily replied.

Note to self. In Sesame Street terms explain to Lily the vast difference between a lady and a harlot...

Ennis practically gave himself whiplash spinning back to our daughter, "What!?" Floundering now, he demanded, "Caught me how?"

I remained calm, "Honestly, Ennis. If I kicked you out, what do you *think* I caught you doing with this... *lady?*"

Incredulous, he stared at Lily, "You're only four–"

"Halfway to five," I interjected, still trying to rope in my stomach.

"Doesn't matter. How does a four-year-old know this stuff? How did she cook up a story about that?"

"It's not a story, Daddy. Mama caught you with a lady and her name was..."

At this point, Lily's voice slowed down as if someone changed the record's speed from forty-five rpm to thirty-three. The kid's voice warped its way down to a deep, James-Earl-Jones-as-Satan voice, painfully dragging out each word, "Herrrr... naaame... waaas... Lela."

I watched my daughter say these words, her lips moving at usual speed but the sound lagging behind. Only when I heard *Lela* did her voice return to normal. I tried swallowing but my mouth went cotton dry. I took a sip of my drink – the second it hit my stomach it bounced slightly, threatening a return trip.

"Who's Lela?" Ennis demanded. "Do we know a Lela?"

He asked me this question to which I shrugged, "Don't think so." At least not yet.

Lily maintained, "You and Mama fought and when you left you said you'd never come back."

Ennis, realizing the gravity of the situation, wiped his hands down his face. He whispered low in my ear, "We gotta do something about this. She needs help if she's imagining us separating or worse, divorcing."

"What does divorce mean?" Lily returned to her original question.

I shouldered the responsibility of explaining since confusion and disbelief sidelined Ennis. "Divorce is when a mommy and daddy stop living together and live in separate houses. They–"

"But what about me and Anna? Who'll take care of us?"

"Honey, we're not divorcing." I clasped her hand, "Daddy and I are fine. No one's angry, no one's leaving, no one's divorcing, and we've never met a woman named Lela."

"Wait," she said. She screwed her mouth to the side the way Ennis did on occasion. This indicated intense concentration. "Lela wasn't her name. It was She–"

I pushed back from the table when a rush of sickness barreled up my throat. I clamped the back of my tongue to the roof of my mouth, slammed a hand over my pursed lips.

Unable to stem the approaching tidal wave any longer, I bolted through the living room (with Ennis right behind me wanting answers), down the hall and hung a sharp left into the bathroom. I sank to my knees just in time. Gripping the cold porcelain for round two, I groaned my relief afterward then leaned back on my heels. The day ranked in my top ten for stress with Ennis accepting the Zone 5 job (or planning to), Darren and Shaun Ellis' antics, getting grazed by one of their poorly aimed bullets and now the big, fat crowning glory – if things didn't change, Ennis and I were headed for divorce and our little girl witnessed it.

An ice cold cloth pressed to my throat, raking a violent shudder through me. Ennis gathered my hair, held it out of the firing line. "Still sick?" he asked, bathing my throat and nape with the washcloth.

"Not as bad," I flinched. A small riot lingered in the pit of my stomach alerting me that it wasn't yet safe to abdicate the porcelain throne.

"Mama?" It was Lily. She stood at the door, head hung low.

"Yes, honey," I croaked.

"I'm sorry."

I waved her closer. I felt like shit however I felt less like shit the longer Ennis mopped me off. Taking Lily's hand I explained, "This isn't your fault. It's been a long day and I'm just tired. Don't worry."

The assurance helped ease her wrinkled brow. Ennis asked her to check on Anna. She dutifully left to fulfill his request.

The sour taste of stomach acid, ham, cheese and sweet tea inspired a subdued heave. I hung my head over one more time but nothing happened. Ennis ran the cloth under the faucet again. I welcomed the cold despite my shivering.

"You're sure it's stress?" he asked, apparently not convinced.

"Sure as I can be."

"Georgia said you were tired and your back ached the other day. Think you caught a bug?"

"I don't think so." I pressed a hand to his at my throat. The cloth found the perfect spot that provided instant relief and I wanted it to stay there.

"No other problems that could be causing this?"

"Besides being in a gunfight and Lily's unexpected apocalyptic prophecy, no." Okay, I stretched the truth but who in their right mind felt confident or comfortable enough to confess their journeys in a time-travel mirror? The listeners would summon the men in the white coats and funny looking paddy wagon. Nope, I was sticking to lying, thank you very much.

My stomach finally eased up. Shoulders slumping, I silently

lamented how weary – and ganged up on – I felt.

Ennis crouched beside me, handed me the washcloth, "What got into Lily? A magic mirror? And that talk of us splitting up. That's outrageous."

So much for a calm stomach. It kicked up a mild fuss at his revisiting the prior several minutes. I pressed the washcloth to my throat again, "Maybe our tiff this morning affected her more than we thought."

"We've argued worse than that in front of her and certainly nothing to spark assumptions of us divorcing. And where'd she hear that word?"

I shrugged, "Maybe the same place she picked up the F-bomb. We don't know what she hears at school or what triggers her fears. We do know it's easy for a kid's fears to be exaggerated. She's just scared we'll break up if we argue. I guess most kids worry about that."

"I guess." He sat down beside me now, leaned his back against the vanity. "I hate to mention it but could you be pregnant?"

My eyes closed on a groan. If the mirror's prediction panned out, no. At least not yet. If Ennis failed to salivate over Sheila Bennett and divorce me, then yeah, supposedly we'd have a son named Daniel. But as I figured out, one change in the timeline affected the whole future.

Like the way of all idiots, I hadn't considered the obvious possibility that I might be carrying a baby. If so, what altered the future's timeline to allow this to happen? In my latest vision, Lily and Anna never heard of Daniel. So I halfway hoped the rabbit died and halfway didn't. I wasn't ready for another kid, not yet – but I sure as hell wasn't ready to lose my husband to a slut either.

Then it hit me. My period. Late again. That fact meant nothing, I assured myself. It ran late when stress took over. I mean, my cycle was erratic since Jeffrey Holland's last stand...

My stomach lurched in mild protest. I plastered the cold cloth against my throat, remembering years ago – the first time Jeffrey abducted me. Once home and healed, Ennis and I celebrated selling the old house and suddenly my monthly went AWOL and the rabbit died. Enter Lily. After last July's encounter with Holland, what if the same thing happened again? Only this time our blessing's name would be Daniel. So, "No, I hadn't considered pregnancy." I made a mental note. Pick up a test early in the morning.

"Hey, I meant to tell you. Before we left the station this afternoon, Captain Shaw told me Lieutenant Ramsey is retiring. I suppose today's events only reinforced his decision. He put in his papers today."

My stomach, three quarters this side of calm seas, suddenly pitched and rolled at his news. Lieutenant Ramsey, the lieutenant at Zone 5. Mid to late fifties. Prime retirement age for law enforcement officers. "Word is," he continued, "a female lieutenant might take the position. I think they mentioned someone named Bennett."

The name caused another heave. It was too late to stop Bennett from entering our lives. The only thing left to do: minimize the damage.

The mirror merrily steamed ahead with its premonition, letting me know I'd changed the future by removing Darren Ellis from the picture. His brother Shaun grabbed an assault rifle a few years ahead of schedule, thereby scaring Zone 5's current lieutenant into retirement. Once Ramsey left, Sheila Bennett took over in more ways than one. By solving one problem, I'd created another. No doubt about it. I was a real genius.

16

Monday

Morning dawned grim and dreary, similar to my mood. Light drizzle floated through the air like thick, heavy fog and by the time we dropped the girls off at school, the clouds opened up. The storm whipped wind-driven rain in sheets so hard I could barely see to drive. I followed Ennis's Ram, careful to avoid backwash from his wheels and tidal waves from passing cars.

We made our way to the station in the deluge, armed ourselves with umbrellas (we still got plenty wet) then ran for the door. We weren't the only drowned rats walking in. Seconds later Mathis literally squished in, his gray suit drenched and his usually coiffed shortened version of a pompadour plastered to his scalp.

He scowled at our stares, "What? *Someone* kyped my parking spot." He leveled the scowl on the "someone". Me.

His parking spot, huh? "There's no assigned parking, John."

"Seniority, Prince. I got seniority. Common courtesy says I get the closer parking place."

"Since when?" I curbed a laugh at actually hearing the term "common courtesy" fall out of his mouth.

A nearby uniform saw John's soggy condition and cracked up. Mathis glared at him while answering me, "Since when? Since I practically died in that flood out there. Why didn't you two carpool today? Geez, save the poor saps who are old, fat and can't run fast. And don't whine about that flesh wound you got either. It's not as if the guy shot your toe off." Berating concluded, he softened his tone, "How is your arm anyway?"

"Sore but okay."

He leaned down, groaning as he wrung out his pant cuffs, "Good work on that Ellis thing. Not even your case and you found him."

Ennis couldn't stand it any longer, "Mathis, don't you have an umbrella?"

The question tweaked John's aggravation, "Does it look like I have one? It broke in the last storm we had. Never got another." He said to me, "Just for stealing my place, you get the leg work today. Make you exercise your backstroke while you're out. It'll give me time to drip dry."

We headed to our offices. Mathis produced a comb from his suit jacket, ran it through his hair. When he finished, he looked like a wet, middle-aged, overweight James Dean.

"Don't you have a change of clothes in your locker?" I expected a "yes". Most cops kept a change handy for convenience or unexpected accidents.

Mathis fired another glare my way. Well, I did say *most* cops...
My hands lifted in surrender, "Sorry. My mistake."

I dedicated the first half hour of my shift to calling Zone 3 where
Bennett currently worked. I asked about her demeanor and what others
thought of her as a person and a cop. I got more than I bargained for. A
few uniforms and detectives alluded to the fact Bennett cozied up to
certain men (usually married). A female detective kindly shared that a
colleague's wife complained to the captain about Bennett's affair with her
husband. After the captain met with the female lieutenant, Sheila headed
out to meet with the wife. No one knew what happened except the wife
clammed up and filed for divorce. I ran across one other chatty lady
detective whose partner fell for Sheila. Again, the wife brought the affair
to the captain's attention and again the wife went silent shortly afterward.
Tragedy struck another detective's family when he found his wife dead of
a gunshot wound – shortly after she'd complained to his captain about
Sheila. Without saying as much, the chatty lady detective volunteered
that it wasn't a closed case and I could check into it myself if I chose to.
No thanks, I told myself. I had enough info to tell me Bennett was
trouble with a capital T. Snooping into investigations and department
records caused too many headaches for cops.

Ennis and I went about our business on the home invasion
homicide case. He checked what few leads might have popped up
overnight and I reviewed the witness and neighbor statements. Mathis
busied himself with jacking up forensics for pending DNA results.

Joseph and Lisa Stewart, both bigwigs at a major bank serving the southeast, raked in millions every year and believed in bountiful philanthropy. They supported the arts, Boys & Girls Club, St. Jude and other organizations. On paper they sounded almost Mother Teresa-like – if Mother Teresa had lived in a palace and spent her Wednesday evenings watching History Channel and Discovery. People we interviewed spoke highly of the Stewarts. Family, friends, employees, maintenance workers and neighbors lauded them as the salt of the earth. They also described them as quiet and unassuming.

The couple lived on Pineland Road located in the Chastain Park area where homes ranged from a cool one and a half million dollars to double that. A person saw everything from Colonial, Federal and Georgian homes lining the long, winding road. Two story homes (sometimes three) towered over lawns only kids could dream of and husbands dreaded mowing. Only in this neighborhood no self-respecting husband dared venture out with his own Toro TimeCutter. These people had landscapers on speed dial.

The houses on Pineland Road sat back from the scenic street. The problem with scenic in Atlanta: sometimes it meant remote. Huge front yards and large trees insulated and isolated homes from traffic as well as next door neighbors.

The surrounding three story homes overshadowed the Stewart's two story. It was as if God put a little modesty into the rich man's neighborhood, reminding the world wealthy folk don't always need exorbitant Taj Mahals to live in.

The crime report in the Chastain Park area remained below

average. Mostly car burglaries, general mischief by bored teenagers and theft – never know when that lawn guy might want an extra weed whacker or the maid might boost the silverware or diamond bracelet. Not exactly a high crime area. That's why the murder of a couple in their early fifties raised such a ruckus with locals. No one saw a connection to anything except senseless violence. Even I began to think the murders were a crime of opportunity in some way. That perhaps a gang of assholes prowled the neighborhood for a viable target. They saw a nice house and crept to the window which was open an inch to feel the cool October air. They saw the Stewarts sitting on the sofa watching TV. The gang appraised the house from their meager vantage point. Polished hardwood floors and cream colored walls. An ivory sofa sat on one side of the room. Across from that sofa was a fifty-five inch high definition television and two gray tweed upholstered armchairs. Expensive paintings hung on the walls – these were later stolen by the killers along with cash and Mrs. Stewart's jewelry. To the assholes lurking outside that window, the place reeked of money – or *enough* money.

I could only guess how they forced their way into the home. Ringing the doorbell. A ruse about needing to use the phone. Or, as society seemed to be turning, just forgo all the formalities and shove their way inside, maul the occupants and/or kill them and the criminals take what they damn well please.

A distinct *squish, squish, squish* padded down the hallway near my office. Mathis. He leaned in the door, "No results yet on the DNA. I think they sent it carrier pigeon."

"It flies as fast as it can, John. Be patient." DNA took forever so I attempted in my own futile way to settle him down.

I pointed to his shoes, "You might consider taking those squishy things off. I hear trench foot is rather unpleasant." Yes, I overdramatized the situation but wet, pruny feet sounded gross, plus hearing him slosh around day would push *my* patience over the edge.

"Trench foot?" He scoffed, "You can't scare me, kid. I got an ex-wife who's worse than any wartime disease."

I returned to reading witness statements, "Okay, but don't blame me if your feet come out of those things swelled, wrinkled and smelly."

In true John Mathis style, he dismissed the subject by redirecting it, "You find anything in those statements we can use?"

"Besides the two neighbors citing the 'two thousand eight or nine white Chevy without a driver's side hubcap' parked at the Stewart house that night? Not really. People around there aren't forthcoming with us law enforcement folk. Half of them never opened their door when we canvassed the area."

According to the few who did crack their door for us, not one heard a peep despite a shotgun being fired inside the house. I wanted to arrest the whole block for being liars. First, the evening of the murders the weather cooled down to the mid-seventies, normal October temps for the city. Southerners, rich or not, usually opened a window or two to enjoy the fresh air. Second, the blast not only tore through Mr. Stewart's chest, peppering both lungs and his liver with bird shot, it shattered the front window. We found bits of his insides in the lawn and boxwoods beneath the destroyed window. According to the coroner, Joe Stewart died after watching one of the aforementioned assholes slice his wife's throat deep enough to expose bone. And the neighbors heard nothing? Sure.

"We should go back and show them what their tax dollars are paying for," Mathis suggested. "This time we'll make pests of ourselves."

"We? Did that rain cause you to sprout a twin?"

"You can handle it. I can't get out in these clothes. I'll catch my death. And trench foot." He winked at me, "See ya, kid."

I rolled my eyes, thumbed through the interviews, wishing for one, just one tiny clue to break the case in our favor.

"I got a call from Captain Shaw."

But I'd never find a break if people kept interrupting me. Ennis leaned against the door frame in his brother Dane's casual manner. "And?" I asked.

"Ramsey's replacement is a lieutenant from Zone 3. I was right. Bennett's the last name. Forgot her first."

"Sheila," I volunteered, mainly to see his reaction.

He seemed surprised, "You know her?"

I shook my head, "I've heard about her though." Oh yeah, I heard a lot about her. Sheila Bennett. A thirty-seven-year-old assertive hotshot with sustained winds strong enough to destroy families, careers and – rumor hinted – maybe bump off people who stood in her way.

To be honest, from Ennis's point of view, I could see the allure of a young, ambitious lieutenant. Currently he limped along with a regular old detective wife, not a swanky sergeant or lofty lieutenant. Plus I was, as my daddy put it, *gettin' up there* at thirty-nine. And here came a gung-ho thirty-seven-year-old that leap-frogged from patrol then detective to sergeant to lieutenant.

Ennis eased into the chair facing my desk, waited for me to elaborate which I did not except to reveal her age. Otherwise I kept a stoic expression.

"A lieutenant at thirty-seven," he repeated. "She's pretty driven to fly up the ranks at that age. That's just two years younger than you."

"What's that supposed to mean?" I snapped. That I hadn't applied myself or sought promotions and raises fast enough? That by forty I should be running the department?

He recoiled slightly, "Nothing. It was only an observation. Why are you so touchy about it?"

I glanced over my glasses at him, "I can't imagine. Only that you'll be working with Wonder Woman, that's all." I parroted his previous statement, "'*A lieutenant at thirty-seven.*'" Two years younger. Feh. This old lady could still kick her ass, lieutenant or not.

He laughed, "I'm not interested in some hoity-toity brass ass. I'd rather stay with my Soon-To-Be-Sergeant."

That was good to hear. "You better. Remember, Soon-To-Be-Sergeant *does* pack a gun and one hell of a temper."

"What else have you heard about Bennett?"

This was getting tedious already, "Rumor has it she gets whatever or whoever she sets her sights on. That's about all." I only wish.

He seemed to consider that with pensive silence, "She might be hard to work with if she's too aggressive."

You have no clue precisely how aggressive that bitch is, my dear, but I do. I merely shrugged a shoulder.

"Who you talkin' about?" Mathis stepped in my office. He traipsed in wearing his slacks, dress shirt and (mercifully) only black socks. No squishy shoes. Better. Much better.

Ennis's bubble of excitement sprung a leak and fizzled, "Ramsey's replacement in Zone 5. A Lieutenant Bennett's taking over."

For the first time I realized how humorous it sounded. I constructed an impromptu (and quite appropriate) rhyme. *Ladies, keep your eyes on Lieutenant Bennett or she'll have your husband in a New York Minute.*

"Sheila Bennett?" Mathis sounded almost mortified. "The broad from Zone 3?"

Ennis nodded. I stayed quiet. For some reason Mathis switched to me, "You've heard the rumors, right?"

Who needed rumors when the mirror provided a crash course on the infamous lieutenant? I equipped my best innocent poker face anyway, "Rumors?"

"Yeah," he said. "She fell from the top of the tramp tree and banged every guy on the way down. Especially the married ones."

Ennis snorted his disgust, "Mathis, that's a rotten thing to say. You don't know the woman."

A hot arrow of jealousy pierced my heart. Ennis defended her without even meeting her. I nearly grabbed a Tums from my desk drawer. The ride downhill had officially begun and someone broke the emergency brake. Time to belt in and hang on, my instinct said.

John removed his reading glasses, "How long have I been a cop?" This was his lecturing mode. Ennis should have capitulated at that point but stood his ground instead. John proceeded, "I had a badge before either of you hit puberty."

He nodded to me, "Present company excluded, females on this job have been known to climb the career ladder by way of climbing their superiors. Why do you think Bennett's at Three anyway, Rutherford?"

Ennis had no clue. His frown deepened at Mathis's disparaging remarks which served only to upset my stomach further. This was going to be a nightmare.

John rolled his eyes, "Ennis, she's already slept her way through all the other precincts except this one and Five. She's a plague of locusts wrapped up in a size eight and a D cup." He glanced at me, his tone defensive, "No offense to females in general and FYI, I took a wild ass guess at her measurements."

His *wild ass guess* overshot the mark *and* missed the broad side of the barn too. Bennett packing a pair of D cups? Hardly. God blessed her with a very conservative B. The Big Man endowed me with a respectable B so nope, the only things of Ms. Bennett's that were larger than mine were her paycheck and ego. "Did I say anything?"

"No," he seemed to read my mind, "but you thought it."

From there, the conversation digressed. His mama may have

named him after the singer Johnny Mathis but when his mood soured, the last thing I heard was the song "Wonderful, Wonderful". My mood also teetered on the dark edge because of this Bennett woman. I needed a change of topic so I tapped the folder on my desk, "You interviewed the Stewart's kids, right? What was your impression?"

Ennis sighed, crossed his arms – his way of protesting my decision to redirect the subject. To appease him I suggested, "Ennis, perhaps a phone call is in order. Call Zone 3 and talk with the patrol sergeant and detectives. Get their perspective of the bit–" my mouth slammed shut. I nearly said *bitch*.

Mathis wheeled to me as if I let the epithet fly in its grand, offensive glory. I regrouped fast, "Sorry. I've been reading those interviews too long." Then I pointed to the exact word I'd practically let slip. One of the witnesses called the Stewart's daughter (actually Mr. Stewart's daughter and his wife's step-daughter) a bitch. I used that as an excuse for my Freudian slip. Ennis appeared preoccupied and didn't seem to notice. Mathis, of course, leaned closer to see if I lied about seeing *bitch* in the interview. He nodded his approval with a sly wink. I minded my tongue now, "Ennis, call and ask about Bennett."

He'd begun gnawing his thumbnail. Perhaps a seed of doubt germinated about accepting the transfer, I hoped? Bennett's gung-ho attitude not setting well with him?

He stood up, nodding absently, "I think I will."

Once he left the room, my shoulders slumped, "Shit, John. I nearly blew it."

"You know about Bennett?" He, like my husband, also sounded surprised.

Why did the men in my life think I lived under a rock? No, *my husband* required educating on floozy homewreckers, not me. "Who the hell doesn't besides Ennis? I don't want that slut anywhere close to my husband but what can I do? He's determined to take the job."

John stepped closer, put a hand to my shoulder, "He ain't committed yet, kid. Fate might step in soon."

"Can't be soon enough. I'm sick of her already. Let's get back to the case. What about the Stewart kids?" I asked because at the scene, Mathis assigned me to the crime scene first then told me to join him and Ennis for interviewing witnesses later. I had first-hand knowledge of the carnage but not of everyone who interacted with the Stewarts.

Dr. Bret Stewart, a gynecologist, was the oldest of the two children. Short brown hair, five eleven, trim and athletic. He lived in the upscale Tuxedo Park not far from Buckhead. If money trees existed, Tuxedo Park would have been an orchard of them. During the initial interview I overheard Bret begrudgingly disclose his address to Mathis. I'd sneered. Where else would a doctor hang his hat except an exclusive edition where a square foot of anything cost more than a month of my salary?

When I saw them at the scene, Dr. Bret's wife clung to her husband, not leaving his side but not speaking much either. By no means a beauty queen, she held her own in the looks department – and the designer clothes, high heels and bleached hair departments as well.

I read through John's notes, taking in the highlights but wrinkled my brow at his chicken scratch. Deciphering it proved too complicated for my addled "Sheila Syndrome" brain.

If I read correctly, Bret Stewart's blonder half helped fund the Georgia Aquarium and was on the Board of Trustees with the Atlanta Performing Farts. Wait... *What?* "Atlanta Performing *Farts?*"

John jerked the folder from my desk, "You know better than that. *Arts*, Prince. *Arts.* The pen slipped but gimme a break."

I removed my glasses, "The pen slipped, huh?"

"Okay," he confessed. "A private joke then. You know I can't stand that opera and ballet crap."

"Clean up the notes before Hunter sees them."

"Yes, Sergeant Spoilsport," he harrumphed in rare good humor. "About the Stewart's daughter-in-law. She's too busy being popular with her Artsy Fartsy friends to care about anyone but herself. You saw her with her husband, the almighty women's healthcare professional from on high. He came off as one too. Snooty and too busy to be bothered."

His attempt at political correctness amused me, "Women's healthcare professional? I remember when you called gynecologists a far harsher name, even X-rated names."

"That's when my wife's 'healthcare professional' kept telling her she was pregnant. I began wondering who fathered 'em all, me or him. Plus, I don't trust doctors. Their hands are always soft and they give limp handshakes. Wussies."

I begged to differ on the "wussy" label, "Jeffrey Holland's hands were soft but a person doesn't really care when those soft hands are trying to kill them. And his handshake? Solid as a rock. Tell me about the daughter." I referred to the notes again, "Tessa Campbell. She's full-time as a waitress at The Farm House Restaurant downtown and her husband Stan is a used car salesman."

His lip curled, "He's a typical shyster salesman."

"And you know this because..."

"His job. Going to a used car lot is like going to a whorehouse. You know you're gonna get screwed. If his alibi wasn't so airtight I'd arrest him for menacing the public."

My mama always said life was too short for grudges. She never met John Mathis, Grudgemaster Extraordinaire. He crafted grievances into a fart – or *art*, I should say. I did, however, understand his animosity toward used car salesmen. "Still smarting over that Cavalier?" Or, as he not so lovingly referred to it, the Commode.

Mathis's over-the-glasses stare basically called me a moron. "You're kidding, right? The car you squeezed and got lemonade? Have you forgotten being my ride for two weeks while the mechanics put it on life support? I shoulda pulled the plug on the damn thing before they hauled it in and charged me a grand to fix it. Probably just needed a screw tightened."

In those days Mathis and I spent a lot of time together. Chevy christened it the Cavalier but John's car developed a penchant for stranding him on highways and busy streets. Until one day it blew the transmission and he needed a ride to and from work. Enter Savannah's

Taxi Service. His payback to the fickle four-wheeled nightmare was to name it the Commode then point to the turn signal lever and tell anyone within earshot, "And this is where you flush it."

"You've got a nice car now," I said, wanting respite from his are-you-stupid glare.

He granted my wish, "At least it runs."

Mathis drove a blue Volkswagen Jetta and for a man accustomed to good old American BST (Mathis-speak for Blood, Sweat and Tears), the defection sent the whole station into turmoil with one officer predicting the end of times. What's next, he asked, the Four Horsemen and famine?

A subject change seemed in order, "Tell me about Tessa."

John's finger circled his temple, "That one's a few clowns short of a circus, lemme tell you. Making basically minimum wage and buying on credit until the cards bleed. She and her husband have a kid, a boy. He's older than Lily, probably about six or seven. The woman buys that kid whatever he wants. Prince, do everyone a favor. Don't buy your kids everything they want. It makes 'em idiots."

No problem there, "We can't *afford* everything they want." Back to the original topic, "Did the parents give her money to bail her out of debt?"

"Not according to the financials. If they did, they used cash."

"I think I'll try my hand at talking to Bret and Tessa, see if anything new crops up."

"Be my guest. Take Rutherford with you. Make him earn his

paycheck today."

I let that slide, realizing Mathis felt abandoned by Ennis the way I did. We'd been a trio for years and he chose to break up our group for a few extra bucks.

"Speak of the devil," Mathis mumbled, hitching his thumb at the door.

Ennis strutted into my office. He appeared no longer perturbed by a thing. In fact he seemed (I hated to say) euphoric.

"What did you find out?" I asked, my gut winding in another knot. I prayed the guys and gals at Zone 3 took pity on Sheila Bennett's future victims, most especially their wives, and forewarned Ennis to duck the coming storm and decline the transfer.

He sank into the chair across from me. He fought the beginnings of a smile, "I took your advice, called Zone 3 and talked to a couple of officers. Even talked to Bennett herself. She was still on shift."

I puckered in places that made me cringe. "Yes?" was all I could say.

Ennis's grin broke free to stretch the width of his face, a toothy grin reserved for his happiest moments. "The officers said she's fair but tough. Bends the rules but not too far. As for her, I considered her very personable and chatty. Very open."

Like her legs, I assume. My lips clamped tighter to avoid *that* blunder. Instead I chose to stew.

"So are her legs, Rutherford, so be careful around her or your wife'll perform an impromptu amputation." Mathis must have read my mind again, especially when he pointed at Ennis's crotch.

Ennis shot him a dirty look, "You're jaded, Mathis. Jaded by gossip. One juicy morsel gets passed around as true and it's not. Rumors and lies." He glanced to me, "That's what happens to women on the job, isn't it?"

"Some women, yes." *But in her case it's true.* God, I'd never struggled so hard to keep my words tactful. It was excruciating.

My husband stretched out, laced his hands behind his neck with a wistful, "I believe I'm gonna love it there."

The remark sprinkled salt in our already open wounds about the transfer. Surprisingly, I held my tongue. Not surprisingly, Mathis didn't, "I hope Texans run faster than they talk because your spouse is about to strangle you and I might help her."

17

Monday

I left the station before I lost my mind and the firm grip on my tongue. To John's dismay, I left Ennis behind singing the praises of Zone 5 and his soon-to-be new lieutenant. *Personable and chatty*. Ooh, I wanted to hit something – and hard.

The trip to Sandy Springs calmed my nerves. The rain stopped half an hour earlier, leaving the air fresh, heavy and muggy. Ponds stretched across main thoroughfares and gutters still ran deep with water. At least no one had to build an ark.

Dr. Bret Stewart's practice was located a few short minutes from Georgia's house. Today was her morning off from the bakery to do housework and catch up on errands. The near proximity tempted me to drop by and cry on her shoulder about the day's events. Once I explained about the new lieutenant's penchant for poaching husbands, I envisioned her serving up a generous helping of chocolate cake and pouring me a tall glass of cold milk with permission to drown my sorrows. While keeping me supplied in her mouthwatering goodies, my dear sister would proceed to assure me that Ennis loved me and would rather yank out his eyeballs and/or hack off his right hand before lusting after or touching another woman. I needed my sister's moral support but I'd tend to business first.

When I pulled into Dr. Bret's parking lot, cars occupied seven of the ten parking spaces. I took the eighth. Posters of babies in cute poses and some with Mama, Papa and Baby together hung on the waiting room walls. It gave the impression that having these pint-sized humans equaled bliss twenty-four hours a day. Obviously the images were targeted at new mothers who might buy that line. Two months into motherhood and the woman would be lucky to remember her name or lace her shoes every morning. She'd be too busy cleaning, feeding or rocking the baby. And doing *lots* of laundry. But the rewards were enchanting and extraordinary. Toothless smiles and goofy giggles. Adoring eyes staring up at Mama and Daddy. A tiny hand grasping Mama's thumb. No, it wasn't bliss 24/7 but the good times made the stressful ones worthwhile.

I walked into a setting not depicted on Dr. Bret's posters. Harried mothers (half of them bulging with another baby) bribing their crying toddlers with food or toys to shut up. In other words I walked into the equivalent of my own home when the girls went on a rampage. The difference was the knee-high imps in the waiting room ran amuck on Dr. Bret's earth tone carpet and climbed the beige chairs and coffee tables like wild monkeys.

The sight of those besieged mothers-to-be reminded me I still needed to pick up that pregnancy test. I started toward the check-in desk when a towheaded toddler charged in front of me, bringing me up short. He made a beeline to his mom but took a moment out of his young existence to berate me, "Watch it, lady."

"Robert, that's not nice," Mother scolded – but not too harshly. She offered her apologies on his behalf.

Ennis and I never claimed to be great parents but our kids would have earned more than a *that's not nice* if they got nervy with a stranger for no reason.

At the check-in window, a young brunette tapped away on a keyboard. Without looking up, she acknowledged my presence simply by saying, "Good morning."

I held my badge discreetly for her to see, "Good morning. I'm here to–"

"Fill out the first three pages." She grabbed a clipboard with a half dozen forms and shoved it through the window by rote – without glancing away from the monitor, "Make sure you list all medications including supplements. And I'll need your insurance card."

I slid the clipboard across to her until she finally looked up. Her vision centered on the shiny gold badge. Good. That got her attention so I started over, "I'm not a patient but I need a quick word with Dr. Stewart."

I might as well have asked to see the Pope. "I'm afraid he's terribly busy today," she said. "A patient went into labor and he's over an hour behind on appointments." She looked past me to the women behind me, including Robert's mother.

I kept my voice low, sympathizing, "Yes, those delays happen at my doctor's office too. If you'll let him know the police need a moment with him, I won't take much time."

"Right now?"

I nodded. The woman sighed, "He won't like this." She slunk away like a teen off to inform Daddy she wrecked the car. Meanwhile interest in the new face demanding to see their already late physician increased. Two women checked their watches. Robert's mother sighed with a stern *stop that or else* to her hyperactive son. By the time Dr. Stewart rounded the corner, no one – patients, kids, doctor or detective – was happy.

Dr. Bret smiled anyway, shook my hand. That handshake matched his smile. Fake as my Aunt Katherine's mink coat but it paid to keep up appearances, especially in front of his patients. He cut off my introduction, motioned me to his office, "I have a patient prepped in an exam room so please make it brief."

Since when did doctors give a rat's ass how long a patient waited? When they had a cop in their face, that's when. "I understand. No woman enjoys waiting in that position." As if these guys cared. OB/GYNs were a necessary evil. By the time they finished with a patient, what modesty she scraped together measured the size of an atom.

I quickly reviewed the basics of Mathis's original interview then moved on to my own questions about money. He peeked at his watch as a silent nudge to move along. When he spoke, I resorted to shorthand to keep pace with him. Halfway through, the redundancy of his answers and veiled reminders of "his patients' time" chafed me. The visit shaped up to be a waste of time.

A hesitant knock on the door suspended our conversation. Brunette poked her head in, "Dr. Stewart, your sister is on line one. She's very upset."

The doc clenched his teeth. His cheeks surpassed rose and peaked at scarlet. "This won't take long," he snatched the phone from the cradle, stabbed the appropriate button for the call, "What is it, Tessa? I've got patients waiting, another in stirrups and a police detective in my office. Make it quick."

I busied myself studying his diplomas hanging on the wall. Harvard. Well, *that* university certainly grounded a person. Another certificate, this one from Massachusetts General, stated in a grand flourish that he'd finished his residency at their illustrious facility.

"For the second time, no. I'm not giving you the money." He toned down to a near whisper, "You married the loser so why make us pay for it?"

I heard the phone drop in the cradle. Dr. Bret chuckled, "Bingo."

That laugh warranted a comment. I turned, confused, "I'm sorry. 'Bingo'?" He celebrated because his sister hung up on him? That stunt usually incited a riot in my family, not laughter.

The man sounded positively proud, "That's the key to shutting my sister up about 'borrowing' money. Mention Stan the Man and his lack of ambition and inability to support his family. Gets her every time."

Nice intro, Doc. Thanks. "She ask for help often?"

Bret rolled his eyes, "Over the course of her life Hard Luck Tessa has perfected the art of creative solicitation, Detective. She'd ask a homeless person for his last quarter and make him feel guilty for not having two."

I played along, "I guess every family has their Tessa."

He crossed his arms in protest, "Does your Tessa beg for two grand every three months or so? Mine does. It depends on Stan's income, you understand. He works on commission at the car dealership but he's not very successful at it. I don't know why they don't fire him. Well, he's good for those humiliating commercials, I suppose. With two paychecks Tessa still cries to me for rent money or to pay the water bill. They barely scrape by yet neither of them are motivated enough to find better paying jobs to feed themselves and their boy. And the word *is* motivated. She went to Georgia Southern. Majored in environmental sciences. Surely somewhere there's a whale in need of saving or a tree requiring a hug. If nothing else she could join that bogus 'If Trees Could Sing' nonsense."

I hated to enlighten the doc but "If Trees Could Sing" highlighted musicians, not Tolkien creatures in a forest *or* environmental science majors. Famous artists recorded songs to benefit nature conservation. A worthy cause in my opinion and we all knew how much Dr. Bret valued either one, the cause or a cop's opinion.

This guy's ego barely fit in the same room with him. He really looked down on anyone not in possession of that medical degree. *Eat my shorts, Harvardite. Any guy can touch a woman <u>there</u>, you know. No high-dollar degree required.* "Did she ask your parents for money?" Of course she asked. If she repeatedly hit her brother up, that meant she tapped the whole family.

"Always before calling me. And for the record," he pointed to my notepad, "Lisa was our *stepmother.* Our mother died twelve years ago." Yeah, Mathis jotted "stepmom" down in his notes. I nodded as Bret continued, "Lisa wouldn't give Tessa the time of day much less any money. No, she kept us in line by saying when Dad died, she'd get everything. As though being his wife entitled her to the whole estate, not that it'll be worth much."

Probably on a doctor's salary, the Stewart estate added up to a mere pittance. Dr. Bret lived in Tuxedo Park where houses sold for over five million bucks on average. Chastain Park real estate raked in around two to three million per home. Not much, the doctor said. Yet another lesson in perspective, I groused. Ennis and I scrounged money from bank accounts, some savings, sofa cushions – *anything* to buy our little slice of heaven in Dunwoody – and we still needed a loan. Our net worth would send this clod into hysterics. I think I had enough education in Dr. Stewart so when his nurse peeked into his office as a silent cue to hurry up, I put my notes away while Dr. Bret excused himself, "Detective, I need to go. As you know, those stirrups can be very uncomfortable after a point."

I wanted to slug him because his expression showed no empathy (in fact, did I see the beginning of a grin?) for women in that position. Mathis's X-rated term for gynecologists soared to the forefront. This guy was the definition of that pornographic word. I smiled at the thought of the smug, almost nefarious Dr. Bret's jaw dropping upon hearing it. "Thank you for your time, Dr. Stewart," I turned and while making my way through the crowded waiting room, said a prayer for those poor women about to saddle up on his exam table.

o   o   o

Tessa Campbell worked as a waitress at the Farm House Restaurant, a nice little standalone eatery downtown that served traditional Southern food. The interior décor suited the name with ceiling fans, wooden floors and homey dining tables covered in red and white checkerboard tablecloths. Outside, an A-frame chalkboard placed outside the door of the hunter green roofed building informed masses:

"In the South…
Our tea is sweet
Words are long
Days are warm
And our faith is strong."

I'd eaten there twice and realized that on the addictive scale the Farm

House's chicken fried steaks rated up there with booze and marijuana. Even Georgia raved over the food. They specialized in chicken fried steak smothered in cream gravy with sides of mashed potatoes, corn, green beans and buttermilk biscuits as big as a fist – all served with a glass of ice cold sweet tea, the house wine of the South. They could whip up a mouthwatering meal in mere minutes that left a lifetime of lip-smacking, savory memories and an extra inch on the hips. What they couldn't whip up: Tessa Campbell. Apparently she called in sick that morning. Funny, I thought. She didn't sound very ill when she hung up on her brother earlier. She sounded volcanic.

I spoke to a waitress named Nicole who worked with Tessa. When interviewing people, I filed them into two categories. Clams or slot machines. I hit the jackpot with Nicole Baker.

We reviewed what Mathis wrote in his notes which covered the bare basics. So basic in fact I questioned how long John spent with her. Nicole reluctantly admitted the "pot-bellied detective came across as mean as a mama wasp" (no offense she said). I mentally rolled my eyes. Classic Mathis. He hated doing interviews and his attitude showed it.

In her mid-thirties, Nicole's outspoken demeanor reminded me of a woman who'd waited too many tables and didn't mind letting anyone know it. She seemed at ease with me, volunteering boatloads of information Mathis could have finessed from her if he'd tried but his definition of finesse meant swinging a sledge hammer. He blamed age, not personality, on his lack of patience. The day I met him he was a detective in his early thirties and already a crusty sourpuss. Age had nothing to do with it.

Nicole and I spent several minutes talking about Tessa. The two spent their breaks together when possible but weren't close enough friends that they went bowling on Saturday nights. Then Nicole mentioned, "To my knowledge the family got along fine. Tessa, Stan and her parents. Now her brother? He treated her wrong." She wagged her finger, "That man needs a Come to Jesus meeting regarding Genesis 4:9. It does not apply to only brothers, y'know. Sisters need help too."

Yes, Georgia regularly applied the "Brother's Keeper" verse regarding my life. Most times I appreciated it, other times not.

I wondered if Nicole might have reconsidered her judgment if she realized how often Tessa supposedly tapped the trough. If Georgia or Seth suffered financial issues, Ennis and I would gladly pitch in and vice versa. But continual support strained bank accounts and relationships, sometimes damaging both beyond repair.

Nicole continued, "The poor girl just needs a few bucks once in a while. They're trying to raise that boy. Her daddy was good to help her. Well, until he found out."

"Found out?"

"About her affair. The boy isn't Stan's. When Joey found that out, he cut her off. What a shame too. The kid's cute. Looks like his mama – and Brad Pitt."

Brad Pitt? I doubted the Hollywood heartthrob took time out of making movies to do the horizontal tango with a used car salesman's wife however it was interesting news. An affair with a Brad Pitt clone. "And who was the affair with again?"

"The Stewart's neighbor. Mr. Moore."

And my hamster fainted on its wheel. She compared Shane Moore, the owner of the car dealership, to Brad Pitt? Hardly. Moore, in his late forties, shared exactly two features with the movie star. Sandy hair and an angular jaw. The big payoff of the interview wasn't the comparison but the revelation that Mr. Moore played with fire and got burned. I'd bet a year's salary that whatever friendship he and the Stewarts shared went straight to hell after that.

Nicole proved to be a font of information, "I thought it was weird since Mr. Moore hired Stan about the time Tessa told everyone she was knocked up. I mean *Stan*? A car salesman? A florist, maybe, but that schlep couldn't sell a bucket of water to a guy whose pants were on fire." She leaned forward with a conspiratorial whisper, "Have you seen those stupid commercials he does?" She slashed a manicured fingernail from ear to ear, "No hope. Plus he spends money on old baseball trinkets. Some defunct team no one's heard of since The Great Flood. Drives Tessa nuts."

So Moore hired Stan about the time he bedded Stan's wife...

My phone rang. I excused myself, retrieved the cell phone from my belt. It was Lily's teacher.

"Mrs. Rutherford," the usually soft-spoken lady in her mid-twenties sounded flustered and uneasy, "we have a problem with Lily."

"What kind of problem? The virus?" I expected this call last week when a rash of back door trots hit the classroom. Kid after kid fell victim to it and had to be sent home.

"No ma'am, she's not ill. She, um… She hit another child."

I came to my feet, "She what?" I hadn't intended to practically shout into the phone but according to the heads swiveling in my direction, I'd basically done just that. For whatever crazy reason, our calm, cool and collected little girl took to delivering uppercuts and jabs instead of using charm to make her point.

Memories roared back of my own mother receiving such a call about her "darling baby girl" Savannah. Around Lily's age I'd been a terror and yes, I belted a boy or two for various, perfectly valid reasons, at least to me. One kept yanking my ponytail, another talked non-stop and the other boy kissed me – or I should say the *wrong* boy kissed me. Mama's firm hand on my backside and unquestionably firmer words convinced me knocking someone's nose off really wasn't worth the punishment. It seemed as though my daughter now required a lesson or two about social graces and civilities.

I was crushed and embarrassed, "I'm so sorry." My mama said that a lot too. Telling the teacher she was sorry for my behavior, as if her debutante-in-training flipped out and mooned the whole kindergarten class.

"It's just so uncharacteristic of Lily. She's normally well behaved."

Uncharacteristic to say the least. Our kid personified polite unless provoked. That brought one particular dark-haired brat to mind. "Who did Lily hit? Brooke Van der Meer?" Because I wanted a heads-up on whether I'd go toe to toe with Brooke's mother again. A month earlier Brooke began a campaign of bullying her classmates – Lily in particular and later shoved and knocked her down. Lily missed hitting her head on a desk by scant inches. Brooke's mother treated the situation with less concern than a hangnail – until I stated shoving was considered assault. A few exchanges later, the mother promised a stern talk with Brooke. I dreaded the upcoming meeting – if the tables turned and I faced this woman once more – all because my girl exercised her right hook. Unless the Van der Meer kid goaded Lily, my child's punishment required plenty of deliberation. I wanted her to defend herself but not knock out half the class.

"No, this was Lauren Powell," the teacher replied. "The children said it was unprovoked. Lauren's mother is on the way to pick her up."

I exited the restaurant, "Is Lauren hurt?"

"She's okay, just a mark on her cheek." She hesitated, gathering courage to utter a statement I recalled from my own childhood. The one saying the offending kid got expelled. "As for Lily," she said regretfully, "I'm afraid we're sending her home for the day. I can call your sister to pick her up if you can't leave work. I notice she's listed as next of kin."

This was no job for an aunt. A mother signed up for these situations when the pregnancy test turned positive. Everything from sleepless nights to tending skinned knees to dealing with them punching classmates in the face. Plus, if anyone faced the girl's irate mother, it would be me. "No, I'm leaving work now."

Since Ennis preferred cloud surfing about Sheila that day I called

Mathis on my way to the school. I updated him on Tessa Campbell's affair with her daddy's neighbor and asked him to check out the car dealership Moore owned. No one wrung answers out of a person the way John Mathis could – when he put his mind to it. Some people excelled at math, others English or science. Mathis's specialty was squeezing blood from turnips. I hit the road with three wishes. One, that Mathis cracked the case with this new information. Two, that my kid stopped socking her classmates, and three, that my husband forgot about Sheila Bennett and the transfer altogether. How "Wonderful Wonderful" it would be...

18

Monday Afternoon

Thankfully the girl's mother accepted mine and Lily's apologies. After seeing little Lauren Powell's cheek, I sighed with relief that the mark faded a bit. Chances of a black eye verged on nil. My mama's wish had come true. I had a daughter just like me. A veritable hellion with a pretty decent straight punch.

I called Josh Hunter, updated him on my latest crisis and asked for lost time to compensate for my three hour absence. I made the most of it by having a stern chat with Lily. You can't go beating on other kids, I said. It's not only wrong but rude. I reserved spankings for huge violations and yes, belting another kid fell into that category. But Lily rarely acted out. I wanted to talk to her, find out the reason for her tantrum then decide whether to put her on parole or condemn her to a visit to the woodshed. "Why did you hit Lauren?" I asked her. "She's your classmate."

She crossed her arms and puffed up. The sight would have been comical had the situation not been serious. Her don't-be-stupid Mama expression kinda caught me off-guard. She should have been timid and contrite, even nervous over her impending punishment. Instead my little girl brazenly challenged me, jutting her chin, setting her jaw. She was angry – and put out with my ignorance. "She's not a classmate, Mama. She's a girl from another class."

Semantics. Great. That trick never worked with my mama and it sure as hell wouldn't with me either. "My mistake. So why did you hit Lauren *from another class*?" I wasn't used to this boldness. Lily always expressed herself in gentle ways, not this in-your-face insolence.

"Because."

"That is *not* an answer, young lady." I saw her about to argue that yes, it was an answer so I cut her off, "It is not an *acceptable* answer. Why did you do it?"

In a surprising but welcome move, her shoulders slumped. She stared at the floor, "Because she looked like Sheila."

Because she looked like Sheila. Perfect kid logic. No, perfect *Prince* logic. My daddy and his brothers used it as had I until Mama got hold of me. "So you lay people out who kinda resemble someone you don't like?" Personally, I failed to see Lauren's resemblance to Sheila but who was I? Just the mother of a future Ultimate Fighting Champ if I couldn't derail the Prince logic and quick. "Remind me again. At what point did I say 'when in doubt, knock 'em out'?"

Ah, a breakthrough. Her lower lip quivered. She sniffed back growing tears, "She wouldn't share the crayons. She said they were hers and she was keepin' them, just like Sheila said me and Anna were hers and you couldn't have us back."

Oh, *that's* what instigated the punch. The mirror's vision threw her in the middle of our venomous custody battle. But still... "Honey, you realize that little girl isn't Sheila, right?"

"M-hmm, but she made me mad."

I tipped her chin up until we met eye to eye. A single tear slid down her cheek. I thumbed it away, "You can't go off and hit people because they remind you of someone you don't like. There'd be a lot of black eyes in this town if I did that."

"But *you* hit Sheila. I saw you."

Another prediction from my old pal The Nameless Mirror. Explaining an event I'd yet to experience (or how it came to pass) posed a unique problem. I dumbed my way through a reply, "I'm sorry you saw that but I'm trying really hard to prevent that from happening."

"I don't wanna live with Sheila. I wanna live with you and Daddy."

"You're staying right here," I promised. "I'll try to keep her from taking Daddy away." Why deny the mirror's visions to her any longer? She saw what I saw and we both knew what was at stake. Our family.

The second I admitted knowledge of Sheila's intent, my girl's expression evolved from defensive to utter relief that I hadn't dismissed her statement as child's folly. Her big blue eyes again filled with tears, "Daddy never believed me."

I curled a lock of hair behind her ear, "Don't cry, baby. Daddy didn't believe you because he doesn't know about the mirror. And we need to keep that our secret, just you and me, okay? Not even Aunt Georgia can find out."

"Okay," she bravely sniffed back the emotion, scrubbed a finger beneath her nose.

"Good. Now I can't promise anything but I *am* trying to protect our family and stop Sheila. I'll do my best to keep us together."

Her eyes brightened, "Can I help?"

"Yes. You can help two ways. One, don't clobber anyone else at school and two, when Sheila does show up in our lives, don't bust her kneecaps. Leave that to me if it's gotta be done." I stuck my hand out, "Deal?"

The earlier Resentful Lily transformed into Loving Lily again. She ignored my hand, leaped from the chair and hugged me tight, "Deal."

O   O   O

We concluded our discussion about punching people out or generally maiming them because we disliked Sheila Bennett. I agreed to soft-pedal the incident at school this time only because Ennis wouldn't understand about the Sheila lookalike. But one more screw up, I warned Lily, and she was toast.

I dragged out an apron and a casserole dish. Lasagna sounded too good to pass up. Soon the house smelled of onion, garlic and Italian seasoning mixed with tomatoes, hamburger and sausage. It promised a tasty supper for those souls busy devising a plan to rid ourselves of a two-legged, high-ranking rat.

Lily sat up shop at the dining table. She brought along her crayons and colored construction paper. Sorting her crayons with the keen eye of a true artist, she lined up her choices straighter than soldiers assembled for battle. Done choosing her arsenal, she picked up the bright canary yellow, "I'm makin' Uncle Dane's birthday card."

That was nice but, "What about Uncle Seth? His birthday is next week." Dane's followed two weeks after. My brother, born a Scorpio, displayed traits of a Taurus or Aries – moody, serious and driven. Dane's birthday fell in November (also a Scorpio) but he acted more like Ennis's Libra – easygoing, fun and a big ol' kid at heart. Seth and Dane shared the same zodiac sign but possessed polar opposite personalities. I attributed the difference to their raising. Like me and Georgia, Seth grew up with Daddy's drinking and suffered his wrath throughout our younger years. Dane's father was a gentle man who, according to the brothers, loathed even the mildest argument. My brother faced issues head-on and rarely backed down from a confrontation. Dane, the laidback cowboy, let things work out on their own but intervened if need be. Dane was the playful uncle who told jokes, helped build snowmen, and enjoyed giving piggyback rides. Lily loved Seth but she adored Dane.

She reinforced that fact by wrinkling her nose at my reminder, "I don't know what Uncle Seth likes. Uncle Dane loves horses and so do I."

"Uncle Seth is in the Army Reserve. How about drawing him in his uniform?"

That lead balloon we all heard about? It didn't fly with my kid either. I kinda understood. The last time she tried drawing camouflage, Seth resembled a green and black Dalmatian. The sight, entertaining to everyone else, caused him to mask his chagrin. Lily's lack of enthusiasm inspired me to offer, "I'll help you with the uniform if you want."

She blew out a resigned breath, "Okay, but can I do Uncle Dane's card first?"

Of course, I said. Who was I to inhibit creativity? By the time she finished Dane's she might actually decide to tackle grumpy old Uncle Seth's card. Well... I could hope.

After fifteen minutes she yawned, gathered her crayons and headed to the living room. "'My Little Pony' is on," she said.

She climbed into my recliner and switched the channel to her show. I stole a peek toward the table at what she'd drawn. A sun in the corner of the page, sprigs of green grass lined the bottom and smack in the middle? Dane Rutherford on a giant brown German Shepherd. The brown-haired lady riding behind him I assumed might be Georgia. They smiled as they moseyed around on the overgrown Rin Tin Tin (Lily's interpretation of a horse, of course) and enjoyed the boundless flat Texas Panhandle landscape. Ennis always joked they took levels to the Panhandle to test them for accuracy. I did not argue. Between that, the heat and the dust storms (better known as "Panhandle rain"), a person wondered why the hell anyone voluntarily settled there. Then they met the residents and understood why.

I resumed my work in the kitchen. Anna preferred to watch the cartoon following "My Little Pony" so I'd wake her from her nap in another twenty minutes.

Ennis was an hour later than normal. Had they stumbled on a break in the case? I debated about calling for an update then glanced at the lasagna ready to bake. The salad makings sat on the counter, the last item on the evening's menu. Once I chopped the salad and put the lasagna in the oven, I'd call him and give him directions home in case he forgot where he lived.

I busied myself with the lettuce when my phone rang. It was Mathis who lectured, "If you don't take that sergeant's exam, I'll never speak to you again."

What the hell. He called to tell me that? "What?"

"You had me check out Moore, the Stewart's neighbor, and his dealership. I got an employee list. He's paying three salesmen and four guys to repair and detail the rejects when they're brought on the lot."

"We'll check out the salesmen tomorrow and try to interview them and the detailers. Did you ask Moore about the car at the curb the night of the murders?"

"Said he saw it briefly between nine and ten that night. A newer car, light color, maybe white. I'll bet you a box of éclairs that conceited bastard is behind the murders. Probably tired of Tessa's mooching so he gave himself a nice early Christmas gift. Financial freedom."

John's experience at the job paid off more often than not but on occasion his animosity overshadowed his instincts. And he literally hated car dealers with an extraordinary passion. "Don't concentrate too heavily on him," I cautioned, "not until we check out his employees. But if you're right about Moore I'll buy you two boxes of éclairs. For now, if you get time, recheck Tessa and Stan's financials and their phone records."

"Sure thing. And here's a word of advice from an old dog. Brush up on your command skills, kid. Sergeants give orders, they don't make suggestions. This *if you get time* crap has to stop."

I slid the lasagna into the oven, "I'm not a sergeant yet, John."

"Like my mama always said. 'Don't practice till you get it right, practice till you can't get it wrong.' Or something like that. Either way, keep studying."

Arms slid around my thighs and cinched down tight, hobbling me from walking. Lily's face peeked from beneath my elbow, "Mama…"

"Mathis, I gotta go. My rug rat has a problem."

"Yeah, from what I hear, she's got her mother's temper. One more thing. Take that sergeant's exam or answer to me. Bye." The line went dead.

I stared at the phone wondering why he wanted me for his boss. It took him four months to remember my last name instead of settling for *Hey, Stretch* (because of my height) and took me two years on the job to gain his respect and trust. Now he campaigned for Stretch to become Sergeant Stretch?

Eee-yowch… Lily squeezed until the bones in my knees ground together. "Honey, ease up, okay? It hurts."

"She's here," was the covert whisper.

"She who?" I baby-stepped to the sink, washed my hands then began chopping the romaine lettuce.

A key turned in the front lock then the door squeaked open. "Sugar, I'm home."

Well, imagine that. My cheerful, wandering spouse decided to grace me with his presence. "In the kitchen," I called back, feeling petite but lethal arms constrict python tight again. I cringed down at her, "Lily, what is wrong with you?"

She held on for dear life, her wide blue eyes staring up at me. "Make her go away, Mama," she begged in a small frightened voice. "You said you'd protect us."

I busied myself trying to ease not only her panic but her killer grasp – until I heard Ennis, "Sugar, I'd like you to meet Lieutenant Sheila Bennett. Lieutenant, my wife Savannah."

Make her go away Lily begged moments earlier. I looked up from our daughter's terrified expression to see "her" standing right in the middle of my dining room. If the older version of her sparked the green-eyed monster in me, the modern day version infused it with steroids. I pushed back images of Ennis threading his fingers through her luxurious dark waves (the way he did mine), then leaning in to plant a knee-weakening kiss on her. Unlike her future form, *today's* Sheila Bennett scared the hell out of me. Her slim, toned body crowned with surprisingly attractive features… I felt, for lack of a better word, inadequate. Infinitely inadequate.

At least her garb rated less than spectacular. Navy blue pantsuit and white button down blouse and dress shoes with a chunky three inch heel. Her belt displayed the usual – badge, gun and cell phone. She'd obviously come off shift for the day but the question remained – why was she with my husband?

Bennett's hand extended to shake mine. I still held the chef's knife in my right hand. I won't bother explaining my inner struggle while grasping that thing.

Playing nice, I switched hands to give her hand a solid shake. Sheila's mouth broadened into a cordial toothy curve that outright chafed me. *Terrific. She has perfect teeth and a charming smile too.*

"It's a pleasure to meet you, Savannah," she said. "Ennis has told me a lot about you."

Bet he hasn't told you I'm an expert shot. Or was until a few months ago but I'm still accurate enough to knock your nose and that grin off your face.

I forced a smile, "Lieutenant, good to meet you." People said practice made perfect. At that rate, I'd be a top-notch liar by the weekend.

My vision shifted to Ennis, praying the man read every injurious thought storming through my mind. He ambushed me by dragging her home. And where the hell had he been for over an hour anyway? Not on shift, apparently, so I posed the question, "What delayed you getting home?" *And why the hell did you bring her along? And today, no less, when our baby threw such a tantrum over this woman that the school booted her for the day.*

He tried that aw-shucks shake of his head, "The lieutenant stopped by the station after work, offered to buy me a drink and get acquainted."

I sat the knife aside before going samurai on our guest. *A drink* and *acquainted* normally led up to no good, especially if one participant made a habit of wrecking marriages. "That's nice." Not.

Bennett laid a hand on his arm, patted it warmly, "Ennis, please. Call me Sheila." She turned her deceptive, casual smile on me, "I'm not a stickler for formalities. We're all friends anyway. We'd better be, right?" She bobbed her brow, "Since I'll be spending most of my time with your husband." The woman actually laughed.

The knife's siren song grew louder. So sharp. So convenient. So... tempting. Common sense temporarily replaced my homicidal tendencies with a reminder children should not witness such bloody carnage, particularly initiated by their mother. I eased my hand away from the cabinet and forced a congenial, "Right."

She slapped Ennis's back "ol' buddy, ol' pal" style, "This guy can toss back the hooch too. You had, what, three or four shots?"

"Two beers," he nervously averted his gaze from mine. "Just two."

"So did you get acquainted after those two drinks?" I asked, trying oh-so-hard not to sound like a jealous shrew.

Bennett answered for him, "Sure did. We'll work very well together, won't we, Ennis?"

He shrugged, his cheeks tingeing red. I turned back to the oven, appraised our supper. Bubbling hot – a lot the way Ennis's current wife felt. Still, I held my tongue, "Good. So you're all squared away for the transfer then?"

"Babe, she was just being friendly," Ennis explained.

With Lily clinging to my jeans' belt loop, I towed her along while transferring the large wooden salad bowl to the dining table. I tried keeping my mood upbeat while arranging the smaller salad bowls at each plate, "Ennis, I didn't say a word. You've met everyone else at Zone 5, you needed to meet your new lieutenant." *Meet, not doink her. Remember that, darling.*

Sheila nudged him with her elbow, "See? I told you she'd be alright with it." She shrugged a shoulder at me, "He thought you'd get upset that I took him out for a drink."

Two drinks and no, I'd get pissed off if you took him to your bed. I used my sister's favorite phrase, "Heavens, no."

"You've got a pretty cool wife, Rutherford. I like her already. Most women would blow a gasket because we were drinking together."

I straightened the place settings, specifically the forks and knives. "I'm not most women. Lily, honey, want to help me set the table?"

Her fingers closed in a fist on my belt loop. She shook her head.

Bennett stared at the countertop beside her. I'd moved the sergeant's study guide there, along with my other study materials. She thumbed through a few pages, "Ennis said you're studying for the sergeant's exam. How's that coming?"

Boy, oh boy. Had he opened the Encyclopedia Savannah for her?

Tell her my bra size and monthly cycle too? "Fine. Still waffling on whether I'll try for it now or later," I said, hoping my husband caught that curveball. *See? I can surprise you too, dear.* "When you've got kids, they keep you busy."

"Having kids never appealed to me. Too career-minded, I guess." She added as an afterthought, "But it's good that you enjoy being a wife and mother. Someone has to, right?"

Don't make me poison your coffee, lady. I gritted my teeth to bear this visit. Similar to root canals, a person forced themselves to endure the pain. This felt like four root canals at once without Novocain – and it only got worse.

"Uh," Ennis chanced speaking, "Hunter said you took lost time this afternoon. Something about Lily. What happened?"

Lily abandoned the belt loop to resume hugging my thighs again. I took it as a reminder not to blab about her whopping little Lauren. I patted her hands, "Oh, nothing serious. A misunderstanding is all. Everything's fine now."

"Mama," Lily whined into my thigh. She peeked around my leg again, this time shooting the evil eye at Sheila. "Make her leave."

Sheila chuckled, crouched to Lily's level, "What's wrong, honey?" She asked me, "Lily, isn't it?"

I nodded, put my hand to Lily's shoulder, "It's okay, sweetie."

She shook her head in response, whispering *no, it's not.*

Bennett waved her over, "My name's Sheila. Your daddy's told me all about you and your sister Hannah."

"Anna," I gently corrected despite seething inside. At least get the kids' names right, I thought. "Her name is Anna."

Lily progressed to using me as her personal shield, bobbing and weaving to avoid Sheila's gaze, "I don't like her."

For Bennett, what began as amusement evolved to confusion, "Why don't you like me, Lily?"

Being my kid, she of course chose that moment for brutal honesty, "Because you're gonna take my daddy away–"

"Honey, we discussed this," I tried diffusing the increasing tension between Bennett and Lily. "He's going to work in a different part of town, that's all." To Sheila I said, "She doesn't want him to transfer."

"No," my kid hammered away. "She's gonna–"

I slapped my hand over her mouth, "That's enough, sweetheart. Go check on your sister for me. Make sure she's still in her bed." My face burned from ten degrees of dismay and embarrassment. Lily squirmed beneath my hold so I took a firmer tone, "Okay, we'll both go. Excuse us, please."

I hustled the mouthy child out of Bennett's earshot. That meant Anna's bedroom.

On the way I whispered to Lily, "Don't say that out loud again. Understand?"

She nodded, finally surrendering to my hold. Safely in Anna's room, I kneeled to face Lily, "Listen, *we* know what's happening but don't let Sheila know, okay? I can't fix this if you tip her off."

She toed the carpet, hung her head, "Sorry."

"Just be quiet around her, that's all I ask."

Anna sat up in bed holding her teddy bear Dallas (wonder where she got *that* name, Ennis). The beady-eyed bear stared at us as if expecting an explanation for the intrusion. If so, he would be sorely disappointed. One kid knew about Sheila and that was one kid too many. Controlling Lily was hard enough but corralling a young toddler's mouth? Might as well try squirting toothpaste back in the tube.

I lowered Anna beside Lily, gave her kiss and a hug. I did the same to Lily and asked that she look after her sister.

Holding Anna's hand, my oldest voiced her disapproval, "Where are you going?"

"To the mirror right quick. Tell Daddy I'm in the bathroom if he asks and for goodness sakes don't speak to Sheila."

I hurried to the master bedroom determined to get answers from the mirror. Many reasons spurred the need. The sight of Bennett in our house. Her faux *nice ta meetcha* attitude. Ennis's ridiculously euphoric grin as he flanked another woman – the same grin he flashed at me before we said our I Do's.

I closed the bedroom door and swiveled to face the old, rabble-rousing antique. I scowled at the cloudy image staring back, "Give me a heads-up on this bitch."

19

Monday Evening

My last words distorted into an echo. The mirror obliged my request and yanked me through again. This time my transition from present to future in became almost painful, like being stretched through a small hole. Voices from the other side grew louder. Bennett and I exchanged vicious threats.

The mirror dumped me in the middle of a heated argument. In a new and surprising move, this trip meshed my body with the Savannah standing and holding Lily's hand. My daughter looked around five or six, not a whole lot older than her current age.

Sheila pushed me, knocking me off balance. It was then I discovered I had no actual control over my body or actions. The mirror limited me to spectator again except this time I watched through Future Savannah's eyes, felt her emotions and the fact she stumbled backwards after Sheila's attack.

Lily's hand constricted on mine and kept pulling me backward while cradling her left wrist against her chest. She screamed at Sheila, "Leave me alone! You're not my mama and I'm not going with you!"

Transitioning into the crazy scenario, I tried gaining my bearings and control of my body and tongue but I was only along for the ride. A frightening rage swelled inside my future self even as she calmly assured Lily, "Don't worry. She's not taking you anywhere." I watched the scene unfold through Future Savannah's eyes, heard every word fall from her lips, felt the hot, violent fury flowing through her.   To Bennett she warned, "Touch my kids again and you'll be carried out of here on a gurney." Then to Lily, "Take Anna and go to your room. Shut the door."

Lily raced for her bedroom, crying and holding her left wrist. Apparently in the seconds prior to the mirror dropping me into the argument, Bennet hurt Lily in her haste to steal the children.

My mood ramped into an increasingly murderous rage. It happened in an instant and it happened automatically despite my own attempts to remain cool and clearheaded. The escalation scared me since I could not control it. My brain pulsed in harmony with my heart, giving me a normally crippling granddaddy of a headache. Rigid muscles strained to their limits. Adrenaline and chaste hatred coursed in my veins. Before my arrival the fight escalated to the point Older Me wanted to kill Sheila Bennett. Not just kill her but tear her to pieces.

Apparently Older Savannah's opponent shared the same sentiment. Kill the bitch across from her. She stalked toward me, "Ennis wants those kids and he's going to get them."

"If he wants them so much why'd he send you?"

"Personally I think he's scared of you but I'll go *through* you to get those brats if need be. He wants full custody, no more joint custody bullshit, and I'll make sure it happens."

I rooted to the spot, blocking the hallway entrance. Good move, I told my older self. If she charged, I'd have room to beat the shit out of her without the kids seeing it from the bedroom. "Over my dead body," Older Savannah dared.

A curl of a smile deepened her smug expression, "Your choice." She shouted past my shoulder, "Girls, front and center now! You've got five seconds or I'm coming after you!"

The bedroom door squeaked open an inch. I turned toward the hall, ordering, "Stay put and keep the door closed." The door latched shut again.

I looked back at Sheila when something crashed against my cheek, sending me sideways a step. Tears blurred my vision, my palm raced to my cheek in a decidedly gentler fashion than the back of her hand struck me.

Bennett leaned in, her fists clenched. In a low, almost quiet voice she said, "Stand in my way and I'll bring you to your knees. Now back away and let me by."

My cheek and jaw ached and burned as if clocked by a hot iron. If I'd seen the attack coming, I'd have ducked in time but ambushing (in every respect) was her specialty.

When I asked the mirror for a preview of mine and Sheila's

confrontation, I expected to interact freely – perhaps to change the future again. The mirror, however, locked my present self in my future version's body, unable to speak or act of my own accord. In this case it didn't matter. Whether I was twenty-nine, thirty-nine or ninety-nine I'd react the same way.

I swung back, fingers rolled tight until the knuckles blanched, then put my rage to work. I drove my fist into her right cheek. Bone struck bone. Pain exploded in my hand, traveled up my arm in a white hot bolt of lightning. Bennett's head snapped sideways and with a brief, sharp shriek, she fell against the wall, colliding with a portrait of the girls, knocking it askew. An old adage came to mind while watching her surrender to surprise and pain. *He who hesitates, meditates in a horizontal position.* She may have slapped me but I leveled her.

Sheila Bennett crumpled to a weak kneeling position, one hand cradling her jaw, the other bracing flat against the floor. I thought I heard a whimper. That lone punch expelled a modicum of my boiling rage – rage so foreign to me I felt as if I slipped into someone else's skin – and I had. A homicidal lunatic's skin.

I stepped closer, the venom so scalding and bitter, the words themselves stung when I spoke, "Get out of my house and stay away from my kids. *Do you understand?*" Older Savannah bent closer to deliver one last threat, "Tell Ennis if he wants my girls he, not you, will try to get them and that will not be easy. Tell him to remember all my trophies. I didn't win them playing bingo."

It finally registered. She wanted this confrontation. Planned an

altercation. Baited me to the point of losing control for one instant –
then she'd snap pictures of the bruise, show the judge and I was screwed.
The woman played me perfectly and I fell for it.

A tiny alarm in the back of my own brain wailed away. *Shut up,*
it warned. *Shut up _now_. You risk losing what's most precious to you –
Lily and Anna – and God only knows what else this bitch will take.*

Bennett slowly pushed to her feet, wobbled until steadying herself
on the sofa's armrest. She worked her jaw, winced. A drop of blood
bubbled in the corner of her mouth. She touched it, studied it then lifted
her gaze to mine. A contemptible smile crossed her lips, "You've got
quite a temper, Sergeant. I'm not sure those girls are safe with you. The
judge might agree with me once he sees this bruise. And I sincerely
doubt the job would consider you stable enough to carry a weapon…"

The world faded white while the mirror switched scenes. With
my luck I'd be sixty-five and behind bars.

When I arrived at my new destination, I sneezed. The
overpowering woody scent of men's cologne permeated the air, agitating
my nose and constricting my throat. My eyes watered behind closed lids.
Polo cologne. Great. The only men's fragrance (especially in that
quantity) that summoned my beastly allergy.

Opening my eyes, I blinked to clear my vision. I sat in an
uncomfortable metal folding chair in an interview room at my station.
Across the table from me were two detectives I recognized from Internal
Affairs. Bill Robbins and Thomas Greene. About thirty-seven, Robbins
presented a commanding air with his impeccable posture and confident,

almost cocky, expression. He dressed smart in a gray suit and burgundy tie but looked like he had a hard-on for the world – or perhaps just the sergeant in the room.

Lazily leaning back in his chair, Greene topped my age by ten years and wore his graying hair in a side part. He reminded me of a high school teacher in his dark slacks, white shirt and camel colored sport coat.

Greene reached behind him for a box of tissues, slid it across the table to me. I stripped one, dabbed my eyes, blew my nose. Then I realized – the mirror turned me loose. It no longer tethered my present self to Older Savannah. I could say and do anything I desired and I sincerely desired to flee the room. My head ached, my heart still pounded from fighting with Bennett and thanks to the lack of fresh air, my breathing suffered too.

But the true misery lay ahead. Robbins and Greene earned reputations in IA as careless cowboys, roping officers by way of doubletalk, twisting words and turning a clear cut case of self-defense into assault, punishable with suspension, lost pay or dismissal. No cop came away unscathed with them.

The two stared in silence, their scrutiny causing me to squirm. The Hot Seat. It should have been called Old Sparky. Any cop sitting there could describe the inner terror of occupying that seat and the animosity toward the so-called "colleagues" grilling them. The poor victim just waited for IA to throw the switch on his or her career – and sometimes their freedom, depending on the severity of the offense. Judging by the two stern faces across the table, I was a goner.

In the past, the small interview rooms rarely affected my claustrophobia because I sat on the other side of the table. At that moment I felt weak, faint and scared. Making matters worse:
Another sneeze caught me off-guard.

Robbins leaned back with a curled lip as if I'd exposed him to the plague. "Sergeant," he said, "Lieutenant Sheila Bennett filed a formal complaint against you." He reviewed the forms in his hands. He clucked his tongue, "Assaulting a superior officer is a serious charge."

Greene – apparently not worried about contracting my "deadly" allergy – bent forward with a secretive whisper, "She also mentioned smelling liquor on your breath." He pretended to give a shit about me, as if using that ridiculous hushed tone might keep the accusation from seeing daylight despite the camera mounted in the upper corner of the room. He played the good old boy, the cop's best friend. Those were the most dangerous IA cops.

I gave Sheila credit. She built a solid case against me. The belt across her jaw and now a cunning lie about me drinking. I was stone cold sober when I clobbered her.

Greene took the paperwork from his partner, scanned down the page, "Says here you and your ex-husband are fighting for custody of your two children." He looked at me, "That can bring on some heavy-duty stress."

I just stared at them, trying to reign in my fear and failing.

Mr. I'm-Your-Pal Greene continued, "Savannah – may I call you Savannah?"

I shrugged the "whatever" shrug. He proceeded, "We don't care about the drinking. You drink at home, that's your business and according to the lieutenant, this incident occurred at your home. We've got her side of what happened, now we want yours."

No, they didn't. Their faces labeled our meeting a simple formality to close their case. I expected them to check their watches or perhaps Greene to call the wife and say he'd be home early.

Besides Internal Affairs, I sat alone in that room. No allies, no delegates, no one. Had I lost my marbles not having a representative with me? Another sneeze tickled my nose. I wiped it with a tissue, hoping to ward off the blast. "Could we crack the door please?"

"No," Robbins replied. "Tell us what happened."

Asshole. I coughed again, blew my nose, "Where's my delegate?"

Greene poured a glass of water from a nearby pitcher, "You said you didn't want one, remember?"

No, of course I didn't remember. If I asked for one now, I'd look guilty, crazy or just plain stupid for refusing one in the first place. I weighed my options and decided a delegate could not help me tell the truth, because that's what I intended to do.

I took a sip of water and delved into the nightmare (at least the part I personally experienced), "Bennett came over to take the kids – by force if need be, she said. She grabbed my daughter Lily too hard and hurt her. I stepped in, ordered the girls to the bedroom. When I turned, Bennett struck me. I defended my kids and myself against an aggressive individual," I stared directly at Robbins, "superior officer or not. And I had *not* been drinking."

"The lieutenant said your interactions have always been acrimonious. When she arrived alone why did you invite her inside? Because to the average person that looks suspicious, like you lured her into an altercation." Robbins snuggled into his role as Bad Cop. He seemed to enjoy playing the part, interrogating cops and dangling their career over a bottomless pit.

I wished for one more sneeze. A real doozy. I'd be tempted to neglect catching it in a tissue and blast that bastard with my best effort. But I hated to shame my Mama by resorting to childish behavior. There was enough in the room already. "Pardon my French but that's utter bullshit. I may have *allowed* her into my home but not to waylay her and certainly not to let her run off with my children *or* hit me."

"Bennett said the attack was unprovoked. That you, and I quote," Robbins made sure to read it slow and precise as if I suffered from Dim-Wit Syndrome, "'Hauled off and knocked the shit out of me for no reason.'"

"If you call quid pro quo 'no reason'," I shot back.

"She's got a hell of a bruise on her jaw. I don't see a scratch on you. Can you explain that?"

I hated this condescending, overdressed jackass, "Sorry. I'm afraid it slipped my mind to take photographic evidence of her assault." I returned the favor of careful enunciation, "She hit me first. She tried to kidnap my children. If someone tried taking your kids would you stand aside and let them?" I glanced at his left hand. No ring. The jerk had no clue about being a parent. I crossed my arms, "I was protecting my children. I make no apologies for that."

"She also said you threatened her husband."

"You mean *Ennis*?" I reciprocated with the same are-you-stupid tone he'd used on me seconds earlier.

Robbins frowned, "Detective Ennis Rutherford, yes." He read back through the complaint, "The lieutenant quoted you as saying 'Tell Ennis if he wants my girls, he, not you, will try to get them and that will not be easy. Tell him to remember my trophies. I didn't win them playing bingo.'"

Wow. Verbatim. Did she wear a tape recorder at the house that day or possess an elephant's memory? Whatever the case, the bitch didn't get to lieutenant by being incompetent.

Robbins retrieved a pen from his suit jacket, poised it over his notepad, "What trophies were you referring to?"

"Savannah," Greene said, topping off my glass of water. "I've got three girls. They're grown but I understand how you feel. I'd do anything to protect them from what I considered a threat."

I set him straight, "I don't *consider* her a threat. She *is* a threat."

"The trophies, Sergeant." Robbins impatiently reminded.

I dropped the words like boulders, "Golf. Trophies."

His brow shot up in a manner suggesting my sanity teetered on the precarious edge of shooting him and Greene on the spot. (The thought *had* crossed my mind in a moment of folly). "So," he said, "you threatened to take a golf club after him? Is that correct?"

My unblinking stare answered his question. Rising to his feet, he closed the folder on the table (along with my career, I assumed) and opened the interview room door. For a fleeting instant I saw Sheila Bennett casually leaned against the wall across from the room. Our vision locked. The bruise-free corner of her mouth lifted in a smug half-grin as Robbins approached her, closing the door behind him.

Mumbled exchanges – hers and Robbins's – caught my attention but the voices were subdued, their comments indistinguishable. Greene leaned back again, his hands behind his head and yawned. A cop's career hung in the balance of covert whispers and a bored yawn. Perfect.

Robbins opened the door. Bennett was gone. Without sitting down or ceremony of leading up to the decision, the grim-faced detective simply announced, "Sergeant, you are suspended without pay pending further investigation of this matter. Surrender your shield and all on and off-duty weapons." He thumbed through the folder again, "Department records show two thirty-eight caliber revolvers. Is that correct?"

The suspension wasn't surprising. The "without pay" was. "It isn't procedure to consult with the complainant before determining disciplinary actions. Why were you talking to her?" Because she ran the show, I told myself. She'd slept with both detectives and Robbins consulted with her on what to do next. Like fire me which came later I assumed.

He tapped the table, "Badge and guns. Now. Unless you'd prefer an indefinite suspension or termination. Your choice."

The final two words said everything. It was his way of saying *whatever Sheila wants, Sheila gets.* The woman wrapped up my life and career with a neat little bow. My expression relayed my feelings on his ultimatum. I shifted to Greene who apparently decided his fingernails required a thorough examination. He and Robbins blew off the backbreaking suspension because they'd receive their paycheck that week. I wouldn't.

I reached on my belt, retrieved my .38 which I took my time unloading. I placed both it and my badge reverently on the table, figuring this was our final goodbye. "My off-duty gun is at home."

"Get it here before five," Robbins ordered. "I'll be waiting."

I bet you will, you unscrupulous lowlife. By now Bennett's probably got herpes and the little fellas haven't arrived for the party in your pants just yet. But you'll deserve it. Both of you will deserve it.

I exited the interview room, my head held high. She'd screwed me too, but at least I'd not suffer the wrath of STD's for my trouble. Nope. I'd just have to find a lawyer, apply for unemployment (which officers suspended without pay could do), and get with God on a lot of prayers.

The finality sank in the further I walked. *I'll bring you to your knees* Sheila promised. I wasn't there yet but I knew the bitch was far from finished. Ennis wanted the kids. She swore to get them any way possible.

The steps I took past my office and the desk sergeant's area might well have been my last as a sergeant, a detective, a police officer. Shoring up my courage and stemming the rising tide of tears, I pushed my shoulders back, marched to the front door. An uneasy hush fell over the room when I crossed the catching area's threshold. Officers and the desk sergeant watched as I strode past but I felt dozens of eyes following my trek to the door. John Mathis and I locked gazes. Compassion softened his usually surly features as he motioned for me to call him. I nodded.

They all realized what happened in that room. Sheila Bennett spread the news faster than flu in a preschool class.

The moment I stepped outside, hot humid air broiled my already scarlet red complexion. Reflections off windshields burned laser bright and waves of summer Atlanta sunshine undulated across the parking lot in desert-like mirages. I wanted out of the stifling heat, the invasive stares and the humiliation of the last several minutes.

I scarcely held my emotions in check while fumbling through my purse for the car keys. A potent mix of desperation, fear, and anger welled in my blurring vision. How would I feed the kids? Keep the mortgage paid? Find other employment that offered health benefits? How could I stop this rollercoaster called The Sheila Bennett Express to Hell?

This isn't real, at least not yet. This is your map to use upon returning home to your husband and family. Find a detour on this map. It's here somewhere.

A small cluster of officers gathered outside the station's entrance, watching me, exchanging comments among each other. A sergeant suspended without pay for assaulting a superior officer was rare – and damned humiliating for the sergeant who felt wronged.

Heat radiated off my blue Charger (thank God *that* was paid for and all mine). I dreaded getting inside that oven on wheels. The temperature must have topped ninety-five with air so wet a person could wring it out. I imagined the sauna awaiting me inside the car but to escape the invasive stares and whispers at the station entrance, I unlocked my car, careful to avoid touching the searing handle until preparing for an impromptu branding. When I braved it, a woman's hand pressed against the door denying me entry. The palm pressed solidly against the hot metal and remained unmoving. I stared at it, waiting for Sheila Bennett to retreat and sling out the pain.

Only when I swiveled to face her did her hand withdraw. She ditched her smug grin for a narrow, green-eyed glare, "Tough day, wasn't it? You think you're crying now? Keep fighting me."

Don't flatter yourself, bitch. "My teary eyes and stuffy nose are the result of your bootlicker Robbins bathing in his nuclear cologne."

"Throw in the towel, Savannah. Let us have the girls and I'll drop the charges. You worked hard for that sergeant's promotion. You can retain that title and your job if you listen to me. I'll tell Internal Affairs I overreacted and our squabble was a misunderstanding. You can be reinstated tomorrow if you sign the custody papers right now."

She was insane. I'd never sign those damn papers and she and Ennis knew it. I yanked on the door handle. Baking in a hot car sounded better than going to prison for murder. The uniforms continued watching the confrontation. Citizens meandered in and out of the station. There'd be plenty of witnesses for the prosecution if I acted on the desire for revenge.

Sheila pushed the door shut, "But if you refuse, I'll bury you. Today is just the beginning."

"Unless you've got a tow truck ready to steal my car too, get your hand off that door."

She didn't move, "Did you hear me? Give up the girls or I will crush you in every way possible."

"Your hand. Now."

Her hand finally retreated, "Remember this conversation. Keep crossing me and you'll lose more than your job and your girls."

Another blinding flash of light mercifully ended the vision. The comfort of a soft bed replaced the heat, humidity and fanatical hussy. I recognized the feel of my own bed. I was home but in what time, the present or future? I kept my eyes closed to listen and analyze my surroundings. For a house normally brimming with children's laughter, their constant chatter and frequent arguing, the place sounded too quiet. No kids. No blaring TV. Nothing but silence. Where were my girls?

Subdued voices at the bedroom door caught my attention. Georgia and Dane. They alternated between low tones and whispers.

"That despicable woman has nearly destroyed her," Georgia said. "A civil suit after having her suspended. If she loses the kids, the house, her savings–"

Dane shushed her, "We're not letting that happen. Between us, Seth, Leah and Ma, we'll figure something out."

Georgia sounded skeptical, "What's your mother planning to do?

Ennis is her son."

"She's flying out to talk with him. Sheila keeps running interference when Ma calls. Cal's coming with her so it'll be hard for Sheila to buck three of us. I intend to be there too."

Long seconds passed. Georgia finally spoke, "What does Ennis see in that woman? He had a good family and turned his back on them. I don't understand."

"None of us do." Dane paused again. "She's really passed out."

Georgia whispered, "She should be. I gave her enough Valium to knock out a rhino. I had to do something. She went crazy when the lawsuit papers arrived. Thank God Seth was here. He's the only one who can physically handle her when she loses control."

"Pretty bad, huh?"

She blew out a breath, "Nearly a rerun of Mama's funeral. Screaming, fighting, flailing. Giving her the Valium was like bathing a cat but she finally relented."

"At least the department took her guns. Less chance of a massacre that way."

"They only took her department guns. You forgot the .38 Special she bought a month before Jeffrey abducted her. She'd given me the combination to her gun safe so I opened it and gave the gun to Seth until things cool off."

"Smart move because Ennis still won't listen. I tried talking sense to him but he says it's Sheila's decision whether the charges are dropped."

"Sheila better back off because Savannah nearly made it out the door twice, vowing to kill 'the bitch' for suing her. If we're not careful we *will* have a murder on our hands." She blew out a breath, "I'm thankful Leah had the girls this afternoon. At least they didn't see their mother lose her mind. Maybe when she wakes up and sees them, she'll settle down a bit."

"You staying the night?"

"Good Lord, yes. Seth and I both are. The kids can't keep her from rummaging the house for the car keys and racing over there to kill Sheila. I'm telling you, Dane, I'd better not see your brother for a long time. He allowed that woman to set Savannah up. He'll probably get the kids and if she loses that civil suit, she'll lose her job and probably her pension."

"She found a lawyer yet?"

"Seth met with one this afternoon. We're splitting the retainer. We'll see where it goes from there…"

The darkness behind my eyelids brightened. I braced myself for the next jump into the future and thoroughly dreading it. I'd probably be on the streets begging for food or worse I'd land in prison, an ex-cop convicted of whatever crime Bennett framed me for. Nothing struck abject fear inside a cop as going to prison.

I'd sit in a six by eight cell equipped with a stainless steel sink and toilet, a steel cot with a thin mattress reminiscent of a gymnasium floor mat, and a metal door with two small portals to the outside world: a small safety glass window and a flap for serving meals. I'd seek refuge in that tiny cell, battling constant claustrophobia, then the second that door opened I'd face another threat. Inmates who knew I'd been a cop. I wouldn't survive a week.

Wherever the mirror sent me, I was lying down. Eyes closed tight, I concentrated on what I heard. No sounds of heavy metal doors slamming and locking shut. No shouting or cursing. No gym mat for a bed. I felt comfortably warm in the silence surrounding me. Soft, thick carpet met my touch. I smelled Italian food – lasagna. I was home. *Really* home now.

Tears sprung to my eyes. Sheila Bennett would destroy my family and steamroll me in the process. And laugh every step of the way.

"Mama, what happened to your cheek?"

Lily bent over me, hands on her knees. Her young upside down image brought the gravity of the situation painfully to heart. Our beautiful girls did not deserve to be pawns. I would not allow it.

I swiped away a tear, flinching at the first touch on my cheek. It ached. For some reason something changed during that last foray into the mirror. In previous visits, injuries (like the gunshot wound to my leg) disappeared upon my return to the present. Not this time. The hot sting of Bennett's powerful backhand lingered, probably as a convenient reminder to keep my cool around her. The trollop's strategic skills far outweighed mine when applied to the darker side of human nature. She'd bulldoze her mother, the Pope, God and Lucifer to get what she wanted. And soon she'd want me gone from Ennis, the girls, my job and, I supposed, life in general.

Lily wanted an answer so I stammered, trying to create one, "I, um, well…"

She kneeled beside me whispering, "You went in the mirror. What happened?"

After what I experienced, I shook my head. I refused to tell this innocent angel what lay ahead of her, of us all as a family – if I failed to fix it. "Nothing good."

Lily placed her cool hand on my flaming hot cheek. The soothing gesture brought more tears to my eyes. I could not, *would not*, lose my girls or my husband to that Jezebel in the dining room.

If anyone questioned the intelligence of a near-five-year-old, they needed to witness my kid. I swore an adult stared back at me when her small hand caressed my cheek. "Don't cry, Mama," she said. "We'll make it okay."

I prayed she was right.

20

Tuesday

The rabbit died. Or as my niece Lindsey so eloquently phrased it with news of Anna's conception, my eggo was preggo. I determined my new condition that morning with two separate tests that bore the same results. An hour later, I sat at my desk, head in hands, my brain spinning with disbelief. If the antique mirror's prediction came true, little Daniel floated in a nice warm cocoon inside me, high-fiving his daddy from afar for his hearty swimmers.

I counted back on the calendar. Ennis and I went a bit crazy once I requalified for reinstatement. That meant my baby bun only measured the size of a gnat's eyelash. Even so, the pregnancy qualified as the strangest. With Lily I harked my guts up enough people at work probably pegged me as bulimic until the pregnancy started to show. With Anna my back hurt as if she'd grabbed my spine with both hands and tried cracking it over her knee. The third pregnancy so far hadn't done much to alert me yet. Sure I puked but those episodes stretched far apart, plus anyone would barf if they'd been in a gunfight. Yes, I felt fatigued and my back tired out quick but a flashing neon sign announcing "Pregnant" it wasn't. The eeriest part – Ennis suggesting I might be knocked up even before I gave it any consideration.

I looked forward to meeting Daniel or whoever occupied that space. Visions of our girls spoiling their little brother brought a tiny smile to my face. Then Sheila marched through the happy family like Sherman through Atlanta, wrecking and ruining, destroying our marriage, putting us at odds regarding custody.

I placed a hand to my belly, imagining the little boy (or perhaps girl) growing inside. I remembered the mirror's version of our future. Sheila. Divorce. A custody war for two girls – Lily and Anna. Not a boy in sight. Not a *third child* in sight. In those peeks into tomorrow, Daniel was never born, not after Sheila entered the picture. A terrifying possibility struck me harder than Bennett's backhand to my cheek. It robbed my breath, briefly stilling me behind the desk. No, *no, NO...* Please no, I prayed, placing a hand to my belly. Not a miscarriage. That, unfortunately, could have explained Daniel's absence in those visions with Bennett. Had I been pregnant with a boy and stress (or Sheila herself) caused me to lose the baby? My mind went wild with notions including one that Sheila physically assaulted me, triggering a miscarriage. The mirror possessed the answers I needed – and I needed them to protect my family. A family that now hopefully included a son.

"You feeling bad?"

I snapped from my daze. Mathis stood at my office door. His girth spanned most of the width until he entered my domain. He peered over his reading glasses, motioned to the hand still cradling my stomach, "You got problems? Your face is white as my shirt."

Which said a lot considering his "white" shirt verged on the grayer side of ash. I peered around his ample form checking for eavesdropping husbands or crazy lieutenants. I crooked my finger at him. He bent closer as I whispered, "I'm pregnant and don't tell a soul. Ennis doesn't know yet."

Mathis's brow drew downward, "Don't you two realize how this is happening? Are you shooting for a world's record or something?"

I ignored the crass comment. "The goal I'm shooting for is getting Ennis away from Sheila Bennett. I don't need a damn divorce on my hands along with carrying a bun in my oven."

Mathis stepped back, temporarily slack-jawed, "You two already talking divorce?"

"No, John. I don't want one but we've all heard about the paths of destruction she leaves behind. Well, except Ennis, of course. She still hung the moon according to him." That ate at me too. After supper Ennis recited Bennett's illustrious career detail by agonizing detail. For me it was like being pecked to death by chickens.

His "heroic" spiel about her caused me a sleepless night and plenty of worries. I'd lost all but one hour that night. That name and face consumed me in my waking and sleeping hours, and especially in the sparse, illogical dreams I mustered during those sixty short minutes.

I slumped at my desk, leaned my head in my hand.

John settled his sizeable self in a chair, "You really do look horrible, kid. No sleep, huh?"

I shook my head, "He brought *her* over yesterday to meet me."

"He told me. So if you're convinced she's moving in on him, what are you planning to do?"

"Besides the obvious that lands me in prison, I don't know."

"Has he officially accepted the job in Zone 5 yet?"

I accessed my top left drawer. Tums, aspirins, Tylenol, antihistamines and Band-Aids. All the helpful items a person might require to limp through a hard day – or deal with a floozy named Bennett. All the helpful items except a bazooka. For a brief moment I entertained searching internet auction sites for rocket launchers or flamethrowers. Then that good old guilt hit, reminding me that seeing Mama behind bars might be a bad influence on the kids. I debated over an aspirin or Tylenol. Maybe in a minute, I decided, then answered John, "According to him, no, but he only has until mid-week next week to commit. Otherwise Christine gets the job – if the rumors are true."

"Rumors," he snorted. "He'll believe anything about sports, news and politics but one rumor backed up by a dozen cops and he rejects it. You married a real weirdo."

"I married a trusting man, that's the problem. He likes Bennett, thinks she's nice, funny and probably easy to work with."

"She's easy alright."

I bowed up – but mildly, "That's not funny, John. I'm getting hives and migraines over this. I'm knocking on the door of a nervous breakdown." From the corner of my eye, I saw Ennis strolling toward my office. That silly smile brightened his face. I also knew who put it there and it wasn't me.

"Good morning, everyone," he basically cheered. Mathis and I returned the greeting with a grumble that dialed down his smile's wattage. His brow dipped, "What's wrong?"

Mathis whispered, "Begins with 'B' and ends in divorce if you're not careful."

I rolled my eyes, thankful Ennis hadn't heard him.

My hubby centered on me, "You not feeling well? You look tired."

Mathis cleared his throat. I shot him a withering scowl that said *don't make this worse than it is*. "Spoken to 'the lieutenant' this morning?" I asked Ennis, hoping to change the subject off my questionable constitution. I'd tell him about the baby in my own time. Depending on his stance regarding a certain superior officer, I'd either present it to him or bludgeon him with it.

All innocent-like, Ennis inquired, "Who? Sheila?"

My lip curled, "Oh, so it's *Sheila* now, is it?"

"Prince," John's cautionary scold volleyed back the *don't make this worse* inference.

I took his advice, toned down the rancor, "How is the lieutenant doing?"

Ennis swung his attention between me and Mathis. He sensed something amiss, "I haven't spoken to her since last night when I dropped her off at her house."

Lurid images of Ennis and Sheila tangled together in the throes of sex squeezed my already cramping gray matter. My right hand instinctively fisted around the pen in it.

Mathis saw it, "There's my cue." He rose to his feet and headed for the door. "You two? You're comin' to blows whether you know it or not. Just make sure you leave a will for the kids." Before ambling away he took a perilous step by preaching, "Better watch those hormones."

And like that, my ally abandoned me. Ennis slid John's chair closer then sat down, "What's he talking about? Hormones and coming to blows?"

I waved it off, "I don't know. He's in one of those moods."

"You seem uptight about Sheila."

Don't get me started... "Just not used to you answering to a female superior officer, I guess."

"I do it every day here and at home."

My husband. The silver-tongued devil. "Really? Is that how you feel? I run roughshod over you?" Superman was faster than a speeding bullet but my tongue was faster than the speed of light. *Oh my God, Mathis is right about the hormones...* Appalled with myself, I uttered an apology.

Ennis sat, stupefied at my outburst. The remnants of his smile disappeared, "I was teasing you," he explained. "Sugar, you honestly look worn out. Let me and Mathis drive the ship today. You take it easy."

As if. "I'll be okay." *If I don't lose my mind first.* Rummaging the top drawer again, I shook two aspirins in my hand and tossed them back with a swallow of water. Good for headaches and preventing heart attacks, the experts said. Those experts must have married a person like Ennis Rutherford because I already suffered headaches and really despised the idea of suffering the other.

"You're not very convincing."

"I got one hour of sleep so if I seem testy about you leaving for Zone 5 and working with some young upstart lieutenant, give me a break."

Mr. Silver Tongue found that humorous, "Young upstart? She's only two years younger than you."

Pregnant or not, no woman took the "age" subject well. "Do I consider that an insult or a compliment?"

My grim expression should have advised him to rein in his fanciful reactions. I guessed his survival instinct took a coffee break because he chuckled, "I've never seen you so jealous."

He really skated on thin ice with me, "Excuse me?"

"Why are you so sensitive about her? Because she's younger and a lieutenant?"

His attempt to diffuse the conversation backfired. It riled me instead of joked me out of my mood. I said nothing and settled for staring at him, daring him to continue.

He did. "Sugar, it's different for her. She's not married and doesn't have kids so she's got time to excel at the job. She spends her off-duty hours at the gym working out and running the treadmill. She kinda reminds me of you before we got married."

Before we got married? Really? My husband tended to suffer from hoof-in-mouth disease. Today it turned into a near terminal case of it. Yeah, I was married and had kids. Last I looked, *he* had plenty to do with both. My off-duty hours consisted of childcare, husband-care, cooking and cleaning but that did not mean I was a flabby, out-of-shape detective. I still ran to stay in shape but I ran around the neighborhood, not at a pricey gym. With his dissertation, he'd hurt my pride and my feelings.

I shot to my feet, fighting the urge to simultaneously explode *and* cry, "Well, good for Sheila. She's driven, young, beautiful and unattached." I marched past him, fully intending to hole up in the restroom for a good cry. Forget the bazooka. I wanted a nuke.

21

Saturday

Monday's good cry repeated itself on Tuesday. Wednesday caused a surprising upheaval of tears both at home and work. Thursday I barely kept a straight face. Hormones and paranoia hijacked my life. Friday was a washout on mood and, like a lot of the week, the case stalled too. Moore gave Mathis the employee list on Monday. We'd scoured his and his salesmen's backgrounds and alibis until the bones were dry and blanched. Trying to get the names of his detail personnel was a whole other story. He'd left that duty to Stan, the master of procrastination, who took his sweet time producing it. By Saturday, Mathis and I put asses and elbows to work on those while Ennis chummed around the station with who? Sheila.

They spent alternate evenings together after work for drinks. When he crossed the threshold those evenings slightly tipsy but far from drunk, I viewed him with a jaundiced eye, wondering if they'd hit the sack yet or not. His suit jacket slung over his arm, his tie always loosened but no lipstick on his collar. As for me and Bennett, we rarely interacted.

Her transfer took effect the upcoming Wednesday – Ennis's transfer would kick in the following Monday if he formally accepted the job. The deadline loomed in three days. She did her best to court him into her lair at Zone 5 (and her bed as well, I guessed), buying him drinks, keeping him out late and calling him at home with cloying, unnecessary reminders that "we need detectives like you at Five".

The constant contact poured fuel to my insecurities. I'd lost so much sleep, I developed dark circles beneath my eyes, my mood sucked and I couldn't concentrate my way out of a simple game of Go Fish. The brightest spot of the week came when we discovered Shane Moore hired ex-cons to do his dealership's detail work. Ex-cons with serious records. Assault and battery, robbery, and *murder.*

Mathis's reaction reminded me of a kid on Christmas morning after seeing all the loot Santa left behind. "We got 'em." He plopped in the chair across from my desk. "This is the jackpot. I can feel it. Maybe Mr. Junk Dealer paid these mutts to wash the cars, vacuum the carpets, steam clean the engines then polish off the Stewarts."

"Reason?"

"Because Joe and Lisa were all over him about his affair with Tessa. Once I braced him about it, he admitted they split the friendship sheets six years ago and the animosity got worse. There was even talk of Stewart filing a lawsuit over property line infringement. The crown jewel? I found out the Stewarts began a campaign with their homeowner's association to fine Moore for planting the wrong trees and installing lights on their tennis court."

"Yeah? Our homeowner's association is picky too but would that be enough to provoke homicidal tendencies toward the Stewarts? If Joe and Lisa hadn't tattled about the trees and lights, some other neighbor would have. No one in that neighborhood likes the Moores as far as I could tell."

With an arrogant lift of his chin, Mathis brushed imaginary lint from his sleeve – at least I thought it was imaginary. "You do realize who the president of the Snob Society was, right? The head of the homeowner's association was Joe Stewart. And he threatened to foreclose on Moore's house for failure to pay last year's dues – and other offenses. Moore's going broke in a hurry, Tessa keeps nagging for cash and her daddy won't take his foot off Moore's neck."

"How long has the homeowner's association's nitpicking and harassment been going on?"

"Six long years."

About the time the boy was born and the affair was exposed. When Mathis first mentioned it, I halfway dismissed the idea of Moore murdering his neighbors. Tessa and Stan stood more to gain – or thought they did until the lawyer probably explained the will. The Stewart's will disproportionately divided the estate's millions. Dr. Bret stood to receive a fourth of a prearranged amount (probably pocket change for him). The remaining three quarters of the allotment went to Tessa. They bequeathed most of their estate to charities and trusts. Not a happy financial ending to Tessa or Stan's cash-strapped dilemma. Problem was no one except the Stewarts and their lawyer knew the will's details. What happened if Tessa or Stan saw a golden opportunity to cash in early on the supposed inheritance?

With this new information, Mathis made me rethink my stance. Moore tolerated constant threats and harassment from not just the almighty homeowner's association but complaints from neighbors as far as five doors down – or had he? No one approved of the lowly Deerwood lotto winner *movin' on up* to Chastain Park. The possibility of losing his home plus having his steadily declining business shrink into near obscurity probably put a lot of strain on Moore's last nerve. Add some tension with that affair and the resulting pregnancy and viola, maybe Shane Moore deserved the VIP seat in the interview room for a while.

"There's the gal I'm looking for."

My lips thinned in exasperation at that voice. They pressed tight to prevent myself from blurting everything from cuss words to death threats. Helping clamp my mouth tight? Memories of Sheila's pals Robbins and Greene and the screwing they gave my career. That was a rerun I planned to skip.

I turned as Sheila sashayed in decked out in a beige pantsuit, a black blouse revealing ample cleavage and waves of thick, dark hair cascading past her shoulders. The fourth Charlie's Angel, complete with a beaming mile-wide Farrah smile that dimmed upon viewing our sour expressions, "Wow. Bad day, huh? Well, cheer up, Sergeant Savannah." She plopped a small English ivy on my desk. Small as in the terra cotta pot measured two inches in circumference and each green tri-lobed leaf was smaller than a dime. Sheila crowed, "Maybe this'll perk you up. Ennis said you'd been under the weather lately. This is a get well gift as well as a thank you for letting me steal your husband most of the week."

Lovely how she called me Sergeant Savannah then added insult to compliment by using the phrase *steal your husband*. And why, in the name of everything holy, did Ennis confess I'd not been feeling up to par?

I stared at her peace offering that stood shorter than the five by seven of my family sitting beside it. Oh, yippee. I rated an ivy. Not such an even trade, I told myself. An ivy for a husband.

I scooted it to the middle of my desk in prominent view. Anyone who asked, I'd tell them with her generosity, big-hearted Sheila Bennett could put Santa out of business. But I held my tongue and made my mama proud. I thanked the smiling bitch for her gracious gift.

Sheila waved it off, "No problem. Ennis said you like plants."

Plants. Not seedlings. "He's right."

Mathis smirked. I, however, found no humor in the moment.

Sheila touched a leaf, "I bet it needs water. Looking sorta droopy."

I'll fetch my eyedropper. "I'll get on that," I stood up, cradled the peewee plant in my palm and hightailed it to the restroom before I collapsed in tears. Again.

Once safely inside, I placed the sprout on the sink and headed for the toilet. A sudden sickness overwhelmed me in those few minutes but it relented once I calmed down. Then I pointed my other end down for a pit stop. Pressing the toilet lever and watching the water swirl down gave me an odd sense of satisfaction. Too bad I couldn't drop a certain woman down there, pull the lever and score a jackpot.

I hung out in the stall a good ten minutes, dialing down the urge to maim that shameless woman. In the midst of wearing off her "thoughtfulness", I heard a continuous knocking on the restroom door. I figured it was Ennis since he'd been known to (in rare fits of mindless concern) barge into the ladies room to check on me but not before annoying occupants with his imitation of a woodpecker first. The person currently rapping on the door gave up, choosing to open it instead, "Hey, Prince. You done with your constitutional?"

Judging by his voice, Mathis leaned in the restroom far enough to rouse complaints from a female officer and an understandably upset civilian who busied herself washing her hands.

"The door's there for a reason, Detective," the female officer griped.

I held my breath, waiting for the backlash of her admonishment. Mathis replied, "Was I talking to you? *Prince?* You still in here?"

"Yes, John. Be out in a minute." I washed my hands then watered my Lilliputian plant, all while wondering what possessed him to poke his nose into the women's restroom.

The female uniform at the mirror applied her mascara then appraised the ivy with the same squinty look – probably because she could barely see the tiny sprig. "Nice, um..." she hesitated, "plant. A gift from your kids?"

I wish. "A lieutenant in Zone 3."

Her brow shot up, "Bennett?"

I nodded, recognizing incredulity when I saw it. She stared at the plant like it was a pot of ragweed now, "Good luck."

"Thanks. I'm gonna need it." I gathered the little thing and opened the restroom door only to come face to face with my older colleague. We stood inches apart until I stepped back, blushing at the weird sideways glances passing officers gave us. Oddly, I felt dumber holding Bennett's green sprout than nearly rubbing noses with John. "What is so important you chase the women from the restroom?"

"I was wrong."

Well, *yeah*. No one enjoyed their restroom visits interrupted – for obvious reasons. "Then next time wait for me to come out."

He stared at me in his unique don't-be-a-smartass manner, "About the case, kid. While you were indisposed, I called Moore to ask him some questions. Remember my first interview with him? He copped an attitude and told me to talk to his lawyer next time?"

Yes, unfortunately I remembered it. We wrote it off to ten percent not wanting to get involved (a broken record cops heard a lot) and ninety percent snobbery.

Mathis continued, "He said the same thing this morning only he used disparaging remarks to describe me as a person."

The gleam in John's eyes warned of repercussions for those "disparaging remarks". If Mathis came face to face with Moore, my friend might do more than "disparage" the dealership owner. Mathis had ways of making people miserable without laying a hand on them. "What did you do, John?"

Mathis straightened his crooked tie, bragging, "The second he pulled outta his driveway, he was mine. I had a uniform pull his ass over and arrest him."

"You *what*?" My stomach dropped. With a hand to my gut (which heard the beckoning call of the toilet again), I swallowed hard. Apparently Mathis went mad while no one was looking – and he expected congratulations for the feat. "So now what? If he gives us attitude we kick his ass six ways from Sunday? John, I can't believe you had him arrested for calling you names." There'd better be more to it than that, I finished, or nuclear explosions paled in comparison to the captain's lecture on legalities and police procedure.

"Yeah, Prince, that's what I do. Arrest people because they piss me off." He rolled his eyes, "This whole Bennett thing's turned you schizo. You know me better than that."

"M-hmm. That's why I asked."

His offense faded to an awkward, "You crucify me over one time?"

"If you hadn't asked *me* to bring the guy in... Mathis, I was a rookie. I trusted you."

"Aw, c'mon. Hunter only yelled at you. He tarred and feathered me."

I could imagine my life as a sergeant with Mathis under my command. Chaos and nervous breakdowns... The reasons for Josh Hunter's gray hair and perpetually frazzled appearance dawned on me.

They both stood right outside the women's restroom, chatting about arresting people. "John, do me a favor. Explain this in small words and convince me Hunter won't tar and feather us both this time."

Mathis sighed, "How's this? Moore had an outstanding ticket from three years ago. I thought the bastard needed to pay his bill."

"So did the president of his homeowner's association," I reminded, "and you see what happened to him." Sometimes I worried about John's outlook on subjects. Arresting Moore for one unpaid ticket? The "unpaid" part *might* save an ass chewing from Hunter however the "one" seemed iffy. Ten unpaid tickets carried more weight. One meant pray and pray hard.

"You want something to really worry about, kid?" He hitched his thumb at my plant, "Make sure your new little buddy ain't poison ivy."

22

Saturday

Moore stormed around the interview room thundering threats and raining down fists on the metal table. He glared into the one way mirror, a red-faced madman, shouting lofty promises that his attorney might have found difficult to fulfill (and some impossible to defend).

Once John told Moore we knew about his affair with Tessa *and* knew about their son, the car dealer went ballistic about his right to privacy and included a generic "you violated my civil rights" as most idiots did. I explained he kept exceptionally mouthy company and information obtained via interviews did not violate his civil rights. As for his privacy, either live right or tell people to keep quiet.

People with Moore's attitude assumed their boisterous rants, offensive words and hand gestures were new, unique and speechlessly shocking to law enforcement. Fact was we saw and heard it all from both genders, in various languages, and every socioeconomic status. Abuse was abuse, an insult an insult and the middle finger meant the same whether the individual made minimum wage or owned a global business. Moore's claim to fame? A lucky draw on the lottery. Five minutes at a Pump & Stop to plunk down a buck for a ticket (his *customary* numbers, he'd said in the newspaper) and moments before Channel 2 Action News aired, Moore and his wife were millionaires. Moore quit his job and "on a whim" bought a car dealership selling brand spanking new Jags and Beemers. He and the wife promptly abandoned the middle class suburb Deerwood for hoity-toity Chastain Park. The nouveau riche, I told Mathis who battled a snarl at my recalling of the Moore family fairytale. He labeled it something less G-rated and reminded me Moore now sold Chevy Commodes and Ford Failures to an unsuspecting public now, not sparkling silver Jags. One year after acquiring the exclusive dealership Moore discovered hustling other rich folk had a price. They boycotted his luxury car racket thus relegating him to specialize in used, less lucrative vehicles.

Moore's tantrum extended from exasperating to outright ridiculous. The ranting and whining rang a familiar bell. I lived with two young hellraisers myself – granted their tirades revolved around toys, not murders, and their vocabulary certainly fell short of Moore's cesspool language – but enough was enough.

I cracked open the interview room door. Moore wheeled from the mirror, his face now a deep, impressive shade of crimson. His face twisted into such rage, I dared not step inside. I took only enough time to level my own ultimatum, "I've got plenty of experience with children so here's the deal. Until you reclaim your decorum, no one will speak with you. That means a very long day in a very small room. Alone."

Another half-hour later he believed me. For two minutes. We were forced to transfer him to another interview room as per Captain Hunter's orders. People at the patrol sergeant's desk complained about the noise and vulgarity. Moore's spectacle wasn't a great community relations advertisement, Hunter said, so *kick him to the back room.* Mathis and I debated over taking our boss literally. Punting Shane Moore through the door of an interview room tempted the most even-tempered cop – which neither of us was.

I grabbed Moore's left elbow, Mathis his right to help expedite our travels from one room to another, this one a usually short thirty feet away. Today we agonized every inch with Moore's hollering louder than a howler monkey in heat. Somewhere the man dredged up a second wind and proceeded to rail at the top of his lungs again. In his ravings, he managed to spit on Mathis who took the accidental assault well for a man blessed with virtually no patience.

Moore guaranteed us that once his attorney finished with us, we'd be on Medicare before we found gainful employment again. This threat – declared with hellfire and brimstone any reverend would admire – rendered the immediate area silent. Officers stood aside, flattened their backs against the wall to let us pass. Josh Hunter poked his head out his office door. I sneered at him, halfway praying he read my mind. Since marrying Ennis I tried refraining from striking a smartass or stubborn suspect upside the head but I really wanted to slap the shit out of Shane Moore and probably would have if I'd still been single *and* we hadn't encountered Ennis and his shadow Sheila Bennett.

Bennett did not look happy. She blocked our path, slipped into her lieutenant's role, "What's the problem?"

She specifically addressed me. I intended to answer only to have Moore intrude with a demand, "I want my phone call. I'm allowed a phone call."

Bennett crossed her arms, ignoring Moore's outburst. "Is this individual under arrest?"

I took offense to her tone. She lifted a brow, waiting for my reply. Meanwhile memories of my rookie year swept in. Hunter reaming me out for not getting the details from Mathis on that "arrest" he'd ordered. The shame of being lied to, of believing Mathis. He'd apologized but it took a long time to trust him again. I was older now and had a family to support. I knew better than to blindly go along with Mathis and his wild ideas. I couldn't jeopardize my paycheck...

"Detective Prince?" Bennett dragged me from the embarrassing past. "Is this individual under arrest?"

I looked at Mathis, expecting a firm, decisive *yes*, not a firm, decisive, "No."

Shock tried to slacken my jaw. We skated on paper thin ice arresting Moore based on one unpaid ticket, particularly without an actual warrant. But outright lying? To a lieutenant no less – and of all the lieutenants he chose to lie to *her?* My head began aching just thinking about IA's forthcoming fiesta as they threatened to use our pensions as piñatas. My brow quirked with the question of the ages. *Have you lost your mind?*

John's lie sent Moore into a hysterical rage, "That's not what the cop said–"

Bennett's piercing green eyes mercifully shifted from me to John, "Then why is he crying for a phone call?"

"Dunno." Mathis shrugged it off, "Had him brought in for further questioning on our case."

"I'm free to go?" Moore took advantage of the strained conversation. "Really?"

Mathis shrugged again, "We'll see after you answer our questions."

Bennett turned to Moore. Her tone sharpened, "Sir, I strongly advise you to calm down, cooperate with the detectives and allow them to do their jobs. You'll find your stay is more pleasant if you do."

"And if I don't?"

Finding my voice, I warned, "I'll charge you with obstructing an investigation."

The corner of Bennett's mouth curled into a shrewd smile, "She took the words right out of my mouth."

With his cherry red face and squinted eyes, he reminded me of a squawking Angry Bird when he mimicked Bennett, "Yeah, *cooperate with the detectives. Allow them to do their jobs.* You mean railroad me? Are you even a cop?"

Bennett's left eye twitched. The cold, penetrating stare evolved to dangerous one – one conveying inner rage waiting to be unleashed on anyone stupid enough to oppose her. "I am indeed, *sir.* My name is

Lieutenant Sheila Bennett. I work out of the Zone 5 station which, if you don't know, is located on Spring Street. If you intend to file a complaint, my captain's name is James Shaw. For the record, it is crude, demonstrative residents like you that make me wonder what the hell I was thinking when I applied to the police academy. But I am sworn to protect and serve everyone in this city and I do so with utmost pride and passion. Remember. Lieutenant Sheila Bennett, Zone 5, Spring Street station. Now, can you remember all that or should I write everything down for you and your lawyer?"

They locked gazes for another several seconds. Bennett never blinked. Not once. Moore, though, closed his mouth and trudged toward our destination, defeated. The Angry Bird had been plucked.

Safely in the new interview room with the door closed, Mathis exhaled long and low, "Geez, she's got a set, doesn't she? Bigger'n mine, probably."

I couldn't care less about her chutzpah or if a set of brass balls really were tucked in those designer slacks. I took John aside – away from the one way mirror and camera – and whispered in his ear, "We lied to her."

"Nope. I did. You froze, remember? Thanks a million for that too."

"She'll probably check it out–"

"Prince," he changed to the abrasive, patronizing Mathis of old, "take a pill. It's okay."

Somehow I doubted that. Bennett appeared less than convinced at John's answers, plus my silence hadn't helped matters. Mathis had no clue about Sheila's capabilities – or reach in the department. All the way to IA. Thanks to my antique mirror, I got the crash course. The woman destroyed lives for a hobby.

Moore also appeared shell-shocked. Bennett's tongue-lashing deflated his bluster to a mere pittance of its former glory. He lumbered to the closest chair, eased into it quiet as a mouse and watched Mathis grunt into his seat and sort paperwork to prepare his questions. Nerves prevented me from sitting. Mathis looked at me then the available chair. I shook my head.

He sighed then fired the first shot at Moore, "Once we wrung the whole employee list from you, we discovered you're not discriminating about who you hire."

"Who? Stan? He needed a job, I gave him one. I can't help that he's lousy at selling cars. I did it as a favor to Tessa."

"I'm not talking about Stan." He sifted the papers until settling on four. Each page had a photo on it. A photo not from the DMV but the Georgia Department of Corrections. Scott Arthur (the only black individual in the group) and Alex Hayes easily passed for ordinary, non-assuming citizens. Upon first glance a person might peg them as married with a mortgage and a kid or two. The third photo revealed a hatchet-faced individual (Blake Hill) whose mug could scare Dracula back to his coffin. Last but not least, Carlos Oritz, a typical, tattooed gang member.

Mathis fanned each page on the table in front of Moore, "I'm talking about voluntary manslaughter, Shane. I'm talking assault with a deadly weapon, four counts of aggravated robbery, and a thing we call larceny."

Bennett shut Moore up but John drained the color from his previously scarlet cheeks. "Wh-wh…" The word bounced inside Moore's mouth once more forming itself good and solid. "*What?*"

"You're a regular humanitarian hiring these guys after what they've done."

I joined in, "Not to mention who they did it to. Blake Hill used his Ford F-150 to run over his girlfriend after she had lunch with a male colleague. Turns out he thought she was stepping out on him." I lifted another page from the table, "And this fella. Carlos Ortiz. He just got tired of taking the Nike Express and helped himself to a brand new Lexus. After an hour long, three county high speed chase he wrecked into a tree. Said he needed a beer. His blood alcohol level was already nearly twice the legal limit." I pointed to a different face, "Scott Arthur isn't exactly an angel either, just ask his ex-wife who needed seven reconstructive surgeries to look like a human again. Not a woman. A *human*."

Moore pushed back in his seat, growing greener by the second. I tapped the next page on the table, "This one's even better. Read what Alex Hayes did to a tourist before he stole the guy's wallet and rental car."

Moore eyed me then gave the page a quick scan. He pressed a hand to his stomach, swallowed hard, "I'm gonna be sick."

I scooted the trash can beside him with my foot, "Live it up. We'll wait."

He held off on doing the Jersey Yodel long enough to swear, "I-I don't hire criminals."

I leaned onto the table, looked him straight in the eyes, "Your payroll says you do. You hire the whole rainbow Georgia DOC has to offer. None of these guys have lightweight records."

"Prince, jailbirds need jobs too," said the detective who'd eat dirt before actually believing that sentence. Mathis believed in chain gangs and prisoners breaking rocks in the blistering sun. After witnessing society's cruelty over the years, I agreed with him on certain points. If he wasn't already dead, I'd have given my right arm to see Jeffrey Holland spend his existence bashing rocks in Atlanta's blazing sauna called summer.

I felt Bennett at the mirror, her emerald gaze boring into the back of my skull. The brass watched interviews for various reasons. I suspected she parked at the mirror to see how Mathis and I handled Moore but also to catch us in a lie about his arrest.

Shaking free of her intrusive and intimidating presence, I focused on Hill to see Moore's reaction to, "Guess what Blake Hill drives, Shane? A two thousand eight white Chevy Cobalt bought at your dealership. Only he didn't pay for it. Records show you did. Was it a down payment for murdering the Stewarts? Did you need out from under Tessa's constant nagging for more money? Thought you'd help her win her own lottery?"

Mathis took over, "Or maybe it was a twofer. Knocking off the head of the homeowner's association removes the thorn in your pocketbook two ways. One, Tessa gets a fat inheritance and you might keep your house – or buy you enough time to gather the cash to pay the dues. Makes sense to me." He looked to me, "How 'bout you?"

I nodded, "Absolutely."

Shane Moore's green tinge blanched. His wide eyes darted across the small room, centered on the camera mounted in the upper right corner. He looked ready to bolt. "I-I didn't buy anyone a car. *I didn't even hire these people.* A-a-and *what?* I didn't knock anyone off *period.*"

"Why doesn't that reaction surprise me?" I asked Mathis. "Oh yeah. Because I hear denials from anyone sitting in that chair."

Moore squared his shoulders. "Listen, the dealership's going to crap. Losing money each month. I'm trying to unload it so while I locate a buyer, I let Stan hire the detailers. The others quit since I couldn't pay them what they wanted. Stan can't sell cars worth a shit but I thought he could find decent detailers for me, certainly not felons. And I don't care what you say. I didn't buy any of those guys a car and no, I didn't have anything to do with Joe and Lisa's murders. I helped Tessa only by hiring her husband, that's it. And the fight with the HOA is over. I paid the dues and fines the other day."

Convenient, I thought. Come into serious cash lately, have you?

"Let's assume my colleague and I are turnips for a minute," Mathis said. "Say we believe you allowed Stan to do your job – because his title don't say *manager* or *owner* anywhere on the deed to that joint. Can you prove you didn't hire them or buy that car for Hill? Cause the signatures read Shane Moore and they look pretty authentic to us compared to your driver's license. While we're at it, where did you magically find the cash for your HOA dues? Tooth Fairy leave it under your pillow?"

"I knew it! I knew you were framing me for this! I knew that bitch cop would let you!" He shouted at the mirror, "Lieutenant Sheila Bennett at Zone 5, Spring Street station, Captain James Shaw! Detectives John Mathis and Savannah Prince, at the freakin' Twilight Zone, Maple Street station, *I want their captain and I want my lawyer!*"

Of course he hadn't said *freakin'*. The word he actually used deserved to have a bar of Dial soap shoved between his molars. I forced myself not to look at the mirror. I sensed Bennett's smile – the vicious one she'd used when demanding I surrender custody of my girls. Moore's "bitch cop" reference was sure to endear him to her in a special "go postal" kind of way – but at least for now the target landed on him and not me.

Mathis kept the ball rolling, "Our captain ain't coming, dummy. You already pissed him off with your girly screams earlier. You want your lawyer? Fine. But if you're so innocent, help us out. Let's play 'what if'. What if you're square with the HOA again? What if you had a perfect friendship with the Stewarts and what if Stan hired those assholes to detail cars like you say? What if he also wanted to kill the Stewarts but Tessa got there first?"

Moore screwed his mouth to the side in disbelief, "What?"

"Well," John continued, "think about it. Stan hires 'em, Tessa takes advantage of their, let's say, 'unique skills'."

Mathis struck a nerve with Moore who straightened in his chair. A slow burn, my brother would have called it and he'd know since he spent his youth perfecting them.

John charged ahead with his scenario, "She probably met them when she dropped by with Stan's lunchbox one day, struck up a conversation with these guys. Doesn't take much to convince an ex-con to fall off that wagon, especially when they see a huge payday ahead." He paused half a beat, "You know, Prince? I think we solved the case." He removed his glasses, nodded me to the door, "Pick Tessa up."

Moore rose from his seat, "Leave Tessa alone."

I stabbed a finger at his chair, "Sit your ass down and behave yourself or that obstruction charge will become reality, lawyer or no lawyer."

He put us on notice, "One more word about me or Tessa hiring those thugs to kill the Stewarts and I swear I'll sue the lot of you. I mean, you're hanging us out to dry. Have you even looked at Stan?"

"Nah," Mathis dismissed the idea. "Rumor has it he's as sharp as a meatball. How's he gonna set up a double homicide? Cause he ain't gonna walk in and blow the Stewarts away himself."

Moore's hands rolled to fists, his breathing hard and deep like a bull about to charge. He enunciated like we were the idiots, not Stan, "Listen to me. Stan hired those guys to work at the dealership. I always run background checks on potential employees and as for Tessa–"

"Hey," I pointed to the chair again while practicing my own

articulation, "Sit. Down. Now."

Reluctantly he eased back down. Between the time he blew his top and my last warning, something clicked in his mind. Odds were he measured the depth of shit he stood in. Neither Stan nor Tessa sat in the police station answering questions. He did. Question was, did he continue harping about suing us or go ahead and cooperate?

To avoid the former, I mellowed my parental tone to a more cordial one, "Keep talking but keep it respectable."

He closed his eyes, inhaled long and slow. "Stan wanted more responsibility and hours for extra money. I let him hire people to wash and detail the cars. It stopped him from asking for an advance on his paycheck at least. He thinks I'm a bank. I mean, I won the lottery. I don't keep winning it." He shoved a hand through his sandy brown hair, "He must have forged my signature on the car papers because I don't buy cars for anyone but me and my wife – or I did until I paid those thieves from the HOA. And I sold what stocks I had to get that cash. I can show you proof."

Now he wouldn't shut up, "Tessa said for the last month Stan stays two hours after closing – until ten o'clock – then goes home. I mean, what's the point?"

"The detail guys stay after hours too?" Mathis again.

Moore's hands turned palm up in an "I don't know" gesture. "Tessa mentioned Stan got along with them. Go figure, right? He can't stand his in-laws but he chats it up with felons."

"I'll check it out," I told Mathis so while he wrapped up the interview, I made my way toward my office, passing the observation room door. It opened as I breezed past. "Hey," Ennis leaned out, gave me a thumbs up, "good work."

"Thanks. I'm checking on the Felonious Four. See where they're living these days."

Sheila Bennett peeked out the door, "Nice job, Detective. Keep this up and Sergeant Savannah is in your near future."

So were a couple of other significant events. My husband's adultery, our divorce, their marriage and the fight of a lifetime…

23

Saturday Afternoon

One call to the Foursome's parole officer garnered their addresses. Another call, this one to the dealership, yielded the fact they weren't working that day since business slowed to a crawl.

Mathis joined the parole officer in rounding up the four ex-cons. My overbearing colleague used the pregnancy against me to keep me locked between the walls with Ennis and his newfound buddy Sheila. Her chummy façade sickened and disheartened me. I considered her deceptively appealing smile, the feather-light brushes on his arm and persuasive words falling from her soft-spoken honeyed voice to be the beginning cracks in our marriage. She waged a silent war, one she assured herself she'd win because wives were easy to intimidate and/or eliminate. Soon she'd see me as a threat, just another basic hurdle in her race to bed every married male in the detective division. But unlike the other wives, *this* one carried a badge. I presented a unique problem. Cops didn't easily intimidate so how did she plan to keep me quiet about their affair? The mirror never showed me that important detail. I'd have to watch my back while suppressing the urge to plunge a knife into hers.

After a long, tense wait, Mathis located half our payload of parolees. Ortiz and Hayes – The Grand Theft Duo I called them. Unfortunately knife happy Scott Arthur wasn't home. On their last stop, Mathis found Blake Hill (Mr. Chevy Cobalt), the Don Juan convicted of mowing down his girlfriend. Not content to obey three armed police officers, Hill dashed for his tiny apartment window, threw it open and aced a jaunty swan dive from the second story and got away – but not before leaving something behind. A cell phone.

Mathis returned with his trophy, leaving the parole officer scratching his head over what went wrong with his ex-cons. John alerted the patrol division to keep an eye on the two apartments and to pick up Hill and Arthur if they saw them.

Trolling the phone's previous calls we noted several made to one mystery number. Few things sparked a detective's interest more than seeing a parolee repeatedly dial one number. A flurry of calls started weeks before the Stewart homicides then slowed to a trickle a couple of days afterward.

I slipped on my glasses, opened the folder listing our suspect's phone records, including the Moores and Tessa and Stan Campbell. I cross-referenced Hill's number to everyone else's in this case. No match. I ran the mystery phone number expecting it to be a burn phone like Hill's. Surprisingly a name popped up. "Pete Modica?"

Mathis jotted the name, "No burner phone? I lost that bet."

The name sounded familiar to me. It nagged at the back of my brain like trying to recall obscure song lyrics. The old gray matter kicked in while I typed Pete's name into the computer, "That's it. The Atlanta Crackers."

Mathis thumbed through his own copy of our suspects and their phone records, "The Quackers?"

I removed my glasses, pinched the bridge of my nose. Did he ever really listen to me? "Mathis, you truly need a hearing aid."

He frowned, "Why would I need a hand grenade?" A second later a bemused, crooked grin curled his mouth.

Mathis and joking went together like vodka and tightrope walking. Sighing, I tried again, "The Atlanta *Crackers*, not Quackers, was a baseball team many years ago. I'm running the address registered to the phone."

"Allow me. It'll make up for the hand grenade comment." John rounded my desk, leaned over to hunt and peck the number into the computer. "Pete Modica. 521 Capitol Avenue Southeast."

I groaned, "That's not a residence. That's Atlanta-Fulton County Stadium. The Crackers played there until nineteen sixty-four. This is crazy. Using a deceased player's name and the address of the stadium where he played."

"How the hell do you know this baseball stuff? And why?"

"Seth is a true blue fan. He can quote chapter and verse about the Crackers and the Braves day and night. He's a walking encyclopedia."

"And you remembered those names?"

I nodded, unsure if he was amazed or skeptical. Since childhood my brother rambled in an endless loop over his favorite teams, listing ERAs, RBIs, HRs, SOs and everything short of M-O-U-S-E. His exhaustive recitation caused my eyes to glaze over and my brain to shift into neutral but his nonstop chattering finally paid off. I now appreciated my brother's obsession a little more.

"You really need a hobby, kid. One that doesn't involve baseball or sitting in the floor with toddlers singing *the wheels on the bus go round and round.*"

I chose to ignore him. Yes, it was redundant but the girls loved it, it was catchy and its biggest attribute? It was one song I never forgot the lyrics to. "Maybe we can tear Ennis away from his obsession with Zone 5 long enough to check into how Modica pulled a Lazarus and got himself a cell phone. In the meantime, let's check the GPS on Hill's phone. Maybe the genius left it on for us and we can see where he's been."

O   O   O

Baseball. True blue fan. I'd used the phrase to describe Seth's passion for the game so why did it keep nagging me like a low level ache in the back of my mind? Something a person couldn't quite shake but also not put a finger on. A subject I'd heard lately but couldn't place where. Ugh. I hated getting older. Grandma Culberson said one of the keys to happiness was a bad memory. If so then why the hell wasn't I euphoric by now? Probably because my job depended on having decent recall.

I closed my eyes, grumbling the basic words that got me into this obsessive mess. Baseball. Fans. Teams. History. Memorabilia. Wait... Hold that thought. Memorabilia...

Taking my time, I walked back through my conversations in the last few days, the ones at home, the ones at work, the interviews with Bret and Nicole. *Nicole, the waitress at the Farm House Restaurant.* Bullseye, baby. I remembered the gist of her statement being – *He spends money on old baseball trinkets. Some defunct team no one's heard of since The Great Flood.*

"Look," John handed me a computer printout. His enthusiasm sparked hope we hadn't rolled snake eyes with Hill's cell records.

The dates, times and locations of those calls. Fate gifted us with a trifecta. If we could find Blake Hill, he had tons of explaining to do.

"That's no coincidence," I said, still riding high on my epiphany. "According to these he was *on* Pineland Road before and after the murders. Listen, we've got a few minutes to squeeze Ortiz and Hayes for info. I have a good idea who Pete Modica is."

"I ain't gettin' the two boxes of éclairs, am I?"

"If I'm right, 'fraid not. But I'll buy you one to celebrate if I'm right. Deal?"

We shook on it. Mathis stepped aside, "Lead the way, Sarge."

The dialogue with Ortiz and Hayes started rough. Neither said a word except to look at each other, shrug and occasionally smile.

I tried a different approach, "And you speak English?" Of course they did. Otherwise, why would they taunt me with those smiles? One more try, "*Hablas ingles? Sprechen Sie Englisch? Parlez-vous anglais?*" That pretty much ran the gamut of my foreign language skills except for the more colorful phrases schools never taught. *C'mon guys,* I complained inwardly, *work with me.*

They looked at each other again and chuckled. I did not find any humor. "Okay, then listen up. You heard what I said earlier and apparently understood it so tell me about Blake Hill's phone. Who gave it to him? Who did he call and receive calls from? Give me something or you'll be spending Christmas back in Norcross. I'm trying to help you guys so how about helping me?" Lame attempt and probably hopeless but worth a shot anyway.

Ortiz leaned across the table, "You screwin' with us? You cops'll toss us back no matter what we say. I have a crap job but it pays for my food and rent and I'd like to keep it."

I rolled my eyes, "And you *can* keep your crap job or find another one if you explain Blake Hill and the mystery man on the phone he called."

Hayes crossed his arms, snorted, "Ain't no mystery, lady. The last month or so the boss and Blake stayed in close contact during work and off hours using those dinky idiot phones."

He flinched when Ortiz stabbed him with his elbow, warning in a Cheech & Chong accent, "Hey man, what the hell you doin'? Cuttin' our throats?"

"C'mon, we didn't do nothin'. We didn't have a burner phone and we weren't up the boss's ass. Blake and the boss spent all their time talking baseball. Always the Braves and some team I've never heard of before."

Ortiz continued to sit in disbelief that his compadre sold out so quick. I urged Hayes to remember the team name. He thought for several seconds when Ortiz blurted, "What the hell. The Crackers. It was the Crackers. I mean, how racist is *that?*"

"You keep saying 'the boss'. Who is it?" Mathis asked to be absolutely sure despite the fact we already figured it out.

Mr. Ortiz put the cherry on our day. "Stan Campbell the Gopher Guy."

Mathis and I conferred outside the interview room. He shook his head, "We got the name and two witnesses with records to verify a few conversations about baseball. Not exactly a homerun, kid. How we gonna prove Stan's the brains, such as they are, behind the murders?"

"Bring Stan in, John. Tell him we have more questions about the Stewarts. Get him here then you work on him. If anyone can get him to talk, you can."

Mathis gave his tie an impromptu primp then buttoned his suit coat, "My pleasure, Sarge. Once we prove Stan's the chump who arranged the murders, he'll be singing The Wheels on the Bus Roll Directly to Prison."

O   O   O

I'd never met Stanley Campbell but I'd seen his DMV photo and watched the silly TV ads for Moore's Quality Cars. Thirty of the most excruciating seconds of my life occurred when Stan traipsed out in a giant gopher costume declaring "Don't go in the hole to buy a car!" I told Ennis at the time it took guts, blackmail or total desperation to subject himself to such ridicule because I'd only do that to save my family from starvation.

An up close and personal view explained why Shane Moore recruited Stan for his commercials, corny as they were. For all his personality shortcomings (and when he wasn't parading around in a gopher getup), Stan's looks far outshined Moore's. Not a knockout by any means but ladies probably considered him nice looking and the men didn't feel threatened. A win-win for the boss.

Stan's demeanor suggested Mathis used his softer side to lure this catch, instead of slapping cuffs on him and dragging him into the station kicking and screaming (à la Shane Moore). I, along with everyone else inhabiting the building, was grateful.

I watched John's interview from the observation room. Ennis and Sheila left earlier which escalated my paranoia to unfathomable proportions. I called him, praying he didn't answer the phone panting or scrambling for excuses why my call nearly went to voicemail. He hadn't. He explained they went to the Zone 5 station to meet with Captain Shaw. To shake hands on his transfer, I assumed though he never actually confirmed my suspicion.

Adding to my frustration, Stan exhibited a surprising cool

confidence I hadn't expected. Crossing his arms, shooting back denials at
Mathis. Here we go again, I thought. Another brick wall. Until we
connected the Pete Modica phone to Stan or got a confession, we worked
on circumstantial evidence and hearsay because I figured he chucked that
phone after the murders.

A loud slam shattered my concentration. Stan's fist pounded the
metal table with a Moore-like flair. Difference was Moore didn't flinch
afterward, Stanley did. I had a feeling beneath his bluster and passable
looks resided an overly timid man, otherwise how had Moore suckered
him into wearing that stupid gopher costume? I studied Mr. Campbell
through the mirror, analyzing the man's posture and reactions. At one
point, he started chewing his nails then stopped, slanted a narrow glance
at the mirror as if sensing my presence. Faint dewy perspiration gleamed
at his hairline and his eyes blinked the telltale S.O.S. that any trained
detective recognized. His nerves ran the way of my hormones – full
speed ahead with no stops in between. No matter what his mouth said,
Stan teetered closer to breaking.

He denied forging Moore's signature and providing Blake Hill
with a set of wheels. But time ticked by and the sheen of sweat glistened
brighter under the room lights until he wiped a hand down his face.
Beneath the table his right leg bounced up and down in a frenetic steady
rhythm.

He ignored John's accusation that he created a fake cell phone
account with the name of a long deceased baseball player. He refused to
admit he received numerous calls from Hill during the days leading up to

the murders and three times the night the Stewarts died, the last two in the critical window when the neighbors saw the Chevy Cobalt at the curb. The first call registered at 8:45, the last two at 9:25 and 9:34. Moore's company computer records showed Stan logged off at 9:41 and set the building's alarm system. At 9:57 he left the dealership. Security cameras verified Stan driving off the lot at 10:00.

We approached a critical time in the interview. The one where we either kept hammering, hoping Stan might tire of the questions and of sitting in that chair, getting hungry, frustrated and/or angry – then confess. Or we backed off to regroup. I voted for getting creative.

The observation room door opened. Josh Hunter came in holding a manila folder, "Phone records and GPS on Pete Modica's cell." He handed them over, watched a minute of Mathis spinning his wheels with Stan, "Not going well, is it?"

I glanced over the calls. As with Hill, only one number was ever dialed. Blake Hill's. Incoming calls: Blake Hill only. The GPS, though, proved the gem we longed for. Every call made came from the dealership's location. Not exactly rock solid evidence but enough to work with. I answered Hunter, "Actually, things are looking brighter now. Thanks for the help."

"Anything to wrap up this mess. Well, not *anything*. You know what I mean." He headed to the door, "Give me an update later."

"You're first on the list." Now I could move things along. Mathis carefully avoided certain details of the investigation, namely that we'd missed nabbing two of the paroled car washers, particularly Blake

Hill. That gave me a wild idea (and I blame the hormones for it). Since Stan hadn't met me, I figured my plan might stand a chance of succeeding.

I left the observation room, headed to the uniform officers' desk area. I located Officer Miles Raynor, exactly the fella I needed. Mid-twenties, clean cut with NBA basketball height, Raynor busied himself at a desk, filling out a report.

"You still bring that briefcase to work with you?" I asked him.

He looked up, mildly confused at the odd question, "Yeah. Why?"

"Mind if I borrow it? Won't take twenty minutes and I'll have it back to you."

He shook his head, "I don't mind." He rose from his seat, his beanstalk physique towering at least seven inches over me. I felt like one of Snow White's dwarfs against his Jolly Green Giant. Raynor looked intimidating but he possessed a soft-spoken, courteous nature reminding me of Ennis. He asked, "You need the combination too? I can take out my study material for my night classes."

"Nope, just the case is fine. Oh, and can I borrow your pen and a slip of paper real quick?"

I jotted a note before we headed to the locker room. On the way I spied another uniform officer that possessed a talent I sought. Officer Debbie Parsons, the officer who commiserated with me over Bennett's ivy in the restroom. She stood shorter than me, had cute features and her hair done in an elegant bun. I waved her over, "I love your hair. Would you do mine?"

Fifteen minutes later, I was set. I stood in front of the locker room's mirror while my impromptu hairdresser put the finishing touches on my brand new bun. She rivaled Georgia on expertise and speed. I buttoned my gray suit jacket halfway, "Convincing?"

Parsons stepped back appraised my outfit with a stylist's keen eye. She motioned to my blouse, "Mind if I..." .

I nodded her to go ahead. Once I explained my odd requests to them, both wanted every detail perfect too. Raynor unlocked his briefcase on the off-chance I needed it. Parsons kept tweaking my hair and attire.

She unbuttoned my black blouse one more button, left the jacket as is, straightened the shoulders a tad then handed me the briefcase. She still wasn't happy. "Don't you wear glasses?"

"For reading, yes."

She nodded for me to try them. I slid them on. Parsons reached up, pulled the specs down my nose a bit. "Look," she nodded to the mirror.

I did and was amazed. Ennis really went for this look in the past. He called it the "sexy librarian". I decided to resurrect it soon to keep the home fires burning and keep Bennett at bay.

I smiled at my fashion whiz, "This might actually work. Thanks a million, you two." I handed her my gun and phone for safekeeping and pocketed my badge. "Y'all wish me luck."

Raynor nodded, smiled. Parsons waved me out the door, "We'll be watching from the observation room."

On the way to the interview room, I reviewed my plan and heard John's discontent carrying through the closed door. People walking by gave the immediate area a wide berth – and my appearance a cock-eyed glance. No, I never revealed that much cleavage or wore my glasses John Mathis style but to be convincing I needed every shred of help for this charade.

I grasped the doorknob, preparing my intro and gathering my courage to face Mathis, the man who verbally deep fried people of the profession I imitated.

One... two... three... I barged into the room. The unexpected interruption cut John off in mid-sentence.

His vision snapped to me. I swore he fought between bawling me out for intruding or letting his jaw drop in speechless shock. He chose stunned disbelief while his vision trailed from my glasses to my revealing cleavage and finally settled on the briefcase. "What the hell..."

"I want my client released immediately," I demanded. To punctuate it, I slapped the folded handwritten note on the case folder in front of him, "My client's name – in case you forgot. I *printed* it especially for law enforcement."

By his frown, he did not appreciate the last comment. His mouth twitched. Oh, he wanted to shoot a sharp comeback at me. Once he viewed the message reading *Sock it to me*, he understood. "Sorry, Counselor," he crumpled the note in his fist, pocketed it. "Where he's going, that fella'll need a candle to remind him what light looks like."

If he asked me what firm I worked for I'd say "Allen & Allen" (which was located somewhere on this continent) but his mood indicated he didn't give a shit where this bold lawyer came from – however, he'd be happy to tell her where to go, "So I assume you're representing both those idiots?"

"He's not an idiot and he's my only client – *so far.* If you cared to check, his record is squeaky clean since his parole. You and your department are not railroading that young man on a double homicide. I promise you that."

At the beginning of our exchange, Stan's disinterest rated ten on the scale. By the conclusion of my Law & Order-worthy declaration, Stan's cheeks drained of color. The nervous little man inside him slowly emerged.

Beside the folder I saw Hill's cell phone sealed in an evidence bag. I reached for it, "He said you took his phone. Is that it?"

Mathis slapped his meaty hand over it before I got a chance. "That phone is evidence, Counselor. No touching." He smiled at me. Not a friendly smile either. His eyes flashed with unspoken promises of bodily harm if this bold "attorney" pushed her luck.

Which I immediately did, "I want an inventory of every item you people removed from his apartment." I leaned a tad closer, "And if you leave even one lint ball unaccounted for–"

"Get out of here," he stabbed a finger at the door. "You have no business in this room. Lemme deal with my schmuck and you deal with yours. Go wet nurse your client. Tell him he won't feel a thing when

they slide that needle in his arm on Judgement Day. Unless they miss
the vein, that is."

Act or no act, I heeded his tone – but not before blistering him
with my own glare. I about-faced to the door when I stopped with a
sidelong glance at Stan. "Hey, aren't you the gopher guy on TV?"

Oh my God, Mathis complained under his breath.

I proceeded, "Selling those broken down heaps, I bet you'll need
my services pretty soon. Here, take my card." I reached toward the
briefcase latch, waiting for Mathis to lose his cool. It did not take long.

"*Out,* Counselor," he rose from his seat, "Or I'll help you out."

Leaving now, I took only enough time to grumble in a most
unflattering inflection, "Cops."

The moment I closed the door behind me, I pressed an ear to it,
listening. Had I overplayed it or had Stan taken the bait? I wanted a
confession, not a cat and mouse game. Stan Campbell made the world
believe he verged on stupid when in fact he planned and orchestrated two
murders. Two very brutal murders. I wanted to bag this asshole and
ship his sorry butt to the far corner of the nearest prison.

In the interview room, Mathis cranked up in rare form, "You
know how an apple and a lawyer are alike, Stan? They both look good
hanging from trees."

"Was she talking about Joe and Lisa?" Stan asked.

I barely heard Mathis who lowered his voice to a hush-hush tone.
Hush-hush for Mathis meant anyone within five feet heard him. I fell
into that category. "I'm not supposed to say, Stan," my colleague began.

"But between you and me, yeah, that's who she was talking about. What that broad don't realize is, her client spent an hour turning stool pigeon on his cohorts. She's wasting her time. The guy's bound for the death chamber."

"What do you mean 'his cohorts'?" Stan turned very chatty – and concerned – all of a sudden. And plenty interested in "my client".

"That's what I've been trying to tell you, Stan, and your IQ falls short on reach. I'll give it one last try. Your secret cell phone and the phone calls leading up to the murders, plus the rash of calls after Joe and Lisa were killed. The broad's client is pinning everything on his partner in crime and *you*. He said you're the head honcho of the whole thing."

I imagined Stan's mouth fell open into a dark, gaping cavern. "B-b-but I didn't kill anyone. Surely you've checked my alibi."

"Yeah, yeah. We know you left work at ten the night of the murders. Still doesn't change the fact you paid these guys to kill your in-laws."

"With what? I'm broke! Haven't you checked my bank account?"

"Sure. We checked your financial records. No weird activity, no large amounts of money withdrawn, yada, yada, yada. But there are other ways to pay people. We know that."

Yeah, we knew that but we didn't know how Stan paid the guys.

"Such as? Listen, I'm scraping by as it is. I need every penny I make or I wouldn't be working at that stupid dealership. What's he saying I supposedly paid him with? Good wishes?"

"Can't tell you that, Stan. I'd get in trouble with my boss if I did. Fact is, the broad's client is the only one talking and she'll let him yammer till his tongue falls out as long as he gets immunity."

"But what about me?" Stan nearly shouted. Nervous Stan evolved to Fearful Stan. The one I predicted might make an appearance before day's end.

"Since you've been here, you shut tighter than a clam's ass at high tide. You'll be spending your days behind razor wire and hiding from sleazy guys the size of small planets wanting to play a whole different version of Cornhole. Keep your keister against the wall and you'll be fine. At least that's what I hear – but I have been known to be wrong."

I hurried into the observation room. As promised, Parsons and Raynor watched at the mirror. We returned our respective properties – I retrieved my phone and .38 then handed Raynor his briefcase – while the two offered congratulations on my performance. I hadn't anticipated the kudos nor the sight of Ennis and Bennett also standing at the mirror to watch the show. Ennis offered an exuberant high five. I halfway expected Bennett to offer another pocket-sized plant.

She swiveled from the mirror, arms crossed, "I underestimated you, Detective."

Why did that sound ominous? "How so?"

"Going to these lengths to mislead a suspect? You're toeing a thin line."

Boy, I thought. She flipped her Bitch Switch quick. She put me on notice in front of my husband and two other cops. Parsons and

Raynor politely excused themselves.

For the last few hours, I stewed and obsessed over her and Ennis being alone so much for days on end. *Now* she questioned my methods of closing homicides? Mathis was right. Her set of balls put any man's to shame. Slipping my badge and phone on my belt, I calmly squared off with the lieutenant, "What's the problem? There is no law saying we can't mislead a suspect. Are you saying you've never done that?"

Ennis stepped between us, drawing out a laid back, "Sheila, give her a break..."

That teed me off. "There's no break to give. I did nothing wrong."

He eased me back a step while he pled my case, "We've been bogged down on this case for over a week. Pressure from city hall, the chief, it's been—"

"After that spectacle you think you deserve a position of authority," Sheila pressed, ignoring Ennis's presence.

This inquisition could mean only one thing. "Are you on the oral exam board?" The gravity of that question hit me harder than Bennett's slap during the mirror's grim preview of my future. If she sat on the exam board, my aspirations of sergeant vanished quicker than Parsons and Raynor when they vacated the room.

Sure enough the glint in her eye said she smelled blood in the water, "I'm friends with two captains on the board."

Captains. Code for "conquests". Voices in the other room raised in volume and intensity. I cut my eyes to the window to see Mathis on his feet, leaning over the table and shaking his finger at Stan. Campbell pressed back in his seat, weathering his dressing down better than the female detective in the adjoining room. Stan gaped in bewilderment at John, as if a cop wasn't allowed to shout at a citizen. Mathis temporarily suspended his tirade, his scarlet complexion darkening while he huffed and puffed Big-Bad-Wolf-style at Campbell. Stan took that moment to refute whatever Mathis said then added fuel to the fire by wagging his own finger at John.

Someone better get in there and separate them before Mathis kills this guy. I turned to leave, to go save Stan from Mathis and Mathis from a coronary.

"Savannah, we're not done." Sheila's voice dropped to that antagonistic tone from the mirror's vision. "Mathis can fend for himself. Now, I'm asking you one last time. Do you believe you deserve a promotion and do you condone what you and Detective Mathis did?"

"Yes and yes." I tried moving Ennis aside to avoid speaking around his shoulder. He refused to budge so I proceeded, "For the record John is blameless. This was my idea alone." *In case you intend to lynch him alongside me... And for the record, I've got Fifty Shades of Bitch too and she doesn't play nice either so watch it.*

"Didn't look that way to me and I guarantee Captain Hunter would agree. The first rule of supervising is that your detectives' actions reflect on you and yours reflects on them."

I'm sorry, I wanted to say, *do I look like a member of the 40-Watt Club to you?* The old Savannah would have lunged already but sergeants weren't awarded the title using their best roundhouse. And now, for some silly reason, I *really* wanted the promotion so no amount of goading would bait me into belting her.

A quick look revealed Mathis and Stan both on their feet yelling at each other. My impatience erupted, "My colleague is alone in there with a livid, desperate, *unpredictable* individual. I'm not letting Mathis drop of a stroke because you want to grill me right now. I'll talk to you when I put those two in their corners."

I'd grabbed the doorknob just as Mathis shouted "sit down" at a decibel South Florida heard him. Stan obeyed. He sank into the chair, shoulders slumped, head in hands. I leaned against the door and finally breathed. One disaster averted, one more to go... "Lieutenant, if you have a problem with me, feel free to bring it to Captain Hunter's attention. I stand by what I did and believe it or not, I did it on my own."

Ennis joined the argument, albeit in a less heated way, "Sheila, our boss doesn't have a problem with Savannah's work." He made solid eye contact with her, "And don't threaten her or her career. She's my wife and I won't tolerate it. I haven't committed to transferring yet so if this is how you supervise your people, I'll stay here."

Seconds drew out. Bennett contemplated her next move, staring. Scrutinizing.

I held her steady gaze with my own but inside I rioted. What was she thinking? *Planning?* Was this her first step to having me fired?

Bennett's mood flip-flopped from accusatory to careful

consideration, "Actually, I will have a word with Hunter."

I stiffened, bracing myself for the battle ahead. Step one. Round up the witnesses. Step two. Get a delegate that hopefully hasn't been in her pants.

"I want you both as a package deal. I'll talk to Hunter and find out the earliest date he can replace you," she said.

"What?" was the extent of my current conversational abilities. She wanted Ennis *and* me? Together? Working with her?

She finally smiled, "Savannah, I could use you over at Five. You're loyal to your people, skillful and creative, you take chances and you're not afraid to buck the brass. I want you on my team."

Ennis appraised my stunned expression. Neither of us expected that bombshell but he jumped right on board, "That'd be great. We could still work together." He asked Sheila, "If she made sergeant, though, would she be able to stay at Five?"

She tossed a confident wink at me, "I know someone who could make it happen."

I'll bet she did. But before Ennis pictured our little trio being cozier than a Norman Rockwell Christmas card, I burst his bubble, "I'm fine here, but thanks for the offer."

Ennis deflated. Sheila gave him a subtle *I'll handle this* nod then in her annoyingly graceful stride while approaching me. Her arm slid across my shoulders and squeezed them accordion style, "I'm pretty persuasive when need be and I won't be happy till I get my way. I'll go ahead and talk to Hunter and you think about it." Another squeeze,

"Think *seriously*, okay?"

I'd rather crawl naked through a mile of barbed wire than have her hug me up so I nodded to appease her.

She mercifully retreated toward the door, "Excellent. Hey, let's go for drinks after your shift. We can talk about it then."

"Can't," I said. "I'm picking up the girls from school."

"Then I'll take Ennis out and he can drink on your behalf. We'll chat about how to pull off this threesome." She looked to him, "You up for that?"

Why did everything she said sound sexual? And of course her suggestive expression drove those supposed innocuous words deeper into my insecurities.

And *of course* Ennis answered, "Count me in." He signed up for tossing back firewater with her while his wife collected their offspring and took them home to feed them. Somehow the arrangement lacked two important aspects. Common sense and fairness. On second thought, spending the evening hearing about the kid who ate glue and the one who carried on a conversation with his thumb sounded better than sharing drinks with Lieutenant Easy Lay. To be honest, I'd had enough of spending evenings without him. It was time my hubby shared our supper table again… "But hon," I used my sweet voice, "we have that thing at church tonight."

"What thing?" he asked.

Days ago we'd discussed the "thing" at church which consisted of an evening social for kids and their parents. Like a Baptist block party.

At the time Ennis and I decided to skip it. A sudden resurgence for mingling with our religious brethren and sistren struck me with a genuine Bible-thumpin' epiphany – just long enough to pry that bitch away from Ennis, "You don't remember? Two weeks ago at Bible study?"

He struggled to recall the evening in question so I verbally nudged him, "The Parent Council's Family Night Dinner? After Lily's tantrum, I think we should attend. That way everyone will think we're normal parents and not training our kid for the Golden Glove championship." To tilt the situation in my favor, I released my hair from the tight bun, shaking the waves loose again. Ennis preferred my hair down and I needed every weapon in my womanly arsenal to combat Sheila. Indeed, the move inspired him to fuss with the waves, smoothing them into order.

A mocking smile touched her lips. I didn't care if she was onto me. "It's kinda like a PTA meeting at church," I explained. *Y'know, family business. No homewreckers allowed, that sort of "thing".*

Bennett humored me, "Sounds very... spiritual. I'm sure he'll have fun."

Ennis's brow suddenly dipped, "But I thought we decided not to go."

"That was before Lily lost her temper in class," I reminded. "Sorry, babe. But there'll be other nights to have that drink." *Mark it on your calendar the day pigs fly...*

"You're right," he conceded. "Maybe we should go. I'll pass on drinks, Sheila. Thanks anyway."

She shrugged, "Well, another night then. You can grab a babysitter and the three of us can throw back a few together. And Savannah, think about my offer. I don't give up easily. When I want something I get it." She winked, "Keep that in mind." She stepped toward the door then turned back. "One quick thing. Just for kicks, was Shane Moore really under arrest? Mathis said he wasn't but," she hinted, "you didn't seem convinced."

Ennis stunned me by saying, "Mathis doesn't lie to other cops."

He and I both realized he did – but Bennett refused to accept his answer. He wasn't stupid. He realized where the conversation headed.

Sheila leaned closer with a secretive, "C'mon, just between you and me. He wasn't, was he? Mathis didn't have cause or a warrant to arrest him but he did anyway, didn't he?"

Between you and me, huh? Riiight... I scrambled for a suitable response that prevented me and Mathis from being skewered by Internal Affairs. My mouth opened to speak when the interview room door slammed open. It smacked Bennett squarely in the ass. She jumped out of the way, rubbing her rump that suffered a rather brutal shot from the door handle. She tossed a glare at Mathis who bulled into the room, ignoring the fact he'd smashed a lieutenant with the door.

Like a man who'd matched every lotto number he waved the Stewart case folder while literally dancing across the floor, "We did it, kid, and we did it together. With your plea peddler act and my polished persuasion, he's dead meat."

No witnesses. That was my first thought. We had no witnesses to John acting goofy and boogieing his fat self around the room. Not a soul would believe us if we told them. Frankly, society wasn't prepared for this John Mathis, not his Jackie Gleason grin, twinkly-eyed giggle or dorky little dance. Our girls would have doubled up in hysterics. Hell, *anyone who knew him* would have. And Bennett wanted me to give *this* up? Not on her life.

Only one thing explained his uncharacteristic mood. "You mean Stan actually confessed?"

And just like that, Regular Everyday Mathis replaced Jolly Old St. Mathis. "What? You missed it? Were you gettin' a pedicure?"

No, I was being cross-examined by a lieutenant not even assigned to our station. "The lieutenant and I were having a discussion at the time." A discussion involving possibly drawing and quartering her two favorite detectives...

"He told me he let Blake Hill and Scott Arthur keep the money in the Stewart's safe as payment. Musta been ten or fifteen grand or so, he said. Also, and I'm rather proud of this fact, I pried the location of the murder weapons from him too. We're looking for a shotgun, a 9mm and a butcher knife."

The revelation rendered us all mute. Even Bennett paused coddling her kiester for several seconds. Mathis took advantage of the silence, "It's an abandoned elementary school in Zone 1." He handed me the address, "He said we might even find the guys there since Arthur's brother is in the Black Mafia. He's been known to hide out there so maybe Hill's with him."

One look at the address caused me to flinch. The old school resided in not just gang territory but an area where three gangs constantly warred – but the Black Mafia was by far the biggest.

Bennett and Ennis bantered back and forth about the break in the case while Mathis pulled me aside, "You're staying here while Ennis and I search for those weapons."

I bowed up at his bossy attitude, "Like hell I am." I regretted telling him about the pregnancy already. The Stewart case was only my second since returning to work. I fought too hard on it to bounce myself from it – or be bounced by well-intentioned males.

John's vision dropped to my belly, "Geez Prince, you know why you need to stay here."

Make no mistake, my expression said. "I'm. Going."

Ennis nestled behind me, his hands settling at my hips, "We can handle the search." His right hand slid across my tummy, his fingers spanning right where Baby Daniel hung out, "It won't take that long."

What possessed him to say that? Two things came to mind. One, he'd rather not have me along since he found his new friend or two, Mathis suffered a Freudian Slip and told him about the baby. John was older but no airhead. He'd kept secrets before – usually from Georgia and only because I promised to tell her soon – so I blamed my sudden excommunication on my husband's infatuation with Sheila. He just didn't want me along.

I resented the fact Ennis spent his time chatting her up instead of working the case. While Ike and Mike watched from the sidelines,

Mathis and I hoofed it around Atlanta until our legs ached, interviewed people, made calls, and searched computer records until our eyes crossed. Topping it off, we brainstormed together until we wrung our gray matter dry. In short, Mathis and I worked the way Ennis and I used to. So in my humble opinion, John and I deserved this trip and nothing short of the Second Coming would prevent me from going.

As if we asked for it, Bennett offered her contribution, "Let's all go. Unless Savannah or Mathis object, I'd love to join in."

"Why would they object?" my naïve Texan inquired.

Sheila chuckled, "Well, they did the lion's share of the work. Detectives always feel possessive of a case."

Yeah, like the detective feeling possessive of her husband too, you horrid tramp–

"Savannah's not like that," Ennis assumed. "Mathis, you mind if Sheila comes along?"

John raised his hands in his signature don't-involve-me gesture, "Your wife's decision, not mine."

Bennett's brow lifted in a lofty expectation of my consent – as if my input mattered. As an afterthought she added, "I only figured since Ennis and I will be working together anyway–"

"Saddle up, Lieutenant," Ennis butted in. To me he said, "This is perfect. With Sheila along you can stay here and keep giving Stan the third degree."

Pay attention, Ennis. "Mathis already did that. Since cops aren't allowed to use the fourth degree, I'm going."

"You're staying."

His tone rang with authority. Enough I switched my theory. Mathis tattled about the baby. I'd bet my next month's salary on it. "I'm not staying. As for the lieutenant, it's her decision whether she goes." I huffed past the trio when I felt (what I considered) a patronizing pat on the back.

"Aw," drawled Bennett, "he's looking out for his girl. How sweet. Savannah, don't get bashful about it. It's cute. And call me Sheila, already. No formalities between us. After all, we'll be family over at Five soon, right? Till then I'll basically be Ennis's second wife."

I stiffened. The infernal patting suddenly ceased. "At work, I mean," she amended.

Alarm registered on John's face. He shook his head at me. Don't lose it, he seemed to say. I hoped Mathis might take a hint and speak up about Sheila tagging along but he defected to Ennis's camp, "Prince, you can wait for Stan's mouthpiece while we round up the weapons."

My teeth clenched as Sheila volunteered, "Well, if she wants to miss out on the fun, sure, but Savannah's no benchwarmer."

"No, I'm not. Ennis," I nodded toward the door.

"Oh," Bennett said, "I thought Ennis and I would ride together." She challenged, "If you don't mind, that is."

I do mind. I mind a lot.

"She's fine with it," Ennis shot me a fierce stare, "aren't you?"

His undertone? No reply except yes sufficed or there'd be hell to pay. The man acted like I peed in his Post Toasties by insisting I go

J. L. Lemon

along.

I countered with my own glare and pursed lips.

"No objection?" Bennett waited a beat. "Great. Thanks, guys." She clapped me on the shoulder, "See, Savannah? We're already a team."

Ennis threw open the door and stormed out, "Let's go."

Leaving the room, I felt sick to my stomach. This woman might as well crawl between us in bed at night. She shadowed Ennis worse than a stalker. They marched in step together ahead of me and Mathis, our little foursome heading out the front door to our detective's sedans.

At the end of the sidewalk, Sheila stopped our procession. "Give me a sec. I need to run to my car right quick."

The lieutenant winked at me, this one a devious message gloating *Sheila – One, Savannah – Zero.* "Y'all don't leave without me," she beamed, trotting off to her car.

"Wouldn't dream of it," Mathis replied. Then grumbled in my ear, "Let's toss her in the trunk. We got plenty of room in there." He walked ahead, "Meet ya at the car, kid."

I paused beside Ennis who ignored my presence. When we split up on a case, we always made an effort to tell each other "I love you." He kept track of Bennett who sashayed to the far end of the parking lot.

"Ennis—"

"You should stay here." He was still blistering mad. He turned to face me, lecturing, "Why can't you listen to me?"

"Because Bennett's right. Mathis and I worked hard on this case. We deserve to go after those weapons. We earned it."

He shoved a hand through his hair, "Yes, you earned it. But why can't we get them and you still get the credit for the case? Won't that work?"

"No. I'm doing my job."

"A job that'll get you killed if you're not careful. It's a dangerous area. Gangs, shootings, rapes." He turned from me, "You're impossible."

I touched his back but he shrugged away. The urge to cry swelled in my throat. Since we met, Ennis never rejected my touch. Not until now. Not until Sheila arrived. It absolutely devastated me.

His attention riveted to the lieutenant rummaging the trunk of her black Chevy down the way. She practically bent double trying to find whatever she searched for, giving my husband a full, obscene eyeful of her Brooks Brothers-clad ass.

I wanted to sob my eyes out *and* slap the snot out of him. It took extraordinary effort to curb both and stay with our routine. "I love you, Ennis." Despite my best efforts, my trembling voice betrayed me. I walked away, unable to bolster the courage to see if he returned the sentiment.

Halfway to my car I heard him call my name. I turned. The anger vanished from his handsome features. Defeat sagged his shoulders, "I love you too but I wish for once in your life you'd listen to common sense."

24

Saturday Afternoon

Daddy's favorite phrase seemed appropriate right about then. *Shot at and missed and shit at and hit.*

I trudged to my detective sedan only to see it empty. A short horn blast directed me three cars over where Mathis signaled me to his car. He'd settled behind the wheel by the time I got there. I climbed in the passenger side, "I wanted to drive."

Incredulous laughter spilled out, "You gotta be kidding. In your mood? I wanna spend the evening with a TV dinner, a beer and TIVO, not being interrogated by IA about why you drove over Bennett."

He cranked the engine, backed out of the parking space. Down the way, Bennett slammed her trunk, hurried from her car to Ennis's sedan.

Mathis slowly rolled past the pair. Bennett smiled, waved. John nodded while I returned her gesture with less – but just enough – convincing enthusiasm.

"What did she mean you'd be family at Five? You leaving too?"

Not if I could help it. "She wants me to but I'm staying even if I have to chain myself to Josh Hunter to do it."

"This day went to hell in a hurry. After all these years I finally get you broke in and now this."

"I'm not transferring to Five, John." I switched to watching the Bobbsey Twins. Bennett said something to Ennis who tossed her the car keys and swapped places. She relegated him to riding shotgun in his own sedan.

Mathis stopped, waited for Sheila to pull in behind us before gunning the engine. The force pushed me back in the seat. I checked my seatbelt. Yes, securely latched. "This is why I hated riding with Ennis years ago. Ease up or I will *demand* to drive."

"Only way you're driving my car is if I'm unconscious or dying."

"You're really afraid I'll mow her down?"

"No," John said. "I'm afraid you'll mow the bitch down then back over her for good measure."

Good ol' Mathis. He knew me so well...

We drove for twenty minutes, leading the charge to find the murder weapons. Behind us, Ennis and Bennett jawed up a storm. Every glance in the rearview mirror found them talking and/or laughing. I boiled while Mathis sped down the streets. Bennett tailed him close enough to make me nervous. Ennis didn't seem to notice their front bumper getting fresh with our rear end. Nope, he busied himself yucking it up with her while treating me like a petulant child.

Resting his elbow on the window, Mathis leaned his head in his hand, "You shoulda stayed behind. This is driving you nuts."

I stared in the rearview mirror again, "Yes, it is."

"She can see it too."

I snapped around to him, "What?"

"She's needling you on purpose. Yeah, she wants Rutherford for a night or two, but she sees how this is tearing you up. You're letting it show. Hell, if it's obvious to *me*, it's a beacon to her."

Another brief appraisal in the mirror showed Ennis engrossed in telling a story and Bennett laughing. Then she did something unexpected. She turned straight ahead and met my gaze in the mirror. Mathis was right. She knew. And I was an idiot.

A touch of nausea stirred at the base of my throat. With the stress level lately, it didn't surprise me but the pinging reminded me of Ennis's determination to leave me behind. "Did you tell Ennis about the baby?"

Steering one-handed, he rounded a corner too fast. I scowled at him. He scowled back, "Do I look suicidal to you? If I learned anything from my marriage, it was to keep my mouth shut. He told you to stay behind because of the gang activity. That's all. Not because he wants to bone Bennett on a dusty school desk in the middle of Watts."

I pointed ahead, "Watch the road and slow down. There's no need to—"

"Hold on," he punched the gas. The car roared through the busy intersection just as the light turned red. Behind us, Bennett ran the light altogether. Cars squealed to abrupt stops to allow the vehicle through —

but not without a symphony of honking horns.

I glared in the rearview mirror, shouting, "Hey, try not to kill my husband, you crazy–"

Our car suddenly swerved partway into the adjoining lane. I braced against the dashboard while Mathis straightened the car. He blurted the granddaddy of curses then scorched me with a glare so hot I leaned away from him. "Do you mind? I'm driving a car here," he bludgeoned, leaving off the "*are you stupid?*" postscript – but not the inflection.

I recoiled from his tone, muttering a timid, sincere *sorry.*

He rubbed his forehead, "You women run on drama and hormones, dontcha? There's a reason Adam ate the apple. He was trying to kill himself cause Eve drove him nuts nagging and yelling. Women never stood a chance, not with her being the prototype." His dressing-down suddenly turned personal, "So I say this with all due respect, but you come unglued every time you get knocked up."

It escaped me how the ex-Mrs. John Mathis kept from duct-taping her husband's mouth during their marriage. "You done yet?" I deadpanned.

"Are *you?*"

"She blew through that light, John. Ennis and I might be at odds but I want to make up with him. Hard to do if he's six feet under *because of her.*"

"Take a breath. She don't drive any worse than any other cop."

I harrumphed, still steaming over that Adam and Eve bullshit.

"If Eve nagged and yelled at Adam, he was sitting on his sorry, naked ass too much." Ha. Take *that*, Mr. Chauvinist.

To my utter surprise, Mathis snickered. So far three people got my goat that day. I vowed three was my upper limit.

We entered a part of the city resembling what people associated with a ghetto. Venturing further into the bowels of gang territory revealed an eerie ghost town atmosphere. Not a soul roamed the streets or hung out around the buildings.

The thirty acre housing development opposite the school appeared empty and abandoned. Barbed wire fences cordoned off the buildings slated for demolition. The schedule for razing ran late by nine years so far. Block after block various colors of gang graffiti overlapped on brick walls, marking and remarking supposed turf borders. This area was a miniature version of the five families of New York, except instead of the names Genovese, Gambino and Lucchese, they carried monikers such as Black Mafia, Hustler Bloods, and Money Boyz.

John eased the sedan down the street. We both searched the empty streets for activity. Bennett and Ennis followed close behind, scouting the neighborhood along with us. The area may have appeared deserted but no one traveled those streets without being observed. Invisible eyes tracked us from the "empty" windows across the way, watching our every move. In this neighborhood a cop's sedan stood out like a circus wagon in an Amish village.

Mathis pulled to the curb, threw the gearshift into Park. "Here," he reached to the back seat and shoved a bulletproof vest at me. "I oughta make you wear two of 'em." He grumbled under his breath, "Comin' out here pregnant. What the hell is wrong with you?"

I regarded Mathis from the passenger seat, speechless that he'd lecture me and amazed that I halfway enjoyed the idea. "Thanks, Dad."

"Call me that again and I'll pistol whip ya. I'm just looking out for my future. You gotta make sergeant so don't get killed."

It touched me that he cared. All grousing aside, Mathis and I shared a bond formed over many years that began with a simple question in my rookie-dom. When my ex-boyfriend slugged me, Mathis inquired about the bruise darkening my jaw the next day. He asked, "Nobody taught you to duck?" And the rest was history.

We climbed out just as Bennett pulled up, killed the engine. Mathis donned his own vest while I wrestled mine on. Bennett tossed the keys over the hood to Ennis, "Grab a couple of vests for us, babe."

My jaw tightened. *Babe?*

"Don't react," Mathis mumbled to me.

Like throw up, you mean? A rise of nausea nudged the back of my throat. Bad timing and I shared a lifetime of memories. Why now, I asked myself. Why get queasy now? I couldn't tell if it was Bennett's constant aggravation or my pregnancy kicking in good and hard. Either way, harking my toenails up left a bad impression on homewreckers and everyone in general – plus it gave credence to John's campaign to leave me at the station.

Ennis and Bennett equipped their vests then she exercised her authority by assigning us partners (she took my husband, of course) and a search grid for each person. She scanned us mere lowly detectives, "Everyone on board with this?"

We nodded and headed toward the old, abandoned (at least by the city) school. Since the city closed the U-shaped, two-story red brick building, the neighborhood declined, leaving families no choice but to seek safer accommodations than the crumbling nineteen sixties housing project. The criminal elements took the opportunity to swoop in and take over the area since the city didn't seem to care. Beer cans and illegally dumped tires littered the area. Weeds surrounding the sixty thousand square foot complex grew taller than me in some places. Windows were boarded – well, the ones gang members, vagrants and drug addicts hadn't pried off.

Ennis and Bennett took the upper floor while Mathis and I traversed the ground level. The stench of urine, vomit and feces overpowered the sour mildew of wet wood and sheetrock, forcing me to hold the back of my hand to my nose. If Bennett's antics failed to inspire a spew, the smelly building would not.

Mathis soldiered on without flinching. His nose clearly had an "out of business" sign on it somewhere. Any normal human's stomach retched at the thick fetid odors.

With guns and flashlights we moved in methodical silence, stepping over scorched spoons and used syringes strewn across the floor and dodging old damp newspapers and nests of ratty, roach ridden blankets. Above us, stained ceiling tiles sagged and dangled above us like mobiles, secured only by thin strands of metal. Others had given up the fight long ago and fallen to the floor, leaving gaping black holes overhead.

Our flashlight beams crisscrossed, looking for not only the murder weapons but faces hiding in the dark. We ventured further into the building, passing by the office. It looked as if a bomb exploded. Plaster, dirt and dust layered the floor. Old textbooks and loose pages littered the area. The door hung askew on the hinges, and light fixtures dangled from the ceiling by an electrical cord. We found no murder weapons.

A few doors down we discovered what once was the music room. Urine-stained sheet music scattered the floor. The upright piano that years ago played tunes to young children now lay in ruins with the keys stripped from the busted case and piano wire strung across the room. Stair-stepped risers used for choir practice had been reemployed as beds or chairs. More scorched spoons, used syringes and newspapers. Still no weapons.

We made our way through three more rooms, one filled with furniture and fixtures, the others the boys' and girls' bathrooms where nature began reclaiming the rooms with moss and thick fibrous stalks of kudzu snaking through the windows.

The whole building was an obstacle course and the boiler room presented its own unique challenge. "Watch your step," Mathis warned, sweeping his light across the floor. "There's glass everywhere." Each step resulted in crunching over remnants of shattered fluorescent lighting tubes. We tiptoed and sidestepped our way across the room that once housed water heaters, air handlers and electrical equipment. Vandals and thieves ravaged the cavernous room, stealing every machine and potentially valuable item the city left behind. We found broken glass, more drug paraphernalia, roaches the size of Rhode Island and rodent feces but no weapons.

My throat tightened from the continuous battle with nausea, "Did Stan give a ballpark location for the weapons?"

"Just the school. I shoulda beat it outta him. He probably withheld the info as payback."

"This'll take forever," I wiped my brow. In the midst of our search a hot sheen of perspiration rose on my skin. Teasing halos of light outlined the board covered windows, amplifying my claustrophobia. Tormenting images abounded of suffocating inside the stuffy, squalid room, of struggling to breathe or call for help. The perspiration turned cold when fear rooted in. I shivered, trying to shake off the worst of the irrational thoughts. My mind centered on the baby and keeping him safe from this real life haunted house where creatures lurking in the darkness really *could* kill you.

"I don't like the idea but maybe we should split forces," Mathis mentioned. "I'll take the east side and you the west. Are you comfortable with that?"

A subtle reference to my pregnancy. I appreciated his concern and no, I wasn't comfortable with it but, "I'll be more comfortable when we're done. Let's just do it."

"Yell if you need help." He shuffled off to investigate on his own, repeating his earlier caution, "And don't get killed."

"You either."

Heading off alone scared me. The adage *two heads are better than one* applied to guns too, particularly with cops searching in a known gang area. It was the first time John's admonishment *what the hell were you thinking* hit home. I relied on my gun, flashlight, and instincts only. My partner was seconds away but seconds stretched to a lifetime in tight situations.

With gun and flashlight leading the way, I braved the next room, walking over broken tiles that crackled with every step. The tremble in my right hand returned full force. Between the day's stress and the strain of holding the .38 (light as it was), I fought to steady the weapon in my hand.

The flashlight illuminated a second doorway at the back of the room. Erected in the middle of the floor stood a veritable monument of old school desks stacked in a Tetris-like block. The structure appeared stable enough, probably held together with the archaic wads of gum I saw mashed on the undersides of the desktops.

A subtle scraping sound wheeled me to the left. The tremble worsened, wobbling the snub nose a bit too freely for my comfort.

The sudden, crippling fear waned upon sight of a rat scurrying toward the room's rear doorway. A deep breath later (one I nearly regretted when my gut clenched from the foul room), I cobbled together my courage to forge ahead but not before holstering the gun to exercise and limber up my hand. I shook out the tremors as best I could, equipped the gun and resumed the search.

On the negative side, I found no weapons. On the positive side, I found no gang members ready to kill me.

Moving slowly to the next room via the back doorway, I heard the rat rustling around somewhere to my right. The flashlight beam passed across him hiding behind one of the piles of books stacked along the wall. I aimed the light straight at the little beast. Beady eyes stared boldly back at me, daring me to venture closer. *No thanks, buddy. This is your territory, not mine and I'm just passing through...*

This room would drive me nuts. Being small anyway, the contents shrank it to an abysmal size for a claustrophobic person. It served as another repository for rusting file cabinets and old dusty books lining walls in perilous, uneven pillars. Dozens of sagging, water-stained boxes marked "Textbooks" rose six feet high, some listing toward collapse. In the middle of the room, rows of those hazards created tricky pathways with only a tight corridor for navigation.

I inched down one row, finessing my way around one precarious leaning tower of books. The claustrophobia dug in degree by degree, speeding my heart, squeezing my lungs in its fist. *Do not lose it. Breathe and concentrate. And stabilize your weapon, for God's sake, or you'll accidentally shoot yourself...*

With the flashlight still in my left hand, I braced the wrist beneath my right hand to reduce the shaking somewhat.

Another sound spooked me. This was not the scurrying of animal feet but when I aimed the flashlight across the room nothing seemed amiss so I proceeded. At the row's end I turned, swept the flashlight down the aisle between another narrow lane of books. Nothing.

A distinct sound behind me sent torrents of adrenaline coursing through me, sharpening senses, kicking in instinct. Shoes scraped the floor once more. Cops never crept up behind other cops. I was in trouble – big trouble – and alone.

I swiveled, shouting for Mathis at the same time. Halfway into the turn, a debilitating pain caused the gun and flashlight to slip from my grasp, the former clacking to the concrete, the latter winking out upon impact. I went to my hands and knees with a whimper while sheer panic and the room's darkness engulfed me. The room spun in a sea of dizziness as I groped the damp floor for my .38 before ending up dead.

Yell for John. Yell again. I did, or thought I did. Through the pounding headache and ringing ears, my voice sounded muffled. Had I shouted or groaned his name?

A gun barrel pressed at the base of my skull, keeping me on my hands and knees.

Fingers jerked the Kevlar vest's straps loose, stripped it off then flung my only protection into the room's abyss.

The gun relocated between my shoulders at the same time a flashlight bathed the area in eerie, elongated shadows. "You've been checking up on me."

I froze. Muffled hearing or not, Sheila Bennett's voice registered as unmistakable as the gun shoved in my back. The forays into the future replayed at fast-forward speed, reviewing every encounter I'd had with her. None revealed this horror show. On my knees in the ghetto, *pregnant* and held at gunpoint. I was on my own in this real life nightmare – no mirror to help, no Cliff Notes, no Mathis or Ennis, nothing.

The harsh truth gradually dawned on me. Somewhere, somehow I'd changed the future. Instead of growing old as a divorcée, I'd likely die here at thirty-nine – with my unborn child.

Again I'd underestimated Bennett. She organized this plan in mere minutes after learning about the weapons stashed at the school. First she volunteered to help search the building, then when Mathis and I separated she must have tracked me down and pounced.

Sheila's weapon kept steady pressure and an equally steady hand. She leaned closer, trained her flashlight directly on me, "Don't bother calling for Ennis or Mathis. I sent them on a wild goose chase in the building next door. I'm your backup now and we're taking time to resolve our issues."

Resolve our issues. What a strange euphemism for murder, I thought. Her inflection indicated these "issues" rated as high as a forgotten loaf of bread at the store. Such pesky inconveniences, these wives of cops she intended to bed. One, two, three, poof! No more wife. No big deal. Life goes on.

But sociopaths perfected calm under pressure. I learned that with Jeffrey. He hadn't killed over twenty women in a span of five years by being flighty or stupid. Bennett successfully silenced the other cops' wives by intimidation and God knew what else, maybe even by *resolving their issues* John Gotti style. I doubted Ennis might find her current persona cute, entertaining or fun. Behind me stood the monster from my journeys into the future, not his chummy, lighthearted pal Sheila.

I tried playing ignorant and incredulous despite the terror raging through me, "What *issues* besides the fact you assaulted me and are holding a gun on me?" I spied my .38 against a box two feet away. Too far out of reach before getting a hole blown in my back.

Bennett saw it too. She stepped forward, kicked it away. I watched it skid ten feet across the floor and ricochet off the wall. "I'll spell it for you, Savannah. You screwed up. Cops don't check on cops unless they're Internal Affairs. Asking about my personal life? That's none of your business." She punctuated the final words with a generous stab of the gun barrel.

I begged to differ with the bitch but, "Ennis is my business. I wanted to know who he was dealing with. Who *I* was dealing with." A punishing blow between the shoulders took me to the floor. I curled on my side before white pain exploded beneath my shoulder blade. My cry split the silence. If that sound didn't alert my husband and Mathis, nothing would.

Reason, focus and religion temporarily abandoned me. Hot tears slipped from my eyes as one image raced to mind. The mirror's vision of a smiling little boy with a cowlick who'd greeted me with a cheerful, "Good morning, Ma." *Daniel. Shield Daniel.*

Bennett leaned to my ear, "Do you know who you're dealing

with now, Savannah?"

My eyes squeezed tight against the throbbing, the tears coming in a stream now. I nodded.

"It took the other wives longer to catch on but not you. I barely shook hands with Ennis before you started asking around about me. You're either too smart for your own good or too insecure to deserve a man like him."

"I'm protective of my family. That's why I asked about you." Okay, it wasn't the only reason but I'd eat razor blades before confessing the truth.

"The other wives were easy to control," she continued. "Threaten their husband's job, or describe how simple it is to set someone up. A cop's wife being tossed in prison for dealing dope – now that's when the others shut up. But you being a cop presents a challenge – or it did until today. I can't believe my luck. This is the perfect place to solve my problem."

I shakily pushed onto all fours again. This woman was crazy. Crazy enough to kill another cop. I spaced the words between the pain's ebb and flow, "Ennis won't give you the time of day. You're nuts if you think he will."

"This isn't just about Ennis. It's about what you learned with your snooping." She leaned to my ear, "You know what I did and I'm not foolish enough to let you live."

"What are you talking about? I only found out about the affairs." From the corner of my eye I saw her foot swing back and I turned and crouched to duck the attack if possible. Her foot collided right beneath my shoulder blade again. Another, more subdued, cry split the silence. Neither Ennis nor Mathis came running to help.

"Stop lying, Savannah. You accessed my department records. There are three Rutherfords on the job. One is older than Moses, one is Ennis and he's too busy preparing for his transfer then there's you. You got in the records and you know what Turner's daughter accused me of."

"On the job I go by Prince, not Rutherford, and had I accessed your records, I wouldn't hide behind my married name. I learned about your affair with Turner through word of mouth." I'd never called up her department history because I realized it would alert her. As for Turner's daughter, she'd outright accused Sheila of blowing her mother's brains out and blamed Internal Affairs of sweeping the murder under the rug.

"Then you also know when his wife found out, she tried tattling on me and I had a little chat with her, similar to the one we're having right now. Poor woman. They found her the next day. Someone put a bullet right between her pretty blue eyes."

Yeah, "Someone named Sheila Bennett."

"Tsk-tsk, Savannah. You sound like their daughter. Officially, that murder is unsolved." The gun barrel sank deeper behind my heart. I arched against the pain as she proceeded, "Internal Affairs did a thorough investigation. I was cleared. There was no evidence, no witnesses, nothing tying me to her death."

"Are Robbins and Greene going to clear you of my murder too?" I knew the instant it left my lips I'd signed up for another attack – but it never came. I'd hoped to catch her off-guard with the information I'd gleaned from the trips into the future. The two IA cops who railroaded me out of a job held a more instrumental role in Bennett's life than I thought.

Instead of surprise, Sheila Bennett calmly and quietly replied, "And that, Detective, is the reason you'll die in this rat infested shithole. You know too much."

I heard the metallic click of a revolver's hammer. Bennett normally carried a Glock, not a revolver. At first I assumed she brought a throw down gun to kill me then I recalled the murder weapon in the Turner case was never recovered. Sheila probably obtained an untraceable gun through her "special" network of contacts. She had them everywhere and unfortunately my murder wouldn't raise many eyebrows anyway. A rough part of town. Gangs. Drugs. Turf wars. It happened – a cop getting shot searching a building in the local war zone. Sheila would shoot me, blame a thug, attend my funeral then try to ride off into the sunset with Ennis and our kids. Happily ever after. For her.

I had two choices. Be a good little victim and stay nice and still for the psychopath or I could try to save my baby and myself. I stared longingly at my .38 so far from my reach I stood no chance of touching it without dying first. A quick glimpse revealed the immediate area devoid of items to use as a weapon. The filthy room full of dusty, water-damaged boxes lent no help to an ambushed, terrified, pregnant police detective so I improvised.

My left hand curled into a fist. One good bash in the knee.

That's all I needed to knock her off balance – and pray both the baby and I lived through it.

A sudden blinding light illuminated our position. "Drop the gun, Bennett."

Oh thank God... I practically fainted at the sound of my husband's voice. My knight in shining armor had a Texas twang, a sharpshooter's aim and plenty of practice expediting destructive vermin. I instantly expelled a long, unsteady breath while my body relaxed, succumbing to the crippling anxiety and panic. From head to toe I shivered like a newborn foal on wobbly legs. Tears blinded me as I wept aloud on all fours in that filthy, smelly classroom.

Ennis kept the bright light aimed at Bennett's face. She blocked the glare with her forearm but the grip on the gun never wavered.

"I said drop the gun," Ennis's voice deepened to a threatening, don't-screw-with-me tone.

Bennett jammed the weapon's barrel in my back then answered Ennis with a defiant *no*.

Shoot her, damn it, I wanted to scream. *Wing her or wound her – otherwise I'm a goner and so is your son.*

"*I'm* the Rutherford who accessed your records, not Savannah," he confessed. He maneuvered closer behind us to gain full view of our positions.

From the corner of my eye I silently implored Ennis to please shoot the crazy bitch so I could finally, totally collapse. Cold sweat surfaced on my face and back. The shakes worsened. And the nausea?

J. L. Lemon

Well, if my hubby didn't speed things along, there'd be a call for cleanup on aisle nine.

Ennis, on the other hand, seemed content on chatting her into submission, not pulling the trigger. "I'm the one who discovered your involvement with Robbins and Greene. I also know you're holding the weapon that killed Turner's wife. *Put the gun down now.*"

The magnitude of my husband's temper far outweighed Sheila Bennett's common sense. Bennett pressed her luck by ignoring him. She'd soon regret it and if he'd known about the baby, she'd already have been dead.

Making matters worse, she laughed, "And I thought you were a hayseed from Texas. You're not so dumb after all."

Hayseed? Nice move, moron. Throw gasoline on the flames. As for me, I ducked closer to the floor, giving Ennis a clearer shot because I felt his finger slowly tightening on that trigger.

Several feet in front of me, Mathis guardedly peeked around the corner of a wilting tower of boxes. *Help me,* I mouthed to him. He nodded then retreated out of sight before Bennett spotted him.

"Let Savannah go or I *will* kill you," Ennis forewarned. "And hayseeds from Texas kill with one shot."

"Sorry, Ennis," she casually dismissed the demand as if declining a lunch date. Sorry, her inflection said, but I already have plans to murder your wife then I'm scheduled for a spa treatment. "And you might want to reconsider killing me. You'll go to prison, your wife will be dead then who will raise Lily and Hannah?"

For the love of God, "It's *Anna*," I corrected. "Not Hannah."

Her grip on the gun firmed, pressed harder against my back until I wormed from the pain. "No one cares," she squeezed through clenched teeth, "what that brat's name is."

A shot rang out, dragging that split second into one of the longest of my existence. I'd braced for the hot, shocking impact of a bullet tearing through vital organs. I waited for the explosion inside my chest and for the power of the shot to drive me against the floor. For weakness to set in and my heart to pump frantically for a few brief seconds then surrender to the inevitable as life blinked out like my flashlight had. Memories played in disjointed clips from childhood to now where I waited to meet my mother at the end of the long, bright tunnel leading to Heaven. To run into her welcoming embrace and hold her tight once again.

The gunshot's sharp, deafening report echoed off walls and boxes. A short shriek (was that me?) registered past my ringing ears. An instant later I collapsed. Bone painfully collided with concrete and a sudden cumbersome weight drove me to the cold floor, compressing the air from my already struggling lungs.

It took a long moment to realize my lungs weren't filling with blood nor had I felt the pain of impact from a gunshot. Only the backbreaking weight crushing me to the concrete. It felt like a piano fell on my back. In reality it wasn't a Steinway but a Bennett. The shriek and unmerciful weight belonged to the crazy woman. Like my flashlight, hers fell to the floor but hers blazed bright, revealing the bizarre scene unfolding around us. The woman sprawled atop me in a perverse and ridiculous position resembling (I was quite sure) a deranged wrestler pinning her opponent. She pushed against me, one hand on the floor, the other braced on my neck to right herself. The warm, wet sensation of blood dripped down her hand to my shoulder.

Mathis converged on us, his gun aimed in our general direction, "You okay, kid? Hurt anywhere?"

I fought to draw a decent breath, "I'm okay I think. Except for the bitch parked on top of me."

He leaned down to retrieve the revolver Bennett dropped, whispering, "Is *everything* okay?"

I took a quick inventory. Ribs – hurt like hell. Back – achy, thanks. Nerves – AWOL. I squirmed beneath Bennett to free myself. Thanks to her I hit the floor harder than anticipated and now I obsessed over the baby, "I hope so."

"Lemme get a bus for you." He'd already reached in his gray suit jacket for the portable radio.

"She doesn't need the ambulance," Bennett growled like Mathis was dense. "*I* do. I could die from this wound." Adding insult to my already humiliating position, she mashed my head against the concrete floor, dug her nails into my scalp until I winced.

She complained of being *injured* when her sole purpose for joining our search was to *kill* me? Once I pried myself from beneath the lead caboose pinning me, I'd show her the definition of murder, "John, get this arrogant hag off me."

Mathis grabbed her arm and yanked. Bennett stumbled, the momentum ramming her headlong into a water-stained box across the aisle. John smirked then extended his hand to help me up.

"Stand up, Bennett," Ennis ordered. "I'm not finished with you."

I paused in mid-reach for John's hand. I did not recognize my husband's voice when he spoke. It combined ten percent Ennis Rutherford with ninety percent homicidal maniac.

"Ennis," I cautioned, wanting to stop him before he walked out in handcuffs along with Sheila.

He loomed over Bennett who cradled her injured shoulder. He'd pocketed his Maglite, leaving hers the only adequate light source in the room. One hand held his .38, the other clenched and released as if he debated when to launch the first punch.

Sheila flinched as blood slowly seeped between her fingers. Mathis seized my outreached hand, effortlessly lifted me to my feet. He recognized Ennis's temperament right away and urged me, "You're the only one who can get through to him. Talk. Quick."

Ennis jerked Sheila upright by her wounded arm. Her cry pierced the thick, dank air. For the first time since I'd met her, her tough façade yielded to genuine fear when Ennis shoved her against the wall of boxes. He advanced on her, nostrils flared, the gun in his right hand and his left solidly doubled in a fist. Those didn't set off my internal alarm. His expression did.

"Say something," Mathis urged. "He's losing it."

Yes, thanks to Bennett, Ennis reached the threshold of unleashing his personal, inner beast. The one we all had but kept tucked away unless certain circumstances unlocked its cage. That monster who justified any deplorable, unthinkable act by cheering us on and ramping up our rage. *Do it. It's okay. They deserve it...* Bennett unlocked his door and kicked it open. Now I had to try and talk down his savage side and retrieve my sweet, loving husband.

"Ennis, whatever you're thinking, stop before it's too late." I stepped closer until our vision met. Instinct warned me to turn and run from the stranger staring back. This wasn't the man I shared a bed with. This person standing before me certainly hadn't fathered my girls. The cold eyes devoid of any emotion except rage. The tendons in his neck stood out and a vein on his normally smooth forehead pulsed. Rock solid muscles tensed, ready to bruise and break bones. Something commandeered my husband and that something was temporary insanity. I backed away two steps, used a softer tone, "Babe, listen to me. She's not worth it. Let Mathis cuff her–"

"I nearly lost you in July because I didn't kill Holland when I had a chance. I'm not making the same mistake twice."

His guilt resurfaced from never exacting revenge on Jeffrey Holland. Memories from three months earlier – and five years prior – still lay open, raw. If I wasn't careful, Sheila would end up dead and Ennis would be carted off to Norcross, probably to Holland's old cell.

"Ennis, calm down," I pleaded. "She's going to jail."

"No." He thrust his .38 beneath her chin, "She's going to hell."

He turned back to Bennett, "So you wanted to kill my wife?" The question dared her to reply. She wisely kept quiet.

"You wanted to destroy the woman I love?" His thumb gradually eased the revolver's hammer back until it clicked.

"For God's sake, stop," I implored. The longer he stood there the more I worried he'd follow through on his promise. He tuned everyone out, even me. "Ennis, if you pull that trigger, we'll never be together again. *Think* about what you're doing."

A chilling smile crossed his lips, "Oh, I am. I'm ensuring this bitch doesn't come back the way Holland did."

Mathis nudged my side with his elbow. After Sheila's beat down, such a light tap still fired a healthy pain throughout my midsection.

I rounded on him, mildly lashing out, "That hurts, you know."

His brow lifted, apparently with a bright idea. "Do that again. If he thinks you're hurt, he might stop. You gotta go to the hospital anyway."

I cradled my aching ribs then turned his phrasing against him, "Do *that* again and you'll join me." And what did he mean *if Ennis thinks I'm hurt?* They both saw that lunatic basically body slam me with her butt.

I tried once again, this time using my Mama Ice voice. The girls heeded it so I prayed he did too. "Ennis, back off and let Mathis handcuff her."

The lieutenant pressed against the boxes, meeting Ennis's gaze and muttering a weepy plea not to shoot. Blood soaked her blouse and trailed along her right arm. Sheila grew pale from pain and blood loss but mostly chaste fear. Her wide, watery eyes shifted from him to me. "Please take the gun," was the tremulous whisper.

"Do not speak to my wife," his hand clamped around her throat. His vision cut to me, "Savannah, stay put. I see you moving in."

I stopped, shook my head with a mental sigh. Well, so much for Mama Ice. *Help me get through to him*, I prayed. *I need him to understand what's at stake.* Five years ago Ennis prevented me from killing Jeffrey. At the time I didn't understand why because Jeffrey's death equaled freedom and peace of mind for me. I resented Ennis's interference for months. Eventually I forgave him for making that decision. I only hoped he'd forgive me if I pried that firearm from his grasp.

Mathis mumbled, "C'mon, kid. What're you waitin' for?"

Apparently a miracle. For my husband to reclaim his right mind and put the gun down. *Help me, Lord*, I repeated. *Help me to convey what he will lose – what we all will lose if he pulls that trigger...*

One last try. "Ennis, you stopped me from killing Holland–"

"Five years later we regretted that too. But not this time."

"And I'm stopping you from killing Bennett. Give me that gun now. Don't make our children visit you in prison. Don't make me do it either."

Mathis grumbled, "Sorry, kid, but..."

A flaming spear of pain shot through my side. I yelped in earnest while holding a trembling hand to the ache blooming in my chest and back. I drilled Mathis with a venomous glare for bumping my wounded ribs. He retreated a step, extending a quiet apology for his little stunt. No, it wasn't a brutal blow but it got my attention in a bad way. However it affected Ennis exactly the way John predicted.

My husband wheeled to us. I ensured to convey enough discomfort to convince him that helping me was far more important than blasting holes in that bitch.

The violence faded from his eyes, "What's wrong?" He glanced at my stomach for some reason then withdrew the .38 from Bennett's jaw. He instantly transformed to my gentle, loving husband again as he headed toward me, "Where are you hurt?"

I flinched for good measure, "Ribs."

His hand eased over my belly, "And here?"

Why the sudden concern – especially there, I wondered. So I simply asked why.

"Making sure." My hubby wrapped me in a warm, tender embrace. Now this was more like it. I closed my eyes, savoring the security of his arms and the fact he hadn't executed Bennett as well as our future.

John slapped cuffs on Bennett who protested about the strain on her wounded shoulder. "No habla Whinese so get hustling," he replied. "You got a date with lots of cellmates who treat cops extra special."

"Other than your ribs, you're really okay?" Ennis asked me.

"Yes." At least I had no hole in my back – or my head for that matter. Things were looking up.

Ennis descended on me, his lips claiming mine in a long, possessive, almost desperate kiss that left me clinging to him for stability. He eased from the steamy liplock, caressed my cheek with a trembling hand, "I was nearly too late."

He sounded almost apologetic. I, however, expressed my sentiment by smiling, "I thought you had perfect timing."

Behind us, Mathis examined the revolver Bennett brought along. He cut loose with a string of profanity he reserved for only special occasions. The crowning glory of his spiel concluded with a stunned, "Hollow points. Geez Prince, they coulda flown a 747 through the hole this made in you."

"Two lousy seconds," Sheila glared at me, "and you'd have been dead."

Ennis's muscles tightened beneath my touch. I shook my head in a warning to ignore her. No more guns or shooting, I'd say. He stripped from my grasp, his complexion blanched pale as a ghost.

"Ennis..." Don't kill her, was on the tip of my tongue – but I stopped upon realizing his urgent need lay in the one activity I managed to curtail the last several minutes.

He took three steps and doubled over to heave once then twice and ended the spectacle on a guttural groan.

I rushed to his side before the second uprising, ready to phone for help. He put a hand to mine, refusing the call. "I'll be fine," he assured, holding my hand. He chanced straightening up, "But she's right. Two seconds is all you had left."

25

That Evening

After the hubbub died down, Ennis called his brother to pick up the girls from class as uniforms swarmed the school searching for the murder weapons. Uncle Dane babysat while their mama and daddy hung out at the hospital along with "Uncle" Mathis. John took charge once we arrived, grabbing the first doctor he found and telling him to check me out. I'd seen grown men shrink back from Mathis. This fella thought about reading John the riot act, appraised the three detectives in front of him then waved me back — to the grumblings of other people in the crowded waiting room.

By five o'clock, one lucky officer hit the jackpot on the school's second story. Tucked in a dark corner of what used to be an art classroom, he found a shotgun, a 9mm handgun and a bloody butcher's knife.

By seven o'clock, officers tracked Blake Hill and Scott Arthur to Hill's brother's house on the west side of town. They found both Blake and Scott hiding in the basement, one sandwiched between a mattress and box spring, the other cowering behind a shelf loaded with jars of chow-chow, bread and butter pickles and corn ketchup. By eight o'clock, the two felons sat behind bars charged with the murders of Joe and Lisa Stewart and since Stan Campbell orchestrated the plan, he joined them.

The big bonus for the day – the one that meant more than winning the Georgia Lottery? Sheila Bennett also resided in a cell. The mirror's prediction – thank God – had been wrong. Ennis and I would remain happily married and she'd sleep in a concrete bedroom by herself for years if the trial went right. Things were looking up for everyone except the bad guys. Finally.

By a quarter to eight, we arrived home with the girls and ate a light supper. The girls went to bed at a later than normal 9:30 while we retired early at 10:00. Ennis and I held each other for a time, gazing into each other's eyes with quiet intimacy. The tiny crinkle between his brows deepened, making me wonder what crossed his mind.

He caressed my back with a touch so light it lulled my eyes closed, relaxing and coaxing me nearer to sleep.

He traced around the tiger tattoo at the small of my back. Long before we married, I got the tattoo to hide scars from my rebellious youth. Seth, Georgia and I sported scars from a whip-thin willow branch Daddy used for punishment. At his pickled best, he wielded the branch with an occasional misguided aim, missing my backside and scarring my lower back. I was lucky the tattoo artist's skills outmatched Daddy's drunken anger. He aligned the stripes so the scars blended and the results lessened my self-consciousness somewhat.

The tiger looked pretty good until Jeffrey Holland beat me within an inch of my life. He used a rattan cane and those, I could safely say, caused a special hellacious agony that lit bone marrow on fire and used lacerated skin, nerves and muscle for kindling.

After his handiwork, the skin never meshed together quite right again, leaving my tiger with one ear askew, a crooked nose and one eye that would forever wink.

Ennis drummed his fingers where my tiger's lopsided nose was. My eyes slowly parted, drowsy from receding stress. "Sorry," I apologized. "I drifted off."

It seemed to please him. "It's been a rough day for everyone." He paused rubbing my back. "The doctor wouldn't let me in the exam room and you didn't argue about it. Why?"

Okay. That was the reason for the wrinkled brow. It took a grand total of five hours and fifteen minutes for him to broach that subject – a veritable record for my husband. Why had I left him out of the exam room? Answer – because I laid on that table trembling and waiting for the emergency room doctor to complete his exam. I was literally terrified. The nurse held my hand, reassuring and talking sweetly to me the way my mother would have. I'd told the doctor about the baby and what happened at the school. I told him I tried my best to protect my little one. My very best. Then I cried, begging the man in white to say my baby was okay, that one bad decision hadn't doomed a life I'd help create, that it hadn't destroyed a child I'd never see or hold.

In reality the whole exam lasted thirty minutes. It felt longer than a year. Only when I saw the smile on the doc's face did I breathe again. Truly breathe. Then I cried again. Not from hormones or stress. These tears I dedicated to God for the blessing in my belly. I thanked Him for a second chance with this child. I vowed to stop taking stupid risks – and to get rid of that blasted mirror.

No, I hadn't argued when the doctor asked Ennis to stay in the waiting room. Because for all my bluster, I was still a woman who cried and fell apart when she feared losing someone she loved and if I lost the child I couldn't bear if Ennis watched me go to pieces.

I propped on my elbow before once again succumbing to slumber's siren song. Ennis's concern required full consciousness to explain without revealing the whole truth. I didn't want him feeling left out yet that's exactly what happened.

I cupped his cheek, pressed a kiss to his lips, "There was a reason I wanted to do it alone. I know you wanted to be there but..." I steeled myself when the urge to cry rose in my throat. Between the day, the stress and my pregnancy, I'd be lucky not to need windshield wipers for the next seven or eight months. I threw up with Lily, continually walked with my hand bracing my back with Anna and now bawled my eyes out with the third kid. I was hopeless.

To my surprise, Ennis eased off prying an answer from me. "You were traumatized. I understood that." His voice softened to the point I lost my battle with tears.

Ennis thumbed them away as they slipped down my cheeks, shushing me with a whispered *it'll be okay.*

But it wasn't. I'd excluded my husband on purpose, refusing to have him there while the doctor checked me. I'd settled for a stranger's compassion rather than the comfort of my husband's hand, his boundless encouragement and love.

Ennis changed the subject – sort of, "Mathis chewed his nails the whole time you were gone. Hadn't seen him so worried since, well..."

"Jeffrey." I swept away the last of my tearful spell.

He nodded. "He brightened up after he heard you were okay."

It was true. To see John Mathis actually smile and outright laugh rated as rare as a moonbow. By the time we exited the facility, he proved Scrooge was human after all. "He's mellowing in his old age," I joked.

We spent a long moment in silence, holding each other. His fingers continued in small circles, working on the tension in my back. My eyelids grew heavy.

"How are your ribs?" he asked.

"Sore but they'll be okay." I ran my fingers over his hairy chest. That chest and every strand of hair on it belonged to me, Mrs. Ennis Rutherford, not some snake in the grass harlot. Whatever happened, I owed something or someone a hell of a thank you for changing our future. I leaned in for a kiss.

He'd calmed down since that afternoon, changing from the raging, trigger-happy maniac to my sexy Texan, the epitome of calm and reason. The man who, I'm proud to say, saved my life that day. Once my ribs quit nettling me, this rescued damsel in distress planned to show him my gratitude. I'd told him earlier about the between-the-sheets raincheck, redeemable once my creaky old bones stopped aching.

"I'm not transferring to Zone 5."

No more droopy eyelids for me. Well *that* statement certainly woke me up. After the hemming and hawing, fretting, discussing and arguing, my better half chose to stay "home" at Zone 2. I imagined John Mathis breaking into his own unique rendition of the Hustle to celebrate. If that happened, I'd join him and make a complete fool of myself. "You're not?"

Ennis chuckled at my surprise, "No. You and I are a damn fine team. Why spoil a good thing, right?"

I felt almost giddy, "I couldn't agree more."

His warm hand eased over my hip to my belly, held it there, "You're sure you're okay? The doc gave the all clear?"

"The doc said my ribs will be fine. I'm bruised but not broken."

"No," he traced my belly button, "I mean is Daniel okay?"

Oh... My... God... "You know?" How *could* he know? Unless...

His gaze dropped. After several moments, I tipped his chin up, arched a brow, "Ennis?"

Chagrined, he mumbled, "Mama's magic mirror."

I feigned dismay, "You didn't."

"I did. That's why I insisted you stay at the station today. I knew what Bennett had planned. Thankfully you changed the outcome by turning away from her when she kicked you. In the mirror's version..." his voice tightened. He looked away.

"Miscarriage?" I asked.

He shook his head, averted his gaze down again, "That's only the beginning." Muscles in his jaw tensed as he spoke through clenched teeth, "I should have shot her sooner."

Once more I urged his vision to mine. Tears glistened in his eyes. I smiled, "Ennis, *you saved my life*. I survived because of you."

He reluctantly continued, "That hour in the waiting room was one of the longest of my life. I worried you were seriously hurt, worried about the baby, and I was upset because I didn't pull the trigger earlier. I figured you chose to be alone for the exam because I waited."

"Good Lord, no. I didn't want you to see me crying my eyes out from the stress. That's all."

His shoulders relaxed. He blew out a long, relieved breath, wiped a hand down his face, "I've worried all night about why you left me out."

I snuggled to him, "I was worried about the baby. I couldn't bear the thought of losing him or facing you if I did. At that point I felt guilty – and stupid – for not staying behind at the station."

He gently swatted my behind with a rare chauvinist flare, "I'll teach you to listen to me, woman."

"Don't get your hopes too high, buddy. I'm always subject to be stubborn." Since he possessed foreknowledge of Bennett's attempt on my life, I wondered how much information he really had. "During your trip, did the mirror show you that Stan hired those guys to kill his in-laws?"

"No. The mirror tossed me in the middle of everything at the school – that was my second trip into the mirror."

"You said she was right, that I only had two seconds to live."

He retreated into pensive silence for a short time. "In the mirror's version I was too late. You died in my arms. The coroner discovered the pregnancy at the autopsy."

A violent chill strafed down my back. I came thisclose to dying and hadn't realized how close until now.

"I went to the mirror a few times," he confessed, probably to divert me from the grim, vivid images of death. "The first time I accidentally fell in." He rethought that, "No, it *pulled* me in."

"Powerful bastard, isn't it?"

"Damn thing about broke my arm yanking me through. I wanted to move it closer to the corner, it grabbed me and wouldn't let go. It took me to Lily's wedding reception. God, even at that age you looked stunning and our girls were the most beautiful women on the planet besides you."

I bobbed my brow, "Flattery will get you everywhere with me."

"I'm collecting on your raincheck ASAP too," he winked. Then, like a child marveling at a wondrous illusion, he returned to his story, "You were talking with a big fella – blue suit, graying hair, boisterous laugh. You pretended to enjoy yourself – I can tell when you're uncomfortable with people. You were okay with him until he kept offering you a drink and you had to keep declining."

"Tony's uncle. An ex-cop from Birmingham. Lily and Tony insisted I meet him."

He seemed surprised, "The mirror took you to the reception

too?"

I nodded and let him continue, "Once the guy went to the john, I approached you but Dane stopped me halfway, told me to leave you alone. Then he mentioned how acrimonious our divorce had been." He shook his head, "*That* blew me away because we'd never divorce – but according to the mirror we had. You were very polite for someone ambushed by her ex-husband."

I shrugged a shoulder then wished I hadn't when my ribs pinged, "Didn't want to ruin the wedding."

He smiled, "You mentioned that. Actually you said, 'I'm not destroying our daughter's wedding. Are you?' You were apprehensive around me and that downright killed me. You were leery of everything I said and weren't comfortable when I brushed your hand. I'm not used to that. We chatted a while and everything went well until Sheila showed up. Then everything blew up."

"I remember." Oh boy, did I remember.

"When the mirror tossed me back out I figured I'd make a change to see if it affected our future. I guess when I poked into Sheila's department records, it wrecked us completely because when I tried the mirror again, that's when I saw the shooting at the school. I didn't sleep much last night. When I did, I had nightmares so today I mulled over how to change the future to our benefit. I decided to confront her at the school but you insisted on going with us. That's why I got mad – plus I knew about the baby. The whole thing made me crazy."

"So you went through the mirror more than twice?"

"When I returned I wanted to learn how I got involved with Bennett so I asked the mirror to show me."

"What led up to you sleeping with her?" Because it consumed me. For days it preyed on my mind, undermining my confidence as a wife, as a woman. How had she so easily lured my husband – a man who loved, cherished and protected me – between her sheets and later coaxed him down the aisle?

"Apparently it began when she bought me that first drink and I was clueless until I saw the mirror's prediction."

My mouth dropped. That quick? I tried propping onto my elbow again but eased back to the pillow with a groan this time. Sheila may not have shot me but she left lasting bruises on my ribs *and* my ego. The *first* drink? Good God...

Ennis patted my hand, "Settle down. In the vision Sheila bought me enough shots of tequila to get me feeling good but not drunk. That's why the day I brought her here to meet you I opted for just two beers at the bar. I knew her plan. Because the mirror forewarned me that after my transfer we'd meet again for a friendly drink but she'd get me so greased up she'd drive me home."

"Except she took you to her home, not yours."

"And I went down in flames. Unintentionally. You came to Sheila's apartment and found us together. She answered the door wearing a flimsy little number and I was still unconscious in her bed. That saying 'hell hath no fury like a woman scorned'? Doesn't come close to your temper."

His lips touched mine like a whisper, "I never want to lose you. I love you too much."

I answered with my own kiss, this one long and lingering that left me wanting more. "We're going to grow old together, Ennis. We'll rock our grandkids to sleep on a porch swing, complain that there's nothing on TV, finish each other's sentences and ask each other where we left our glasses. Then we'll go to bed and sleep in each other's arms."

"Damn right we will," he proudly agreed. "Because today I knocked Sheila Bennett in the corner pocket." He kissed me on the nose, "By the way, not that we'll ever experience the mirror's version of Lily's reception but I changed the future there too."

"What did you do?"

"Y'know when Tony's uncle basically escorted me and Sheila out the door? Well, I waited for her to get in the car then I turned and popped Tony's uncle in the jaw for moving in on you. I told him you were mine and we were getting back together."

26

Wednesday

In my youth Daddy said no one had to lead me into temptation because I knew a shortcut. I suppose he understood his baby daughter better than anyone. After all, he provided half my genetic code.

As a youngster I managed to frustrate the majority of the family on a regular basis. When the school called, Mama eventually resorted to one simple question – *what did she do now?* Daddy snapped so many branches off our willow tree for my punishment, I prayed the damn thing might die from exposure or lose the will to live. When I was about seven, I asked Mama, "What if I get kidnapped?" (Thinking of course this might inspire an answer akin to "We'd search the world over and never stop until we found you.") But Mama hesitated which gave my brother, nine years my senior, the opportunity to offer his two cents. "Trust me, Van, they'd bring you back 'cause you'd drive 'em nuts."

Daddy reacted, Mama fretted, Seth gave up but only Georgia, bless her heart, discovered a way to deal with me. She realized I led a socially dyslexic life at times, particularly when it involved trouble. So she harangued me with Confucius-type sayings that actually worked on occasion (at least it made me think). Mark Twain's "It's easier to stay out than get out" was her favorite and most overused pearl of wisdom.

Since childhood, Georgia honed the annoying habit of spouting little tidbits of enlightenment. From slumber parties to dating to marriage advice, throughout her life she accessed her vast library of information, experience, advice and adages and came through for me. God blessed me with a personal Yoda and everyone knew Yoda was almost always right – but he was no fun either.

She whipped out sayings faster than Billy the Kid drew his gun. No doubt she'd reserved a special nugget of Yoda-like wisdom for the idiot standing in front of the mirror.

I stared at the cloudy mirror and the reflection of Older Savannah looking back at me. Do I or don't I take one last plunge into the unknown? I toyed with the idea for days. Ennis and I decided to get rid of the gremlin infested mirror the next day but first we'd attend Wednesday Bible study, praise God, sing a few songs then come home to rest.

With thirty minutes to spare before we left, I went to my jewelry box for the sapphire necklace Ennis gave me two Christmases ago. Diamond chips outlined the dainty heart shaped blue stone. It harmonized with my blue sweater perfectly plus, to be honest, I loved wearing it. Female cops (including us regular old detectives) tired of wearing the formal attire and the authoritative demeanor required of our job. We enjoyed letting down and being ourselves, even if that meant jeans, a sweater and a delicate sapphire necklace.

I left the girls with their daddy who let his inner little boy out to play. When I strolled to the bedroom, the three settled at the table for an exhilarating game of Go Fish. Lily propped onto her knees in the chair then leaned on the table to play the normally placid game. Our oldest was ruthless and personally I felt convinced she used the posture to intimidate other players. That excuse salved my ego since I rarely won a game of Go Fish against her anyway.

I heard Ennis join in Lily's revelry, vowing he'd win and promising chocolate milk for everyone after church. It was no coincidence he won more games than I ever did – Lily succumbed to his charm easier than mine. The chocolate milk, I thought, was a nice touch of bribery.

Anna approached the game with a laid back attitude of an expert poker player, biding her time and playing at her own pace. She relied on her woobie Dallas to help decide what number to call for next. But after two games (as usual Lily won both), Anna hugged her bear to her chest, her eyelids grew heavy and her enthusiasm (and participation) dwindled. It seemed she preferred napping over getting sacked by her card shark sister.

For a moment I stood at the dresser listening to the happy voices in the other room. I smiled, delighting in the sound then opened the jewelry box, latched the necklace's clasp behind my neck then took a moment to admire the lovely gift my husband bestowed on me and not that rat Sheila Bennett.

Giggling erupted in the dining room as Ennis accused Lily of hiding a coveted card behind her ear or up her sleeve. Peals of wild kid laughter ensued – Ennis, no doubt resorted to tickling her for a "confession".

Standing at the antique mirror, I debated whether to chance fate one last time. In my mind Yoda and my sister shook their heads, Mama shook her finger at me, telling me to leave well enough alone while Daddy threw his hands up in defeat. Pissin' up a rope is easier than dealin' with that kid, he used to say.

This time I'd surprise them by resisting temptation. I stepped back. The mirror revealed enough dismal events to convince me its bark *and* bite were pretty much deadly.

I reached down to move it from the wall. I planned to flip the mirror to the "past" side, thus preventing another accidental FUBAR until we could haul the thing off somewhere safe. If Lily visited the mirror again, she'd likely see a birthday party or Christmas morning, not Daddy and Mama strangling each other over bills and money problems or some other disaster.

The mirror easily slid across the carpet when I scooted it toward me. I carefully clasped the frame's edge (again, trying to avoid the potential nasty pickle known as my future). The pivot uttered one small creak while smoothly swiveling to the other side. A warm invisible force clamped around my wrist, tugging on it. "Oh no, you don't," I pulled at my hand. "You're outta here tomorrow so leave me alone. Ennis and I are happy."

The grasp cinched down hard then jerked me forward like an angry parent dealing with a rebellious kid. My free hand braced on the nightstand as I fought the relentless, mysterious force. The bones and tendons in my arm and shoulder stretched to painful levels. My shoes slipped an inch on the carpet. For a fleeting instant I entertained calling for Ennis then thought better of it. I didn't want to scare the kids if they witnessed the absurdity of Mama wrestling with her mirror and losing.

My feet scooched two more inches, my hand slipped off the nightstand, leaving me flailing to find purchase any way possible. The mirror took advantage of my plight, yanking me harder until the bright light of the future engulfed me. I quit struggling but dread set in about the situation awaiting me. The mirror never forecasted pleasant events. Only sorrow and suffering. I was convinced the damn thing was a torture device from the Spanish Inquisition.

I opened my eyes to an unfamiliar living room and the sound of a baby crying. The room, modest and nicely decorated with a cream and white color palette, offered a comfortable vibe. Two cushy vanilla ice cream colored chairs and matching sofa centered around a flat screen TV mounted on the wall. Framed pictures adorned the mantle above the fireplace to my left, including one of me and Ennis. We were much older in the five by seven portrait, around our late fifties or early sixties. The couple still appeared happy in each other's embrace. Whew... One hurdle cleared. We were both alive and still married. The biggest surprise so far – five inches of length went missing from my older self's silver hair. I expected the color change but not to see my tresses barely touching my shoulders. It looked nice but considering I lopped that much off, it presented quite a shocker to my thirty-nine-year-old self. Age also rewarded me with enough lines at the eyes and a few around the mouth to unsettle my ego. Ennis, of course, possessed the genes of Adonis and looked stupendously sexy even later in life.

A woman's voice drew me from the image of mine and Ennis's golden years. She tried speaking over the baby's wailing, asking her little girl to go "sleepy-bye". In a peach pullover and jeans, a bleary-eyed Lily plodded into the living room holding a pink bundle in her arms. She tried baby talk once again, this time with a hint of desperation parents used just before resorting to the granddaddy of all ploys. Begging. I'd done my share of begging Lily and later Anna to *please* grab forty winks before I fainted from exhaustion. Lily looked close to that herself.

She came right up to me but never acknowledged me. I was back to being a spectator, unable to interact with others in the vision.

With a fluid, gentle motion Lily rocked the infant in her arms, "I wish I had Grandma and Grandpa's touch. They must have the Sandman on speed dial."

She laid the baby in a crib beside me. A small diamond ring glimmered on her left hand. I looked around, finally seeing a framed photo of her and her hubby on their wedding day. Not everything changed from the mirror's prior journeys. In the picture Tony Stafford enfolded Lily in a loving embrace. This one common thread intrigued me. Where, I wondered, had she and Tony met? Work, school, church? A chance meeting at a park or supermarket?

The baby voiced her discontent by screaming. It broke my heart to see the baby struggle to settle down and Lily's futile attempts to calm the child. My oldest daughter looked wrung out. Dark circles under her bloodshot eyes, the fatigue in her voice, the slump in her shoulders. No sleep, no rest for the new mother. I remembered those days with my babies and now I'd signed up for another round with Daniel.

For the heck of it, I bent over the crib with a smile and placed my hand at the baby's tummy. The fuzzy fleece of her pink bodysuit warmed my palm but my hand passed through the baby's image. The cries paused momentarily as if she was suddenly startled. Her eyes flared open, searching around her. Had she felt my presence? The baby wiggled beneath my hand and I swore she looked right at me with those sweet, innocent blue eyes.

I stood in awe of that tiny cherub – so animated and incredibly loud. What a set of lungs she had! A true Prince trait if ever I heard one. But she truly hit the jackpot on looks – I could tell she inherited a good deal from the Culberson side.

No matter which parent the child favored or what side of the family her genes leaned toward, besides my own children I'd never seen such pure perfection. Downy golden brown hair, a little turned up nose and the bluest eyes this side of God's vast sky. My granddaughter. I cooed and marveled at her, trying to quiet her if possible, "Hush, little one. You need rest and so does Mama."

The baby wailed again. Oh yeah, I cringed. That scream was pure, potent and unadulterated Prince.

Lily came back with a bottle only for the baby to turn away from the offer. Lily closed her eyes on a sigh, "Faith, I'm officially at my wit's end. I might as well call your grandma."

"It's probably colic," I said as if she could hear me. Leaning over the crib again, I reached toward Faith (an ideal name for such a gorgeous girl), "Try keeping her tummy warm, see how she does." I settled my hand close to her stomach once more. The pleasant fuzzy warmth rewarded my effort and once more the baby's sobbing paused a beat. Lily turned to her daughter, amazed at the sudden silence. I tenderly rubbed Faith's belly (or the image of it), singing "You Are My Sunshine". Faith's blue eyes darted around until centering on my position. Whether she saw, heard or sensed me, I didn't know.

For a total of twenty seconds my little girl enjoyed peace and quiet. Then *her* little girl wound up crying all over again.

Exasperated, Lily winced, rubbed her forehead, "Let's call Grandma. She'll know what to do." She turned to reach behind me for the phone. Amazingly she hesitated before walking right through me – yes, *through* me.

"Lily," I said, hoping she caught even a few words, "swaddle her in a blanket and snuggle her against your chest. It worked when you had colic."

Her brow wrinkled. She glanced back at the crib. "I think Mama said I had colic as a baby. But what did she do for it?"

Her response encouraged me to repeat myself. Maybe she heard me after all.

She puttered down the hall, returned a minute later holding a
bubblegum colored blanket, "Let's try this." She wrapped the blanket
around Faith, "If this doesn't work, I *am* calling your grandma. She's got
the magic touch and I seriously need some sleep."

The phone rang which intensified the crying to a desperate
screaming. Faith's chubby little cheeks went from cherry red to crimson
in a split second.

Lily shushed her to no avail and I could see her frustration of
dealing with a call at a most inopportune time, at least until she
discovered the caller's identity, "Daddy?"

I heard Ennis speaking so fast no one could understand him, not
even me. Lily pressed the cell phone closer to hear over the baby's crying,
"Daddy, calm down and say that again. What happened?"

The color drained from her face, "I'll meet you at the emergency
room. No, I'll call Anna and Daniel. You call Aunt Georgia and Uncle
Seth. I'll be there soon." She disconnected the call, bowed her head in
brief prayer. The baby wailed for her mother, the insistent mournful
cries drawing Lily to hold her. "Shh, baby, shh. I need to leave for a
while." She wiped away a tear, scrolled through her phone contacts,
settling on one, "I'll call Leslie. She can babysit you while I'm gone."
She dialed while whispering, "Hang on for us, Mama."

My shoulders drooped and now I rubbed *my* forehead, defeated.
The phone call not only deflated the earlier poignant and precious
moments but shot them all to hell. Judging by Ennis's voice and Lily's
reaction I'd dropped of a heart attack or fell victim to some other

affliction or accident. Perfect. Another five star someone's-gonna-die vision, brought to you by my no-name, pessimistic, Inquisition mirror. Nothing the mirror chose to share ended well. I expected nothing less now.

The fading surroundings warned me of an imminent change in time or venue. This one occurred quickly. I stood in an apartment charmingly furnished with tasteful colors and furniture, these considerably more subdued and conservative than Lily's brighter, more modern décor.

"Stop that," a woman scolded with a *come hither* inflection.

"Make me," a deep, husky voice murmured.

I searched out the couple, praying not to walk in on *too* private a moment and questioning why the mirror dumped me right here, right now. A moan redirected me toward the kitchen. Surely the two wouldn't resort to hanky-panky in the kitchen. Then memories of me and Ennis stopped me cold. One turn of a corner and I'd likely get an eyeful.

"Hey," the guy protested with a soft, "no fair."

"Serves you right," she said. I heard a smile in her voice. "You don't play by the rules either."

Anna. I recognized her voice from the wedding reception. I dared a peek around the wall separating the kitchen from the living room where I stood.

It still amazed me how this little girl Ennis and I held in our arms now boasted a height rivaling mine. That meant Lily only bested her by an inch or so. Both girls looked trim and athletic (Lily still carried some baby weight) but Anna showed the results of regular workouts including running and weight training.

I cherished these priceless sneak peeks at our children, to see their personalities, interactions and their lives but by far – on this trip – it was Anna's attire that staggered me. Our baby daughter – the kid who still called a flashlight a "frashright" and had an occasional unfortunate "whoops" (she called it) wiping her own behind – wore a dark blue Atlanta Police uniform. The blouse and slacks fit her in an entirely more attractive fashion than they ever had me. If I'd looked half as good as she did in a uniform, I'd have fallen to my knees in eternal gratitude. Our kid should have been the poster child for becoming a cop.

The duty belt fastened around her slim hips revealed her attention to detail – and the fact she was (like Mom and Pop) right-handed with her gun, an interesting development considering at nearly three she waffled between her left and right hand, depending on the task.

A proud smile curved my lips upon viewing that shiny silver badge and polished nameplate inscribed "Rutherford". I couldn't wait to tell Ennis when I got back. Anna followed in our footsteps.

Then a mother's innate anxiety set in. Our baby girl assumed the responsibility of chasing thieves and catching rapists and murderers. In my younger years I hadn't fully understood the burden my mother shouldered when, as a teenager, I went on ride-alongs with my cousin Bobby, the Richmond County sheriff. I was unarmed and patrolling Augusta's streets, reliant upon Bobby's judgement, instinct and aim if we found ourselves in danger. Anna had training and a gun, yes, but any mother worth her salt would worry herself into an ulcer with her baby facing that danger every day. *I get it now, Mama. I realize why you couldn't sleep at night and why those lines furrowed deeper between your brows when I'd leave with Bobby on those Sunday afternoons...*

Anna leaned against a counter beside the stove. She muttered another halfhearted protest to her boyfriend whose hands cradled her face while moving in for a kiss. Not a long one, thank goodness, for I already felt out of place watching them. "Don't get me worked up," she finished with a wide grin. I saw Ennis in that smile, and maybe just a hint of me as well.

Her companion, a tall, wide-shouldered guy with short curly brown hair pinned her against the counter and promptly planted such a steamy kiss on her that *I* broke a sweat. I averted my gaze thinking, Oh Lord, this is *so* not right...

From the corner of my eye, I saw Anna twine her arms around his neck and I turned back, focusing on her left hand. The "married finger" as Lily once called it, shined as naked as the day Anna was born. My eyes narrowed at the young man, "Boy, for passion this intense, there'd better be a wedding ring on that finger soon or I'll *find* a way to slap you."

No one heard me of course. Nope, they kept right on smooching like the drapes were closed and Mama wasn't anywhere around. I went from embarrassed to protective pretty damn quick.

Mr. Touchy-Feely let his hands migrate south to her breasts which he gave a little squeeze. I wanted to punch him out. *That's my child you're groping, buddy, and I don't give a shit if she's two or twenty-two. Keep your mitts off her till you're good and married.* Sounded good but it was a case of *Hello, Pot. Meet Kettle.* Around Anna's age, I dated a guy named Toby Jackson and we'd done more than neck in a kitchen. If my daddy saw us, he'd have ventilated Toby with his twelve gauge and whupped me until I had no backside left to whup. And Mama? She'd have fearlessly chased Toby around the block with her broom, beating him all the way to South Carolina then towed *me* along by the ear preaching *remember your raisin', young lady.* Our parents cared not about age. Daddy thought boys were threats to "his girls" until they collected pensions. Mama wanted me and Georgia to uphold our reputations, i.e., act like ladies *and* keep our knees closed. But they both loved us dearly. I loved my girls too and watching this scene out of "Carnal Knowledge" was killing me. I couldn't even grab Anna's arm, much less her ear. As for Mr. Handsy? He should have thanked God my .38 was still locked up back home in the present time. (Never thought I'd say it but Daddy had the right idea.)

Crossing my arms, I watched this guy's fingers migrate to Anna's duty belt. They converged on the buckle. Anna parted from the kiss with a teasing smile, "Mama and Daddy'd kill you if they saw you right now."

She got that right.

He shrugged off the comment, "I'm not scared of them."

You should be.

"Yes, you are," she chuckled. "Always the perfect gentleman

around them. They'd never guess you're a scoundrel in disguise."

I would now. If only the mirror allowed me to interact, I groused. I'd strip the cuffs off Anna's belt and chain this guy to an F-16 bound for Antarctica.

Anna glanced at her watch, "I gotta get going. My shift starts at four."

Mr. Handsy's lips grazed her jaw, worked down her throat while his hands settled at the buckle on her duty belt.

Finally she put a firm grasp on his greedy (and amazingly dexterous) fingers, "Baby, I'd love to but honestly, do you know how long it took me to get into this monkey suit?"

"A lot longer than it'll take me to get you out of it."

"It's hard enough to dress once, much less twice. I mean, do you realize it takes a female officer twice as long just to *pee* because of all this gear? It would take forever to redress after sex."

Nice one, kid, I smiled, proudly leaning against the wall. She learned well from Aunt Yoda. I carried a loaded .38. Georgia packed a cannon loaded with guilt.

Anna continued, "Men have it easy. Unzip, aim and go. Instant relief."

"Are we still talking peeing or sex?" He added a purring caveat, "I promise to help you get dressed again. I'm an expert at gun belts, you'll see."

Anna cocked a brow, "So you're dating more than one Atlanta cop, are you?"

His forehead rested against hers, "Only you, Officer Anna Rutherford. Only you."

She smiled again (our girl wielded a heartbreaker of a smile), wrapped her arms around his neck again, leaned in for a lip-lock.

I wanted to look away, to give them privacy for the passionate kiss (and perhaps other subsequent activities). I turned for more reasons than one. I saw their embrace tighten and her fingers thread his hair. Get me outta here, I implored the mirror while seeing her companion's amazingly dexterous digits attack the duty belt's double latch. The desire to slap those hands away kindled into an inferno until I reminded myself of my daughter's age and remembered life in my early twenties. I proceeded to talk myself down from committing homicide in the future. No shotguns, .38's, brooms or ear-pulling necessary. Anna was not two (nearly three), not here. She wasn't a horny teenager, running on unfamiliar feelings and budding hormones. No, she was a full grown woman with desires, a boyfriend, a career and the freedom to make her own choices. *And Mama has no business taking a front row seat to* this *choice. Hint, hint, mirror...*

A cell phone rang. She reached to her pocket but he gently captured her hand and held it. "It's not," he kissed her between words, "important."

"Let me be..." she barely fit in between smooches, "the judge of that." She placed a hand on his chest to hold him at bay while checking her phone.

Focused on the call now, her shoulders sagged, "It's Lily." Anna clicked on, "This is not a good time, sis." A second passed when her eyes rounded and she swatted her boyfriend's hand away with purpose, "When? Was he there when it happened?" A pause then, "What hospital did they take her to?"

The boyfriend's mood sobered from lusty lover to reliable partner when he gathered his jacket and Anna's purse. He retrieved car keys from a gold key shaped key rack on the kitchen wall then put a hand to Anna's shoulder, leading her to the front door. "Where do we meet Lily?" he asked.

"Atlanta Medical. Mama had a heart attack." Into the phone she said, "We'll pick Daniel up. If you hear anything before we arrive, call me..."

My surroundings brightened. I shielded my eyes and kept them closed tight against the glare. When the light receded, I heard birds chirping and singing. Voices and occasional laughter drifted in. A car drove past, slowing to a stop somewhere ahead of me. In the distance, highway traffic sped past at a steady clip. Nearby a loud bray of twanging guitars opened my eyes and sent me back a step, searching for the source.

A college age guy in a blue checkered shirt and jeans reached in his pocket for a phone. The tinny ringtone droned on about catfish on a trot line and mud on the tires before the young man clicked on, "Hey, you wanna grab a beer before the game?"

A woman about the same age dressed in a beige sweater and Levis sidled by me clutching two textbooks to her chest. She too had a cell phone pressed to her ear, only she sported a languid grin much like

Anna's minutes earlier.

I took a second to study my surroundings. The mirror brought me to a grass-lined sidewalk. A few hundred yards away stood a huge building with four or five floors. The outer walls were glass and the sloped roof gave the facility a modern look, like a dome cut down the middle. I recognized the building from the ninety-six Olympics where they held the aquatic events. I'd read that after renovations it boasted not only swimming pools but also a fitness center and tennis courts. The mirror dropped me on the Georgia Tech campus, in front of the recreation center. The emerald grass bordering the building began fading for fall's transition to winter. The trees still clung to their burgundy, burnt orange and honey yellow leaves, refusing to surrender to the harsh upcoming season. The university was gorgeous this time of year – and bustling with students preparing for the holiday break only weeks away.

Half a dozen students exited the recreation center, most carrying gym bags at their sides. A few stragglers ambled from building to building, each one holding a cell phone to their ear or chatting with a friend. Others passed by me, conversing about classes or Saturday's football game against Clemson. When a pair of students walked right through me, I discovered my status remained the same. An invisible spectator.

Another couple from the recreation center sauntered toward me. They looked postcard perfect, he in dark jeans and pine green polo and she in a cardigan and slacks. He carried a black gym bag in his left hand while curling his right arm around his girlfriend. Cute with a charming smile, the girl stood half a foot shorter than him which reminded me of the height difference between Ennis and myself.

To my utter shock, as they approached me, I recognized the handsome young man with a trim waist, short mocha colored hair and semi-bashful smile. Our son Daniel favored his daddy, standing tall and regal with sun-bronzed skin and his shoulders spanning the breadth of Ennis's. He went from a plump, vocal toddler that sucked his thumb to this magnificent man filled out in hard, defined muscle, a gentle touch and soothing voice.

I could see these two standing at the alter exchanging vows – except I doubted I'd witness the happy occasion if the mirror had its way.

Daniel leaned in, whispered something to her. She blushed then playfully elbowed him, "You're a rascal."

My son reached down to tickle her waist. She wriggled free, keeping him at arm's length while wagging her finger, "Not on your life, mister. You know I hate tickling."

Daniel broke into a huge grin, reached and seized her hand. One gentle tug and she gladly returned to his arms. He squeezed her against him, "You don't hate all my tickling."

She settled into his embrace as they resumed their trek down the sidewalk, "No, not *all* of it. But you better stop tickling me around your parents. It's embarrassing."

"Speaking of my folks, Ma invited you to Sunday supper. She's making pot roast."

The young woman paused, a frown shadowed her features.

The action surprised Daniel, "What's wrong? You don't like pot roast?"

"It's not that." She worried her bottom lip with her teeth, clearly debating her reply. "You know I like her," she continued reluctantly, "but I'm kinda uncomfortable around her."

Amusement crooked his mouth in a half-smile, "Why? She's just my mother."

I wasn't sure whether to be offended or not. *Just his mother?* What kind of statement was that? And as for his girlfriend, I couldn't imagine what I'd done to spook her. Georgia claimed I never stopped being a cop. Had I asked this girl too many questions when Daniel brought her home to meet us? Or, God forbid, made her feel unwelcome in any way? The mere idea demoralized me. Even my best behavior (which I knew I would've employed) apparently failed to measure up.

Nervous, she soldiered on – sort of, "Your mother is very…"

I walked alongside them, cocking an ear to catch her personal assessment of me. This eavesdropping gig was fast becoming bullshit. Nothing but misery came from it. Now the mirror (in its infinite wisdom) planted me in the middle of my son and his girlfriend, the latter of whom was probably about to nuke my ego.

This attractive young woman (a woman who my son clearly cared for) took that instant to hesitate. I held my breath, waiting. His mother was *what?* Overbearing? Abrupt? Mouthy? All the customary terms used by various people to describe me raced back in living color.

Daniel took a stab at answering for her, "Lemme guess. My

mother is very assertive and sometimes intimidating?"

Neither of those sounded complimentary at the moment. He said it with the beginnings of a grin so I had hope he meant well.

"Yes," she sighed, apparently relieved that he said it instead. "I feel so... inadequate around her."

Daniel's brows drew together, "What for?"

"The woman can do anything. I mean, she was a sergeant with the police department," she said in a manner suggesting he was daft. "Remember when I called you after I broke down on I-85? You called her and she had two units dispatched to help me. *In four minutes.*"

"It was rush hour and she didn't want you hurt or killed. 85 is one of the busiest and deadliest interstates in the country. Ma said nearly three million drivers a day use it. You were in real danger."

I nodded with pride, gave myself a mental pat on the back. *Chalk one up for Ma.* He wasn't lying about Interstate 85, though. Back home in the present time, approximately two million drivers traveled the highway each day. And yes, studies concluded it already rated as the deadliest in the country.

The girl accepted his reasoning but wasn't quite finished, "She also helped my father with that speeding ticket..."

"He was driving a friend to the hospital. It was a life threatening illness. That rookie shouldn't have ticketed him. Ma righted a wrong, that's all."

"That's my point. She can do anything. She asks and it's done. But she's so laid-back at family dinners and get-togethers you'd never guess she'd been a cop. It's amazing."

Sounding better, Savannah. Apparently, you'll do good in the future. At least then *Georgia won't say you never stop being a cop.*

"Daniel, your whole family is a Hallmark movie. Your father and uncle can build anything and run a ranch. Your aunt is a popular author *and* owns a bakery and your mother helps run it and still makes time for church charity work. Who wouldn't be intimidated?"

He chuckled, "This is kinda funny."

"Funny how?" she wanted to know.

He chuckled, "Because a few weeks ago Ma told me she admires *you*. In a way I think you intimidate *her*."

Her eyes rounded, "She admires me?"

"Yeah. We discussed the hours you put into cramming for exams and writing papers, especially in biochemistry and microbiology. I showed her your paper on the P53 gene and it blew her mind."

"She read that?"

"Yeah, but she didn't understand much of it. I told her it involved cancer research."

For whatever reason, the young lady failed to grasp the fact I liked her. She stammered, "How could she possibly approve of me, much less admire me? Your mother *hates* doctors."

Daniel had an easy laugh similar to his daddy's. He gently braced her shoulders with his strong hands, "No honey, she hates *her* doctors. That's just Ma. Hates for anyone else to run her life. But she told me you weren't only beautiful, you were also packing serious brains and charm. She likes you, get it?"

She giggled a little, "I've always liked her too. I just felt uneasy around her because of my choice in profession."

"Oh, I see. You think my mother is the one in a kabillion who doesn't want her son to marry a smart, beautiful doctor?"

She nudged him with her elbow, "Stop that. You're making me blush."

"Can you finally relax around her? She wants you to enjoy yourself when the family gets together. After all, you'll be part of the family pretty soon anyway. She's no fool. She sees how close we are."

Was that a hopeful glimmer in the girl's eyes – or the fight or flight instinct rearing up? "You didn't tell her, did you?"

Daniel shook his head, "No, but as you pointed out she is a retired detective. She's seen the signs so she sat me down for a long chat about our future."

"But we decided to wait another year–"

"Calm down. I told her that and she encouraged us to hold off a while. She realizes how committed we are to each other *and* how important your premed studies are. She wants us both to concentrate on our education for now."

The girl blew out a relieved sigh, "God bless her." She went to tiptoe and pecked a kiss to his lips, "I love your mother."

"What a coincidence. So do I."

"And I can't wait to be Mrs. Sheila Walsh Rutherford."

My jaw and stomach dropped. *Sheila? Sheila Rutherford?* Fate really had a screwy sense of humor. Once the shock subsided, an uncontrollable urge to laugh bubbled to the surface. It figured, right? Why the hell not? At least it wasn't Sheila Bennett Rutherford. And hopefully Daniel's fiancée wasn't a card carrying member of the Crazy Club.

The couple turned in my direction, visually searching out something or someone. Or had they heard me laughing the way Faith seemed to sense my presence?

Somewhere nearby a driver floored their vehicle, gunned the engine then hit the brakes until a quick screech of tires turned every head within sight. A black sedan rounded the corner with deadly precision despite the driver slamming the gas again.

Daniel released his fiancée, handed her his gym bag and made a beeline to my location. He was more than unhappy with the driver. He was furious.

He marched toward the curb and judging by his posture he meant to confront the person and set them straight about endangering the public. His carefree mood darkened as he waved the driver down, "Hey! Slow down!"

The car roared to the curb with another brief screech. Daniel stooped to the driver window, glaring at the tinted glass sliding down. I winced at his bravado, afraid (and halfway expecting) the reckless driver to point a gun at my son's nose.

Indeed, Daniel's eyes bugged, "Anna?"

"Do you *ever* turn your phone on?" she griped. "We've been driving around this campus for ten minutes looking for you."

"Why the hell are you driving so crazy? You coulda killed—"

"Get in," my youngest daughter demanded, hitching her thumb to the back seat. "We're going to the hospital."

Without hesitation, he followed his sister's orders, opening the door for Sheila then climbing in beside her, "What happened?"

Anna's main squeeze answered for her, "Your mother had a heart attack. We're meeting Lily and your father at the ER."

Both Daniel and Sheila buckled up tight. Anna took off at a speed that sent a shiver down my back. I prayed the mirror hadn't brought me here to witness the death of two of my children because I watched the modest (yet powerful) sedan race down the street at a rate no mother should witness. My heart ached and it had nothing to do with a heart attack. I felt simultaneously terrified that my kids loved me enough to risk their lives in this situation and also dreaded to see what they ultimately faced when they arrived...

The trees vanished, the sidewalk faded to bright white. Here we go to the final moments of my life, I assumed. I closed my eyes, braced for images reminiscent of several days earlier when I stared at a coffin, obsessing over who occupied it. This time I'd know.

The air smelled pungent and clinical. The sound of a soft, rhythmic beeping encouraged me to sneak a small, cautious peek. I was in the hospital – amazingly still breathing and my heart ticking as steady as a Swiss watch.

Well, I exhaled with relief, at least I'm not dead. But an

inexplicable fatigue wore on me. My arms and legs felt weighed down like lead, not blood, coursed through them. A low level ache thrummed in a constant current through my left leg. I started to bend my knee, hoping to relieve it.

A soft yet unrelenting grasp seized my ankle, immobilizing it in a gentle hold. I was an active participant in this vision now, not a spectator anymore. What I said would be heard and what I did they would actually see.

The person attached to that warm grasp spoke in a rich, soothing voice that instantly comforted and calmed me. It was Daniel, "It's okay, Ma. I know your leg hurts but don't bend it."

Lily backed him up, "Doctor's orders."

"I don't think she's awake yet," Anna said. "She doesn't realize she's doing it."

"She moved and groaned," Daniel argued. "I'll bet she's awake. Nudge her a little, see if she is."

"What am I? Stupid?" Anna's incredulous tone nearly made me laugh. Same kid, no matter her age. Had a quip for everything. She expounded on her comment, "I'm not jabbing our mother just because you want her awake."

"You two cut it out," Lily scolded with a whisper. "Mama doesn't need this."

Besides the kids, I heard two others carrying on subdued conversations. Daniel's fiancée and Anna's beau then another familiar voice, "Be patient, kids."

Georgia! It was such a joy to hear her, even if she did sound bone weary. Judging from the pictures at Lily's house, if I hovered around sixty, that put Georgia in the neighborhood of sixty-six.

As usual my sister played peacekeeper, "The nurse said she's been sleeping since the surgery. We'll let her rest."

What *surgery*? If I suffered a heart attack, why did my leg and groin ache? Whatever happened, I thanked God (and the mirror) I didn't experience it during this vision. I only knew the lethargy could cripple an elephant and a wave of wooziness toyed with my stomach. I felt crummy but at least the thick fog settling over me dissipated and my hearing and mind sharpened nearer to full consciousness. I'd heard my kids and Georgia in the room but where, I wondered, was Ennis?

Daniel's defensiveness shifted to cold sarcasm, "She did everything the doctor said to. Now this happens and *then* he decides to do something when it's nearly too late. So yeah, Anna, I want to make sure Ma's okay."

"Honey," Georgia interjected, "we knew this was a matter of time." God bless my sister. I could always count on her to wrangle my kids (and me) back to stability. She heaved a weary sigh, "But the doctor did wait longer than he should have. I'll try again, hopefully she'll consider changing cardiologists."

Someone brushed a lock of hair from my forehead. "We'll help any way we can," Lily's voice and touch lulled me into a twilight sleep. Whatever the doctors sedated me with needed strict warning labels about time-traveling heart patients.

Daniel's frustration darkened to anger, "If I see that doctor, I'm gonna–"

"You're gonna what?" Anna dared him to continue.

Their outbursts stirred me awake but I kept my eyes closed. Before I conversed with anyone, I wanted more information to get my bearings. What happened, what surgery and where the hell was my husband?

Anna bulled on, "You see this badge I'm wearing, Danny Boy? Who do you think's gonna have to drag your butt to jail when you jump this guy? Daddy'll have to post bail and won't Mama be proud of you then? Wake up from this to learn her son's breaking bread with drunks and wife-beaters." That was my baby girl. Brusque but honest.

"*Kids*," Georgia's impatience emerged, "*please*. You hardly ever argue like this."

Anna dialed down her indignation, "Settle down, Daniel. Mama and Daddy need us – out of jail, preferably. Besides, the doctor said the operation went well. That's all that matters."

Seconds passed when he capitulated, "You're right. I'm sorry."

"My God," Lily's voice rose with surprise. "I can't believe it. A truce."

"Shut up," her siblings drawled in unison. I detected a hint of teasing in their response, as if the reaction was a customary response to their big sister's wisecracks.

Daniel offered an apology to Georgia as well. My boy might have had my temper but he exercised his daddy's manners. Thank goodness for that.

Georgia's mood mellowed again, "I understand you're worried and upset, sweetie. We all are but the important thing is to focus on your mother's recovery."

Heavy footsteps – a man's gait – caught my attention. Hard heeled dress shoes clacked across the tile in a steady cadence. Cops developed an acute sense of hearing over the years, one that centered on new noises as threats in unfamiliar situations. Everyone did it but cops honed it because their lives depended on it.

I listened closer, searching for telltale signs of my husband in the long strides. It was not Ennis. Due to a horse riding accident in his youth, my hubby's right leg had a slightly shorter gait than the left. The mystery man did not.

"Is she awake yet?" was the semi-whisper.

My heart sank. No, the visitor wasn't Ennis but a younger man around Lily's age. Maybe even Anna's.

"Not yet," Lily replied. "But soon we think. How's Faith?"

"Fine. Mother got her settled down."

"Tony," Georgia called, "if your mother is busy, Dane and I can take Faith for a while. You and Lily need time with Savannah."

Both Tony and Lily thanked her. A hand scooped mine into a cozy, velvety hold. Delicate fingers stroked the skin. The touch belonged to Lily. "Daddy's been gone fifteen minutes. How long does it take to get coffee?"

Anna replied, "Forever apparently."

Lily ignored her, "She'd wake right up if she heard him."

The room fell silent. With Lily's rhythmic caresses, I drifted to sleep. A blank white view with no images or sounds surrounded me. I went to sleep asking myself questions I had no answers to and curious why the mirror refused to return me to the present. A shred of doubt wormed into my brain. The same doubt that plagued me in the other vision when Ennis was killed. Was I stuck here indefinitely? I groaned at the mere notion. What a way to spend my golden years. Twenty years ahead of schedule.

"She moaned again," Daniel said. "Ma, are you okay?"

He suddenly grunted as Anna warned, "Stop nagging her."

"Stop shoving me," he shot back. "I'm worried about her."

"I'll be happy to give you something else to worry about if you aggravate Mama anymore."

I heard Georgia sigh. Lily joined her, "So much for a truce."

"Listen," my sister transformed to General Georgia, Commander of Good Conduct and Ardent Protector of P's and Q's, "if you insist on arguing, take it outside, please. Savannah needs rest."

"Georgia's right," a man said. "Pipe down and clam up. Your mother's had a rough day. Let her sleep."

No need to analyze footfalls or strides. *That* was Ennis, the love of my life – literally the beat in my heart.

The heart monitor's tempo kicked up a notch upon hearing that beautiful baritone voice. My eyes eased open to see him holding a cup of coffee in each hand. He looked as rugged and handsome as the day we met. I fell in love all over again. I adored every silver strand evenly threading his chocolate brown hair and each tiny crease at the corners of his eyes.

He handed a coffee to Georgia who thanked him. He nodded, "Sorry for the delay. The line for this stuff stretches to Alabama. Did I miss anything?"

"Daddy, Lily was right!" Anna exclaimed.

Ennis snapped around to scold her but she pointed to me, "She said the second Mama heard your voice, she'd wake up and she did."

"I'm always right," Lily winked at her sister. "Remember that."

Ennis abandoned his coffee to Georgia who placed it on the tray table. If our mama had lived to see her sixties, she'd have looked exactly like Georgia sitting in that chair. My sister broke into her signature Rita Hayworth smile, "Welcome back, hon. You've been missed as you can tell."

The sight of my family and forthcoming family (including a young woman named Sheila) bolstered my spirits, reminded me how blessed I was to be loved by so many. But it was seeing Ennis that sprung tears to my eyes. I needed to touch him to be sure. To be absolutely sure he was there with me and not some figment of my murky, drugged imagination. Despite the hurdles of my heart issues, I prayed this visit into the mirror accurately depicted our future. Ennis and I were, as we planned, growing old together. Thousands of tomorrows awaited us, countless embraces and kisses, infinities of smiles and laughter. I *wanted* this future.

I reached for my husband, desperate to feel his touch, to have him hold me and say no matter what happened everything would be okay.

Ennis held my hand, his grasp still warm from carrying the coffee. His lips descended on mine with a kiss so sweet and tender my tired soul melted into it and begged for more. His mouth raised from mine with a smile, "Slow down, young lady, or you might strip another gear."

Still suffering anesthesia hangover with droopy eyelids and a rasping voice, I vowed with all my hopefully-not-so-ailing heart, "I don't want to miss a moment with you."

His smile turned thoughtful, his touch trailed along my left brow and temple, "Count me in, sugar." He gave my hand a little squeeze, "How are you feeling?"

"Tired and my leg aches."

With a smug arch of his brow, Daniel needled Anna, "See? Her leg *is* hurting." His hold on my ankle remained solid. Without a doubt I had the straightest leg in Atlanta Medical.

Anna rolled her eyes, "If you'd let go of it, it might *stop* hurting so much."

I lay there wondering how I gave birth to this soap opera. Once thing was certain. I'd bet a hundred bucks our family get-togethers weren't dull – or quiet.

Daniel ignored his sister, "Ma, do you need something for pain?"

I shook my head as Georgia cleared her throat, "Hate to interrupt Abbott and Costello but my brood will be here this evening. The kids are scattered around the city at tournaments and Dane's the cheerleader. Seth and Leah send their best and will see you when they get back. They'll call later to check on you."

My brain stopped at "kids". Plural. She and Dane had more than Eden? My heart filled with joy, wondering what their children looked like, how they matured over the years. Georgia and Dane had *kids*. The idea seemed so hopeless in the present time. The two continued trying to get pregnant and I planned upon my return home to tell her *keep trying, sis, just keep trying and don't give up...*

"Let's plan our own trip to Hawaii." Ennis bobbed his brow at me, "I'd love to see you in a grass skirt," his lips brushed my ear when he whispered, "and nothing else."

"Daaaddy," Lily wrinkled her nose, "don't."

"You couldn't possibly have heard that," Ennis said.

"I see Mama blushing. That's all I need."

I laughed at her discontent that sounded reminiscent of our four-year-old lodging the same complaint when Ennis and I kissed. Some things never changed. I was grateful for that too.

Ennis pressed a kiss to my forehead where he lingered a moment. His scratchy five o'clock shadow, the caress of his soft lips and his nearness sent spirals of divine bliss through me. He was love, home, and pure perfection wrapped up in one person.

"You scared the bejeesus outta me," he said. "When you went down in the floor, I thought I'd lost you."

"I'm not done with life yet. Just glad it's not done with me." I cringed, "What did they do to my leg? It feels weird all the way up to my... my... my girly parts." In the muddled mess called my mind it took forever to find a G-rated term for the nether region.

Georgia rose to her feet, put a hand to my left calf and nodded for Daniel to finally surrender my ankle, "Once they stabilized you, they went through your groin to put in a stent so you need to keep this leg straight and still. And don't get any jailbreak ideas either. Flat of your back for another," she referred to her watch, "three hours and you'll be staying here a few days."

"That's not as bad as dying, at least," I muttered.

"That's a subject we need to talk about," Lily spoke first.

"Death?" I asked.

She nervously shrugged, "In a manner of speaking, yes."

For some reason Tony, Anna's boyfriend and Daniel's sweetheart retreated to the back wall. My immediate family, meanwhile, surrounded the bed like Indians circling a stagecoach. Before they said a word they needed to back off before their hovering roused my claustrophobia. I recoiled against the mattress (keeping the leg board straight as ordered) but held a hand out to halt the advancing tribe, "You know I hate being hemmed in so stop and just tell me what's wrong."

Ennis's linguistic abilities amounted to "um", "er" and "well" while scrubbing a hand along his jaw. Our kids took turns looking to each other with subtle nods, pressuring their siblings to speak up. Daniel put the onus on Lily, "You mentioned it. Go ahead." But she hemmed and hawed too.

Okay, next in line is... "Georgia?" I pressed.

She stared at Ennis, expecting him to break the news. *Moving on then. Let's check the second string of players in this drama.* "Tony? Sheila?" *Or how about you, Mr. Handsy? You were bold enough with my little girl, how about stepping up and sharing this mystery news with her mama?*

"Someone spit it out," I said. Because this was ridiculous.

Georgia finally braved into the subject, "Hon, this heart attack did more damage than the first one with Jeffrey. The doctor thought about bypass and it's still a possibility. He wants to see how the stent does first."

Knuckles delicately swept along my right forearm. Daniel inherited his daddy's large, strong hands and his tender touch. My son gathered my hand in his, "Ma, it's really serious. Things have to change. You could have died." The voice of a mature, adult man but his inflection reminded me of a scared boy.

Anna threatened to sock his shoulder with her fist, "Daniel, you'd lose a war with that runaway tongue."

He backed her off with one look, "It's true. She could have died."

I saw a gleam in her eye. She swiped the tear away in frustration, "Yes, I know but stop saying the word *die*. We don't tempt fate."

Lily pried herself between her brother and Ennis, "Mama, it's important you keep track of how you're feeling day and night. If you continue having angina after this stent, the doctor will talk to you about bypass."

Daniel snorted at the word *doctor* so I decided to use their earlier conversations to my advantage, "Could the attack have been avoided or delayed?"

"Yeah." Resentment fueled Daniel now, "If Harris had put in a stent earlier.   He procrastinated too long and you suffered the consequences."

A genuine grunt of pain filled the room.   Both Anna and Lily elbowed their brother and made it count.

Harris was not my current cardiologist's name.   At least the guy seeing me now wouldn't bungle my future – as far as I knew.   But the moment Dr. Harris (whoever he was) tried entering my life, I'd boot him between the goalposts.   I hated hospitals – and doctors too – but I especially loathed having heart attacks.   I still remembered my first one during Jeffrey Holland's final attempt to kill me.   The crushing pressure, the radiating pain in my arm and back and the inability to draw a decent breath.   Few things terrified me but that had.

I anticipated a brouhaha to ensue with Daniel's candidness. Nope, just that one good shot to his solar plexus with two elbows and Lily's whispered *watch-what-you-say* warning.   No one disputed his comment, not even Georgia who seemed conflicted about expounding on his revelation or keeping quiet.   Everyone stared at me, waiting for my reaction.   All I said was, "Maybe I need a different doctor."

Jaws dropped all around.   The entire group fell speechless except Ennis who looked ready to faint at the declaration.   "Really?" he asked.

Lily shook free of her verbal paralysis, repeating her daddy, "Really? You'd change cardiologists?"

"Mama?" Wide-eyed Anna asked in an almost pleading way, "Do you mean it?"

Tony leaned in beside Lily, "If you do, I guarantee everyone in this room supports you on that decision. You've defended Harris's decisions for years. What happened?"

Georgia and Ennis appeared too shocked to speak. I shrugged, "A big ol' heart attack happened, Tony. Dying really wasn't on my agenda anytime soon so maybe I should listen to my family," I winked at Sheila, "and our budding physician."

My sister's shoulders slackened. She finally breathed, exhaling a long audible breath. "Not to push my luck," she said, "but is it okay if I call Dr. Dara? He's the cardiologist I mentioned last year. He's got an excellent track record. According to the people I've spoken with, he's got a fantastic bedside manner too."

"Dr. Dara?" Really? Why did the name evoke images of a nineteen sixties sitcom? *Calling Dr. Dara, calling Dr. Dara...* I'd gone through my share of strange named doctors. My current cardiologist (in the present time) sported a moniker Juliet Capulet's family loathed. He pronounced it differently but still, anyone not privy to that detail would naturally assume it sounded like Romeo's surname. Now I'd have Dr. Dara because the one heart guy with a normal, unmistakably pronounced name (Harris) twiddled his thumbs while the timer on my life ticked away. Nope, I'd sign on with Dr. Dara, no matter that I envisioned a young Richard Chamberlain prancing across a snowy black and white TV screen topped with rabbit ears.

Georgia rummaged her purse until extracting a small notepad. My sister. Still remarkably efficient after all those years. The world changed, we got older but a person, without a doubt, could not only set their watches by Georgia Rutherford but depend on her in any situation.

After flipping through some pages, she stopped to give a careful recitation of his name, "Dara is his first name. It's spelled D-a-r-r-a-g-h, and his last name is Grawn-yah, spelled G-r-a-i-n-n-e."

Her precise enunciation struck me as humorous. Grawnyah? And the name Darragh? Feh. The whole thing sounded Klingon to me and believe me, with Ennis's fascination with Star Trek, I knew a Klingon name when I heard one.

Georgia must have sensed my parallel to the sci-fi show and clarified Dr. Grawnyah's lineage, "He's Irish and from what I understand, has a charming brogue."

"And an obstacle course for a name. Once I'm sprung from this joint, we'll get Dr. Irish on the horn. I've got a husband, kids and grandkids to spoil. I can't kick off right now."

Ennis kissed me, "No, you can't. You said this years ago and I remember it well. 'We're gonna grow old together. We'll rock our grandkids to sleep on a porch swing, complain that there's nothing on TV, finish each other's sentences and ask each other where we left our glasses. Then we'll go to bed and sleep in each other's arms.' We've got a lot of years left in this marriage, sugar, and we're gonna enjoy every one of them."

27

Thursday

The "Ugly", as Anna christened it, got voted off the island. The kids watched us heft the bubble wrapped, blanketed mirror into the Ram's truck bed. To commemorate the departure of the most hated piece of furniture on the premises we promised them ice cream after our business concluded. They rewarded us with a rousing cheer then Anna proceeded to torture us with the theme song from "Bubble Guppies", one of her favorite cartoons. Lily gleefully joined in and both girls serenaded us all the way to the antique store, stopping just short of Ennis losing his composure and me from losing my mind. Several nights I drifted off hearing that song in an endless loop. I dreamed of goofy little fish-tailed preschoolers and their teacher Mr. Grouper, all of whom acted as if they'd overdosed on anti-depressants and amphetamines. Parents were superhuman souls to survive a kid's repetitive tendencies, not to mention their choice in television.

The kids steamed ahead with another chorus when Ennis rubbed his temple, "What happened to 'Five Little Monkeys Jumping on the

Bed'?"

Just what I needed. Another earworm. Thanks, Ennis. It took months to extricate *that* wretched little ditty from my brain. I literally loathed the monkey song. Now it was back in full living color. For the billionth time, my overtaxed, slightly aching brain produced images of five simians, each one falling off the bed and concussing themselves and the doctor had only one lone remedy for their mother? *No more monkeys jumping on the bed.* Duh. Some doctor he was. With a nonchalant shrug, I replied, "I told Anna the mother should have sued the doc for malpractice."

Thankfully he'd pulled already into the parking lot before turning to me, his eyes wide with disbelief. I smiled, "I'm joking, Ennis. Honestly, I don't know how 'Bubble Guppies' replaced the monkeys." *I'm just glad they did.*

"Bubble Guppies!" Anna cried, making us both cringe.

Well, maybe not so glad, after all...

They cranked up for another chorus, "Bub-bub-bubble!"

"Gup-gup-guppies!" Lily chimed in.

And together, "Bubble, bubble, bubble—"

"We're here." Ennis looked frazzled. "Thank God." He stared into the rear-view mirror, "And no singing in the store."

The thirty minute drive panned out. Mr. Fowler, the store's owner, surprisingly agreed (gasp!) to take the damned old mirror back despite the All Sales Final policy. He'd take it back, he said, but no refund for me. I think he hoped we'd decline the deal but we hadn't. If he refused to take it, we intended to donate it to the landfill.

We unloaded and unwrapped it then waited for the owner to inspect the mirror top to bottom. While I did business with Mr. Fowler, Ennis occupied the girls by showing them antique wind-up toys and cast iron mechanical banks near the store's entrance. The girls yawned.

"Sure you don't want the mirror anymore?" Fowler asked a final time. He gave it another visual going over, slowly easing his hand over the frame the way Georgia did the day I found it. *Careful, mister,* I thought. *That thing bites.*

His hand moved closer to the glass then eased away which gave me pause, reminding me of our last discussion and his reluctance to discuss the mirror. He knew exactly what that thing could do. Probably got himself Hoovered into it too at some point.

"I'm sure," I replied. "It doesn't fit my décor and someone else would be happier with it." Was I a good liar or what? No mention of time traveling or fighting off murderous college kids or insane lieutenants.

"Yeah, I'll bet it fits someone's taste," he agreed, choosing not to disclose our secret. "Well, come on over and give me your Jane Hancock. Gotta keep my records straight, you see."

I followed him to the front counter. He displayed carnival and depression glass on the three shelves inside the glass case. Off to the side on a sturdy wooden stand was an old, cumbersome brass candy store register with pop up amounts like .10, .50, $1, and $2.

Fowler penned an impromptu note that he laid on the display

case then placed a pen on top. Sliding on my specs, I read the form written in passable chicken scratch stating I'd returned the mirror without a cent being refunded (All Sales Final, after all). I didn't care. Being rid of that albatross lifted an enormous burden and if I'd felt any better, I'd have sworn it was a setup. No more "what if" scenarios or worrying about the girls being sucked into its spell. Nope. Ennis and I shook hands on it. We'd wing it from here. Whatever happened happened and we'd live as safely and happily as life allowed.

A slightly liver-spotted hand covered the paper, blocking access to the "Sign Here" line. "Hold on a second," the older guy shook his head. "I can't do this to you. You and I both realize what that thing looks like. There's no damage to it I can see since you've had it so are you okay with getting a hundred bucks back?"

Pleasantly surprised at his change of heart, I slid my hand around his for a good, solid shake, "You have a deal, sir."

He punched a key on the shiny old cash register. A bell dinged and a little orange "No Sale" tab popped up. He opened the drawer, counted out five twenty dollar bills and forked them over, "There y'go. I got a friend in New Orleans who owns an antique shop. I think it'll do better down there."

New Orleans. The land of black magic, voodoo and Marie Laveau. "Yes," I agreed, "it's a much better market for a mirror like that."

"That was your sister with you before? The one who bought the Chippendale table?"

I nodded as he pointed across the store to a small smattering of tables and chairs, "I got a new shipment from the Carolinas and Virginia. Scored a couple of Chippendale tables and four new chairs if she's interested."

"I'll let her know."

Ennis and I walked out with two eager youngsters chanting "ice cream" over and over. It fell much easier on the ears than "Bubble Guppies".

I lifted Anna into the truck, followed by Lily. Ennis took care of belting them in. I climbed in the passenger seat and turned to see both girls laughing and having fun together. Things were looking up. Finally. "You girls were absolutely right," I said. "That mirror *was* ugly."

I spent the trip to the ice cream store with a smile and tons of appreciation to God for my family and the Plus One growing inside me. If it was a boy would he look and act the way the mirror predicted? I lost myself in a long moment of folly, imagining our son from infancy to manhood. I hoped the mirror pegged him accurately. I also wanted it to be a boy because I wasn't sure if Ennis could stay sane with another female in that house.

In less than a week we'd celebrate Halloween. On that spooky, appointed night we'd make the appointed rounds with our ladybug and Sleeping Beauty. First we'd visit the neighbors, then stop by the church for the big annual Fall Festival where candy and Bible related gifts were handed out to the children. Before night's end, we'd visit Seth and Leah then lastly Georgia and Dane who always seemed to decorate more than necessary for giving away treats to little beggars dressed as ghosts and goblins (and a certain ladybug and Sleeping Beauty). The kids enjoyed Uncle Seth and Aunt Leah but inevitably tugged at Mama's blouse or Daddy's hand to hurry us up – as if Aunt Georgia and Uncle Dane might close for business before we got there.

Still high on ice cream, the four of us arrived home two hours later and settled down at the dining table for our homework. Ennis and I decided during my pregnancy with Lily to give our kids a leg up on education if possible. Play music to smarten up infants before birth, the scientists said, however they advocated blasting the unborn baby with Mozart and Beethoven, not Elvis, The Supremes or Rolling Stones. While hanging out inside Mama's belly, our girls heard a lot of oldies while Mama cleaned house. They might not grow up geniuses, but they would be able to shake their booties.

With both kids now old enough for flash cards, we used those to broaden their impressionable, developing minds (Elvis could only do so much). The girls weren't keen on broadening anything except playtime but we insisted. Normally the girls moaned and groaned over the exercises. That day we lucked out. No complaints.

Ennis volunteered for teaching duty that day while I busied myself with the sergeant's study guide. The test loomed on the horizon and I wanted to be extra prepared.

"Seven!" Lily answered a whole lot louder than necessary. "Two plus five is seven!" She leaned onto the dining table, ready for another equation. Our kid loved math, thank goodness, and I prayed she'd do better in the subject than I had in school because Algebra equaled Greek – and Trigonometry amounted to a fancy way to describe triangles and circles.

"That's great, sweetheart," Ennis glowed with pride. "You're gettin' good at these flash cards." He quizzed her on three additional problems (which she aced) then switched to Anna's deck, this one with cartoon animals. He chose a card depicting a monkey and addressed Anna who appeared bored with the entire scene. She yawned, cuddled her bear Dallas while letting her eyelids droop over her peepers.

"Anna," Ennis asked, rousing the child from her lackadaisical state. "What's this little guy called?"

She shifted her vision to the monkey card and answered with absolute conviction, "Daddy."

I tried not to laugh. Ennis did a doubletake at the image then looked at me. He found no humor in the moment, "You think it's funny she calls me a monkey? Watch this." He sorted the cards until settling on one. A lion. He smirked, "What's this, Anna?"

"Mama."

Whereas Ennis took offense to the monkey reference, the lion kinda flattered me. "It's my mane," I joked, tossing back my tresses in a Cher-like fashion. "My wild, bushy mane."

"It's your roar," Lily corrected then tried her hand at ripping a long, deep snarl. "That's why she calls the lion 'Mama'."

Okay, now I didn't feel so flattered. Unlike me, Ennis laughed at the comparison so I asked Lily, "Then why does she call the monkey

'Daddy'?"

Lily snickered, "'Cause he's goofy."

Ennis decided it wasn't so funny anymore and rose to his feet, "School is officially out." He packed up the flash cards to call it a day. His announcement, of course, thrilled the girls. They accepted the home schooling well except when they wanted to spend time playing. But that day I planned to give them a rare thrill. I'd reverse the roles.

I pushed the sergeant's study guide toward the kids, "Anyone want to grill me on the sergeant's exam?"

"I do!" the two imps shouted in unison. Anna exhibited more spirit in that brief second than in the last half hour.

Ennis's tone softened, "Sugar, I told you to hold off on this. You said you wanted to wait."

I half-shrugged, "At the time, yes. Things change and this is one change I don't need a mirror for. Who's first? Ask me anything."

"Can I have a 'Nickers?" Anna inquired, batting her eyelashes. The child tried every cute trick in the book.

Nice try, kiddo... "Anything about the test, sweetie," I amended. "And no, a Snickers will spoil your supper. You've already scarfed down ice cream." Which explained the zoned out, glazed look in her eyes the last hour or so. Too much sugar.

Lily already opened the book, all too happy to turn the tables on Mama. This time I assumed the role of student to her teacher – until she ran across her first very large adult word. Her brow sank while she attempted to sound out two more words without success.

Ennis took over, "Why don't I read the question and you can grade her on the answer? I'll flip through the book and you choose the question."

Lily's excitement mounted. Ennis thumbed through the book then settled on a page. Lily stabbed a finger at a random question.

Ennis cleared his throat, "Okay. 'A police organization is structured by dimensions just as any other organization is structured. Which of the following most accurately describes the dimensions of the police organization? A – Vertical and horizontal only, B – Horizontal and lateral only, C – Vertical and lateral only or D – Horizontal, vertical and lateral.'"

Lily's face went blank. "Huh?"

I smiled at her, "Confusing, isn't it? I'd say the answer is D. The vertical dimension is the rank-ordering structure such as a captain is a lieutenant's superior. The horizontal dimension represents employee relations with others of the same authority such as two sergeants in the same command. The lateral represents employees with the same authority but with different responsibilities such as patrol sergeant with a detective sergeant. D is my final answer." I glanced at Lily, "How'd I do, Yoda?"

Ennis flipped a page or two, held his finger to the answer for Lily. She examined it with a critical eye (she took her job seriously) then burst into a round of clapping and cheering, "Yay, you're right! It's D!"

Anna and Daddy applauded and we all high-fived each other.

Lily assumed command of the thick study guide, thumbing

through the pages until pointing to a question, "That one."

He winked at me, "She picked a tough one this time, sugar, so get ready. 'The issue of a selective enforcement has been a difficult area for the police. An answer to this difficulty has been the use of selective enforcement boards, with some members drawn from the private citizens of the community. With which of the following would such a policy board usually not become involved? A – Enforcement of gambling laws, B – Handling of family disputes, C – Civilian complaints against the police or D – Enforcement of prostitution laws.'"

For effect, I frowned. "You're right. That is a tough one. I'm glad she's not in charge of the real exam." After a silent count to five, I answered the cherry-picked "tough" question. "I believe C is the answer."

Lily waited for him to turn to the answer section. Her face lit up again, "You're right."

"Now ask her why she chose C," Ennis coached.

"Why did you choose C?"

I pretended she represented the oral board of my superiors, and this question was make or break on the coveted promotion, "A selective enforcement board isn't a civilian complaint review board. A selective enforcement board would develop guidelines for police officers to follow when exercising discretionary authority. That's why I chose C."

Again Ennis read the explanation in the book and whispered to Lily who shouted, "Yay! Let's do another!"

He let Lily choose another, recited it for her, again relieving her of pronouncing more burdensome, heavy-duty words. I gave my answer and this time Lily took it upon herself to check my accuracy.

When Ennis gave the thumbs-up she used one of my favorite (and way overused) expressions. "We have a winner!"

Anna's enthusiasm waned after the fourth question. She resorted to daydreaming. Using her arms as a pillow, she laid her head on the table, ensuring Dallas sat in front of her. The longer Ennis and Lily quizzed me, the heavier Anna's eyelids drooped. She sleepily mimicked words we'd say. Sergeant. Enforce. Patrol. Officer. Then she decided she preferred one word in particular. "Po-leece," she mumbled over and over. And over.

I nudged Ennis, "The needle's stuck."

"I wanna be po-leece."

Ennis raised a brow, intrigued, "Or not. Anna, do you want to be a police officer like me and Mama?"

From the drowsy depths of our toddler, "M-hmm."

Incredible. For an instant I basked in that image the mirror presented me the day before. How beautiful our baby daughter looked in that uniform. How confident. How proud to continue the legacy. I geared down my expectations once returning to reality. Anna, being on the cusp of three, fell victim to many aspirations the way most toddlers did. Today a cop, tomorrow a Disney princess, the next she'd announce wedding plans for herself and Cookie Monster with the reception to be held right on Sesame Street.

The mirror showed me one version of my family's future. Things could and would change in ways I decided were best left to fate. I cut my eyes to Ennis, "Mark it on the calendar, Daddy. It might actually happen."

He leaned to my ear with a whisper, "As if we don't have enough to worry about."

The corner of my mouth smiled, "Don't want our kids carrying on the tradition?"

"Not unless I have access to tons of tranquilizers." He looked at the clock, "I'd better mow the lawn before we disappear in the Amazon."

"Daddy," Lily frowned. "What about my golf lesson? It'll be dark soon."

Soon? We had four hours before the first hint of dusk descended on the city. Ennis took her comment well though, "Sweetheart, the day it takes me that long to cut our grass, I'll hang up my mower and retire. You'll get your golf lesson." He bent down to peck a kiss to her cheek, "I promise."

While Ennis mowed, Lily moped. For minutes she stared forlornly out the back door. "Daddy'll be done soon, honey," I assured. "Why don't you find something else to do for a while? Didn't you and Anna plan a tea party before we left?"

Shoulders slumped, she trudged into the living room then plopped down in the floor with Anna. While Daddy cut through our jungle (an exaggeration to be sure), she proceeded with the party looking so low she couldn't jump off a dime.

Anna joined in as little sisters did, excited to be included in whatever Big Sis busied herself with. Once convinced the two got along, I felt safe in tackling the bills.

Paying those monsters felt closer to a punch in the head. I was getting way too much practice subtracting these days and not enough adding. Besides our salaries, the orchards brought in decent revenue to supplement our income. Surprisingly that year the pecan section of the orchards (the smaller section) netted quite a nice sum considering its size. Enough I planned to discuss planting additional trees since the price of nuts skyrocketed the last few years. Four cousins benefited from the profits – me, Georgia, and our daddy's niece and nephew Royal and Vincent, respectively. They'd likely approve the idea since everyone enjoyed making money.

Those orchards provided a little padding for our nest egg but I swore between the insurances and utility bills, everyone tried to steal all our yolks. Both the house and car insurance came due then for an added bonus, Georgia Power wanted their two cents (more like a fistful of dollars) and Atlanta Gas joined the choir. I'd just finished paying the highway robbers when the doorbell rang.

I removed my glasses, grateful for a break. A glance through the peephole revealed a young boy on our porch and a light colored sedan parked in the drive behind my Charger.

I opened the door to a little guy around Lily's age. Super adorable with his proper posture, carefully combed sandy brown hair, blue slacks and blue polo shirt, his head inclined to greet the adult towering at the door. The kid's selling something, I figured, while searching for the requisite flyer kids seemed to tote around these days. Parents gussied up the young 'uns to make good impressions for peddling candy, cookies or magazine subscriptions. And lately we'd had kids in every age range. It got old turning away the hopeful expressions that wanted our money in exchange for an overpriced Oreo. After all, Georgia Power and our other necessary buddies already allocated our income for *their* pockets. But *this* kid… There was something different about him. He was just too cute to refuse. Then I saw an envelope in his right hand. Not a flyer or catalog for ordering, but a simple envelope.

A woman waved from the silver Accord idling in the driveway. I waved back, still wondering who these people were and what the boy wanted.

He met my gaze and began in a polite yet reserved tone, "Mrs. Rutherford, is Lily home? I wanna give her this." Then added *please*, as if remembering his mother's prompt. *Always say please and thank you.*

The boy wasn't only cheek-pinching adorable, he possessed real manners. "Yes, she's home. Come on in," I swung the glass storm door open for him.

"That's okay – I mean, *no, thank you.* My mom said I need a haircut so I want to give this to Lily first."

"Alrighty. Hang on and I'll fetch her for you." I suppressed an amused smile at his hiccup in manners. *Nice recovery, young man. Very nice.* I called my daughter to the door, "Lily, you have a visitor."

Still engrossed in their tea party, Lily tilted the floral patterned teapot into Anna's cup then the cup Anna reserved for Dallas. Baby sister watched the invisible liquid pour into the dainty vessels then took cup in hand for a sip.

Lily levered to her feet, "Who is it?"

"A young man with a delivery for you." I stepped back as she leaned around my thigh to size up the guest. He passed muster so she headed outside.

I tried to give them semi-privacy by standing inside the door out of sight but still within earshot of the conversation. Their exchange sounded friendly but awkward since the boy's mother sat in the car supervising from one side and me from the other.

Georgia called listening in rude behavior. She meant eavesdropping on adult conversations, of course, but when it involved kids I called it necessary. Young voices meant the kids were still there. An adult stepped away for a second and children could disappear – on their own or lured away by a pervert. No thanks. Not on my watch. My kids could expect Mama to nose into their business until such time I either forgot my name or forgot to breathe.

The two chatted a minute then Lily thumbed the latch on the door. Whatever the envelope contained, she'd already ripped into it and seen it.

I held the door open for her, waved again to the mother who returned the gesture while waiting for her son to return to the car. "Who was that?" I asked Lily.

She walked by with an impassive, "A boy from school."

"Is he a friend of yours?" *C'mon, kid. Gimme the scoop.*

She shrugged, "I guess so."

And everyone called *me* difficult. Well, "What did he say?"

"That they're going to Nashville tomorrow to see his cousins."

Surely that wasn't all. "That's all he said?"

"No. He said, 'Here's a Halloween card.'"

My earlier smile broke through and I beamed. That little boy had a crush on my daughter – and my daughter appeared as interested in him as collecting lint. "That was sweet of him. I'll bet it's a pretty card."

Lily thrust the envelope at me, exasperated, "Mama, if you wanna see it, just say so."

I barely curbed my enthusiasm. "You don't mind?"

"Nu-uh."

Before she changed her mind, I accepted. I was more excited about the card than she was. A budding infatuation at nearly five years old. Lily's first admirer arrived earlier than I imagined but hey, who was I to argue? I thought it was capital "C" cute and couldn't wait to tell Georgia.

Lily padded back to the tea party that Anna, in that short span of time, managed to scatter across the floor. "*Anna...*" she complained.

Meanwhile I delved into the envelope the mystery admirer gave Lily. I pulled the card out (a folded piece of notebook paper) and smoothed the neat creases (he was very symmetrical about them). In blue Crayola, he drew two recognizable figures (pretty good for a kid his age). One was Lily, the other I assumed to be him. His artistic flair accurately captured my daughter's hair. The sepia colored Crayola flowed back and forth representing waves in her hair. The two figures stood beside a really fat pumpkin while skinny ghosts floated above them. Across the top of the page in black then underlined it in orange he wrote "To Lily. Boo From Me To You". He'd signed it at the bottom but only God, his mother and Lily could read it. I made out an "O" then a backwards, lowercase "Y" (all his "Y's" were backwards). His mother, bless her heart, filled in the mystery by printing his name below his interpretation of a signature. It read "Tony Stafford".

Find me a chair quick. My knees literally weakened and gravity pulled on my jaw, gaping it open. I leaned against the wall, bracing myself before reading the name again, this time taking careful note to spell it silently to myself. Yep. That was, indeed, the boy's name. I finally found my voice, "That young man is Tony Stafford?"

Still ho-hum about the subject, Lily nodded at me, then commenced gathering pieces of the tea set deposited around the floor. "Annnnaaa," she groaned the name, "where's your teacup?"

Flashes of Lily's wedding came to mind. The big, strapping man at the alter saying *I Do* to my daughter wrote his Y's backwards at four years old. The two hadn't met in college or at work or even the produce aisle at Kroger. They were childhood sweethearts. They grew up, got married and had at least one child. I remembered my words in the vision – *Happy Wedding Day, Mrs. Stafford.* I broke into a girlish giggle. *Well, ring my chimes. I know a secret. A very important secret.* "That really is him."

"What?" Lily heaved a dramatic sigh, apparently resigning herself to Anna's misplaced teacup.

"Do you like Tony?"

"He's okay."

I had it in good confidence that he was better than okay in about twenty years or so.

"He's kinda short," my daughter critiqued.

Just wait, kiddo. That boy grows impressively tall. "He's short now but he'll probably grow this tall." I lifted my hand just below Ennis's height – exactly the height I remembered Tony standing in the vision.

Lily laughed, "Mama, you're funny."

I winked at her, "We'll see who's laughing later on. I have a feeling you and Tony will get along famously."

Epilogue

The sergeant's exam. 100 questions. 2.5 hours. Cut score – 50th percentile. The rest go home. For the other 50%, the next step was the oral exam. 30 to 40 minutes of facing a panel of superior officers who literally held a candidate's future in the palms of their hands. One swipe of a pen and the hopeful officer's hard work and dedication to studying – gone.

I took Daddy's advice to heart. Shit or get off the pot. I got up the day of the written exam, ate my breakfast and while Ennis tended to the girls, I put Josh Hunter's experience to work for me by exercising one hour before the test. Before leaving I thumbed through my study materials, Josh's notes and the ones I made in our various evenings together, him the teacher, me the student. Then I ran across another note. In Ennis's handwriting, it read "Great job, sugar. We love you and good luck! From your three biggest fans." Each of my "fans" signed it, one in blue ink (Ennis) and the other two in green crayon.

The Georgia World Congress Center sat within a block of the CNN Center, Centennial Olympic Park and the College Football Hall of Fame. It looked a little like a small split-level airport from the front with all glass across the front and long walks to anywhere of significance. I hesitated before going inside, wondering if I was making the right decision then bolstered my courage and proceeded inside to take the test. The room brimmed with anxious candidates, men and women alike. I recognized a few. I showed the instructor my ID, signed in and chose a desk in the middle of the room. He handed out answer sheets and test booklets with a reminder of our allotted time and before he started the timer, I took a long, deep breath and chanted the mantra Josh Hunter drummed into my brain. *Never change an answer once you've selected it on the answer sheet and take all the test time allowed.*

Studies showed the failure rate among unprepared candidates stood at a whopping 78%. Yes, the department did studies on this – probably to scare the hell out of anyone considering a promotion. On the other hand (which I prayed included me) another study indicated a remarkable 79% of candidates passed as long as they hit the books steady and hard. I'd find out soon enough what category I fell into.

A few days later I received the results in the mail. I'd passed the written test. Josh and I got together again before the oral exam where we reviewed tips, information and strategies. He also offered two eye-opening, frightening facts. One, the first seven minutes of the exam were critical to receiving a high score. Two, ten percent of a candidate's final score is psychologically calculated before a candidate's first question. I nearly peed myself.

Josh calmed me down and coached me on everything from the second I walked into the exam to the first questions that might be asked. The morning of my oral exam, I walked in dressed in a navy blue pantsuit and mid heels. Shoulders back, confident stride and smile, saluted the panel and shook each one's hand with a sincere *good morning, sir.*

Hunter prepared me for the "ice-breaker" question posed to every candidate. The dreaded *tell us about yourself and why you should be promoted to sergeant.* "State impressive arrests and investigations you led or were involved with," Josh had instructed. "List your awards and commendations. Don't forget family background. Strong family ties count."

I spent 30 full minutes immersed in that pit of hell, sweating every question and picking words carefully yet fluently. To my ears, I sounded capable and qualified. In my heart, I felt ready to keel over from anxiety.

I emerged from the building weak and shaky (both of which hit with crippling force the second I climbed inside my car). The worst were my doubts. Had I done well? Made a good impression? Answered the questions clearly, concisely and correctly with supervisor-quality confidence? Or had I bungled the whole thing, coming across overbearing and bitchy? Oh God, I groaned on the phone to Georgia, "I bombed. I can feel it."

Her answer? "It's nerves. Give yourself time to relax. Go home and run a mile or two before you pick up the girls. Do whatever eases your stress."

"Getting that promotion might ease it but it'll take a while to find out. By then I'll be dead. Georgia, what if I screwed up?"

"Josh told me you were more prepared than anyone he's ever

seen."

"He lies a lot too. To make people feel better."

"Savannah," she chuckled. "Go home and take a warm, relaxing bath. You prepared well for the test. Everyone has doubts afterward but I'm sure you did great."

I followed my sister's instructions. Went home, took a quick run then a long, warm bath. I piled up in my recliner and engrossed myself in her new mystery novel (which thankfully mentioned nothing about a sergeant's exam) until it came time to pick the kids up from school. I convinced myself Georgia, like Josh, placated me with "you'll do fine" and "quit fretting" quips to keep from prying me off the ceiling while I waited. This was my family's future. No one could pry me off until I got the results.

The day they were published, I couldn't bring myself to look. Ennis and Mathis checked the results posted on the bulletin board outside Josh's office. The two came back sullen and long-faced. I hoped Ben & Jerry made extra ice cream that week because I planned to go on a Chocolate Fudge Brownie bender. "I knew it," I griped. "Failed, didn't I? Probably the lowest score ever posted for the sergeant's position."

They heard me out, standing stoic side by side. I'd never seen John Mathis so somber. He actually pitied me and that made me squirm. He shrugged a shoulder, "I'd say you can't win 'em all but…"

Then I watched as they stood at attention, lifted their right hands and saluted me. "Congratulations, Detective Sergeant Savannah Prince," Ennis proudly announced.

"'Bout time the good guys get their due," Mathis added with his own smile. "So anything you need, Sarge, come to us and consider it done."

I could not believe it. Sergeant. All the blood, sweat and tears. The studying. The frustration. The preparation for the oral portion. It was over and along with new responsibilities, I also had a brand spanking new title. I was now Detective Sergeant Savannah Prince Rutherford. Technically, Detective Sergeant Prince – during business hours, that was, and the future looked better than ever. And I still planned to chow down on Ben & Jerry's – and invite everyone to join me. I'd even spring for two boxes of éclairs for my friend John Mathis.

J.L. Lemon lives in Texas surrounded by a loving and supportive family, two adorable and devoted puppies, and hordes of garden gnomes.

Before 2002, J.L. Lemon wrote opinions and product reviews for an online consumer guide. When fellow reviewers cited the author's knack for humor, she decided to return to writing fiction. Along with the standalone title Second Chances, she's published 12 books in the Savannah Stories Series.

www.ingramcontent.com/pod-product-compliance
Lightning Source LLC
Chambersburg PA
CBHW030745030726
47497CB00001B/141

* 9 7 8 0 9 9 0 9 5 8 9 5 6 *